HOME ON THE RANCH:
RODEO REBEL

———— ✠ ————

New York Times Bestselling Author
TINA LEONARD
MARIN THOMAS

⬧ HARLEQUIN® HOME ON THE RANCH

ISBN-13: 978-1-335-02044-4

First published as The Cowboy's Bonus Baby by Harlequin Books in 2011 and A Cowboy's Duty by Harlequin Books in 2012.

Home on the Ranch: Rodeo Rebel Copyright © 2017 by Harlequin Books S.A.

The publisher acknowledges the copyright holders of the individual works as follows:

The Cowboy's Bonus Baby Copyright © 2011 by Tina Leonard

A Cowboy's Duty Copyright © 2012 by Brenda Smith-Beagley

Recycling programs for this product may not exist in your area.

Printed in U.S.A.

™ www.Harlequin.com

CONTENTS

Tina Leonard is a *New York Times* and *USA TODAY* bestselling and award-winning author of more than fifty projects, including several popular miniseries for the Harlequin American Romance line. Known for bad-boy heroes and smart, adventurous heroines, her books have made the *USA TODAY*, Waldenbooks, Ingram and Nielsen BookScan bestseller lists. Born on a military base, Tina lived in many states before eventually marrying the boy who did her crayon printing for her in the first grade. You can visit her at tinaleonard.com, and follow her on Facebook and Twitter.

Books by Tina Leonard

Harlequin American Romance

Bridesmaids Creek

The Rebel Cowboy's Quadruplets
The SEAL's Holiday Babies
The Twins' Rodeo Rider

Callahan Cowboys

A Callahan Wedding
The Renegade Cowboy Returns
The Cowboy Soldier's Sons
Christmas in Texas
"Christmas Baby Blessings"
A Callahan Outlaw's Twins
His Callahan Bride's Baby
Branded by a Callahan
Callahan Cowboy Triplets
A Callahan Christmas Miracle
Her Callahan Family Man
Sweet Callahan Homecoming

Visit the Author Profile page at Harlequin.com for more titles.

THE COWBOY'S
BONUS BABY

TINA LEONARD

Many thanks to Kathleen Scheibling for believing in the Callahan Cowboys series from the start.

I have certainly enjoyed the past five years under your guidance. Also, there are so many people at Harlequin who make my books ready for publication, most of whom I will never have the chance to thank in person, and they have my heartfelt gratitude. Also many thanks to my children and my husband, who are enthusiastic and supportive, and most of all, much appreciation to the generous readers who are the reason for my success.

Chapter 1

"Creed is my wild child. He wants everything he can't have." —Molly Callahan, with fondness, about her busy toddler.

Creed Callahan was running scared. Running wasn't his usual way of doing things, but Aunt Fiona's plot to get him and his five brothers married had him spooked. Marriage was a serious business, not to be undertaken lightly, especially by a commitment-phobe. Aunt Fiona had just scored a direct hit with Creed's brother Pete, who'd married Jackie Samuels and had triplets right off the baby-daddy bat. Creed was potently aware his days as a happy, freewheeling bachelor might come to an end if he didn't get the hell away from Rancho Diablo.

So he'd fled like a shy girl at her first dance. Creed didn't relish being called chicken, but Aunt Fiona was a force to be reckoned with. Creed stared into his sixth beer, which the bartender in Lance, Wyoming, a generous man who could see that Creed's soul was in torment, had courteously poured.

Anyone in Diablo, New Mexico, would attest to the powers of Aunt Fiona. Especially when she had a goal—then no one was safe. His small, spare aunt had raised him and his five brothers upon the deaths of their parents without so much as a break in her stride. She and her butler, Burke, had flown in from Ireland one day, clucked over and coddled the five confused boys (young Sam had not yet been part of the family, an occurrence which still perplexed the brothers), and gave them an upbringing which was loving, firm and heaped with enthusiastic advice.

Creed barely remembered their parents, Jeremiah and Molly. He was the lucky one in the family, in his opinion, because he had a twin, Rafe. It had helped to have a mirror image at his back over the years. Creed was prone to mischief, Rafe was more of a thinker. Once, when the boys had wondered where babies came from— upon Sam's surprising arrival after Fiona had come to be their guardian—Creed had uprooted all of Fiona's precious garden looking for "baby" seeds. Rafe had told Aunt Fiona that he'd seen bunnies in her garden, which was true, but bunnies weren't the reason Aunt Fiona's kitchen crop had to be restarted.

Creed certainly knew where babies came from now. Watching Pete and Jackie go from a casual romance once a week to parents of triplets had underscored for him the amazing fertility of the Callahan men. They were like stallions—gifted with the goods.

With Fiona prodding about his unmarried state, Creed

had hit the road. He did not want his own virility tested. He didn't want a wife or children. Pete was solidly positioned to win Rancho Diablo, for that was the deal Fiona had struck: whoever of the six brothers married and produced the most heirs inherited all five thousand acres.

But he and his brothers had worked an agreement out unbeknownst to their wily aunt: only one of them would be the sacrifice (which had turned out to be the lucky— or unlucky, depending upon how one viewed it—brother Pete), and he would divide the ranch between the six of them. It was a fair-and-square way to keep any animosity from arising between them for the high-value prize of hearth and home. Competition wasn't a good thing among brothers, they'd agreed, though they competed against each other all the time, naturally. But this was different.

This competition wasn't rodeo, or lassoing, or tree climbing. This was a race to the altar, and they vowed that Fiona's planning wouldn't entrap them.

"And I'm safe," Creed muttered into his beer.

"Did you say something?" a chocolate-haired beauty said to him, and Creed realized that the old saying was true: women started looking better with every beer. Creed blinked. The male bartender who'd been listening to his woes with a sympathetic ear had morphed into a sexy female, which meant Creed wasn't as safe as he thought he was. He was, in fact, six sheets to the wind and blowing south. "Six beers is not that big a deal," he told the woman who was looking at him with some approbation. "Where's Johnny?"

"Johnny?" She raised elfin brows at him and ran a hand through springy chin-length curls. "My name is Aberdeen."

He wasn't *that* drunk. In fact, he wasn't drunk at all. He knew the difference between moobs and boobs, and while Johnny had been the soul of generosity, he'd had girth appropriate for bouncing troublemakers out of his bar. This delightful lady eyeing him had a figure, pert and enticing, and Creed's chauvinistic brain was registering very little else except she looked like something a man who'd had six beers (okay, maybe twelve, but they were small ones so he'd halved his count), might want to drag into the sack. She had bow-shaped lips and dark blue eyes, but, most of all, she smelled like something other than beer and salami and pretzels. *Spring flowers*, he thought with a sigh. Yes, the smells of spring, after a long cold winter in Diablo. "You're beautiful," he heard someone tell her, and glanced around for the dope that would say something so unmanly.

"Thank you," she said to Creed.

"Oh, I didn't—" He stopped. *He* was the dope. *I sound like Pete. I need to leave now.* The beer had loosened his tongue and thrown his cool to the wind. "I'd best be going, Amber Jean." He slid off the bar stool, thinking how sad it was that he'd never see Johnny/Amber Jean again, and how wonderfully fresh and romantic springtime smelled in Wyoming.

"Oh, now, that's a shame," Johnny Donovan said, looking down at the sleeping cowboy on his bar floor. "Clearly this is a man who doesn't know much about brew."

Aberdeen gave her brother a disparaging glance. "You're the one who gave him too much."

"I swear I did not. The man wanted to talk more than drink, truthfully." Johnny gave Aberdeen his most innocent gaze. "He went on and on and on, Aberdeen, and so I could tell he wasn't really looking for the hops but for a good listener. On his fifth beer, I began giving him near-beer, as God is my witness, Aberdeen. You know I disapprove of sloppiness. And it's against the law to let someone drink and drive." He squinted outside, searching the darkness. It was three o'clock in the morning. "Mind you, I have no idea what he's driving, but he won't be driving a vehicle from my bar in this sloppy condition."

Her brother ran a conscientious establishment. "I'm sorry," Aberdeen said, knowing Johnny treated his patrons like family. Even strangers were given Johnny's big smile, and if anyone so much as mentioned they needed help, Johnny would give them the shirt off his back and the socks off his feet. Aberdeen looked at the cowboy sprawled on the floor, his face turned to the ceiling as he snored with luxuriant abandon. He was sinfully gorgeous: a pile, at the moment, of amazing masculinity. Lean and tall, with long dark hair, a chiseled face, a hint of being once broken about the nose. She restrained the urge to brush an errant swath of midnight hair away from his closed eyes. "What do we do with him?"

Johnny shrugged. "Leave him on the floor to sleep. The man is tired, Aberdeen. Would you have us kick a heartbroken soul out when he just needs a bit of time to gather his wits?"

"Heartbroken?" Aberdeen frowned. The cowboy was too good-looking by half. Men like him demanded caution; she knew this from her congregation. Ladies loved the cowboys; they loved the character and the drive. They loved the romance, the idea of the real working man. And heaven only knew, a lot of those men loved the ladies in return. This one, with his soft voice, good manners and flashing blue eyes… Well, Aberdeen had no doubt that this cowboy had left his fair share of broken hearts trampled in the dirt. "If you sit him outside, he'll gather his wits fast enough."

"Ah, now, Aberdeen. I can't treat paying customers that way, darling. You know that. He's causing no harm, is he?" Johnny looked at her with his widest smile and most apologetic expression, which should have looked silly on her bear of a brother, but which melted her heart every time.

"You're too soft, Johnny."

"And you're too hard, my girl. I often ask myself if all cowboy preachers are as tough on cowboys as you are. This is one of your flock, Aberdeen. He's only drunk on confusion and sadness." Johnny stared at Creed's long-forgotten beer mug. "I feel sorry for him."

Aberdeen sighed. "It's your bar. You do as you like. I'm going to my room."

Johnny went on sweeping up. "I'll keep an eye on him. You go on to bed. You have preaching to do in the morning."

"And I haven't finished writing my sermon. Good night, Johnny." She cast a last glance at the slumbering, too-sexy man on the dark hardwood floor, and headed upstairs. She was glad to leave Johnny with the stranger. No man should look that good sleeping on the floor.

A roar from downstairs, guffaws and loud thumping woke Aberdeen from deep sleep. Jumping to her feet, she glanced at her bedside clock. Seven o'clock—past time for her to be getting ready for church. She grabbed her robe, and more roars sent her running down the stairs.

Her brother and the stranger sat playing cards on a barrel table in the empty bar. One of them was winning—that much was clear from the grins—and the other didn't mind that he was losing. There were mugs of milk and steaming coffee on a table beside them. Both men were so engrossed in their game that neither of them looked up as she stood there with her hands on her hips. She was of half a mind to march back upstairs and forget she'd ever seen her brother being led astray by the hunky stranger.

"Johnny," Aberdeen said, "did you know it's Sunday morning?"

"I do, darlin'," Johnny said, "but I can't leave him. He's got a fever." He gestured to his playing partner.

"A fever?" Aberdeen's eyes widened. "If he's sick, why isn't he in bed?"

"He won't go. I think he's delirious."

She came closer to inspect the cowboy. "What do you mean, he won't go?"

"He thinks he's home." Johnny grinned at her. "It's the craziest thing."

"It's a lie, Johnny. He's setting us up." She slapped her hand on the table in front of the cowboy. He looked up at her with wide, too-bright eyes. "Have you considered he's on drugs? Maybe that's why he passed out last night."

"Nah," Johnny said. "He's just a little crazy."

She pulled up a chair, eyeing the cowboy cautiously, as he eyed her right back. "Johnny, we don't need 'a little crazy' right now."

"I know you're worried, Aberdeen."

"Aberdeen," the cowboy said, trying out her name. "Not Amber Jean. Aberdeen."

She looked at Johnny. "Maybe he's slow."

Johnny shrugged. "Said he got a small concussion at his last stop. Got thrown from a bull and didn't ride again that night. He says he just had to come home."

She shook her head. "Sounds like it might be serious. He could have a fever. We can't try to nurse him, Johnny."

"We can take him to the hospital, I suppose." Johnny looked at the stranger. "Do you want to go to a hospital, friend?"

The cowboy shook his head. "I think I'll go to bed now."

Aberdeen wrinkled her nose as the cowboy went over to a long bench in the corner, laid himself out and promptly went to sleep. "You were giving milk to a man with fever?"

Johnny looked at her, his dark eyes curious. "Is that a bad thing? He asked for it."

She sighed. "We'll know soon enough." After a moment, she walked over and put her hand against his forehead. "He's burning up!"

"Well," Johnny said, "the bar's closed today. He can sleep on that bench if he likes, I guess. If he's not better tomorrow, I'll take him to a doctor, though he doesn't seem especially inclined to go."

Aberdeen stared at the sleeping cowboy's handsome face. *Trouble with a capital T.* "Did he tell you his name? Maybe he's got family around here who could come get him."

"No." Johnny put the cards away and tossed out the milk. "He babbles a lot about horses. Talks a great deal about spirit horses and other nonsense. Native American lore. Throws in an occasional Irish tale. Told a pretty funny joke, too. The man has a sense of humor, even if he is out of his mind."

"Great." Aberdeen had a funny feeling about the cowboy who had come to Johnny's Bar and Grill. "I'm going to see who he is," she said, reaching into his front pocket for his wallet.

A hand shot out, grabbing her wrist. Aberdeen gasped and tried to draw away, but the cowboy held on, staring up at her with those navy eyes. She couldn't look away.

"Stealing's wrong," he said.

She slapped his hand and he released her. "I know that, you ape. What's your name?"

He crossed his arms and gave her a roguish grin. "What's *your* name?"

"I already told you my name is Aberdeen." He'd said it not five minutes ago, so possibly he did have a concussion. With a fever, that could mean complications. "Johnny, this man is going to need a run to the—"

The cowboy watched her with unblinking eyes. Aberdeen decided to play it safe. "Johnny, could you pull the truck around? Our guest wants to go for a ride to see our good friend, Dr. Mayberry."

Johnny glanced at the man on the bench. "Does he now?"

"He does," Aberdeen said firmly.

Johnny nodded and left to get his truck. Aberdeen looked at the ill man, who watched her like a hawk. "Cowboy, I'm going to look at your license, and if you grab me again like you did a second ago, you'll wish you hadn't. I may be a minister, but when you live above a bar, you learn to take care of yourself. So either you give me your wallet, or I take it. Those are your choices."

He stared at her, unmoving.

She reached into his pocket and pulled out his wallet, keeping her gaze on him, trying to ignore the expanse of wide chest and other parts of him she definitely shouldn't notice. Flipping it open, she took out his driver's license. "Creed Callahan. New Mexico."

She put the license away, ignoring the fact that he had heaven-only-knew-how-many hundred-dollar bills stuffed into the calfskin wallet, and slid it back into his pocket.

He grabbed her, pulling her to him for a fast kiss. His lips molded to hers, and Aberdeen felt a spark—more than a spark, *real* heat—and then he released her.

She glared at him. He shrugged. "I figured you'd get around to slapping me eventually. Might as well pay hell is what I always say."

"Is that what you always say? With every woman you force to kiss you?" Aberdeen asked, rattled, and even more irritated that she hadn't been kissed like that in years. "You said stealing was wrong."

"It is. I didn't say I didn't do it." He grinned, highly pleased with himself, and if he hadn't already rung his bell, she would have slapped him into the next county.

Then again, it was hard to stay mad when he was that cheerful about being bad. Aberdeen put her hands on her hips so he couldn't grab her again. "All right, Mr. Callahan, do you remember why you're in Wyoming?"

"Rodeo. I ride rodeo, ma'am."

Johnny was back. "Truck's out front."

"Johnny," Aberdeen said, "this is Creed Callahan. Mr. Callahan is very happy you're going to take him for a ride. Aren't you, Mr. Callahan?"

"Callahan?" Johnny repeated. "One of the six Callahans from New Mexico?"

"Have you heard of him?"

"Sure." Johnny shrugged. "All of them ride rodeo, and not too shabbily. The older brother didn't ride much, but he did a lot of rodeo doctoring after he got out of medical school. Some of them have been highly ranked. You don't go to watch rodeo without knowing about the Callahans." He looked at Creed with sympathy. "What are you doing here, friend?"

Creed sighed. "I think I'm getting away from something, but I can't remember what."

"A woman?" Johnny asked, and Aberdeen waited to hear the answer with sudden curiosity.

"A woman," Creed mused. "That sounds very likely. Women are trouble, you know. They want to have—" He lowered his voice conspiratorially in an attempt to keep Aberdeen from hearing. "They want to have b-a-b-i-e-s."

Aberdeen rolled her eyes. "Definitely out of his mind. Take him away, Johnny."

Her brother laughed. "He may be right, you know."

"I don't care," Aberdeen said, gathering her self-control. He might have stolen a kiss, but the conceited louse was never getting another one from her. "He's crazy."

"That's what they say," Creed said, perking up, obviously recognizing something he'd heard about himself before.

Aberdeen washed her hands of Mr. Loco. "Goodbye, cowboy," she said, "hope you get yourself together again some day. I'll be praying for you."

"And I'll be praying for you," Creed said courteously, before rolling off the bench onto the floor.

"That's it, old man," Johnny said, lifting Creed up and over his shoulder. "Off we go, then. Aberdeen, I may not make your service today, love."

"It's okay, Johnny." Aberdeen watched her brother carry Creed to the truck and place him inside as carefully as a baby. The man said he was running, but no one ran from their family, did they? Not someone who had five brothers who'd often traveled together, rodeoed together, competed against each other? And Johnny said one of the brothers was a doctor.

People needed family when they were hurting. He'd be better off with them instead of being in Wyoming among strangers.

Aberdeen went to her room to look up Callahans in New Mexico, thinking about her own desire for a family. A real one. Her sister, Diane, had tried to make a family, but it hadn't worked. Though she had three small adorable daughters, Diane wasn't cut out to be a mother. Then Aberdeen had married Shawn "Re-ride" Parker right out of high school. That hadn't lasted long, and there had been no children. And Johnny, a confirmed bachelor, said he had enough on his hands with his two sisters. They had their own definition of family, Aberdeen supposed, which worked for them. If a woman was looking to have a baby, though, Creed Callahan probably ranked as perfect donor material—if a woman liked crazy, which she didn't. "I don't do crazy anymore," she reminded herself, dialing the listing she got from the operator.

The sooner crazy left town, the better for all of them.

Chapter 2

Creed was astonished to see his brother Judah when he awakened. He was even more surprised to realize he was in a hospital room. He glanced around, frowning at his snoozing brother—Judah looked uncomfortable and ragged in the hospital chair—and wondered why he was here. Creed tried to remember how he'd gotten to the hospital and couldn't. Except for a ferocious headache, he felt fine.

"Judah," he said, and his brother started awake.

"Hey!" Judah grinned at him. "What the hell, man? You scared me to death."

"Why?" Creed combed his memory and found it lacking. "What's going on? Where am I?"

"We're in Lance, Wyoming. A bar owner brought you in."

"Was I in a fight?" Creed rubbed at his aching head,

confused by his lost memory. He didn't remember drinking all that much, but if a bar owner had brought him in, maybe he'd gotten a little riled up. "If I was, I hope I won."

Judah smirked. "The fight you were in was apparently with a bull. And you lost. At least this round."

Creed perked up. "Which bull was it? I hope it was a bounty bull. At least a rank bull, right?"

His brother smiled. "Can I get you something? Are you hungry?"

Creed blinked. Judah didn't want to tell him which bull had thrown him, which wasn't good. Cowboys loved to brag, even on the bad rides. He told himself he was just a little out of practice, nothing more riding couldn't cure. "I feel like my head isn't part of my body."

"You've got a slight concussion. The doctor thinks you're going to be fine, but he's keeping you a few hours for observation."

"I've had concussions before and not gone to the hospital."

"This time you had a high fever. Could have been the concussion, could have been a bug. The doctors just want to keep an eye on you. They mapped your brain, by the way, and said you don't have too much rattling around inside your skull. The brain cavity is strangely lacking in material."

Creed grunted at Judah's ribbing. "Sorry you had to make the trip."

"No problem. I wasn't doing anything."

Creed grunted again at the lie. Callahans always had plenty to do around Rancho Diablo. Five thousand acres of prime land and several hundred head of livestock meant that they stayed plenty busy. They kept the ranch running through sheer hard work and commitment to the family business.

"Anyway, it's been a while since anyone's seen you. Didn't know where you were keeping yourself." Judah scrutinized him. "We really didn't understand why you left in the first place."

Now *that* Creed could dig out of his cranium. "I was next on Fiona's list, Judah. I could *feel* it." He shuddered. "You don't understand until you've had Fiona's eye trained on you. Once she's thinking about getting you to the altar, you're halfway there."

"She's thinking about all of us," Judah pointed out. "Remember, that's her plan."

"But it was supposed to be over when Pete got married. He was the sacrifice." Creed took a deep breath. "And then I realized Fiona was running through her catalog of eligible females for me. I could hear her mind whirring. I've known every woman Fiona could possibly think of all my life. And there's not a one of them I'd care to marry."

Judah nodded. "I feel the same way."

Creed brightened. "You do?"

"Sure. Occasionally I think about a certain gal, but then I think, no, she'd never have me. And then I get over it pretty fast." Judah grinned. "The sacrifice wasn't ever going to be me. I'm not good at commitment for the sake of just having a girl around. Heck, I was never even good at picking a girl to take to prom."

"That was an exercise in futility." Creed remembered his brother's agony. "I had to fix you up with some of my friends."

"And that was embarrassing because of you being a year older than me."

"I didn't exactly mind," Creed hedged. "And I didn't hear you complaining about going out with an older woman."

Judah shook his head. "My dates didn't complain because I'm a good kisser. When you're a year younger than the girls you take out, you learn to make it up to them." He grinned. "You know, it's not that I don't like women, I just like *all* women."

"Amen, bro," Creed said happily, back on terra firma. "Women are a box of candy, you never know what you're going to get."

"All right, Forrest Gump. Go back to sleep." Judah smiled at the nurse who came in to take his brother's temperature. "I had no idea the ladies in Wyoming are so lovely," Judah said. "Why wasn't I living here all my life?"

Creed grinned at his brother's flirting. *Now* he remembered who he was. He was Creed Callahan, hotshot rider and serious serial lover of females. Wild at heart. It was good to be a Callahan. He was love-them-and-leave-them-happy, that's who he was.

And women adored him.

Creed never noticed the nurse taking his pulse and his temperature. Somewhere in his memory a vision of a brunette with expressive eyebrows nagged at him. A female who hadn't quite adored him. In fact, she might even have thought he was annoying.

It wasn't likely such a woman existed, but then again, he couldn't remember ever getting concussed by anything other than a rank bull, either. Creed closed his eyes, wishing his headache would go away, but there was greater pain inside him: his last several rides had been bombs. Not even close to eights. On par with unfortunate.

I need a break, and the only thing I manage to break is my head.

He'd just lie here and think about it a little while longer, and maybe the fog would lift. He heard Judah and the nurse giggling quietly about something, which didn't help. Judah could score anytime he liked. The ladies loved all that haunted-existentialist crap that his younger brother exuded. *But I'm not existential. Rafe, he's an existential thinker. Me, I'm just wild. And that's all I'll ever be.*

He felt really tired just connecting those pieces of information. When he got out of here, he was going to remember that a fallen rider needed to get right back up on his reindeer.

Or something like that.

But then Creed thought about dark-blue annoyed eyes staring at him, and wondered if he was running out of good luck.

Aberdeen sat reluctantly at the cowboy's bedside, waiting for him to waken, and not really wanting him to. There was something about him that nagged at her, and it wasn't just that he'd kissed her. Cowboys were typically a good group, but she wasn't sure about this one, though she was trying to give him the benefit of the doubt. She worked to spread faith and good cheer amongst her beat-up flock, and beat-up they were on Sunday mornings. Her congregation consisted of maybe twenty-five people on a busy Sunday, often less. Banged-up gentlemen dragged in for an hour of prayer and sympathy and the potluck spaghetti lunch she and her friends served in the bar afterward. She preached in Johnny's big barn, which had a covered pavilion for indoor riding. The cowboys and cowgirls, wearing jeans and sleepy expressions of gratitude, gratefully headed to the risers.

This man was beat-up, all right, but he didn't seem like he cared to find spiritual recovery in any form. She pondered her transient congregation. Sunday mornings were her favorite part of the week, and she rarely ever missed giving a sermon, though if she did, Johnny was an excellent stand-in, as well as some of their friends. Neither of them had grown up thinking they wanted to be preachers, but missionarying had taken hold of Aberdeen in high school, growing stronger during college. She'd majored in theology, minored in business, and Johnny had done the opposite. The two of them were a good working team. Over the years, Johnny's Bar and Grill had become known as the place to hang out six days a week, crash when necessary and hear words of worship on Sunday. Aberdeen knew many of the cowboys that pulled through Lance. She couldn't understand why she'd never heard of the Callahans, if they were the prolific, daring riders that Johnny claimed they were.

But she'd gotten busy in the past five years, so busy she barely paid attention to anything more than what the top riders were scoring, and sometimes not even that. Her knowledge had ebbed when she started helping Johnny at the bar and writing more of her sermons. She was twenty-nine, and at some point, rodeo had left her consciousness. She'd focused more on her job and less on fun—although sometimes she missed that. A lot.

Plus she had Diane to think about. Diane was in trouble, real trouble, and nothing she or Johnny did seemed to help her. Their older sister couldn't keep a job, couldn't keep a husband—she was on her third—and had three young children, had had one a year for the past three years. Now she was going through a bitter divorce from a man who'd walked out and was never coming back. It had always been hard for Aberdeen and Johnny to understand why Diane made the choices she did.

Recently, Diane had asked Aberdeen to adopt her daughters, Ashley, Suzanne and Lincoln Rose. Diane said she could no longer handle the responsibility of being a parent. Aberdeen was seriously considering taking the girls in. If Diane didn't want to be a mother, then Aberdeen didn't want to see Child Protective Services picking up her nieces. She loved them, with all her heart.

Diane lived in Spring, Montana, and wanted to move to Paris to chase after a new boyfriend she'd met traveling through the state. Aberdeen lived in fear that their elderly parents would call and say that Diane had already skipped.

"Howdy," the cowboy said, and Aberdeen's gaze snapped up to meet his.

"Hi. Feeling better?" she asked, conscious once again of how those dark denim eyes unsettled her.

"I think so." He brightened after feeling his head. "Yes, I definitely am. Headache is gone." He gave her a confiding grin. "I dreamed about you."

Her mouth went dry. "Why?"

"I remembered your eyes. I didn't remember a lot else, but I did remember your eyes."

She'd remembered his, too, though she'd tried not to. "Good dream or a bad dream?"

He grinned. "Now, sugar, wouldn't you like to know?"

She pursed her lips, wishing she hadn't asked.

"Ah, now that's the expression I recall with clarity,"

Creed said. "Annoyance. Mainly because it's not what I usually see in a woman's eyes."

"No? What do you usually see?" Aberdeen *was* annoyed, and the second she fell into his trap, she was even more irritated. Mainly with herself.

"Lust, preacher lady. I see lust."

She leaned away from him. "Ladies do not lust."

He raised jet-black brows. "I swear they do."

"They desire," she told him. "They have longings."

He shook his head. "You've been meeting the wrong kind of fellows, sugar cake."

She got up and grabbed her purse. "It's good to see you on the mend, Mr. Callahan. Happy trails."

He laughed, a low, sensual sound that followed Aberdeen to the door. "Thank you, miss."

He hadn't placed an emphasis on *miss*, but it teed her off just the same. Made her feel naked. She wasn't an old-maid kind of miss; she was a conscientious abstainer from another marriage. *That's right, cowboy. I'm single and okay with it. Almost okay with it, anyway.*

As she rounded the corner, she plowed into a tall cowboy who looked a lot like the one she'd left in his hospital room.

"Whoa, little lady," he said, setting her back on her feet. "Where's the fire?"

She frowned. "You're not one of the Callahans, are you?"

"I am." He nodded, smiling at her. "You must be the nice lady who let us know Creed was down on his luck."

"Yes, I did. He's made a great recovery."

He tipped his hat, dark-blue eyes—just like Creed's—sparkling at her. "My name is Judah Callahan."

She reached out to shake his hand. "Aberdeen Donovan."

"We can't thank you enough, Miss Aberdeen."

He had kind eyes—unlike the flirt back in the hospital bed. "No thanks necessary. My brother Johnny would help anyone in trouble." She smiled at him. "I've got to run, but it was nice meeting you, Judah."

"Thank you, Aberdeen. Again, thanks for rescuing Bubba."

She shook her head and walked away. Bubba. There was nothing little-brother Bubba about Creed. He was all full-grown man and devil-may-care lifestyle. She'd be a fool to fall for a man like him. Fortunately, forewarned was forearmed.

Chapter 3

Judah strolled into Creed's room. By the sneaky smile on his brother's face, Creed deduced that his visit wasn't all about rousing the patient to better health. "What?" Creed had a funny feeling he knew what was coming.

"You've got all the luck," Judah said, throwing himself into a chair. "Finding a little angel like that to rescue you."

Judah grinned, but Creed let his scowl deepen. "She's not as much of an angel as she appears. Don't let her looks fool you."

His brother laughed. "Couldn't sweet-talk her, huh?"

Creed sniffed. "Didn't try."

"Sure you did." Judah crossed a leg over a knee and lounged indolently, enjoying having Creed at his mercy. "She didn't give you the time of day." He looked up at the ceiling, putting on a serious face. "You know, some ladies take their angel status very seriously."

"Meaning?" Creed arched a brow at his brother, half-curious as to where all this ribbing was going. Judah had no room to talk about success with women, as far as Creed was concerned. Only Pete was married—and only Pete had claimed a girlfriend, sort of, before Aunt Fiona had thrown down the marriage gauntlet. Creed figured the rest of the Callahan brothers were just about nowhere with serious relationships.

Including me.

"Just that once a woman like her rescues a man, she almost feels responsible for him. Like a child." Judah sighed. "Very difficult thing to get away from, when a woman sees a man in a mothering light."

Creed stared at his brother. "That's the biggest bunch of hogwash I've ever heard."

"Have you ever wondered exactly what hogwash is?" Judah looked thoughtful. "If I had a hog, I sure wouldn't wash it."

"Hogwash just means garbage," Creed said testily. "Your literal mood is not amusing."

"I was just making conversation, since you're not in a position to do much else."

"Sorry." Creed got back to the point he was most intrigued by. "Anyway, so you met Aberdeen?"

Judah nodded. "Yes. And thanked her for taking care of my older brother. Do you remember any of what happened to you?"

"I don't know. Some bug hit me, I guess." Creed was missing a couple of days out of his life. "I didn't make the cut in Lance, so I was going to head on to the next rodeo.

And I saw this out-of-the-way restaurant on the side of the road, so I stopped. Next thing I knew, I was here."

Judah shook his head. "A bad hand, man."

"Yeah."

"Never want a woman you've just met to see you weak," Judah mused.

"I wasn't weak. I just got the wrong end of a ride. Or the flu." Creed glared at Judah. "So anyway, how are the newlyweds? And Fiona? Burke? Everyone else?"

"No one else is getting married, if that's what you're asking. You still have a shot. Like Cinderella getting a glass slipper. It could happen, under the right conditions."

"I don't want a wife or children. That's why I'm here," Creed growled. "You can be the ambassador for both of us, thanks."

"I don't know. I kind of thought that little brunette who went racing out of your room might have some possibilities."

"Then ask her out." Creed felt a headache coming on that had nothing to do with his concussion. It was solely bad temper, which Judah was causing.

Just like the old days. In a way, it was comforting.

"I don't know. I could have sworn I felt that tension thing. You know, a push-pull vibe when she left your room. She was all riled like she had fire on her heels, as if you'd really twisted her up."

"That's a recipe for love if I ever heard one."

"Yeah." Judah warmed to his theory. "Fire and ice. Only she's mostly fire."

"Hellfire is my guess. You know she's a cowboy church preacher."

"Oh." Judah slumped. "That was the fire I picked up

on. I knew she needed an extinguisher for some reason. I just thought maybe it had to do with you."

"Nope," Creed said, happy to throw water on his brother's silly theory. "You'll have to hogwash another Callahan into getting roped. And you are not as good as Fiona," Creed warned with satisfaction.

Judah shook his head. "No one is."

"I think," Fiona told her friends at the Books 'n' Bingo Society meeting, "that voting a few new members in to our club is a good idea. Sabrina McKinley can't stay shut up in the house all the time taking care of dreadful old Bode Jenkins." Fiona sniffed, despising even saying Bode's name. It was Bode who'd finally closed her up in a trap, and the fact that the man had managed to find a way to get Rancho Diablo from her rankled terribly. She was almost sick with fear over what to tell her six nephews. Pete knew. She could trust Pete. He would keep her secret until the appropriate time. And he was married now, with darling triplet daughters, a dutiful nephew if there ever was one.

But the other five—well, she'd be holding her breath for a long while if she dreamed those five rapscallions would get within ten feet of an altar. No, they'd be more likely to set an altar on fire with their anti-marriage postures. Poof! Up in smoke.

Just like her grip on Rancho Diablo. How disappointed her brother Jeremiah and his wife, Molly, would be if they knew that she'd lost the ranch they'd built. "Some guardian I am," she murmured, and Corrine Abernathy said, "What, Fiona?"

Fiona shook her head. "Anyway, we need to invite Sabrina into our group. We need fresh blood, young voices who can give us new ideas."

Her three best friends and nine other ladies smiled at her benevolently.

"It sounds like a good idea," Mavis Night said. "Who else do you want?"

Fiona thought about it. Sabrina had been an obvious choice for new-member status, because she was Corinne's niece. So was Seton McKinley, a private investigator Fiona had hired to ferret out any chinks in Bode's so-far formidable armor. "I think maybe Bode Jenkins."

An audible gasp went up in the tearoom.

"You can't be serious," Nadine Waters said, her voice quavering. "He's your worst enemy."

"And we should keep our enemy close to our bosoms, shouldn't we?" Fiona looked around the room. "Anyway, I put it forth to a vote."

"Why not Sheriff Cartwright? He's a nice man," Nadine offered. "For our first male in the group, I'd rather vote for a gentleman."

Murmurs of agreement greeted that sentiment.

"I don't know," Fiona said. "Maybe I'm losing my touch. Maybe inviting Bode is the wrong idea." She thought about her words before saying slowly, "Maybe I should give up my chairwomanship of the Books 'n' Bingo Society."

Everyone stared at her, their faces puzzled, some glancing anxiously at each other.

"Fiona, is everything all right?" Corinne asked.

"I don't know," Fiona said. She didn't want to tell them that in another six months she might not be here. It was time to lay the groundwork for the next chairwoman. She would have no home which to invite them, there would be no more Rancho Diablo. Only one more Christmas at Diablo. She wanted to prepare her friends for the future. But she also didn't want the truth to come out just yet, for her nephews' sakes. She wanted eligible bachelorettes—the cream of the Diablo crop—to see them still as the powerful Callahan clan, the men who worked the hardest and shepherded the biggest ranch around.

Not as unfortunate nephews of a silly aunt who'd gambled away their birthright.

She wanted to cry, but she wouldn't. "I think I'll adjourn, girls. Why don't we sleep on everything, and next week when we meet maybe we'll have some ideas on forward-thinking goals for our club."

Confused, the ladies rose, hugging each other, glancing with concern at Fiona. Fiona knew she'd dropped a bomb on her friends. She hadn't handled the situation well.

But then, she hadn't handled anything well lately. *I'm definitely losing it*, she thought. In the old days, her most gadabout, confident days, a man like Bode Jenkins would never have gotten the best of her.

She was scared.

"I'm thinking about it," Aberdeen told Johnny that night. "Our nieces need a stable home. And I don't know how to help Diane more than we have. Maybe she needs time away. Maybe she's been through too much. There's no way for us to know what is going through her mind." Aberdeen sat in their cozy upstairs den with Johnny. It was Sunday night so the bar was closed. They'd thoroughly cleaned it after going by to see the recovering cowboy. He'd looked much better and seemed cheered by his brother's presence.

There wasn't much else she and Johnny could do for him, either, and she didn't really want to get any more involved. She had enough on her hands. "Mom and Dad say that they try to help Diane, but despite that, they're afraid the children are going to end up in a foster home somewhere, some day." Aberdeen felt tears press behind her eyelids. "The little girls deserve better than this, Johnny. And Diane has asked me to adopt them. She says she's under too much pressure. Too many children, not enough income, not enough…maternal desire."

That wasn't exactly how Diane had put it. Diane had said she wasn't a fit mother. Aberdeen refused to believe that. Her sister had always been a sunny person, full of optimism. These days, she was darker, moodier, and it all seemed to stem from the birth of her last child. Up until that moment, Diane had thought everything was fine in her marriage. It wasn't until after the baby was born that she'd discovered her husband had another woman. He no longer wanted to be a father, nor a husband to Diane.

"I don't know," Johnny said. "Aberdeen, we live over a bar. I don't think anyone will let us have kids here. Nor could I recommend it. We don't want the girls growing up in an environment that isn't as wholesome as we could make it. We don't even have schools nearby."

Aberdeen nodded. "I know. I've thought about this, Johnny. I think I'm going to have to move to Montana."

Her brother stared at her. "You wanted to leave Montana. So did I."

"But it's not a bad place to live, Johnny." It really wasn't. And the girls would have so much more there than they would living over a bar. "I could be happy there."

"It's not that Montana was the problem," Johnny said. "It was the family tree we wanted to escape."

This was also true. Their parents weren't the most loving, helpful people. They'd pretty much let their kids fend for themselves, believing that they themselves had gotten by with little growing up, and had done fine figuring life out themselves. So Johnny and Aberdeen had left Montana, striking out to "figure life out" on their own. Diane had opted to stay behind with their parents. Consequently, she'd married, had kids, done the wife thing—and left herself no backup when it all fell apart.

"I've been thinking, too," Johnny said. "To be honest, the red flag went up for me when the folks said they were worried. For them to actually worry and not ascribe to their typical let-them-figure-it-out-themselves theory, makes me think the situation is probably dire."

Aberdeen shook her head. "The girls need more. They're so young, Johnny. I don't know exactly what happened to Diane and why she's so determined she can't be a mother anymore, but I think I'm going to either have to get custody or fully adopt, like Diane wants me to do. They need the stability."

Johnny scratched his chin. "We just can't have them here. There are too many strangers for safety."

"That's why I think I have to go to Montana. At least there I can assess what's been happening."

Johnny waved a big hand at her. "Diane is leaving. There's nothing to assess. She's going to follow whatever wind is blowing, and our parents don't want to be bothered with toddlers."

"They don't have the health to do it, Johnny."

"True, but—"

"It doesn't matter," Aberdeen said quickly. "We just need to think of what's best for the girls."

"We can buy a house here. Maybe it's time to do that, anyway."

She looked around their home. It hadn't been in the best condition when they'd bought the building, but they'd converted the large old house into a working/ living space that suited them. Upstairs were four bedrooms, with two on either side of an open space, with en suite bathrooms in the two largest bedrooms. They used the wide space between the bedrooms as a family room. For five years they'd lived here, and it was home.

"Maybe," she said, jumping a little when a knock sounded on the front door downstairs. Aberdeen glanced at Johnny. Their friends knew to go to the back door after the bar was closed; they never answered the front door in case a stranger might decide to see if they could get someone to open up the bar. A few drunks over the years had done that. She was surprised when Johnny headed down the stairs. Her brother was big and tall and strong, and he wouldn't open the door without his gun nearby, but still, Aberdeen followed him.

"We're closed," Johnny called through the door.

"I know. I just wanted to come by and say thanks before we left town," a man called from the other side, and Aberdeen's stomach tightened just a fraction.

"The cowboy," she said to Johnny, and he nodded.

"He's harmless enough," Johnny said. "A little bit of a loose cannon, but might as well let him have his say."

Aberdeen shrugged. "He can say it through the door just the same," she said, but Johnny gave her a wry look and opened up.

"Thanks for letting me in," Creed Callahan said to Johnny, shaking his hand as though he was a long-lost friend. "This is the man who probably saved my life, Judah," he said, and Judah put out a hand for Johnny to shake. "Hi, Aberdeen," Creed said.

"Hello, Aberdeen," Judah said, "we met in the hospital."

She smiled at Judah's polite manners, but it was his long-haired ruffian of a brother who held her gaze. She could feel her blood run hot and her frosty facade trying to melt. It was hard not to look at Creed's engaging smile and clear blue eyes without falling just a little bit. *You've been here before*, she reminded herself. *No more bad boys for you.*

"We didn't save your life," Johnny said, "you would have been fine."

Creed shook his head. "I don't remember much about the past couple of days. I don't really recall coming here." He smiled at Aberdeen. "I do remember you telling your brother you didn't want me here."

"That's true." She stared back at him coolly. "We're not really prepared to take in boarders. It's nice to see you on the mend. Will you be heading on now to the next rodeo?"

Judah softly laughed. "We do have to be getting on, but we just wanted to stop by to thank you." He tipped his hat to Aberdeen. "Again, I appreciate you looking out for my brother. He's fortunate to have guardian angels."

Aberdeen didn't feel much like an angel at the moment. She could feel herself in the grip of an attraction unlike anything that had ever hit her before. She'd felt it when she'd first laid eyes on Creed. The feeling hadn't dissipated when she'd visited him in the hospital. She could tell he was one of those men who would make a woman insane from wanting what she couldn't have.

It was the kiss that was muddying her mind. He'd unlocked a desire she'd jealously kept under lock and key, not wanting ever to get hurt again. "Goodbye," she said, her eyes on Creed. "Better luck with your next ride."

He gave her a lingering glance, and Aberdeen could have sworn he had something else he wanted to say but couldn't quite bring himself to say it. He didn't rush to the door, and finally Judah clapped him on the back so he'd get moving toward the exit.

"Goodbye," Creed said again, seemingly only to her, and chicken-heart that she was, Aberdeen turned around and walked upstairs, glad to see him go.

Once in Creed's truck, Judah tried to keep his face straight. Creed knew his brother was laughing at him, though, and it didn't help. "What?" he demanded, pulling out of the asphalt parking lot. "What's so funny?"

"That one is way out of your league, Creed."

Creed started to make a rebuttal of his interest, then shrugged. "I thought you said she'd probably feel responsible for me because she saved me."

Judah laughed. "Works for most guys, clearly backfired on you. Good thing you're not interested in a relationship with a woman, or keeping up with Pete, because you'd never get there if that gal was your choice. I don't believe I've ever seen a female look at a man with less enthusiasm. If you were a cockroach, she'd have squashed you."

He *felt* squashed. "She was like that from the moment I met her," Creed said. "I remember one very clear thing about the night I got here, and that was her big blue eyes staring at me like I was an ex-boyfriend. The kind of ex a woman never wants to lay eyes on again."

"Bad luck for you," Judah said, without much sympathy and with barely hidden laughter. "You're kind of on a roll, bro."

"My luck's bound to turn eventually." Creed was sure it would—he'd always led a fairly charmed existence, but when a man couldn't ride and the ladies weren't biting his well-baited hook and he was evading his wonky little aunt's plan to get him settled down, well, there was nothing else to do but wait for the next wave of good luck, which was bound to come anytime.

"Take me to the airport," Judah said, "now that you're on the mend."

"You don't want to ride with me to the next stop?"

Judah shook his head. "I've got a lot to do back home."

Guilt poured over Creed. There was always so much to do at Rancho Diablo that they could have had six more brothers and they wouldn't cover all the bases. "Yeah," Creed said, thinking hard. He wasn't winning. He'd busted his grape, though not as badly as some guys he knew. Still, it probably wasn't wise to get right back in the saddle.

He was homesick. "Maybe that bump on my noggin was a good thing."

"Not unless it knocked some sense into you."

He couldn't remember ever being homesick before. It was either having had a bad ride or meeting Aberdeen that had him feeling anxious. He wasn't sure which option would be worse. With a sigh he said, "Feel like saving on an airplane ticket?"

"Coming home?" Judah asked, with a sidelong glance at him, and Creed nodded.

"I think I will."

"Suits me. I hate to fly. So many rules to follow. And I hate taking off my boots in a line of other people taking off their shoes. I guess I could wear flip-flops or slip-ons, but my boots are just part of my body." He glanced out the window, watching the beautiful land fly past, clearly happy to have the scenery to admire. "Better luck next time, bro," he said, then pulled his hat down over his eyes. "Wake me when you want me to drive."

Creed nodded. He wasn't as sanguine and relaxed as Judah. He was rattled, feeling that something was missing, something wasn't quite right. Creed kept his eyes on the road, tried to relax his clenched fingers on the steering wheel—just enough to take the white from his knuckles. It had been silly to go back to Johnny's Bar and Grill, but he'd wanted to see Aberdeen. He wanted to take one last look at her, at those springy, dark-brown curls, her saucy nose, full lips, dark-blue eyes. He'd been lying, of course. He remembered something else besides those eyes staring at him with annoyance. He would never forget the soft feel of her lips beneath his, printing her heart onto his soul. He'd felt it, despite the concussion, and he had a funny feeling he would never forget Aberdeen Donovan.

Which was a first for a man who loved to kiss all the girls with his usual happy-go-lucky amnesia. He'd wanted one more kiss from Aberdeen, but it would have taken better luck than he was currently riding and maybe a real guardian angel looking out for him to make that dream come true.

He turned toward home.

Chapter 4

When Aberdeen and Johnny got to Montana a week after the cowboy had left town, they found matters were worse than expected. Diane was already in Paris chasing after her new boy toy, and had no plans to return. Ashley, Suzanne and Lincoln Rose had been left with their grandparents—and as Aberdeen and Johnny had feared, the older folk were overwhelmed and looking to hand off the girls. Quickly.

"Why didn't you call us?" Aberdeen demanded. "How long has Diane been gone?"

"She left two weeks ago. With that man." Fritz Donovan looked at her nieces helplessly. "Seems a mother ought to stay around to raise her own kids. Like we did."

Aberdeen bit her lip. *Some raising. You left us to raise ourselves, so Diane isn't all to blame.*

"You still should have called, Dad."

May Donovan jutted out her chin. "Diane said she'd told you that she was leaving. We figured that since you didn't come, you didn't want the girls. And you know very well Diane needs a break. It's just all been too much for her since the divorce."

Aberdeen counted to ten. May's constant blind eye where her older daughter was concerned was one of the reasons Diane continued to act irresponsibly at the age of thirty-five.

Johnny got to his feet, towering in the small kitchen. "There's no need to lay blame. If Diane is gone, she's gone. Now we need to decide what to do with the little ones."

"You're taking them with you, of course," May said. "Now that you've *finally* arrived."

Fritz nodded. "We're a bit old to take care of three little kids. Not that we can't," he said, his tone belligerent, "but maybe they'll be happier with you. Since that's what Diane wanted and all. You should help your sister since she's not had the breaks in life that you two have had."

Aberdeen told herself their parents' words didn't matter right now. They had always been cold and odd, and strangely preferential toward Diane. Aberdeen loved her sister as much as they did, but she wasn't blind to her faults, either. Diane had a selfish side that one day she might, hopefully, grow out of. For the sake of her nieces, Aberdeen prayed she did. "We'll take them back with us," she said finally, glancing at Johnny for his approval, which she knew would be there. "You can come see them as often as you like to visit."

"Ah, well. That won't be necessary," May said. "We don't travel much."

Their parents had never visited their home in Lance.

Aberdeen shook her head. "There's always a first time for everything. I'm heading to bed. We'll be off in the morning."

"That will be fine." The relief on May's face was plain. "You are planning to adopt them, aren't you, Aberdeen? After all, it would help Diane so much. She just can't do this, you know."

Her mother's gaze was pleading. It occurred to Aberdeen that her sister's mothering skills were basically the same as May's. It was always Johnny who kept the family together, Aberdeen realized. Johnny had been adoring of his little sister and helpful to his big sister and they'd always known they had their protective Johnny looking out for them. Not their parents. Johnny.

"I don't know, Mom," Aberdeen said. "We'd have to see if a court would allow it. We don't know what is involved with an in-family adoption when a mother is simply absent by choice. There's finances to consider, too."

"We can't give you any money," May said quickly, and Johnny said, "We're not asking you for money. We just need to proceed in a responsible fashion for the girls' sakes."

"Well, I would think—" May began, but Johnny cut her off.

"Enough, Mom. We have a lot of decisions to make in the near future. For all we know, Diane could come home next week, ready to be a mother. Maybe she just needed a vacation."

Aberdeen hoped so, but doubted it. "Good night," she said, and headed upstairs.

Part of her—the dreamy, irresponsible part she rarely acknowledged—took flight for just an instant, wondering how her life might be different if she, too, just took off, as Diane had, following a man on the whim of her heart.

Like a certain cowboy.

A big, strong, muscular, teasing hunk of six-four cowboy.

But no. She was as different from Diane as night and day. She was a dreamer, maybe, not a doer. She would never fling caution to the wind and follow a man like Creed Callahan.

Yet sweet temptation tugged at her thoughts.

"I've been thinking," Creed told Judah as they made their way through Colorado, "that little cowboy church preacher was a little too uptight for me, anyway."

Judah glanced at him as Creed slumped in the passenger seat, doling out some of their favorite road food. They'd made a pit stop just outside of Denver and loaded up on the junk food Fiona wouldn't allow them to have.

"What made you decide that?" Judah asked, taking a swig of the Big Red Creed had put in the cup holder for him. "Because I was pretty certain uptight might be good for you."

"Maybe in small doses," Creed said, feeling better as every mile took him farther away from temptation. "I'm pretty sure I can't handle uptight in large doses."

"I'd say narrow escape, except I don't think you were in danger of getting caught." Judah munched happily on Doritos from the open bag between the seats. "No, I'm sure you had Free Bird written all over your forehead, bro. No worries."

Creed pondered that. "I've decided to make a run for the ranch."

Judah glanced at him. "Since when?"

Since he'd met the preacher. That was weird, though, Creed thought with a frown. Women usually made him want to get naked, not own a ranch. "I don't know."

"Okay, of all of us, you are not the one to settle down and grow a large family."

"Pete's happy. I could learn by example."

"You ran away from being Pete. Remember? You ran like a hungry wolf to a picnic basket."

Creed considered that as he crunched some chips. "I think I changed when I got my bell rung."

"Creed, you get your bell rung once a year."

"This was different," Creed said. "I saw stars."

"You saw nothing. You weren't yourself for two days," Judah told him. "Anyway, it's not enough to change you. You've always been a loose goose."

"Yeah. I suppose so." Creed lost his appetite for chips and stared morosely at his soda can. "You know, I think Fiona's right. This *is* trash we're eating. I can feel my intestines turning red."

Judah sighed. "This is nectar of the gods."

"Maybe I miss home-cooking. We don't have it bad with Fiona, you know?" The past several months had outlined that to Creed. "We were lucky she raised us."

"Yeah. We could have gone into the system."

"That would have sucked." Creed turned his mind away from thoughts of being separated from his brothers. "Although I met a cowboy who'd been adopted, and he was pretty happy. Things worked out for him."

"It does. But we were in a good place with Fiona and Burke."

"And that's why I intend to fight for the ranch," Creed said with determination. "I just need a woman to help me with this project."

"It'd take you twenty years to *find* a woman," Judah said with some sarcasm, which cut Creed. "I'd say Pete is safe. Anyway, I thought we all agreed that the sacrificial lamb would do the deed, inherit the ranch and divvy it up between all of us. Thereby leaving the rest of us free to graze on the good things in life."

Creed crushed his soda can. "I'm not sure I'm grazing on the good things in life."

"Oh. You want angel food cake." Judah nodded. "Good luck with that. Let me know how it goes, will you?"

Creed rolled his eyes. Judah didn't understand. "I'm just saying, maybe we shouldn't burden Pete with all the responsibility."

"Why not? He's always been the responsible one."

"But maybe some of us should take a crack at being responsible, too. Take the pressure off him. He's got newborn triplets. It's selfish of us to stick him with all the duties."

"I think Fiona's probably realized by now that she can go ahead and award the ranch to Pete. Who could catch up with him? It would take years for one of us to find a woman and then have tons of kids. And what if the woman we found only wanted one? Or none?"

Creed gulped. He tried to envision Aberdeen with a big belly, and failed. She was such a slender woman. He liked slender, but then again, a little baby weight would look good on her. He liked full-figured gals, too.

Hell, he liked them all.

But he'd especially liked her, for some reason.

"It was the thrill of the hunt, nothing more," Judah said, his tone soothing. "Down, boy. It would have come to nothing."

Creed scowled. "I have no idea what you're babbling about."

"We are not settled men by nature. None of us sits and reads a whole lot, for example."

"Not true. Jonas read a hell of a lot to get through med school. And Sam for law school. And Rafe's been known to pick up a Greek tome or two."

"Pleasure reading. Expand-the-mind reading. That's what I'm talking about."

"Well, we're not reading romance novels, if that's what you're getting at." Creed put away the chips, beginning to feel slightly sick to his stomach. "Although maybe you should."

"What's that supposed to mean?" Judah demanded.

"Maybe if you read romance novels, you'd be able to see that which has been at the end of your nose for years, dummy." Creed jammed his hat down over his eyes, preparing to get in a few winks. "Think about it. It'll come to you." He pondered Judah's thick skull for a moment, then said, "Or maybe not."

Judah made no reply, which was fine with Creed, because all he wanted to do was sit and think about Aberdeen for a few minutes. *Judah is wrong. I owe it to myself to see if I can find a woman I could fall for. I owe it to myself to try to figure out if I'd be a good father. Maybe I would. I like kids.*

Wait. He didn't know that for sure. Truthfully, Pete's babies kind of intimidated him. Of course, they were no bigger than fleas. And fleas weren't good.

Pete's girls were cute as buttons. And they would grow. But they still made him nervous. Maybe he didn't have uncle-type feelings in him. He'd been uninterested in holding them. But they were so small and fragile. I've eaten breadsticks bigger than their legs.

Damn. I'm twenty-nine, and I'm scared of my nieces. That can't be good.

"Have you held Pete's kids yet?" Creed asked Judah.

"Nah. They're kind of tiny. And they yell a lot." Judah shook his head. "I don't want kids. I'm a quiet kind of guy. Organized. Peaceful. Small, squalling things are not peaceful."

Creed felt better. Maybe he wasn't totally a heel for not bonding with his nieces. "I just think I could be good at this, if I put my mind to it."

"At what? Being a dad?" Judah snorted. "Sure. Why not? As long as you give up rodeo and getting dropped on your head, you might be all right."

"Give up rodeo?" Creed echoed, the thought foreign and uncomfortable. He planned on rodeoing in the Grandfather's Rodeo, if they had such a thing. They'd drag him out of the saddle when he was cold and dead and rigor mortis had set in. Cowboy rigor mortis. What man didn't want to die with his boots on?

Of course, if he wasn't good at it anymore… "What the hell am I doing?"

"Search me," Judah replied. "I can't figure you out, bro. It'd take a licensed brain-drainer to do that."

Creed decided not to punch Judah, even though he was pretty certain he should. All he knew was that before his concussion, before he'd met Aberdeen, he'd been sure of who he was. He'd had a plan.

Now, he was asking himself all kinds of questions. Judah was right: it would take a shrink to figure out the knots in his brain.

I should have kissed her again. Then I wouldn't be thinking about her. I'm shallow like that.

I really am.

Two days later, Johnny watched as a man he was particularly displeased to see walked into the bar. This reappearance couldn't have come at a worse time. Johnny shook his head, wondering why bad pennies always had to return when a man needed a lucky penny in his boot.

He wasn't surprised when Aberdeen went pale when she saw their customer. But then, to Johnny's astonishment, Aberdeen brightened, and went to hug the tall, lanky cowboy.

"Hello, Shawn," she said. "Long time, no see."

"Too long."

Blond-haired, smooth "Re-ride" Parker's glance slid over Aberdeen's curves. Johnny felt his blood begin to boil.

"Hello, Johnny," Aberdeen's ex-husband said.

"Re-ride," Johnny muttered, not pleased and not hiding it.

"Fixed this place up nicely." Re-ride looked around the bar. "I remember when it was just a hole in the wall."

"How's the rodeo treating you?" Johnny asked, figuring he could bring up unpleasantries if Shawn wanted. When Johnny had bought this place, it *had* been a hole in the wall—and Re-ride had just left Aberdeen with no means of support. Johnny had settled here to help Aberdeen mend the pieces of her shattered marriage, and seeing the cause of his sister's former distress did not leave him in a welcoming frame of mind.

"I'm not riding much these days," Shawn said, staring at Aberdeen, drinking her in, it seemed to Johnny, with an unnecessary amount of enthusiasm. "A man can't be on the circuit forever."

Johnny grunted. He followed the scores. He chatted to the cowboys who came in. Re-ride had never broken out of the bottom of the cowboy bracket. Maybe he had bad luck. Johnny didn't follow him closely enough to know. What he did know was that he seemed to get a lot of "re-rides," hence the name which had stuck all these years. In Johnny's opinion, Shawn could have quit the circuit ten years ago and no one would have missed him. "Guess not. Want to buy a bar?"

Aberdeen scowled at him. "No, he most certainly does not, I'm sure. Shawn, can we offer you a soda?"

Re-ride glanced at Johnny. "Ah, no. Thanks, though. Actually, I stopped by to talk to you, Aberdeen. If you have a moment."

Johnny felt his blood, which was already hot, heat up like he was sitting on a lit pyre of dry tinder.

"Johnny, can you listen out for the girls?" Aberdeen took off her apron, put the broom in the closet, and nodded to Shawn. "I do have a few minutes. Not long, though."

"Girls?" Shawn asked, snapping out of his lusting staring for a moment.

"Aberdeen's adopting three small children," Johnny said cheerfully, instantly realizing how to stop the man from using his soft-hearted sister for whatever reason his rodent-faced self had conjured up. What Aberdeen saw in the man, Johnny would never understand. *Sneaky like a rat.*

"Johnny," Aberdeen said, her tone warning as she opened the door. Re-ride followed her after tipping his hat to Johnny. Johnny ignored it, not feeling the need to socialize further.

This was no time for Re-Ride Parker to show up in Aberdeen's life. He resented every time the man appeared—usually about once or twice a year—but this time was different. He could tell, like a wolf scenting danger on the wind. Shawn was up to no good. He was never up to any good, as far as Johnny was concerned, but the way he'd practically licked Aberdeen with his eyeballs had Johnny's radar up. In fact, it was turned on high-anxiety.

Very bad timing, he told himself, but then again, that was Re-ride. Bad, bad timing.

"I've changed my mind," Fiona told the five brothers who came by for a family council—and to eat barbecue, grilled corn and strawberry cake. Pete was at his house with his daughters and Jackie, probably juggling to keep up with bottles and diapers. Creed had promised to give him the thumbnail sketch of what happened at the meeting.

"I've had a lot on my mind. And I've been doing a lot of thinking about all of you. And your futures." She looked around at them, and Creed noticed Burke give her a worried glance as he served drinks in the large upstairs library. "I can't leave the ranch to the brother who gets married first and has the most children. That was my plan when Bode Jenkins got his cronies to try to legally seize this land for eminent domain purposes. His claim was that this particular property was too large for just one person to own—basically me—when the greater good could be affected by a new water system and schools. So I decided that if you all had children, we could make the case for the greater good, since there were plenty of Callahans. The state wouldn't have the right—nor would they dream, I would hope—of tossing a large family off the only property you've all ever known."

She nodded her head, her silvery-white hair shining under the lights, her eyes bright as she chose her words. Creed was amazed by his aunt's energy. For the hundredth time, he pondered how much she'd given up for them.

He even felt a little bad that he'd tried to thwart her plans. But fate stepped in and, just as soon as he was positive he wanted to thwart her forever, he'd met a girl who made his heart go *ding!* like a dinner bell. Maybe even a wedding bell. That was life for you.

"So," Fiona continued, "I have a confession to make. In my haste to keep the ranch out of the state's hands, and out of Bode's possession, I made a mistake. I played right into his hands by agreeing to sell the land to a private developer. Fighting the state would have taken years in court, and money I was loath to spend out of your estate. So I chose a private buyer to sell it to, and made a deal that they would allow Rancho Diablo to be taken over by an angel investor. My offer was that we would buy the ranch back from them in five years, when Bode had turned his eyes to someone else's property or passed on, whichever came first." She took a deep breath, appearing to brace herself. "However, Bode was ahead of me, and the private investor I thought was absolutely safe and in our corner turned out to be in that nasty man's pocket. So," she said, looking around at each brother, "we're homeless in nine months. Totally. And for that, I can never say how sorry I am. I'm sorry for not being a wiser manager. I'm sorry that you men won't have the home your parents built—"

She burst into tears. The brothers sat, shocked, staring at their aunt, then at Burke, then at each other. Creed took a couple of quick breaths, wondering if he'd heard her right, if he could possibly have just heard that Rancho Diablo wasn't theirs anymore, and quickly realized this was no playacting, no manipulation, on Aunt Fiona's part.

It scared the hell out of him. His brothers looked just as stunned. But their aunt had been bearing an oh-so-heavy burden alone, so Creed got up and went to pat her back. "Aunt Fiona, don't cry. This isn't a matter for tears. We're not angry with you. We would never be angry with you. You've done the very best you could, and probably better than most people could under the circumstances."

"You *should* be angry! If you had an ounce of common sense, you would be, you scalawag." She pushed his hand away, and those of the other brothers when they came to fuss over her.

"But I probably don't have an ounce of sense," Creed said, "and we love you. Rancho Diablo is yours just as much as ours." He gulped, trying not to think about the yawning chasm that their lives had just turned into with a stroke of an errant wand. This was *home*.

Although perhaps not anymore. But he only said, "Let Sam look over whatever papers you have to make certain there are no loopholes. Maybe call in some legal beagles. Right, Sam?"

His younger brother nodded. Creed got down on a knee and looked into her eyes. "You should have told us instead of trying to marry us off. Maybe we could have helped you."

"I wanted babies." She blew her nose into a delicate white handkerchief. "If I was going to lose the ranch, I wanted you to have brides who were eager to marry into the Callahan name, and live at Rancho Diablo. At least get married here, for heaven's sakes. But you're all so slow and stubborn," she said, with a glance around at each of them, "that I realized I was going to have to be honest with you instead of waiting for the spring sap to rise. Goodness knows, even the bulls are looking for mates. But not my nephews."

She sighed, put upon, and Creed glanced around at his brothers with a grin. "We tried to get hitched for you, Aunt Fiona. The ladies just won't have us."

"Well, I certainly don't blame them." She took the drink that Burke handed her, sipping it without energy. "But I'm making other plans. I'm holding a matchmaking ball, right here at Rancho Diablo. I'm inviting every single female that my friends know, and that's a ton, from as far away as the ladies care to come, all expenses paid. It's probably the last big party I'll ever have at this ranch, and I intend for it to be a blowout that will be talked about for years. Your bachelor ball, my going-away party."

"Whoa," Judah said, "there are only five of us, Aunt Fiona. We can't entertain a whole lot of women in a chivalrous manner."

"Goodness me," Fiona said, "most men would leap at the chance to have a bachelor raffle held in their honor."

"Bachelor raffle?" Jonas asked. "That sounds dangerous."

"Only if you're a wienie." Aunt Fiona gave her nephews an innocent look. "And there are no wienies in this room, I hope."

"Definitely not," Creed's twin, Rafe, said.

"No," Sam said, "but as the youngest, I'd like to put forth that I should have the lion's share of the ladies." His brothers scowled at him. "What? None of you wants to settle down. I'm not exactly opposed. At least not for the short term."

"You don't want to settle down," Jonas said, "you want to sow your wild oats. And all of us are ahead of you in the age department."

"Uh-oh," Sam said, leaping at the chance to bait his eldest brother, "do I hear the sound of a man's biological clock ticking? Bong, bong, Big Ben?"

Jonas looked as though he was about to pop an artery, Creed thought, not altogether amused. "We don't need a raffle or a bachelor bake-athon or whatever, Aunt Fiona. We're perfectly capable of finding women on our own. In relation to the ranch, if it isn't ours anymore—potentially—then there's no reason for us to hurry out and find brides. What we need to find are excellent lawyers, a whole team of them, who can unwind whatever Bode thinks he's got you strung with."

"We don't need to hire a lawyer, or a team," Aunt Fiona said, and the brothers looked at her with surprise. "We won't hire a lawyer because I hired a private investigator to keep an eye on him. I'm just positive Bode'll make a slip any day, and I'll be on him like a bird on a bug. And," she said, her doughy little face sad and tearstained with now-dried tears, "it wouldn't look good that I hired a P.I. to dig up dirt on him." She leaned close to Creed to whisper. "However, there's every chance he knows."

Creed winced. "Not unless he's bugged the house." Pete had claimed that someone had locked him in the basement last winter, searched the house and destroyed Aunt Fiona's jars of canned preserves and other stored food in an attempt to find something. What that person could have been looking for was anyone's guess. Nothing had been stolen—no television, none of Fiona's jewelry, no tools. He supposed the house could be bugged, but the room they were currently sitting in was far away from the front doors and not easy to access. Someone would have needed several hours to search the house and plant bugs, and Pete hadn't been locked away that long. "It would be very difficult to bug this place."

"But he might know many things about us anyway," Fiona said, "because he gossips a lot."

"Bode?" Jonas said. "No one would talk about us to him."

"You think Sabrina McKinley might have told him something?" Sam asked, "since she's working as his caregiver?"

"No, Sabrina wouldn't blab," Aunt Fiona said, "because she's working for me."

Chapter 5

"Whoa," Jonas said, "Aunt Fiona, that little gypsy is a private investigator?"

Aunt Fiona nodded. "She's actually an investigative reporter, which is even better because sometimes they're nosier. It's her sister, Seton, who's the actual gumshoe. And don't sound so shocked, Jonas. You didn't think she was a real fortune-teller? She was playing a part I hired her to play."

Creed was having trouble dealing with all this new information. "But didn't she say that our ranch was in trouble, and a bunch of other nonsense?"

"Yes, but I gave her a script. I was trying to warn you, spur you along. As I mentioned, you're all quite slow. Thick, even. Why, I'd say molasses in winter moves faster than my nephews." She gave a pensive sigh. "The problem is, you don't have a home anymore. We don't have a place to run our business. And only Pete got married. At least he's happy," she said. "At least he found a wonderful woman." She cast an eye over the rest of her charges. "The rest of you will have a less favorable position to offer a wife. Your stock has dropped, as they say."

"Okay," Jonas said, "let's not think about our marital futures right now. Let's deal strictly with the business end."

"I say we go kick Bode Jenkins's skinny ass," Sam put in, and everyone shouted, *"No!"*

Sam said, "What a bunch of pansies."

"You have to be more sly than that," Fiona said sternly. "Violence is unacceptable. It's all about the mind, and I simply got outthought."

"I'll have a friend eyeball the papers," Jonas said thoughtfully. "In the meantime, I'm closing on that land I offered on next week. We're not exactly homeless. If we have about nine months, we have enough time to move Rancho Diablo operations there. And build a house. It won't be like this one," he said, glancing around the room, "but it will be ours."

"What would you supposedly get for the house and land—if the deal is for real?" Rafe asked.

"Only ten million dollars," Fiona said. "A half of what it's worth for all the land, the house, and—"

She stopped, glanced at Burke, who shrugged.

"And?" Creed prompted.

"And mineral rights, and so on," she said, and Creed wondered if she'd just hedged some information. Fiona was known to keep her cards close to the vest. "It's a pittance, when you consider that we won't be able even to use the name *Rancho Diablo* anymore. We will truly be starting our brand from the bottom again."

Fiona's cheeks had pink spots in them and her eyes glittered. Creed could see that not only was her pride stung because Bode had outwitted her, she was crushed to have to give her nephews this hard news.

"We'll talk about it later," Creed said. "For now, this is enough to digest. I don't think you should trouble yourself anymore tonight, Aunt Fiona."

Judah nodded. "I agree. My only question is, Bode hasn't been bothering you lately, has he?"

Fiona shook her head. "He's been pretty quiet since he thinks he got me over a barrel."

"About Sabrina," Jonas said. "What happens if Bode finds out that she's actually a reporter?"

They all took that in for a moment. Bode was known for his hot temper and grudges. He was underhanded, unforgiving. The tall, skinny man was unkind to just about everyone he knew; he kept people in his pocket by making sure he had whatever they needed. Bode was a power broker; he liked that power, and no one crossed him lightly.

Creed looked at his aunt. "Do you think involving her was a good idea, Aunt Fiona?"

"She and her sister came highly recommended. They are the nieces of—"

"Oh, no," Sam said, "not one of your Books 'n' Bingo cronies."

Fiona arched a brow at her youngest nephew. "Yes, as a matter of fact. I always hire friends, whether it's for curtain-making, preserving or tree-trimming. There's no better way to ensure loyalty and fairness in a job than to hire one's friends."

Creed's heart sank a little, too, just south of his boots. Aunt Fiona was in over her head. The expressions on his brothers' faces confirmed his own doubts. His cell phone jumped in his pocket, forestalling his worried thoughts. Glancing at the number, he frowned, wondering why he'd be getting a call from Wyoming.

Probably something to do with the rodeo he'd crashed out of. "Excuse me for a moment, Aunt Fiona," he said, and stepped outside the library. "Hello?"

"Creed Callahan?" a man asked.

"Yes. Who's speaking?"

"This is Johnny Donovan. You were at our place—"

"I remember you, Johnny. How are you doing?" Creed's heart jumped right back up into his chest where it belonged as he wondered if Aberdeen might have put Johnny up to calling him. He could only hope.

"I'm fine. In a bit of a tight spot, actually."

"Oh?" Johnny had seemed capable of handling just about anything. "Something I can help with?"

"Actually, yes, perhaps," Johnny said. "You remember my sister, Aberdeen?"

Did he ever. "Yeah." He made his voice deliberately disinterested, not wanting to sound like an overeager stud.

"Well, I'm wondering—jeez, this is awkward," Johnny said. "I'm wondering if I paid your way back up here for a week, could you come keep an eye on my bar?"

Creed's jaw went slack. "Um—"

"I know. Like I said, it's awkward as hell. I wouldn't ask if I wasn't up against it, and if I didn't know that you were taking a bit of time off from the circuit."

"Yeah, I am." Creed sank into a hallway chair, staring out the arched, two-story windows that looked out over flat, wide, beautiful Rancho Diablo. "What's going on?"

"I need to be in Montana for a few weeks. Aberdeen

needs to be there as well. We have a child custody hearing coming up."

Creed frowned. He didn't remember anything being discussed about children. Did Aberdeen have kids? He knew nothing about her personal life—and yet, whenever he thought about her, he got an irrational shot of pleasure. *I'm doomed. I'm damned. She's not only a preacher but one with custody issues. Yee-haw.* "I see," he murmured, not seeing at all, but wanting to prod Johnny into spilling more info.

"Yeah. We can close the bar for two weeks, but I still hate to leave it unattended. This isn't the best area of town, as you know. We're kind of out of the way. I have a ton of friends here who could watch it, but frankly, I was thinking you owed me one."

Creed laughed, detecting teasing in Johnny's voice. "I probably do."

"I believe in doing business between friends," Johnny said. "The pay is generous. My bar's my livelihood. I'd like to keep it in safe hands."

Creed grinned. "And you don't want to keep it open?"

"Not necessarily, unless you want to. You don't have any experience with a bar or family-owned restaurant, do you?"

"Not so much." Creed wondered if he should back away from the offer politely or jump at the chance to see if Aberdeen still smoked his peace pipe the way he remembered she did. He was pretty certain she set him on fire all over. Sure, any woman could probably do that if a man was in the right, open mood, Creed mused—but Aberdeen seemed to do it for him even when she aggravated the hell out him.

He thought that was a pretty interesting juxtaposition.

"We do have a family business, but it isn't in the same field as yours. We don't have strangers knocking on our door at all hours, not often anyway."

Johnny laughed. "So you'll do it?"

"I might. Let me run it past the family."

"Sounds mafia-like."

Creed grinned to himself. "Sometimes it can seem that way to outsiders. I'll get back in touch with you soon, Johnny. Good to hear from you."

He turned off his phone, sitting and considering this new twist for a moment. His gaze searched the wide vista outside, its dusty expanse vibrant even as night was covering the mesa. And then, he saw them, running like the wind across the faraway reaches of the ranch, black as night, fast as wind, free as spirits.

"Los Diablos," he murmured, awed by the hypnotizing beauty. "The Diablos are running!" he called to his brothers, and they came out of the library to stand at his side, watching in silence, shoulder to shoulder, knowing this might be one of the last times they ever saw the beautiful horses materializing across the evening-tinged swath of Rancho Diablo land.

"Are you all right?" Aberdeen asked Johnny as she walked into the upstairs living room. "You look like you're thinking deep thoughts."

Johnny put his cell phone in his pocket. "No deeper than usual."

She smiled at him. "Then why are you frowning?"

"I've just been thinking about how we're going to make this all work out."

"Oh." She nodded and sat down on a worn cloth sofa.

"I finally got all three girls to sleep. They are so sweet when they sleep. They look so angelic and happy."

A small smile lifted Johnny's mouth—but not for long. "Has Diane called to check on them?"

Aberdeen shook her head. "I think she probably won't for a while. I did talk to Mom and Dad today. They said Diane has decided to go around the world on a sailboat with her new boyfriend. They expect the trip to take about a year and a half."

Johnny's face turned dark. "You're kidding, right?"

"I wouldn't joke about that." Aberdeen sighed. "We need her at least to sign some forms that state we can make medical decisions for the girls while she's gone."

"I'm going over to France," Johnny said, and Aberdeen could see his jaw was tight. "I'm going to try to talk some sense into her. She just can't abandon her children. I don't know if she needs medication or what is going on—"

"Johnny." Aberdeen patted the sofa cushion beside her. "Come sit down."

He sighed. "Maybe I need a drink."

"It wouldn't help. I think you going to France is a good idea. I'll stay here with the girls and start looking for a house and school and a doctor."

"Have you ever thought how much having the girls here is going to change your life, even more than mine?"

Aberdeen blinked. "There's no point to worrying about the situation. We love the girls. Diane, as much as I hate to say it, appears to be unfit or unwilling at the moment."

Johnny sat silently for a few minutes. "I'll make a plane reservation. I may drag Diane back here kicking and screaming, though."

"Do you want me to go?" Aberdeen asked, and Johnny quickly shook his head.

"No. You've got enough to do in the next two weeks for the custody hearing." Johnny stood, going to look out a window over the parking lot. "I think I might sell the bar, Aberdeen."

She drew in a sharp breath. "Why?"

He didn't turn around. "I think it's time."

"Is this because of Shawn?" she asked, hating to ask but feeling she had to. She was aware Johnny had been biting his tongue for the past two weeks to keep from complaining about her ex-husband's frequent presence. It would be like Johnny to decide to sell the bar and move the newly enlarged family to Timbuktu if he thought he could get rid of Shawn. Johnny didn't understand her rosy daydreams of romance with Shawn were long evaporated. Shawn was comfortable, someone she'd grown up with, in a strange way.

"No," he said, but she wondered if he was being completely truthful. "But on that unpleasant topic, is there a reason he's suddenly hanging around again?"

A flush ran up Aberdeen's cheeks and neck. "I'm not exactly sure what you mean, or if he has a specific reason for his presence. He says he's changed—"

"Ugh," Johnny interrupted. "Changed what? His spots? I don't think so."

That stung. Aberdeen blinked back tears. "Johnny, he's been through a lot. It's not like I'd remarry him. You know that."

"I just think it's not a good time for someone like him to be in your life if we're serious about getting custody of the kids."

"I think he's lonely, and nothing more."

"You're not lonely right now," Johnny pointed out. "You're busy raising three little girls who really need you."

"Shawn knows me. He's a part of my past."

Johnny turned away. Aberdeen took a deep breath. "So, why are you really thinking about selling the bar? You've mentioned it a couple of times. I'm beginning to think you might really be considering it."

"Aberdeen," Johnny said suddenly, ignoring her question, "if your Prince Charming rode up tomorrow on a white horse, would you want that?"

"I think by twenty-nine a woman doesn't believe in fairy tales. The fairy godmother never showed up for me." She touched her brother on the arm, and after a moment, he gave her a hug. They stood together for a few moments, and Aberdeen closed her eyes, drinking in the closeness.

Just for a few heartbeats, she felt Johnny relax. He was sweet big brother again, not worried, not overburdened by life. She let out a breath, wishing this feeling could last forever.

The sound of a baby crying drifted across the hall. Aberdeen broke away from Johnny, smiling up at him. "Don't worry so much, big brother," she said, but he just shook his head.

"By the way," he said offhandedly as she started to leave the room to check on Lincoln Rose and her sisters. "I've got Creed Callahan coming to watch over the bar while we're away."

Aberdeen looked at Johnny. It didn't matter that her heart skipped a beat—several beats—at the mention of Creed's name, or that she'd thought she'd never see him again. "That's probably a good idea," she murmured, going to comfort the baby, wondering if her brother thought he had to play matchmaker in her life. Johnny was worried she was falling for Shawn again. So had he called in a handpicked Prince Charming?

It would be so like Johnny—but if he was meddling in her life, she'd have to slap him upside his big head.

He just didn't understand that Creed Callahan, while handsome enough to tease her every unattended thought, was no Prince Charming—at least not hers.

Chapter 6

The next day, Aberdeen wondered if her brother understood something about men that she didn't. Shawn sat at their kitchen table, watching her feed the girls and wearing a goofy grin.

"I never thought you'd be such good mother material," Shawn said, and Aberdeen looked at him.

"Why would you think I wouldn't be?"

Shawn was the opposite of Creed in appearance: blond, lanky, relaxed. Almost too relaxed, maybe bordering on lazy, she thought. Creed was super-dark, built like a bad girl's dream with big muscles and a strong chest, and not relaxed at all. She frowned as she wiped Lincoln Rose's little chin. Actually, she didn't know much about Creed. He'd been ill when she'd seen him. But she still had the impression that he wasn't exactly Mr. Happy-Go-Lucky.

Not like Shawn.

"You always seemed too career-oriented to want a family." Shawn sipped at his coffee, and smiled a charming smile at her. "I always felt like you were going to be the breadwinner in our marriage."

"Would that have been a problem?"

"For a man's ego, sure. Some men might like their wife being the big earner, but not me. I have my pride, you know." He grabbed one of the carrots she'd put on the three-year-old's plate and munched it.

Not much pride. Aberdeen told herself to be nice and handed him Lincoln Rose. "Let's test your fathering skills, then."

"I'm a family man," he said, holding Lincoln Rose about a foot away from him. Lincoln Rose studied him and he studied her, and then the baby opened her mouth like a bird and let out a good-sized wail. "Clearly she doesn't recognize father material," Shawn said, handing Lincoln Rose back to Aberdeen.

Aberdeen rolled her eyes. "Have you ever held a baby?"

"Not that I can recall," Shawn said cheerfully. "But that doesn't mean I couldn't learn to like it. I just need practice and a good teacher." He looked at her so meaningfully that Aberdeen halted, recognizing a strange light in her husband's eyes. He looked purposeful, she thought—and Shawn and purposeful did not go together well.

"There was no double meaning in that statement, was there?" Aberdeen asked.

Shawn's expression turned serious. "Aberdeen, look, I've been doing a lot of thinking." Idly, he grabbed another carrot; thankfully, the toddlers didn't seem to mind. Aberdeen put some golden raisins on their plates to keep them happy while Shawn got over his thinking fit. "I know you're determined to adopt these little ladies."

"They will always have a home with me."

Shawn nodded. "I think that's a good idea. Diane is a great girl, but even back when you and I were married, she wasn't the most stable person, if you know what I mean."

Aberdeen bit her lip. She didn't want to discuss this with him. "Diane has a good heart," she murmured.

"I know," Shawn said, his tone soothing, "but you're doing right by these girls. I believe they need you." He gave her a winning smile. "And I know you're worried about the temporary-custody situation. I've been thinking about how I could be of assistance."

Aberdeen shook her head. "Thanks, Shawn, but I believe the good Lord will take care of us."

"I'd like to help," he said. "I really mean it."

She looked at him, her attention totally caught. It seemed the little girls in their sweet pink dresses were listening, too, because their attention seemed focused on Shawn. Handsome Shawn with the charming smile, always getting what he wanted. Aberdeen watched him carefully. "What are you getting at?"

"I just want you to know that I'm here for you." He took a deep breath, and she could see that he meant every word—at least, he did while he was speaking them. "I wasn't the world's greatest husband, Aberdeen. You deserved a hell of a lot better. And I'd like to be here for you now if you need me." He gave her the most sincere look she'd ever seen him wear on his handsome face. "All you have to do is say the word. I'd marry you again tomorrow if it would help you with custody or adoption or anything."

Aberdeen blinked, shocked. But as she looked into Shawn's eyes, she realized he was trying to atone, in his own bumbling way, for the past.

And as much as she'd like to tell him to buzz off, she wondered if she could afford to be so callous. She didn't know how the courts would regard her. She thought they would see her in a positive light, as a minister, as Diane's sister, as a caring aunt.

But what if the court preferred a married mother for these children? Aberdeen looked at her nieces. They seemed so happy, so content to be with her. Their eyes were so bright and eager, always focused on her as they banged spoons or pulled off their shoes and dropped them to the floor. Did it matter that she planned to live with them out of the state where they'd been raised? Would she look more stable with a husband? She and Johnny and Diane knew that even two-parent homes lacked stability—but would a court of law see it that way? For her nieces' sake, maybe she couldn't just write Shawn's offer off as so much talk.

"I would hope nothing like that will be necessary."

He shrugged. "I mean it, Aberdeen, I really do. If you need a husband, then, I'm your man."

"What happened to the man who didn't want to be married to the family breadwinner?" she asked, not wanting to encourage him.

He smiled. "Well, I'd feel like things were a bit more balanced since you need me, Aberdeen."

She pulled back a little and tried not to let anger swamp her. Shawn was pretty focused on his own needs; she knew that. But he was harmless, too—now that she wasn't married to him, she could see him in a more generous light. Sometimes. Creed's dark-blue eyes flashed in her memory. She could see him laughing, even as he was in pain from the concussion. The man had a sense of humor, though things hadn't been going his way. He had a roguish charm, and she'd told herself to run from it.

Because it had reminded her of Shawn. *Crazy*, she'd thought of him. *No more loco in my life.*

And yet loco was sitting here right now offering to give her the illusion of stability for the sake of her nieces. Aberdeen swallowed. Maybe she shouldn't dismiss the offer out of hand. Husband, wife, devoted uncle—not quite a nuclear family here, but close enough.

But it was Shawn. And she wanted something else. "Have some more carrots," she said absently, her eyes on her nieces. She'd been totally attracted to the cowboy from New Mexico, as much as she didn't want to admit it, and no matter how hard she'd tried to forget him, he hadn't left her memory.

But maybe it was better to deal with the devil she knew—if she needed a devil at all.

"Don't mind me," Creed said three days later, as Johnny looked around the bar one last time. "I've got everything I'll need. I'll be living like King Tut here."

"He didn't live long," Johnny pointed out, "and I think somebody might have done him in. Let's hope that your time here is spent in a more pleasant manner."

Creed grinned. "You're sure you don't want me to keep this place open for business?"

"It's too much to ask of a friend," Johnny said.

"Lot of income for you to lose," Creed pointed out. "I'm averse to losing income."

Johnny laughed. "I am, too. But this has got to be done. You just keep an eye on things, guard my castle and I'll be grateful for the imposition on your time."

Creed took a bar stool, glancing around the bar. "You did yourself a good turn buying this place, Johnny. It's nice. Did it take you long to turn a profit?"

"No. Not really. Building business was slow, but it happened over time. People like to hear Aberdeen preach, and then they remember us for snacks and beverages the rest of the week. It's a loyal crowd around here." He took a rag and wiped the mahogany bar with it. "I might sell, you know."

Creed blinked. "Do you mind me asking why?"

Johnny shook his head. "You'll see soon enough."

Creed wasn't sure what he meant by that, but if Johnny didn't want to discuss his business, that was fine by him. He wouldn't want to talk to anyone about Rancho Diablo and all that was happening back home unless he knew that person very well.

Actually, he wouldn't discuss it with anyone but family. Everything had gotten complicated real fast. He looked around the bar, trying to see himself with some kind of business set-up like this, and failed.

But he'd always think of it kindly because it had been his inn in the wilderness. If he hadn't come here—

"Here you go, sweetie," he heard Aberdeen say, and then he heard feet coming down the staircase. He watched the stairs expectantly, wondering how he'd feel about seeing her again. Certainly he hadn't stopped thinking about her. She was a pretty cute girl, any man would have to admit. In fact, probably lots of men noticed. But she was a prickly one. She would never have fitted into one of Aunt Fiona's marriage schemes. The woman was spicy and probably didn't have a maternal bone in her body.

Still, he waited, his eyes eager for that first glimpse of her.

She made it into view with a baby in her arms, holding the hand of a tiny toddler and with a somewhat larger toddler hanging on to her skirt as they slowly negotiated the staircase. Creed's face went slack, and his heart began beating hard in his chest. Three little blond girls?

"Holy smokes," he said, "you guys have been keeping secrets from me." He got up to help the small girls make it down the last few steps so they wouldn't face-plant at the bottom of the staircase. One shrank back from him, wanting to get to the landing herself, and one little girl smiled up at him angelically, and his heart fell into a hole in his chest. They were sweet, no question.

And then he looked up into Aberdeen's blue eyes, and it was all he could do not to stammer. "Hello, Aberdeen."

She smiled at him tentatively. "Hi, Creed. So nice of you to come look after Johnny's bar."

He caught his breath at the sight of those eyes. She was smiling at him, damn it, and he couldn't remember her ever being soft around him. It had his heart booming and his knees shaking just a bit. "It's nothing," he said, trying to sound gallant and not foolish, and Aberdeen smiled at him again.

"Oh, it's something to my brother. He said you're just the man he could trust to keep his bar safe."

Creed stepped back, nearly blinded by all the feminine firepower being aimed at him. "It's nothing," he repeated.

She gave him a last smile, then looked at Johnny.

"We're ready for the road. Aren't we, girls?" She looked at Creed. "I'm sorry. These are my nieces. We're going to Montana for a custody hearing."

"Custody?"

She nodded. "I'm filing for temporary custody of the girls for now. And then maybe later, something more, if necessary."

The smile left her face, and Creed just wanted it back. "They sure are cute," he said, feeling quite stupid and confused, but the last thing he'd ever imagined was that Aberdeen Donovan might one day be the mother of three little girls. He didn't know what else to say. Clearly, he didn't know as much about these folks as he'd thought he had. He'd best stick to what he'd been hired for. "Well, I'll keep the floor nailed down," he said to Johnny, his gaze on Aberdeen.

"I'll check in on you soon enough." Johnny helped Aberdeen herd the girls toward the door. "If you have any questions, give me a ring on my cell. And thanks again, Creed. I can't tell you how much I appreciate this."

"I appreciated you saving my life," Creed murmured, letting one of the tiny dolls take him by the hand. He led her to Johnny's big truck, and watched to see that she was put in her car seat securely, and then he waved as they drove away, his head whirling.

"Three," he muttered. "Three small, needy damsels in some kind of distress." He headed back inside the bar, shell-shocked. Aberdeen had never mentioned children. Of course, they'd barely spoken to each other.

At the moment, his swagger was replaced by stagger, and a rather woeful stagger at that.

"I kissed a woman who's getting custody of three

children," he said to himself as he locked up the bar. "That's living dangerously, and I sure as *hell* don't want to end up like Pete."

Or do I?

Chapter 7

A couple of hours later, Creed was lying on the sofa upstairs, nursing a brewski and pondering what all he didn't know about Aberdeen. He was certain he could still smell the sweet perfume she wore, something flowery and clean and feminine, like delicate lilies and definitely not baby powder from the three little darlings—when he heard a window sliding open downstairs. The sound might not have been obvious to most people, but since he and his brothers had done their share of escaping out of windows in the middle of the night, he knew the stealthy sound by heart.

And that meant someone was due for an ass-kicking. He searched around for appropriate armament, finding Johnny's available weaponry lacking. There was a forgotten baby bottle on the coffee table. A few books were stacked here and there, mostly addressing the topic of raising children.

This was a side of Aberdeen he had totally missed. Creed vowed that if the opportunity ever presented itself, he might ask a few questions about parenthood, a subject he found somewhat alarming. He glanced around the room again, but there wasn't a baseball bat or even a small handgun to be found. If Johnny had a gun, he probably had it locked in a drawer now that he had small angels terrorizing his abode. If Creed had children, he'd certainly have the world's most secure gun cabinet with all things that go pop safely locked away.

He was going to have to make do with his beer bottle, he decided, and crept down the stairs. There he saw his uninvited guest rooting around in the liquor bottles like a martini-seeking raccoon.

And then he spied a very useful thing: a long-handled broom. In the dim light, he could barely make out a shadow investigating the different choices the bar had to offer. The man seemed in no hurry to make his selection; apparently he was a thief of some distinction. When he finally settled on a liquor, he took his time pouring it into a glass. Creed wondered if olives speared on a plastic sword, perhaps a twist of lemon, might be next for his discerning guest.

The thief took a long, appreciative drink. Creed picked up the broom, extending the wooden handle toward the intruder, giving him a pointed jab in the side. His guest dropped his beverage and whirled around, the sound of shattering glass interrupting the stillness.

"Who's there?"

Creed grinned to himself, reaching out with the broom for a slightly more robust jab. The intruder was scared, and clearly hadn't yet located Creed in the dark room. Moonlight spilled through the windows, bouncing a reflection back from the bar mirror, so Creed had an excellent view of his shadowy target. "The devil," he said. "Boo!"

The man abandoned his pride and shot to the door. Creed stuck out the pole one last time, tripping his guest to the floor. "Not so fast, my friend," Creed said. "You haven't paid for your drink."

"Who are you?" The thief scrambled to his feet.

"Who are you?" Creed asked. "The bar's closed. Didn't you see the sign?"

"I—I wasn't doing anything wrong. I was just wetting my whistle."

"Do you do this often?" Creed asked. "Because I think the owners might object."

"They don't care. They give me free drinks all the time." He backed toward the window where he'd let himself in, realizing he wasn't going to get past Creed and his broom.

Creed put the handle out, tripping the man from behind. "Why do they give you free drinks, friend?"

"Because I was married to Aberdeen. And I'm going to marry her again. So I have a right to be here," he asserted, and Creed's heart went still in his chest.

"Are you telling the truth?"

"I never lie," the stranger said. "Anyway, I'm sorry I bothered you. I'll just be leaving the way I came in now."

Creed flipped on the lights, curious to see the man Aberdeen was going to marry. They stared at each other, sizing up the competition. "I'll be damned. I know you," Creed said, "you're that dime-store cowboy they call Re-ride."

"And you're a Callahan." Re-ride looked none too happy. "What are you doing in Aberdeen's bar?"

"Keeping it free of snakes." Creed felt the interview to be most unpleasant at this point. He almost wished he'd never heard the man break in. Marry Aberdeen? Surely she wouldn't marry this poor excuse for a cowboy.

Then again, she'd married him before, or at least that's what he claimed. It was something else Creed hadn't known about her. To be honest, Creed hadn't proven himself to be any more of a serious cowboy in Aberdeen's eyes after his rambling night on the plank bench. Aberdeen probably thought he was just as loose as Re-ride.

That didn't sit too well. "Go on," he told Re-ride. "Get out of my face. I'd beat you with this broom, but I've never roughed up a lady and I'm not going to start tonight. So *git*."

Re-ride looked like he was about to take exception to Creed's comment, then thought better of it and dove out the window. Creed locked it behind him—and this time, he turned on the security system. He couldn't risk more varmints crawling into the bar tonight—he was in too foul a mood to put up with nonsense. He put himself to bed in the guest room, feeling quite out of sorts about life in general.

Babies, beer burglars and a one-time bride—sometimes, life just handed a cowboy lemonade with no sugar in sight.

"I've looked over these papers with Sam," Jonas said to Aunt Fiona, "and I think we're selling ourselves short. Maybe."

His aunt looked at him. "How?"

"We should fight it, for one thing. Not roll over for the

state or Bode Jenkins. And I'm in a fighting mood. Now that I've sold my medical practice, I have more time to help you with things," Jonas said. "I should have been more available for you all along."

Fiona looked at her oldest nephew. "It shouldn't have necessitated your attention. Darn Bode Jenkins's hide, anyway."

Jonas leaned against the kitchen counter, eyeing his small, spare aunt. She was like a protective bear overseeing her cubs, but actually, things should be the other way around. He and his brothers needed to be protecting her and Burke, now in their golden years. Fiona had tried to convince them that she was one foot from the grave, but he'd been keeping an eye on her, and he was pretty certain Fiona was working their heartstrings. She had never seemed healthier, other than an unusually low spirit for her, which he attributed to her concern about losing the ranch.

He had decided to lift those burdens from his diminutive, sweetly busybodying aunt. "You know that land I put an offer on?"

Fiona brightened. "Yes. East of here. How's that coming?"

"I've changed my mind," Jonas said, after a thoughtful pause. It took him a minute to get his head around the words; every day since he'd made the decision, he'd pondered the situation again and again. "I've withdrawn my offer."

Fiona's eyes widened. "For heaven's sakes, why?"

"Because we're not going anywhere," Jonas said. "That's how Creed feels, and I agree with him."

"Creed! He's had a concussion recently," Fiona said

with a sniff. "He's not thinking straight. Then again, when does he?"

"I think he might be thinking straighter than all of us." Jonas reached over and patted her shoulder. "I'm going to need all my resources, both time and money, to fight this theft of our land. I don't regret giving up on Dark Diablo for a minute."

Fiona looked at him. "Dark Diablo? It sounds beautiful."

He thought again about the wide expanse of open land where he could run cattle and horses and have his own place. His own sign hanging over the drive, shouting to the world that this was Dark Diablo, his own spread. But Creed had said Rancho Diablo was their home, and that they should fight for it, and fight hard. They would have to be dragged off their land—instead of rolling over because things looked dark and done. "Otherwise," Creed had said, "we're just cowards. Runners. The family stays together," he'd said. "Sic Sam on them."

Jonas's jaw had dropped. Sam didn't get "sicced" on anyone. Sam liked to ignore the fact that he'd gone to law school, barely broke a sweat passing the bar, and then gone on to prestigious internships, working his way up to cases that garnered him credit for being a steely defender who never failed to make his opponents cry. He'd become famous for his big persona. But only his family had noticed that with every big win to his credit, he became unhappier.

Sam liked winning. Yet he didn't like defending corporate cases where he knew the little guy was getting strung. And after a particularly nasty case, Sam had packed it in. Come home to Rancho Diablo to recover from big-city life. Now he mostly acted as though he hadn't a care in the world.

Except for Rancho Diablo.

Jonas winced. They couldn't sic Sam on Bode, but they could fight. "I've been thinking, Aunt Fiona, and I'm not so certain your marriage scheme doesn't have some merit."

She radiated delight. "Do you think so?"

He shrugged. "It wouldn't be as easy for the state to take a property where there are families. I'm not saying that they care about us, but it certainly makes it easier to win public sympathy when folks realize what happens to us here could happen to them."

"Yes, but Pete doesn't even live here with his family," she said, her shoulders sagging. "And the rest of you are short-timers."

He grinned. "Are you hosting a pity party, Aunt?"

She glared at him. "What if I am? It's my party, and I can cr—"

"When Creed gets back here in a few days, we'll throw that bachelor ball you wanted."

"Really?" Fiona clapped her hands.

"Sure. He needs to settle down."

She looked at him, suspicious. "Why him?"

"He wants to settle down more than anyone. Haven't you noticed? And his days of rodeoing are over, though he'll never admit it. A woman would keep him off the road, and children would keep him busy."

"It's a great plan," Fiona said, "if you think it would work."

Better him than me. With Fiona busy with her usual plotting and planning, I'll try to figure out how to undo this problem with the ranch.

He was going to have to take a firm hand with his aunt and Burke. They weren't telling everything they knew. It was a riddle wrapped inside a mystery, but he agreed with Creed on one thing: it was better to fight than run.

After a couple more beers to help get him over the shock of Aberdeen's babies and the ex-husband who wanted her back, Creed decided maybe he'd be wiser to run than fight. It was three in the morning, but he couldn't sleep, and if he didn't quit thinking about her, he was going to end up having beer for breakfast. Creed sighed, not having any fun at all. Aberdeen tortured him, and she didn't even know it.

"I wouldn't be so bothered if it wasn't for Re-ride," he told a small pink stuffed bear he'd found underneath the coffee table—probably the smallest damsel's bear. He'd placed the bear on the coffee table after he'd discovered it. The bear had looked forlorn and lost without its tiny owner, so Creed had propped it on a stack of books, regarding it as he would a comforting friend. "You have to understand that the man is given to useless. Simply useless."

The bear made no reply but that was to be expected from stuffed pink bears, Creed told himself, and especially at this hour. And the bear was probably tired of hearing him debate his thoughts, because Creed was certainly tired of himself. Everything ran through his mind without resting, like a giant blender churning his conscience. "She's just so pretty," he told the bear, "I don't see what she sees in him. It's something she doesn't see in me." He considered that for a moment, and then said, "Which is really unfortunate, for me and for her. I am the better man, Bear, but then again, a woman's heart is unexplainable. I swear it is."

If his brothers were here, he could talk this over with them. They wouldn't be sympathetic, but they would clap him on the back, rib him mercilessly or perhaps offer him some advice—and at least he'd feel better. It was hard to feel bad when as an army of one trying to feel sorry for yourself, you faced an army of five refusing to let you give in to your sorrows. How many times had he and his brothers dug each other out of their foul moods, disappointments or broken hearts?

There weren't as many broken hearts among them as there might have been because they had each other to stall those emotions. When you knew everybody was working too hard to listen to you wheeze, you got over a lot of it on your own. But then, when it was important, you could count on a brother to clout you upside the head and tell you that you were being a candy-ass.

He wasn't at that point yet. "But she's working on me, Bear." He waved his beer at the toy. "I didn't come here to help Johnny. It wasn't the overwhelming reason I said yes, you know? It was her. And then, I got here, and I found out… I found out that maybe I rang my bell so hard that I didn't really pay attention to her when I met her. I think, Bear," he said, lowering his voice to a whisper, "that I have it *bad*."

Really bad, if he was sitting here talking out his woes on a baby's pink bear. Creed sighed, put the bottle on the table and shut his eyes so he wouldn't look at the bear's black button eyes anymore for sympathy he couldn't possibly find. "Grown men don't talk to bears," he said, without opening his eyes, "so if you don't mind, please cease with the chatter so I can get some shut-eye."

If he *could* sleep—without thinking about Aberdeen becoming a mother, a scenario that in no way seemed to have a role for him.

All Aberdeen could be when the judge had heard her case was relieved. She was sad for her sister and for her nieces, but it was good to be able to have temporary legal custody of her nieces.

"However," the judge continued, "it's in the best interests of the children that they remain here in Montana, where their maternal grandparents are, and paternal as well, who may be able to provide some assistance."

Shock hit Aberdeen. "Your Honor," she said, "my congregation is in Wyoming. My livelihood is in Wyoming."

The judge looked at her sternly. "A bar isn't much of a place for young, displaced girls to grow up. You have no house for them set apart from the establishment where there could be unsavory elements. And your congregation, as you've described it, is transient. None of this leads me to believe that the situation in Wyoming is more stable for the minors than it would be here, where at least the maternal grandparents can be trusted to oversee the wellbeing of the children."

Aberdeen glanced at Johnny. He would have to go back to Lance. She would be here alone with their parents, who would be little or no help. Tears jumped into Aberdeen's eyes when Johnny clasped her hand. She stared at the judge and nodded her acquiescence.

"Of course, should anything change in your circumstances, the court will be happy to reconsider the situation. Until then, a social worker will be assigned to you." He nodded at Johnny and Aberdeen. "Best of luck to you, Miss Donovan, Mr. Donovan."

Aberdeen turned and walked from the court, not looking at Johnny until they'd gotten outside.

"I expected that," Johnny said, and Aberdeen glanced at him as they walked toward his truck. "That's why I said I'd probably sell the bar. I was hoping it would turn out differently, but I knew Mom and Pop know the judge."

Aberdeen drew in a sharp breath. "Are you saying that they talked to him?"

Johnny climbed in behind the wheel, and Aberdeen got in the passenger side. "I don't know that they did, but I know that he would be familiar with some of our situation. To be fair, any judge hearing this type of case might have decided similarly. But I don't think him knowing Mom and Pop hurt them."

"So now what?" Aberdeen asked.

"Now we're custodians, for the time being," Johnny said. "I've got someone looking for Diane, and if they manage to make contact with her, we'll know a little more. I'll sell the bar, and we'll stay here until matters get straightened out. We're either going to be doing this for the long haul, or it could be as short a time as it takes Diane to come to her senses."

"You don't have to stay here," Aberdeen said. "I've taken this on gladly."

"We're family. We do it together." Johnny turned the truck toward their parents' house.

Aberdeen looked out the window. "I think selling the bar is too drastic, don't you?"

"I can think of more drastic things I don't want to see happen."

Aberdeen looked at him. "I think the worst has already passed."

Her brother took a deep breath, seemed to consider his words. "Look, I just don't want you even starting to think that putting a permanent relationship in your life might be the way to salvage this thing."

"You mean Shawn."

"I mean Re-ride." Johnny nodded. "Don't tell me it hasn't crossed your mind. He as much admitted to me that he wouldn't be opposed to remarrying you."

Aberdeen shook his head. "He mentioned it. I didn't take him very seriously."

"Stability might start looking good to you after a few months of Mom and Pop interfering with your life."

"So you're selling the bar to move here to protect me from myself?" Aberdeen sent her brother a sharp look. "Johnny, I'm not the same girl I was when Shawn and I got married."

"Look, I don't want to see both my sisters make mistakes is all," Johnny said. "You're not like Diane in any way, but Diane wasn't like this before her marriage fell apart, either."

Aberdeen sighed, reached over to pat Johnny's arm. "I think you worry too much, but thanks for looking out for me. I know you do it out of love and a misguided sense of protection, which I happen to greatly appreciate."

Johnny smiled. "So then. Listen to big brother."

Aberdeen checked her cell phone for messages, then went all in. "Is that why you brought the cowboy back?"

Johnny glanced at her. "I could pretend that I don't know what you're talking about, but I figured you'd suspect, so I might as well just say it doesn't hurt to have an ace in my boot."

"Johnny Donovan," Aberdeen said, "perhaps I'll start meddling in your life. Maybe I'll find a string of cute girls and send them your way to tempt you into matrimony. How would you like that?"

"I hope you do, because I'd like it very much." Johnny grinned. "Make them tall, slender and good cooks. I do love home cooking, and women who want to cook these days are rare."

Aberdeen shook her head. "Creed has no interest in me. And the feeling is mutual. Besides, he wouldn't solve my problem in any way if Diane doesn't come back. Even if he and I got some wild notion to get married, he lives in New Mexico. I don't know that the judge is going to let me take the girls anywhere if you really believe he's influenced by Mom and Pop."

"Still, he'll keep Re-ride busy," Johnny predicted, "and I won't mind that a bit."

"You have a darkly mischievous soul, Johnny," Aberdeen said, but secretly, she had liked seeing Creed Callahan again. It was too bad she and Creed were as opposite as the sun and the moon.

He could make a woman think twice about taking a walk on the *very* wild side.

Chapter 8

Creed woke up and stretched, hearing birds singing somewhere nearby. It was different here than in Diablo. Everything was different, from the birds to the land, to the—

The pink bear stared at him, and Creed sighed. "Okay, last night won't happen again. You will not be hearing such yak from me again. I had my wheeze, and I'm over it." He carried the bear down to the room where the little girls had been sleeping, and was caught by the sight of tiny dresses, shorts and shoes spread at the foot of a big bed. There were toys scattered everywhere, and even a fragile music box on the dresser top. It was like walking into fairyland, he mused, and he wondered if Aberdeen had had a room like this when she was little.

He backed out of the room after setting the bear on the bed, decided to shower and get cheerful about the day—and there was no better way to get cheerful than to fill his stomach. That would require heading out to the nearest eating establishment, which would be a great way to see Lance. He took a fast shower, jumped into fresh jeans and a shirt, clapped his hat on his head and jerked open the bar door to take in a lungful of fresh, bracing summer air.

Re-ride stared up at him from the ground where he was sitting, leaning against the wall, clearly just awakening.

"Oh, no, this is not going to happen," Creed said, setting the security alarm, locking the door and loping toward his truck. "You and I are not going to be bosom buddies, so buzz off," he called over his shoulder.

Re-ride was in hot pursuit. "Where are you going?" he asked, jumping into the truck when Creed unlocked the door.

"I'm going someplace you're not. Get out." Creed glared at him.

"Breakfast sounds good. I'll show you the hot spots around here." Re-ride grinned. "I know where the best eggs and bacon are in this town."

Creed didn't want the company, but his stomach was growling, and if the eggs were the best… "If you give me any trouble," he said, and Re-ride said, "Nope. Not me."

Creed snorted and followed his new friend's directions to Charity's Diner two streets over. "I'm pretty certain I could have found this place myself," Creed said, and Re-ride laughed.

"But you didn't. Come on. I'll show you some waitresses who are so cute you'll want more than marshmallows in your cocoa."

That made no sense, Creed thought sourly. In fact, it

was a pretty stupid remark, but he should probably expect little else from the freeloader. He followed Re-ride into the diner and seated himself in a blue vinyl booth, watching with some amazement as Re-ride waved over a tiny, gorgeous, well-shaped redhead.

"This is Cherry," Re-ride said, "Cherry, this is Creed Callahan."

Creed tipped his hat, noticing that Re-ride's hand fell perilously low on Cherry's nicely curved hip. "Pleasure," he told Cherry, and she beamed at him.

"Cocoa?" she asked Creed.

"Coffee," he said, wary of Re-ride's cocoa promise. "Black as you've got it, please."

She showed sweet dimples and practically stars in her big green eyes as she grinned back at Creed. "Re-ride, you've been hiding this handsome friend of yours. Shame on you."

Re-ride shook his head as he ran his gaze hungrily down a menu, his mind all on food now, though he still clutched Cherry's hip. Creed looked at his own menu as Cherry drifted away, surprised when Re-ride tapped the plastic sheet.

"She likes you, I can tell," Re-ride said.

"Look," Creed said, annoyed, "it's plain that you don't want competition for Aberdeen, but I don't—"

"Oh, there's no competition." Re-ride shook his head. "I told you, I'm marrying Aberdeen. I'm just trying to find you someone, so you won't be odd man out."

Creed sighed. "Odd man out of what? I'm only here for a few days."

"Really?" Re-ride brightened. "I might have misunderstood Johnny when I called him last night."

Creed perked up. "You talked to Johnny?"

"Yep." Re-ride lowered his voice. "You know Aberdeen is trying to adopt Diane's little girls, a horrible idea if there ever was one."

"Why?" Creed asked, telling himself that the Donovan family matters were none of his business, and yet he was so curious he could hardly stand it.

"Because I'm not cut out to be a father," Re-ride explained. "I don't want to be a father to Diane's children."

"Oh." Creed blinked. "Selfish, much?"

"What?" Re-ride glared at him, obviously confused.

Creed shrugged. "If you love Aberdeen, wouldn't you want what she wants?"

"No, that's not how it works. I'm the man, and I'll make the decisions about what's best for our family. There's no way a marriage can work when there's no chance for privacy right from the start. A man and his wife need *privacy*, and I'm sure you know what I mean, Callahan."

Fire flamed through Creed's gut. *Jealousy. By God, I'm jealous. I can't be jealous. That would be dumb. But how I wish I could poke this jerk in the nose. I should have beaten him a time or two with that broom handle last night, kind of paying it forward. I sure would feel better now.* "You'd be better off taking that up with Aberdeen than with me," Creed said, keeping his tone mild even as his heart had kicked into overdrive. Maybe he was getting a mild case of indigestion. His whole chest seemed to be enduring one large attack of acid.

"You paying, cowboy?" Re-ride asked. "I'm short a few at the moment."

He was short more things than dollars, but Creed just shook his head, deciding it wouldn't kill him to help out the poor excuse for a man. "I suppose," he said, and Re-ride proceeded to call Cherry back over to give her a list of items that would have fed an army.

Creed sighed to himself. If anyone had ever told him he'd be buying breakfast for the ex-husband and current suitor of a woman that Creed had a small crush on, he would have said they were crazy.

"Turns out I'm the crazy one," he muttered, and Re-ride said, "Yeah, I heard that about you."

Creed drank his coffee in silence.

When Creed and his unwanted companion returned to Johnny's bar, Creed said, "Sayonara, dude," and Re-ride hurried after him.

"No," Creed said, shutting the door in Re-ride's face.

"This isn't how you treat friends!" Re-ride called through the door.

"Exactly," Creed said, turning to study the bar. He decided he'd go upstairs and call his brothers, see how the old homestead was doing. He'd only been gone a day and a half—not much could have changed in his absence. He got out his laptop, too, to surf while he chatted. "This is the life," he said, making himself comfortable in the den. He ignored the banging on the door downstairs. Re-ride would go away soon, or he'd fall asleep outside the door again, and either way, it wasn't Creed's problem.

Until Aberdeen came back. Then Re-ride's constant presence would be a problem.

Yet, no. It couldn't be. Aberdeen was nothing to him, and he was nothing to her, and he was only here to pay back a favor. Not get involved in their personal family business.

Or to fall for her.

"That's right. I'm not doing that," he said, stabbing numbers into the cell phone. Re-ride had ceased banging for the moment, which was considerate of him. "Howdy, Aunt Fiona," he said, when his aunt picked up, and she said, "Well, fancy you calling right now, stranger."

"What does that mean?" Creed's antennae went straight up at his aunt's happy tone. Aunt Fiona was never happier than when she was plotting, but surely he hadn't been gone long enough for her to have sprung any plots.

"It means that you must have telekinetic abilities. We just mailed out the invitations to the First Annual Rancho Diablo Charity Matchmaking Ball!"

Creed blinked. "That's a mouthful, Aunt."

"It is indeed. And we are going to have mouthfuls of food, and drink and kissing booths—"

"I thought—" He didn't want to hurt Aunt Fiona's feelings, so he chose his words carefully. "Why are we having a…what did you call it again?"

"A First Annual Rancho Diablo Charity Matchmaking Ball!" Aunt Fiona giggled like a teenage girl. "Doesn't it sound like fun? And it's all Jonas's idea!"

Creed's brows shot up. He could feel a headache starting under his hatband, so he shucked his hat and leaned back in Johnny's chair. Outside the window ledge, a familiar face popped into view.

"Let me in!" Re-ride mouthed through the window, and Creed rolled his eyes.

"Get down before you kill yourself, dummy," he said loudly, and Aunt Fiona said, "Why, Creed! How could you speak to me that way?"

"No, Aunt. I'm not—" He glared at Re-ride and headed into another room. It was Aberdeen's room, he realized with a shock, and it carried her scent, soft and sweet and comforting. Sexy. And holy Christmas, she'd left a nightie on the bed. A white, lacy nightie, crisp white sheets, fluffy pillows…a man could lie down on that bed and never want to get up—especially if he was holding her.

But he wasn't. Creed gulped, taking a seat at the vanity instead so he could turn his face from the alluring nightie and the comfy bed which beckoned. It was hard to look away. He had a full stomach, and a trainload of desire, and if he weren't the chivalrous man that he was, he'd sneak into that bed and have a nap and maybe an erotic dream or two about her. "When is this dance, Aunt?"

"Be home in two weeks," she commanded, her typical General-Fiona self. "We're rushing this because Jonas says we must. I wanted to have it in a month, when I could order in something more fancy than barbecue, but Jonas says time is of the essence. We need ladies here fast. Well, he didn't say that, but that's the gist of it."

Creed sighed. "None of us dance, Aunt Fiona. You know that."

"I know. I never saw so many men with two left feet. Fortunately," Aunt Fiona went on, "you still draw the ladies in spite of your shortcomings. My friends have put out the calls, and we've already had a hundred responses in the affirmative. This should be a roaring success in the social columns, I must say!"

This didn't sound like one of Jonas's plans. "I've only been gone a few hours," Creed said, reeling, and Aunt Fiona snapped, "We didn't have time to wait on you to get back here, Creed, and heaven knows you're not one for making fast decisions. But Jonas is. And he is light on his feet when it comes to planning. I have great hopes for him."

Creed said to hell with it and moved to Aberdeen's

bed, testing it out with a gentle bounce. It was just as soft and comfortable as it looked. "I'm afraid to ask, but why do we need a charity ball?"

"To get your brothers married, of course. And you, but I think you'll be the last to go." Fiona sounded depressed about that. "You're still haring around, trying to figure out what you want in life, Creed."

Right now he wanted a nap in this sweet bed. Telling himself he was a fool to do it—he was treading into dangerous territory—Creed picked up the lacy white nightie with one finger, delicately, as though the sheer lace might explode if he snagged it with his work-roughened hands. "I know what I want in life, Aunt Fiona," he said softly, realizing that maybe he did know, maybe he'd known it from the moment he'd met her, but there were too many things in the way that he couldn't solve. His aunt was right—he was still going after something he couldn't have. "What are we wearing to this shindig, anyway?"

"Whatever you want to wear," Aunt Fiona said, "but I'll warn you of this. Your brothers are going all out in matching black tuxes. Super-formal, super-James Bond. They intend to dance the night away and seduce the ladies in ways they've never been seduced."

Creed stared at the nightgown, seduced already. But what good would it do? There was an eager ex-husband jumping around outside, climbing to second-story windowsills, trying to make himself at home. And Creed was feeding him. "Sounds like fun, Aunt Fiona," he said. "Guess I'll shine up my best boots."

"I'll just be grateful if you get here and ask a lady to dance," Aunt Fiona said, "so hurry home."

"Don't worry. I'll be home very soon."

"You promise?"

"I swear I do."

"Then I hold you to that. I love you, even though you are a wily coyote. I must go now, Jonas is yelling at me to buy more stamps for the invitations. He had them made special in town, and then printed invitations in all the nearby papers. I tell you, your brother's a magician. I don't know why I didn't notice it before."

She hung up. Creed stared at his cell for a moment, finally turning it off. He was dumbfounded, in a word. Aunt Fiona must have worked a heck of a spell on Jonas to put him in such a partying mood. Jonas was not the ladies' man in the family. Nor did he have the most outgoing disposition. Creed frowned. There was something off about the whole thing, but it was Aunt Fiona and her chicanery, so "off" was to be expected.

Still, it made him tired. Or maybe Re-ride had made him tired. It didn't matter. He'd slept on the sofa last night, and he hadn't slept well, and the eggs had filled him up, and Re-ride was quiet for the moment, so Creed took one last longing look at the white lace nightie he held in his hand, and leaned back against the padded headboard just for a second.

Just for a quick moment to see what it would feel like to sleep in Aberdeen's bed. A guy could dream—couldn't he?

His eyes drifted closed.

Creed had never slept so hard. Never slept so well. It was as though he was enclosed in angel wings, dreaming the peaceful dreams of newborn babies. He didn't ever want to wake up. He knew he didn't want to wake up because he was finally holding Aberdeen in his arms. And she was wearing the hot nightie, which was short enough and sheer enough not to be a nightie at all. He'd died and gone to heaven. Everything he'd ever wanted was in his arms.

He heard a gasp, and that wasn't right; in his dreams, everyone was supposed to make happy, soft coos of delight and admiration. Creed's eyes jerked open to find Aberdeen staring at him—and Re-ride.

It was a horrible and rude awakening. There was no hope that he wouldn't look like some kind of pervert, so Creed slowly sat up. He removed the nightie from his grasp and shoved it under a pillow so Re-ride couldn't get more of a glimpse of it than necessary. "Hi, Aberdeen. Did everything go well?"

"Yes." She crossed her arms, glaring at him. "Shawn says you've been running all over town, not watching the bar at all. He says he had to come in and look after it last night because he thought he saw a prowler!"

Creed flicked a glance at Re-ride. The traitor stared back at him, completely unashamed of his sidewinder antics. "Did he say that?" Creed asked, his voice soft, and Aberdeen nodded vigorously.

"And may I ask why you're in my bed?"

It was a fair question, and one to which he didn't have a good answer. And he was already in the dog house. Creed sighed. "You can ask, but I don't have a good reason."

"Then will you get out of it?" Aberdeen said, and Creed got to his feet.

"I guess I'll be going." He walked to the door, glancing back only once, just in time to see Re-ride grab Aberdeen and give her the kind of kiss a man gives a woman when he's about to emblazon her hand with a diamond ring fit for a princess. Creed could hear wedding bells tolling, and it hurt.

All his dreams—stupid dreams—were shot to dust. He slunk down the hallway, telling himself he'd been an idiot ever to have trusted Re-ride. "That yellow-bellied coward. I live with Aunt Fiona and five brothers. How could I have let myself be gamed like that?" Creed grabbed up his laptop and his few belongings, and five minutes later he was heading down the stairs, his heart heavy, feeling low.

Re-ride went running past him, hauling ass for the front door. He jetted out of the bar, running toward town. Creed hesitated in the doorway, wondering if he should check on Aberdeen.

She came down the stairs, lifting her chin when she saw him. "You're still here?"

Creed blinked. "Re-ride just beat me to the door, or I'd be gone already."

She had enough ice in her eyes to freeze him, and Creed was feeling miserably cold already.

"Why were you in my bed?"

"I fell asleep. Is that a crime? It's not like I was Goldilocks and I tried out all the beds in the house and thought yours was the best. Although from my random and incomplete survey, so far it is pretty nice."

"I wasn't expecting to find you in my bed."

"I wasn't actually expecting to be in it, it just happened that way," he said with some heat, still smarting that Re-ride had painted him in a thoroughly unflattering light, and liking it even less that Aberdeen had believed the worst of him. Women! Who needed them? "I went in there, I fell asleep. End of story. And I'm not sorry," he said, "because it was damn comfortable, and I slept like a baby. Frankly, I was beat."

She looked at him for a long moment. "Would you like to sleep all night in my bed?" she asked, and Creed's pulse rocketed. Women didn't say something like that unless they meant something awesome and naked, did they?

"I should probably be hitting the road," Creed said, not sure where he stood at the moment, although the direction of the conversation was decidedly more optimistic than it had been a few moments ago.

She nodded. "Okay. I understand."

He understood nothing at all. "Understand what?"

She shrugged. "Thanks for watching the bar, Creed. And I'm sorry for what I said. I should have known better than to believe anything Shawn says."

"You mean Re-ride?" Creed glanced over his shoulder to see if the cowboy had reappeared, but there was a dust plume from the man's exit. "What changed your mind?"

"He proposed," she said simply. "And I realized he was doing it because of you."

"Yeah, well. I have that effect on men, I guess. They get jealous of me because it's obvious the ladies prefer me." Creed threw in a token boast to boost his self-esteem. Aberdeen had him tied in a cowboy's knot.

"So," Aberdeen slowly said, "the offer's still open if you're not of a mind to hit the road just yet."

Creed hung in the doorway, feeling as if something was going on he didn't quite understand, but he wasn't about to say no if she was offering what he thought she was. Still, he hesitated, because he knew too well that Aberdeen wasn't the kind of woman who shared her bed with just anyone. "Where's Johnny? And the little girls?"

"They're in Spring, Montana. I just came back to get

some of our things." Aberdeen looked at him, her eyes shy, melting his heart. "And then I'll be going back."

She wasn't telling everything, but Creed got that she was saying she wouldn't be around. And she'd just told Re-ride to shove off, so that meant—

He hardly dared to hope.

Until she walked to him, leaned up on her toes and pressed her lips against his.

And then he allowed himself to hope.

Chapter 9

The first thing Creed noticed about Aberdeen was that she was a serious kisser. There was no shyness, no holding back. When he pulled her close and tight, she melted against him.

That was just the way he wanted her. Yet Creed told himself to go slow, be patient. She'd been married to quite the dunderhead; Creed wanted to come off suave, polished. Worthy of her. He would never get his fill of her lips, he decided, knowing at once that Cupid's arrow had shot him straight through.

She only pulled back from him once, and stared up into his eyes. "Are you sure about this?"

He gulped. That was usually the man's question, wasn't it? And here she was asking him like he was some shy lad about to lose his virginity. "I've never been more sure of anything in my life."

"Then lock the door, cowboy. Bar's closed for the rest of the day. And night."

He hurriedly complied, and then she took his hand, leading him upstairs. Creed's heart was banging against his ribs; his blood pressure was through the roof. *Let this be real, and not that horny dream I'd promised myself.* When Aberdeen locked the bedroom door behind them, he knew he was the luckiest man on earth. "Come here," he told her, "let me kiss you."

If he had the whole night, then he was going to kiss her for hours. He took her chin gently between his palms, his lips meeting hers, molding against her mouth. She moaned and he was happy to hear that feminine signal, so he turned up the heat a notch. She surprised him by eagerly undoing his shirt buttons, never taking her lips from his until she had his shirt completely undone. Then she pulled away for just a moment, her hands slipping his shirt off, her gaze roaming over his chest, her hands greedily feeling the tight muscles of his stomach and the knotted cords of his shoulders.

She looked as though she was starving for love and affection. He'd never made love to a preacher lady, but he'd figured she would have all kinds of hang-ups and maybe a go-slow button. Aberdeen acted as if he was some kind of dessert she'd promised herself after a monthlong fast. And he didn't want to get drawn into any lingering firefight between her and Re-ride, if that was what was going on here. He caught her hands between his, pressing a kiss to her palms. "Aberdeen, is everything all right?"

She nodded up at him, her eyes huge. "Yes."

"You're sure you want this?"

She nodded again. "Yes, I do, and if you don't quit

being so slow, I'm going to be forced to drag you into my bed, Creed."

Well, that was it. A man could only play the firefighter so long when he really wanted to be the raging fire. So he picked her up and carried her to her white bed, laying her gently down into the softness. Slowly, he took off her sandals, massaging each delicate ankle. He unbuttoned her sundress, every white button down the front of the blue fabric, patiently, though it seemed to take a year and he wasn't certain why a woman needed so many buttons. He kissed her neck, keeping her still against the bed, his shoulders arched over her body, and still she kept pulling him toward her. In fact, she was trying to get his jeans off, and doing a better job of it than he was doing with the dress, but Creed was determined to have her out of her clothes first and lavish on her the attention he'd been so hungry to give her. Slipping the dress to the floor, he moved Aberdeen's hands to her side and murmured, "Don't worry. I'm going to take good care of you," and she sighed as though a ton of burdens had just slid off her. He slipped off her bra, delighted by the tiny freckles on her breasts, which, he noticed, happened to match the same sprinkles on her thighs. He took his time kissing each freckle, then slowly slipped a nipple into his mouth, tweaking the other with his hand. She moaned and arched against him, but he pressed her against the sheets again, keeping her right where he wanted her.

"Slow," Creed murmured against Aberdeen's mouth. "I'm going to take you very slowly."

She tried to pull him toward her, but there wasn't any way he was going to be rushed. He captured her hands in one of his, keeping them over her head so he could suck on her nipples, lick her breasts, tease her into readiness. Every inch of her was a treasure he'd been denied for so long; he just wanted to explore everything, leave nothing behind. She was twisting against him, her passion growing, and he liked knowing that she was a buttoned-up lady for everyone else but him. He let her hands go free so that he could cup a breast with one hand, shucking his boots with the other, and then started the heavenly trail down her stomach.

There were cute freckles there, too. Aberdeen gasped, her fingers tangling in his hair. He could feel her control completely slipping, which was the way he wanted her, wild with passion. Looping his fingers in the sides of her panties, he pulled them down, bit by bit revealing the hidden treasure.

And there was nothing he could do once he saw all of Aberdeen's beauty but kiss her in her most feminine place. She went still, surprised, he thought, but he had more surprises in store for her. She was too feminine to resist, and he'd waited too long. Her body seemed made for his; she felt right, she fitted him, and he couldn't stand it any longer. He slipped his tongue inside her— and Aberdeen cried out. He spread her legs apart, moving to kiss those pin-sized freckles on her thighs, but she buried her hands in his hair again, and it sure seemed like begging to him, so Creed obliged. He kissed her, and licked her, holding her back, knowing just how close he could get her before she exploded, and then, knowing she was too ladylike to beg—next time, he'd make sure he got her to totally let go—he put a finger inside her, massaging her while he teased her with his tongue.

Aberdeen practically came apart in his hands.

"Creed!" she cried, pulling at him desperately, and he

fished a condom out of his wallet, putting it on in record time. Holding her tightly, he murmured, "Hang on," and kissing her, slid inside her.

She felt like heaven. This *was* heaven. "If I do this every day for the rest of my life, it won't be enough," he whispered against her neck, and when Aberdeen stiffened in his arms, he moved inside her, tantalizing her, keeping her on edge. She was holding back in spirit, in her heart, but as Creed brought her to a crying-out-loud climax, he kissed her, thinking she had no clue that she couldn't run him off as easily as she'd run off Re-ride. He just wasn't that kind of shallow.

"Aberdeen," he murmured, his mind clouding, nature taking over his body. He'd only pleasured her twice, but he couldn't stand it any longer. He rode her into the sheets, the pressure commanding him to possess her, never give her up, take her to be his. She cried out, grabbing his shoulders, locking her legs around him, crying his name, surrendering this much passion, he knew, against her will. When he came, he slumped against her, breathing great gulps of air, and murmured her name again. It was engraved in his heart.

Aberdeen just didn't know that yet. She'd be hard to convince. She'd have a thousand reasons why they couldn't be together.

But if he knew anything at all, if he understood one thing about his destiny, it was that Aberdeen Donovan was meant to be his by the glorious hand of Fate.

And he was damned grateful.

Aberdeen lay underneath Creed practically in shock. Never in her life had she experienced anything like that. She hadn't even known making love could be such...

so much fun, for one thing. If you could call that fun. She felt as if she'd had her soul sucked from her and put back better.

She wiggled, trying to see if he had fallen asleep on her. Her eyes went wide. Was he getting hard again? It certainly felt like he was. He was the hardest man she'd ever felt, like steel that possessed her magically. All she had for comparison was Re-ride, and that wasn't much of a comparison. Aberdeen bit her lip as that thought flew right out of her brain. Creed *was* getting hard inside her again! She'd figured he'd want her once and go on his way, the way her ex had—and then she'd pack the things she needed and head to Montana.

He wouldn't miss her—he wasn't that kind of guy. He probably had women in every town. So she hadn't felt too guilty about seducing him. She'd just wanted a little pleasure, something for herself, an answer to the question she'd had ever since she'd seen his admiration for her burning in his navy gaze. He was too good-looking and too much of a rascal—a bad boy a woman fantasized about—for her not to want the question answered. She wasn't an angel. And right now she was glad of that, because he was hard, and he wanted her, and even if she hadn't planned on making love to Creed twice, she wasn't about to say no.

Not after the pleasure he'd just given her.

He looked deep into her eyes, not saying a word. She didn't know what to say to him. He made all the words she ever thought she might say just dry up. He made a lazy circle around one of her breasts, and she could feel him getting even harder inside her. He kissed her lips, sweetly and slowly, and Aberdeen's breath caught somewhere inside her chest.

To her surprise, he rolled her over on her stomach, and she went, trusting him. He reached for another condom, and kissed her shoulders, as if he wanted to calm her, soothe her. So she waited with held breath as he kissed down her spine, finding points which seemed to intrigue him. He kissed her bottom reverently, took a nip here and there, licked the curve of her hips.

And then the hardness filled her again as he slid inside her. She tried not to cry out, but oh, she couldn't stop herself. He held her gently, not demanding, not passionate and eager as he'd been before, and he rocked her against him, filling her with him. He tweaked a breast, rolling it between his fingers as he kissed her neck, and she couldn't stop her body from arching back against him. She didn't know exactly what she wanted, but when he put a hand between her legs, teasing her, the combination of steel and gentle teasing sent her over the edge again. "Creed," she said on a gasp, and he said, "Say it again," against her neck, and she obeyed him as he drove her to another climax. And when she said his name a third time—she heard herself scream it—he pounded inside her, taking her until his arms tightened around her and his body collapsed against hers.

But still he didn't let her go.

And now, she didn't want him to.

When Aberdeen awakened, Creed wasn't in her bed. She rose, glancing around the room, listening.

There was nothing to hear.

He'd left. He'd gone back to New Mexico. Her heart racing, Aberdeen crawled from the sheets, sore in places she couldn't remember being sore before. And yet it felt good, a reminder of the passion she'd finally experienced.

No wonder the Callahans were famous. She peeked out the window, but his truck was gone. Her heart sank, though she'd expected him to head off. Men like Creed didn't hang around. Hadn't she learned that from Shawn? Oh, he'd come back in the end, but he hadn't really wanted her. She'd figured that out quick enough when Shawn proposed to her.

She'd told him she had custody of her nieces, and he'd told her he didn't want to be a father. That had inflamed her, and she'd told Shawn that if he didn't get out of her room, out of her house, she'd set Creed on him.

Those were the magic words. Her ex had run as though devils were on his tail.

Aberdeen got into the shower, thinking she had a lot to be grateful to the Callahan cowboy for. She'd known there was no future for the two of them—there were too many differences in their lives—but still, she wished he'd said goodbye.

She took a long shower, letting the hot water calm her mind. She didn't want to think about her nieces at the moment, or custody, or cowboys she couldn't have. Raspberry body wash—her favorite—washed all the negative thoughts away, and she grabbed a white towel to wrap around her body and began to dry her hair. If she hurried, she could leave in an hour. She'd close up the bar, put on the security alarm and drive to the next phase in her life. She doubted she'd ever see Creed again. A tiny splinter of her heart broke off, and she told herself she was being silly. Just because she'd slept with him, that didn't mean they could be anything to each other. But still, she'd started to think of him as someone in her life—

She heard the door downstairs open and close. Her pulse jumped. Creed had left, but surely he'd locked the door. She'd seen the closed sign in the window when they'd come home.

Boots sounded on the stairs. Aberdeen froze, holding her towel tightly around her. She could hardly hear for the blood pulsing in her ears.

When Creed walked into the room, her breath didn't release, as it should have, with relief. If anything, she was even more nervous. "I thought you'd gone."

He smiled at her. He'd showered, but he must have used Johnny's room, which made sense. His longish hair was slightly wet at the ends. His dark-blue eyes crinkled at the sides.

"Did you dress for me, Aberdeen?" he asked, his voice a teasing drawl.

Blush heated her face. She decided to brave this out. "As I said, I thought you'd gone."

He nodded. "I didn't want to wake you up when I went out. You were sleeping like a princess."

Of course he was well aware he'd made her feel like a princess. Her defenses went up. "Why are you here?"

His gaze swept her toes, up her calves, considered the towel she clutched before returning to her face. He gave her a smile only a rogue would wear. "Do you want me to leave?"

She wanted him, and he knew it. He was toying with her. "I don't know why I would want you here," she said, "I'm leaving today, and I'm sure you have places to go."

He took off his hat and laid it on her vanity. Her heart

jumped inside her, betraying her inner feelings. "I do have places to go, things to do," he agreed.

She didn't trust the gleam in his eyes. Tugging the towel tighter against her, she lifted her chin. "Where did you go?"

"Out for a little while."

He didn't move closer, so Aberdeen felt on firm footing. "Did you come back to say goodbye? Because if you did, you can say it and go. No guilt." She took a deep breath. "I know you have a long drive."

He nodded. "I do."

She waited, her heart in a knot, too shy suddenly to tell him she wished everything could be different—

"I didn't come back to say goodbye," he said, stepping toward her now. "You need breakfast before you leave, and I need you."

She stood her ground as he came near, and when he reached out and took hold of the towel, she allowed him to take it from her body. He dropped it to the floor, his gaze roaming over her as if he'd never seen her body before. He seemed to like what he saw. He took her face in his hands, kissing her lips, her neck, and Aberdeen closed her eyes, letting her fingers wander into his hair as he moved to her stomach, kissing lower until he licked inside her, gently laving all the sore places until they felt healed and ready for him again. She moaned, her knees buckling, her legs parting for him, and when Creed took her back to her bed, laying her down, Aberdeen told herself that one more time enjoying this cowboy in her bed was something she deserved. She couldn't have said no if her life had depended on it. He made her feel things she'd never felt before, and she wanted to feel those things again, and he knew it.

He took out a new box of condoms. Aberdeen watched him, wanting to say that he wasn't going to need an entire new box since they both had places to be—but by the time he'd undressed and gotten into bed with her, murmuring sweet things against her stomach, telling her she was a goddess, Aberdeen slid her legs apart and begged him to come to her. And when Creed did, she held him as tightly as she could, rocking against him until she felt him get stronger and then come apart in her arms, which somehow felt better even than anything he'd done to her.

She was in heaven in his arms—and she didn't want to be anywhere else.

Chapter 10

Time seemed to stand still for Creed, suspended between what he wanted and what was realistic. The sleeping woman he held in his arms was what he wanted. Realistically, winning her was going to be hard to achieve.

He had to give it everything in his power. There were a hundred reasons he could think of that Aberdeen had to be his—but convincing her would take some serious effort.

It would be worth it, if he could convince her.

He realized she was watching him. "Hello, beautiful," he said, stroking her hair away from her face.

She lowered her lashes. He liked her a little on the shy side; he enjoyed tweaking her, too. She was so cute, tried so hard to be reserved, and then she was all eager and welcoming in bed. "I want you again," he told her. "I don't know how you have this spell on me."

She stroked a hand over his chest. He kissed the tip of her nose, and then lightly bit it. She pinched his stomach, just a nip, and he grinned at her, giving her bottom a light spank. She jumped, her eyes wide, and he laughed, holding her tighter against him. "I could stay here with you for weeks, just making love to you. I don't even have to eat."

He would just consume her. He kissed her lips, taking his sweet time to enjoy that which he'd wanted for so long.

"I have to go, Creed," Aberdeen said, "as much as I would love to stay here with you."

He grunted, not about to let her go this moment. There was too much he still needed to know. "What happened to Re-ride? Why did he take off?"

She gazed at him, and Creed couldn't resist the pain in her eyes, so he kissed her lips, willing her to forget the pain and think only of the pleasure he could give her.

"He got cold feet," Aberdeen said.

"How cold?"

"Ice." She looked at him. "Arctic."

"He said he was going to marry you again." Creed palmed her buttocks, holding her close against him so he could nuzzle her neck, feel her thighs against his. She slipped a thigh between his, and he nearly sighed with pleasure. She was so sweet, so accommodating. He really liked that about her.

"He talks big." Aberdeen laid her head against his shoulder, almost a trusting, intimate gesture, and Creed liked that, too. "He didn't want me to adopt the girls, but I am going to, if I have to. If it's the right thing for them. If my sister, Diane, doesn't come back, then I'll move to the next phase. Right now, I've been awarded temporary custody. Shawn wanted to be part of my life, so he claimed, knew I was going to adopt my nieces if I had to, but when I told him I had to move to Montana, he went cold." She ran a palm lightly over his chest. "I told him if he didn't get out, you'd throw him out. Or something to that effect. I hope you don't mind."

Creed grinned, his chin resting on top of Aberdeen's head. "I never miss a chance to be a hero."

"So that's my story. What's yours?"

Creed thought his story was too long and too boring to bother anyone with. He didn't want to talk about it anyway. "I don't have a story."

Aberdeen pulled away. "That's dirty pool. You can't pull out my story, and then keep yours to yourself."

She had a point. He pushed her head back under his chin and gave her another light paddling on the backside. "Have I ever told you I don't like opinionated women?"

She made a deliberately unappreciative sound which he would call a snort. "I like my women a little more on the obedient side," he said, teasing her, enjoying trying to get her goat, only because he wanted to see what her retribution would be. He liked her spicy. Spice was good.

"I like my men a little more on the honest side," Aberdeen shot back, and Creed smiled to himself.

"That's my sweet girl," he said, and Aberdeen gave him a tiny whack on his own backside, surprising him. He hadn't expected her to turn the tables on him.

"So, your story?" Aberdeen prompted.

"I need to get married," Creed said, his gaze fixed on the vanity across the room as he thought about his life in New Mexico. "My aunt wants all of us to get married."

Aberdeen pulled away from him to look into his eyes. "And do you have a prospect back in New Mexico?"

"No," he said, pulling her back against him, "I don't. So my aunt—who is a formidable woman—is planning a marital ball of some kind to introduce me and my four unmarried brothers to eligible ladies."

"Why does your aunt care if you're unmarried or not?"

"Because she's bossy like that." Creed loved the smell of Aberdeen's shampoo. Raspberry or strawberry— something clean and fresh and feminine. He took a deep breath, enjoying holding her. "And the women she'll have at the ball will be highly eligible. Socially acceptable. Drop-dead gorgeous."

"So what are you doing here?" Aberdeen asked, and Creed grinned, fancying he heard just a little bite in her words.

"Sleeping with you? Oh, this is just a fling." He kissed her lips, though she tried to evade him. "Didn't you say that you had to leave for Montana? So you're just having a little fun before you go back. I understand that. Men do it all the time." He sucked one of her nipples into his mouth, and Aberdeen went still, though she'd been trying to move to the edge of the bed, putting room between them.

"I don't know what this is," Aberdeen said, and he heard honesty in her voice. He released her nipple and kissed her on the mouth instead.

"You were going to say yes to Re-ride."

She looked at him, her gaze clear. "I hate to admit that I briefly considered it."

"But it didn't work out before."

She shook her head. "I suppose I was desperate enough to wonder if it might have been the best idea."

He hated the sound of that. "Because of your nieces?"

"I only have temporary custody. The judge didn't seem to find me all that compelling as a guardian. I feel like I need more stability in my life to convince him. He pointed out that Johnny and I live over a bar, not exactly suitable for children. The clientele is transient. He doesn't know Johnny and me. He does know our parents, and made the assumption that they'll be available to help us out. What he didn't understand is that our parents didn't even raise us." Aberdeen seemed ashamed to admit this, and Creed put his chin on her shoulder again, holding her tight. "So I can't leave Montana with the kids. I think if my marital status were to change, that would be something in my favor."

"And along came Re-ride, and you saw your prince."

Aberdeen shrugged. "It made sense at the time."

Creed could see the whole picture. He understood now why Johnny had called him to come watch the bar. Johnny didn't like Re-ride. Johnny had called Creed in, hoping Creed might have an eye for his sister.

"Tell me something," Creed said, "why are you here to get your things instead of Johnny?"

"Johnny was going to come, and I was going to stay with the girls. But then Johnny said he thought it would be better if he stayed because our folks give him a little less trouble. Very few people bother Johnny. He's always been my biggest supporter."

"Protective big brother," Creed murmured, and Aberdeen said, "Yes."

And so Creed had run off the competition, just as Johnny had probably hoped. Creed could spot a plot a mile away, even if he was late to figure it out. Fiona had given him good training. He tipped her chin back with a finger. "Preacher lady, you need a husband, and it just so happens I need a wife."

She blinked. Seemed speechless. Her eyes widened, like she thought he was joking. He kissed her hand, lightly bit the tip of a finger before drawing it into his mouth. She pulled her finger away, then glared at him.

"That's not funny."

"I'm not joking." Creed shrugged.

"You're serious."

"Men don't joke about marriage." Creed shook his head. "It's a very serious matter worthy of hours of cogitation."

"Are you suggesting we have some sort of fake marriage? To fool the judge and to fool your aunt?"

"*Fooling*'s kind of a harsh word." Creed kissed her neck, ignoring her when she tried to push him away. She couldn't; he outweighed her by a hundred pounds, and he sensed she wasn't serious about moving him away from her delightful body. She just needed distance while her mind sorted the conclusion he'd already come to. "I'm just suggesting we become a stable, responsible married couple for all interested parties."

"You want to marry me just to get your aunt off your back?"

Creed laughed. "You make it sound so simple. Aunt Fiona is not that easy to fool. You'll have to be a very enthusiastic bride. Or she'll find me a better wife."

Aberdeen shook her head. "It's a silly reason to get married. I counsel people on making proper decisions regarding marriage vows. This would be a sham."

"*Sham* is also a harsh word." He kissed the tip of her nose. "I prefer *happy facade*."

Her glare returned. "*Happy facade* sounds ridiculous. Marriage should be a contract between two people who trust each other."

"Think of all the benefits. I'd sleep with you every night, Aberdeen. I promise." He tugged her up against him, so he could kiss between her breasts. "We're a good fit in bed."

"Sex isn't enough." Aberdeen tried to squirm away.

"It's not enough, but it sure is a lot." He rolled her over so he could spoon against her back and nip her shoulder lightly at the same time. "Good thing you like sex as much as you do. I wouldn't want a frigid wife."

She gasped and tried to jump out of the bed. "Aberdeen, you know you like it. Don't try to deny it." He laughed and tugged her against him. "Were you reaching for the condoms, love? If you hand me a couple, I'll give you an hour you'll never forget."

She went still in the bed. He held her against him, stroking her hips, letting her decide if she was going to be angry with him or take the bait. Either way, he had a plan for that.

"You're too crazy for me to marry," Aberdeen said, "even if you're serious, which I don't think you are."

"I'm as serious as a heart attack, love."

She flipped over to stare into his eyes. "Where would we live?"

"In my house in New Mexico. Wherever that's going to be."

"A house?" He could feel her taste the words, and realized having a house was a dream of hers.

"Mmm," he murmured, unable to resist running a

palm down her breasts. "House, yard, school nearby, church, the works. Nothing fancy. But a home."

"Why would you be willing to have my three nieces live with you?" She looked as though she didn't quite believe what she was hearing.

He shrugged. "I don't mind kids. They didn't exactly run screaming from me, and I thought that was a good start. And my aunt wants us to have as many children as possible."

She crooked a brow. "Can't you have your own?"

He laughed. "Come here and let's find out."

Aberdeen squirmed away, studying his face. "Men don't get married and take on other people's children because of aunts."

"Probably not." He could feel her brain whirring a mile a minute, trying to find the trap. She didn't get it, and even if he told her, she wouldn't believe him. *I like her, I honestly like her. I like her body. I like her innocence. I think she'd like being married to me. That's as much as I know about why people get married anyway. This feels good and real, when it's always felt kind of empty before. And I think I'm falling in love with her.* "If you want to make love again, I'll try to think of some more reasons we should get married. There's probably one or two good excuses I haven't thought of yet, but—" He kissed her neck, burying deep into the curve, smelling her clean scent, wanting her already.

"Creed," she said, "I've been through one marriage. And my nieces have already been through marriages that didn't work out for their parents. Do you know what I mean?"

"I do, my doubting angel." He kissed her hand. "You want something solid for your nieces. You won't settle for anything less than a real family. And you think I'm your man. Hand me that bag on the nightstand, please."

"Not right now, Creed, this is serious." Aberdeen melted his heart with her big pleading eyes that melted his heart. She was such a delicate little thing. He wouldn't hurt her for the world. "I feel like you're playing with me."

"Oh, no. I wouldn't. Well, sometimes I will, in fact a lot of times I will, but not about a marriage agreement. I'm very serious about agreements. Hand me my bag, sugar."

She shook her head. "Creed, I can't make love when you've got me tied in knots. I couldn't think. I couldn't focus. I just don't understand why you want to marry—"

He gave her a tiny slap on the backside. "Aberdeen, will you please hand me that sack on the nightstand? Or do I have to get it myself?"

"Here's your silly old sack," she said, snatching it up and flinging it at him. "But I'm not saying yes, so don't even ask."

He raised a brow. "No yes?"

"No. Absolutely not." She looked fit to be tied, as if she'd love to kick him out of her bed.

Creed sighed. "Is that your final answer?"

"In fact, it is. No woman can make love when the man who is in her bed is being an absolute ass."

"Whoa, them's fighting words from a preacher." Creed grinned at her. "Just so I can get this straight," he said, reaching into the bag and pulling out a jeweler's box, which he opened, "you're saying no?"

She stared at the box he opened for her to view. It contained a heart-shaped diamond, which he was pretty proud of picking out this morning on his way for the condoms and granola bars.

"Creed," she said, sounding shocked and choked-up, and he snapped the box shut and put it back in the bag.

"Too bad," he said. "The jeweler promised me no woman could say no to this ring. He said a woman would have to have a heart of stone to refuse it. He said—"

"You're crazy! I knew it when I first met you. I know you're crazy, and I know better than to throw myself to the wind like this, but I'm going to ride this ride, cowboy, and I swear, if you turn out to be a weirdo, I'll be really ticked at you."

He kissed her, and she burst into tears, and threw her arms around his neck. "There, there," he said, "having a weirdo for a husband wouldn't be that bad, would it?"

"Creed, give me my ring," Aberdeen said, trying not to giggle against his neck as he held her.

"Greedy," he murmured, "but I don't mind." He took the ring from the box and slipped it on her finger, and for a moment, they both admired it in the light that spilled into the bedroom through the lace curtains.

"You are a weirdo," Aberdeen said, "and I don't know why I'm jumping off a cliff into alligator-infested waters."

Creed just grinned at her. "I'll let you get on top, future Mrs. Callahan, if you're sweet, and this time, you can ride me bareback."

Aberdeen looked at him, not sure if she trusted him or not, not sure exactly of what she wanted to feel for him. But Creed understood she'd been let down before, so he tugged her on top of him, and then smiled to himself when after a moment she said, "This time, I'm going to please you, cowboy."

Aunt Fiona was right, as usual. This marriage stuff is going to be a piece of cake. I feel like I'm winning again—finally.

Chapter 11

Marriage was *not* going to be a piece of cake. It was going to be as nerve-racking as any rodeo he'd ever ridden in—only this time, he was pretty certain getting stomped by a bull was less traumatic than what he was experiencing now. Creed found himself waiting outside Aberdeen's family home, cooling his heels before the big intro. The girls were inside, getting reacquainted with their aunt and Johnny. Aberdeen wanted to introduce him to her family after she had a chance to go inside and prepare them for the big news.

He was nervous. And it was all because of the little girls. He'd thought they'd liked him for the brief moments they met him before—but what if they'd changed their minds? Kids did that. He knew from experience. He wasn't certain he would have wanted a new father when he was a kid. Maybe he wouldn't. He and his brothers

probably would have given a new father a rough road—
he was certain they would have. They'd given everybody
a rough road on principle, except Fiona. She wouldn't
have put up with that type of nonsense, and besides, she'd
always been able to outthink them.

He was pretty certain the little girlies might be able
to outthink him, too. Girls had mercurial brains, and at
their tender ages, they probably had mercurial set on
high.

He was sweating bullets.

He should have brought some teddy bears or something. Big pieces of candy. Cowgirl hats. Anything to
break the ice and get the girls to see him in a positive
light.

"Creed, come in." Aberdeen smiled out the door at
him, and he told his restless heart to simmer down. It
was going to be okay.

He stepped inside the small Montana house—and
found himself on the receiving end of frowns from everyone in the family except Johnny.

"Good man," Johnny said, clapping him on the back,
and Creed felt better.

"You might have warned me you were setting me up,"
Creed groused under his breath, and Johnny laughed.

"You struck me as the kind of man who didn't need
a warning," Johnny said. "These are our parents. Mom,
Dad, this is Creed Callahan."

He was definitely not getting the red carpet treatment.
Mr. and Mrs. Donovan wore scowls the size of Texas.
"Hello," he said, stepping forward to shake their hands,
"it's a pleasure to meet you."

He got the fastest handshakes he'd ever had. No
warmth there. Creed stepped back, telling himself he'd

probably feel the same way if he had little girls and some cowboy was slinking around. The girls looked up at him shyly, their eyes huge, and Creed had to smile. He did have little girls now—three of them—and he was going to scowl when boys came knocking on his door for them.

"Well," Aberdeen said, "Creed, sit down, please. Make yourself comfortable."

"You're marrying my daughter," Mr. Donovan said, and Creed nodded.

"That's the plan, sir."

"I don't think I care for that plan."

Creed glanced at Johnny, surprised. Johnny shrugged at him.

"I'm sorry to hear that," Creed finally said, trying to sound respectable. "Your daughter will be in good hands, I promise."

"We know nothing about you," Mrs. Donovan said.

"Mom," Aberdeen said, "I'm marrying him. You can be nice, or you can both be annoying, but this man is my choice. So you'll just have to accept it."

"You're not taking the girls," Mrs. Donovan said, and Creed went tense.

"Yes, I am, as soon as I clear it with the judge." Aberdeen got to her feet, abandoning the pretense of a welcome-home party. Creed felt sorry for her. Aunt Fiona had kept them in line over the years, but she'd never been rude to them. He glanced at the tiny girls, and they stared back at him, not smiling.

His heart withered to the size of a gumdrop. He wanted them to like him so badly, and at the moment they just seemed confused.

"The judge won't approve it." Mr. Donovan seemed

confident about that. "He feels they are better off here, near us."

"All right. Come on, Creed." Aberdeen swept to the door. Creed recognized his cue and followed dutifully, not understanding his role in the script but sensing his bride-to-be was working on a game plan.

Mrs. Donovan shot to her feet. "Where are you going?"

"Back to Wyoming," Aberdeen said, and Johnny followed her to the door. Johnny might have set him up, Creed realized, but he definitely had his sister's back.

"You can't just leave!" Mrs. Donovan exclaimed.

"I can. I will. And I am."

"Wait!" Mrs. Donovan sounded panicked. "What are we going to do with the girls?"

"Raise them," Aberdeen said, and Creed could see her lips were tight. She was angry, loaded for bear, and he didn't ever want to see her look at him like that. "Maybe you'll do a better job with them than you did with us."

"Hang on a minute," Mr. Donovan said. "Let's just all calm down."

"I'm past calm," Aberdeen said. "Calm isn't available to me at the moment."

The little girls started to cry. Creed's heart broke. "Oh," he murmured, not sure what to do, completely undone by the waterworks. "I think I'll wait outside," he said, and headed toward Johnny's truck. This was such bad karma that he was going to kiss Aunt Fiona as soon as he got back to Rancho Diablo. He'd never realized before how much her steadfast parenting had colored his existence happy. Of course, she was going to box his ears when she found out he was getting married and she didn't get to arrange it, and that made him feel a bit more resourceful.

He sat in the truck, feeling like a teenager. After a few moments, Mrs. Donovan came to his window. "Mr. Callahan," she said, her eyes bright. He thought she'd been crying.

"Yes, ma'am? Please call me Creed."

"Will you please come back inside and have a cup of tea before you depart?"

He looked at her, and she looked back at him with a sad expression, and he realized she was scared.

"You know," he said softly, "I'm not taking her away from you forever. And you will always be welcome at Rancho Diablo. We like having family around."

Tears jumped into her eyes. She nodded. "Tea?"

"I'd be honored," he said, and followed his future mother-in-law into the house.

"What did you say to her?" Aberdeen asked, watching her mother ply Creed with cupcakes and tea.

"I said I liked tea a whole lot."

Creed filled his plate up with sweets, and balanced Lincoln Rose on his knee as though he'd done it a thousand times before. Aberdeen was astonished. Good father material wasn't something she'd put on her checklist when she'd decided to seduce Creed. The shock of discovering that he might have potential in this area warmed her heart. The most important thing in the world to her right now was the welfare of her nieces—she'd do anything to protect their futures, make sure their lives were as comfortable and normal as possible under the circumstances.

Never had she suspected that Creed might be a truly willing participant in her goal. He sure looked like it now, with all her nieces standing close to him, eating him up with their eyes like they'd never seen a real man before. They'd had Johnny, but she and Johnny hadn't been around much, not knowing that Diane's marriage was in trouble. So Creed garnered a lot of attention from the girls. And he seemed to return that attention, with affection thrown in.

It's an agreement. We made an agreement. He's merely keeping up his part of the bargain. I wanted stability, and he wanted stability, and neither of us ever said anything about permanent. Or love.

So don't do it. Don't go falling in love when you know that's not a realistic ending to the story. Wild never settles down forever—and he never said forever anyway.

"More tea?" she said to Creed, and he smiled at her, his gaze kind and patient as he held the girls, and she felt heat run all over her. And another chip fell off her heart.

"To be honest," Johnny said to Creed when they'd gone outside to throw a ball for the little nieces, "I didn't mean for you to propose to my sister."

Creed looked at him, then back at the porch where Aberdeen was standing with her parents, watching the game. The small house framed them. If he hadn't known better, he would have thought this was a happy family. However, it wasn't anything he wasn't experienced with, so Creed felt pretty comfortable. "What did you have in mind, then?"

"I thought it would be a good idea to give Aberdeen something new to look at. Re-ride was old, you were new." Johnny grinned. "I wanted her to know that there were other fish in the sea."

"I'm sure there've been plenty of fish swimming her way," Creed said, his tone mild.

"Yeah, but she's not much for catching them." Johnny tossed the ball, and the pink toy bounced toward the girls who squealed and tried to catch it with uncoordinated hands. "Anyway, I just wanted you to know that you're taking on a pretty tall order with us."

"Tall doesn't bother me." Creed looked at the girls, then glanced back at Aberdeen. Her hair shone in the Montana sunlight and she was smiling at him. "However, you'll have to come to New Mexico to see her, my friend, so I hope you thought through your plan in its entirety."

"That's the way it is, huh?"

"That's the way it is." Creed nodded. "We've got plenty of space for you, too, if you're of a mind to see a different topography."

Johnny grinned. "I hear New Mexico is nice this time of year."

Creed nodded, but his gaze was on Aberdeen again, and all he could think about was that New Mexico was going to be really nice, better than nice, when he had his little preacher lady sleeping in his big bed. Naked. Naked, warm and willing.

She waved at him, and he smiled, feeling like the big bad wolf. The happiest wolf in the canyons.

After he'd charmed Aberdeen's folks—who warmed to him quickly after their initial resistance—and after he'd cleared hurdles with the judge, Creed placed one last phone call to warn his family of their impending change in lifestyle.

"Hello," Rafe said, and Creed grinned.

"Hello, yourself. If you've got the time, we need a ride."

His twin sighed. "I'm not flying up there just to pick up your lazy butt."

Creed had taken himself out to the small backyard after dinner to have this conversation. Johnny and Aberdeen were tucking the little girls into bed, so he had time to sound the alarm. "You'll be picking up my lazy butt and a few very busy little bottoms."

"Well, now, that sounds more interesting. How are these bottoms? Female, I hope?"

Creed grinned. "Very much so."

"Round and cute?"

"The cutest, roundest tushes you ever saw."

"So I should shave."

"Definitely. You'll regret it if you don't. You don't want to scare them." Creed thought about the small dolls that would be traveling with him and held back a laugh.

"You flying your own entertainment in for Fiona's charity ball?"

"You might say I am."

"Well, consider me your eager pilot. Where and what time do you need a pick-up?"

One of the benefits of having an ex-military pilot who'd spent time flying for private corporations was that the family had their own plane. Rafe was an excellent pilot, and letting him fly them home would be easier on the girls. Creed hadn't yet told Aberdeen, but he was looking forward to surprising her. "Tomorrow, in Spring, Montana. Plan on me, a friend and four damsels, you might say."

Rafe whistled. "You *have* been busy."

"Be on your best behavior. And ask Aunt Fiona to get the guest house ready for visitors, will you?"

"She's going to be thrilled that you're falling into

line." Rafe laughed. "I should have known that all this talk of watching over a bar for some guy was just a ruse."

"Probably you should have."

"I don't know if Fiona's going to be cool with you sleeping in the guest house with a bunch of women. On the other hand she's not totally uptight, and she is hoping to marry you off," Rafe mused. "She did say she thought you were the least likely of all of us to ever settle down. So she'll probably be okay with it."

"My ladies are pretty fine. Aunt Fiona will be all right after the initial shock."

"Bombshells, huh? Are you sharing?"

"You can hold them anytime you like. Except for my particular favorite, of course. Oh, and bring your headset. They can be loud. Girl chatter and all that. Wild times."

"You old dog," Rafe said, his tone admiring. "And everyone says you're the slow twin. Boy, did you have everybody fooled."

"See you tomorrow," Creed said, and turned off his phone. He went to find Aberdeen, who was sitting in the family room alone. She appeared slightly anxious as her gaze settled on him. "Hello."

"Hi." She smiled, but he thought she looked nervous.

"Girls asleep?"

"Johnny's reading to them. Lincoln Rose is asleep, the other two are excited about the trip tomorrow."

Creed nodded, sitting next to her on the sofa. "I hope you don't mind flying."

Aberdeen looked at him. "We're flying to New Mexico?"

"It'll be easier on the girls than a few days' drive."

"Thank you." Aberdeen smiled. "That's considerate of you, Creed."

"It is. I plan to get my reward after we're married."

Aberdeen's eyes widened. "After?"

"Well, yes. You'll have to wait to have me until you've made an honest man of me." He was pretty proud of his plan. He knew she had probably been thinking of how everything was going to work out between them. Sooner or later, she'd get worried about the silly stuff. Like, she wouldn't want to sleep with him at his ranch until they were married; it wouldn't be decent. She was, after all, a minister. She would worry about such things. She was also a new mother to children. She would be concerned about propriety. He intended to take all those worries right out of her busy little mind.

"I think you are an honest man," Aberdeen said shyly.

"Well, aren't you just a little angel cake," he said, pleased, and dropped a kiss on her nose. "But you're still not having me until you put the ring on my finger."

Aberdeen laughed. "You're horrible."

"But you like it." He put her head against his shoulder, enjoying holding her in the quiet family room.

"I'm so glad you weren't bothered by my folks," Aberdeen said softly. "They can be busybodies."

"Oh, I know all about well-meaning interference. I'm an experienced hand. I just hope you know what you're getting yourself into, little lady."

She smiled and leaned closer, and Creed closed his eyes, contented. Of course she had no idea what she was stepping into. He wasn't certain what was waiting back home for them, either. All he did know was that he'd told her she had to wait until they were married to have him again.

But they hadn't set a wedding date.

He felt like he was holding his breath—and he needed to breathe again. Soon.

Chapter 12

When Rafe met them at the plane, he was in full wolf mode. Dark aviator glasses, new jeans, dark Western shirt, dress boots. Even a sterling bolo with a turquoise stone. The kind of lone wolf any woman would lick her chops over.

Only Creed's ladies didn't really have chops yet, just gums. "Here you go," he told Rafe, and handed him the baby. "This is Lincoln Rose. Lincoln, don't be scared of ugly, honey. He tries hard but he's just not handsome like me."

Lincoln Rose stared at Rafe. Rafe stared back at her, just as bemused. Creed grinned and went to walk the next little girl up the stairs. "This is my brother, honey. You can call him Uncle Rafe if you want to, Ashley," Creed said, even though she didn't talk much yet. "Let's figure out how to strap your car seat in, okay? This plane has never seen a baby seat. But I'm pretty sure we can figure it out." He put her favorite stuffed animal and a small book beside her, then went back to the front of the plane. "And I see you've met my last little girl." Creed grinned at his brother, who still held Lincoln Rose as he latched eyes on Aberdeen with appreciation. "And this is the lady I mentioned was my special girl. Aberdeen, this is my brother, Rafe. Rafe, this is my fiancée, Aberdeen Donovan, and this little munchkin is Suzanne. Her sisters call her Suzu. And bringing up the rear is our nanny, Johnny Donovan."

"You look just like Creed," Aberdeen said. "Creed, you didn't tell me you had a twin."

"No reason to reveal all the sordid details." Creed waved Johnny toward the back and took Lincoln Rose from his brother.

"Details like how you travel in style?" Johnny said. "This is a sweet ride."

"Well, it helps to get around the country fast. We do a lot of deals here and there." Creed looked at Aberdeen. "Do you want to be co-pilot, honey?"

"No," Aberdeen said, "Thank you. I'll just sit back and try to decide how I got myself into this."

Creed grinned. "Make yourself comfortable. I'm going to help Rafe fly this rust bucket. Are we good to go, pilot?"

Rafe still seemed stunned as he looked over his new cargo of toys and babies. "Three little girls," he said, his tone amazed. "Are you trying to beat Pete?" he asked, and Creed glared at him.

"Do you see a fourth?" Creed asked.

"Who's Pete?" Aberdeen asked.

"Our brother who was first to the altar, and first to hit the baby lotto," Rafe said cheerfully.

"What were you supposed to beat him at, Creed?" Aberdeen asked.

Rafe glanced at Creed, who wished his brother had laryngitis. "I'm not trying to beat anybody at anything," Creed said. "Don't you worry your pretty little head about anything my numbskull of a brother says."

Rafe nodded. "That's right. Ignore me. I'm a pig at times."

"Most of the time. Let's fly." Creed dragged his brother into the cockpit.

"She doesn't know, does she?" Rafe asked as they settled in.

"I saw no reason to mention the baby-making aspects of Fiona's plan. It had no bearing on my decision."

"You sure?" Rafe asked.

"More than sure. Otherwise, there would be a fourth."

"And there's not?"

"Do you see a fourth?" Creed glared at Rafe again.

"I'm just wondering," Rafe said. "As your twin, it's my duty to wonder."

"Skip your duty, okay?"

Rafe switched on some controls. "I should have known that when you said you were keeping an eye on a bar, you meant a nursery."

"No, I meant a bar. I didn't have plans to get engaged when I left."

"So you found yourself in a bar and then a bed." Rafe sounded tickled. "And there were three bonuses, and so you realized this was a primo opportunity to get out of Fiona's line of fire. And maybe even beat Pete."

"No," Creed said, "because there's nothing to beat

Pete for. We have no ranch, per se. Therefore, no need to have children by the dozen."

"Oh. You hadn't heard. You've been gone." Rafe slowly taxied on to the runway. "We're all supposed to settle down, if we want to, to try to keep Bode from getting the ranch."

"It's no guarantee."

"But you don't know that Fiona says that competition begets our more successful efforts, so he who winds up with a wife and the biggest family will get the biggest chunk of the ranch—if we keep it."

Creed frowned. "That has no bearing on my decision."

"It might when you've had a chance to think it over. You'll probably think about it next time you crawl into bed with your fiancée," Rafe said, his tone annoyingly cheerful.

Creed scowled. "Let's not talk about marriage like it's a rodeo, okay? I'm getting married because…because Aberdeen and the girls are what I need."

"To settle you down." Rafe nodded. "Believe me, I understand. I'd settle down if I could find the right woman."

That wasn't it, exactly. Creed was getting married because he and Aberdeen had struck a bargain that suited them both. He got up to glance out at his precious cargo, wanting to make certain everyone was comfortable, particularly the little ladies. Aberdeen and Johnny were staring at him. Aberdeen looked as if she might be on the verge of throwing Lincoln Rose's bear at him. Johnny looked as if he was considering getting out of his seat to squash Creed's head. "Is something wrong?" he asked, instantly concerned for the babies.

"The mike's on," Johnny said, "or whatever you call that loudspeaker thing."

Creed groaned. They'd heard everything—and probably misunderstood everything, too. "We'll talk later," he said to Aberdeen, but she looked out the window, not happy with him at all.

That made two of them.

Creed went back into the cockpit, flipping the switch off as he sat down. Rafe glanced at him.

"Uh-oh. You may be in trouble," Rafe said. He looked honestly concerned. "Was that my bad?"

"I'm not certain whose bad it was. Just think about flight patterns, bro. The sooner I get her on terra firma at Rancho Diablo, the clearer things will be."

He hoped Aberdeen was the type of woman who was willing to forgive and forget. Otherwise, he might be in for a bit of a rough ride, and, as he recalled, he'd been thrown recently. Which was how he'd ended up here in the first place.

He had no intention of being thrown again.

"This is home," Creed told Aberdeen when they arrived at the ranch a few hours later. Rafe had left a van at the small regional airport where they kept the family plane in a hangar, and very little had been said on the ride to the ranch. The girls had been sound asleep in their car seats. Though Johnny had ridden up front with Rafe, and Creed had sat next to her, neither of them had felt like talking. The bigger conversation was later. If he thought she was marrying him out of a sense of obligation, he was dead wrong. And she had no intention of "settling him down," as he'd told Rafe. He could just go settle himself down, she thought.

Now, at the family ranch, Aberdeen couldn't help but be surprised. She glanced at Johnny for his reaction to the huge house on the New Mexico plains. In the distance a couple of oil derricks worked. Cattle roamed behind barbed-wire fencing. The sky was a bruised blue, and canyons were red and purple smudges in the distance. It was in the middle of nowhere, and a sense of isolation hung over the ranch.

Until, it seemed, a hundred people flowed out of the house, coming to greet them. Creed opened his door, turning to help her out. A tiny, older woman made it to the van first.

"Aunt Fiona, this is Aberdeen Donovan," Creed said. "Aberdeen, this is the brains of the outfit, Fiona."

"Hello, Aberdeen," Fiona said. "Welcome to Rancho Diablo."

Fiona's smile enveloped her. Aberdeen thought that the same wonderful navy eyes ran in the Callahan family. She felt welcomed at once, and not nervous as she had been after listening to the men discuss their "tyrant" aunt. "Hello. Creed's told me so many wonderful things about you."

"I doubt it." Fiona smiled. "But you're sweet to fib, honey. This is Burke, the family overseer. He's the true brains of the outfit, as my rascal nephew puts it."

A kindly white-haired gentleman shook her hand. "It's a pleasure, Aberdeen. And Fiona, I think we have some extra guests." Johnny had unstrapped Lincoln Rose and handed her out to Aberdeen. Fiona gasped.

"What a little doll! Creed, you didn't tell us you were bringing a baby!"

His brothers came forward, eager for their introduction and to catch a glimpse of the baby. Johnny handed out the last two, and Aberdeen smiled.

"This is Lincoln Rose, and Suzanne and Ashley.

These are my nieces, and this is my brother, Johnny Donovan."

Johnny finally made it from the van and introduced himself to the rest of the Callahans. Fiona shook her head at Creed. "You told Rafe you were bringing bomb-shells, you ruffian."

"I couldn't resist, Aunt Fiona." Creed grinned, clearly proud of himself.

"These are the prettiest bombshells I've ever seen," Fiona said. "I'll have to send out for some cribs, though. And anything else you require, Aberdeen. We don't have enough children at Rancho Diablo, so we'll be happy to gear up for these. You'll just have to let us know what babies need. My nephews have been a wee bit on the slow side about starting families." She sent Creed a teas-ing smile. "Is there anything else you'd like to spring on us, Creed?"

"Introductions first, Aunt Fiona." He went through the litany of brothers, and Aberdeen felt nearly overwhelmed by all the big men around her. Johnny seemed right at home. But then, another woman came forward, pushing a big-wheeled pram over the driveway, and Suzanne and Ashley went over to see what was inside.

"Babies," Ashley said, and Creed laughed.

"This is Pete's wife, Jackie. Jackie, this is Aberdeen Donovan."

Jackie smiled at her; Aberdeen felt that she'd found a friend.

"We'll have a lot to talk about," Jackie said.

"Yes, we will," Fiona said. "Come inside and let's have tea. I'm sure you're starving, Aberdeen." She took Lincoln Rose in her arms and headed toward the house. Aberdeen and Jackie followed.

"I'm starving, too," Creed said, watching the ladies walk away.

Sam laughed. "Not for love."

Jonas shook his head. "Did you buy that big diamond she's wearing?"

Creed shrugged. "It isn't that big."

"You're getting married?" Judah asked. "You were only gone a few days!"

"It feels right," Creed said, grinning at them.

"You're trying to win," Pete said. "You're trying to beat me."

Creed clapped his brother on the back. "Nope. I'd have to go for four to win, and I'm pretty good at knowing my limits, bro. The gold medal is all yours."

Pete grinned. "I hope you warned Aberdeen."

"About what?" Creed scowled as he and his brothers and Johnny walked toward the house, each carrying a suitcase. Burke tried to help carry one, but the brothers told him diaper bags were their responsibility, and Burke gladly went to park the van instead.

"About the bet. Which is a really dumb bet, if you ask me," Pete said. "I wasn't even trying, and look what happened to me. I just wanted to get married."

"It's almost like you got hit by a magic spell," Sam mused. "Who would have ever thought you could father three adorable little girls?"

"I don't know what to say about that," Pete groused. "I think it was more like a miracle. But besides that, I'm more than capable of fathering adorable, thanks. You'll be the one who has ugly."

"There's no such thing as an ugly baby." Jonas opened the door. "Have you ever seen an ugly baby? They don't exist. I'm a doctor, I know."

"You're a heart specialist, don't overreach your specialty." Creed shook his head. "But no, we're not going to bring up the baby bet, and we're not going to talk about ranch problems or anything like that. I'm trying to get the woman to marry me, not leave in a dust cloud."

It could happen. Aberdeen could get cold feet. She had that cold-feet look about her right now. Creed knew she was still annoyed about Rafe's conversation with him in the plane. He also knew she'd been a bit rattled by the size of Rancho Diablo. Or maybe by its faraway location. Whatever it was, he needed time to iron it out of her without his brothers bringing up Callahan drama. "So just pull your hats down over your mouths if you have to," he told his brothers, "and let's not talk about anything we have going on that's *unusual*."

"Oh, he likes this one," Sam whispered to his brothers.

"You're talking about my sister like I'm not here," Johnny said.

"Sorry," Sam said. "You look like one of us. You could be a Callahan. We can be easily confused." He grinned. "We separate ourselves into the bachelors and the down-for-the-count."

"I'm not down— Oh, never mind." Creed shook his head. "Johnny, don't listen to anything we say. We mean well. Some of us just blab too much."

Johnny shrugged. "I hear it all the time in the bar. Yak, yak, yak."

Jonas jerked his head toward the barn. "While the ladies chat, let us show you the set-up."

Creed hung back as his brothers headed out. He was pretty certain that if he was smart—and he thought he was where women were concerned—he'd better hang around and try to iron some of the kinks out of his little woman. She had a mulish look in her eyes whenever he caught her gaze, and he knew too well that mulish females were not receptive to men. He sat down by Aberdeen and pulled Lincoln Rose into his lap. "Take you for a buggy ride around the property when you've had a chance to rest?"

Aberdeen looked at him. "Is it story time?"

"I think so." Creed nodded. "Better late than never, huh?"

"We'll babysit," Jackie said, and Fiona nodded eagerly.

"And it's romantic on the ranch at night," Jackie said. "Trust me, Aberdeen, you want to take a spin on the ranch."

Aberdeen looked at Creed, and he smiled, and though she didn't smile back at him, he thought, she wasn't beaning him with a baby bottle, either—and that was the best sign he had at the moment.

"Romance," he said so only she could hear, "are you up for that?"

"We'll see how good your story is," she said, and Creed sank back in the sofa, looking at Lincoln Rose.

"Any tips on good stories?" he asked the baby, but she just looked at him. "I don't know any, either," he said, and Fiona said, "Then I suggest you get it in gear, nephew. Once upon a time, cowboy poets lived by their ability to tell stories. Live the legend."

Aberdeen raised a brow at him, and he decided right then and there that whatever she wanted, the lady was going to get.

Chapter 13

Aberdeen could tell Creed was dying to get her alone. She wasn't entirely reluctant. Story time didn't sound horrible—and in spite of the conversation she'd over-heard between Creed and his twin, she was willing to give him a chance to explain.

And to kiss her breathless.

Burke entered the room with a tall, distinguished-looking guest, and the room went silent.

"Well, Bode Jenkins," Fiona said, rising to her feet. "To what do we owe this unpleasant occurrence?"

Bode smiled at her thinly, then glanced at Aberdeen's daughters. "A little bird told me that you were welcom-ing visitors. You know how I hate not being invited to a party, Fiona." He sent a welcoming smile to Aberdeen, but instead of feeling welcomed, her skin chilled.

Creed stood, and Jonas stood with him. Sam followed,

as did Rafe, Pete and Judah. Aberdeen glanced at Creed, whose face seemed suddenly set in granite. The brothers looked ready for an old-style Western shoot-out, which bewildered her.

"Now, Bode," Fiona said, "you have no business being here."

"You should be neighborly, Fiona," Bode said, his tone silky. "When Sabrina told me you were expecting visitors, I just had to come and see what good things were happening around my future ranch. One day," he ruminated, "I'm going to cover this place over with concrete to build the biggest tourist center you ever dreamed of."

The brothers folded their arms, standing silent. If this man's visit was about her arrival, then Aberdeen wanted no part of it. She grabbed Lincoln Rose and held her in her lap, either for comfort or to protect her from what felt like an oncoming storm, she wasn't certain. Her sisters naturally followed Lincoln Rose, hugging to Aberdeen's side for protection.

But then Ashley broke away and went to Creed, who picked her up in his big, strong arms. Bode smiled, his mouth barely more than a grimace. "Looks like you're growing quite the family, Fiona," he said, glancing at Pete's and Jackie's three daughters. "Another birdie told me that you're paying your sons to get wives and have babies so you can make the claim that Rancho Diablo has its own population and therefore shouldn't be subject to the laws of the nation. It won't work, Fiona, if that's what's on your mind."

"Never mind what's on her mind," Creed said, his voice a growl. "If you've stated your business, Jenkins, go."

Bode looked at Aberdeen. Her skin jumped into a

crawling shiver. She clutched her two nieces to her. "I'm not going without giving my gift to the new bride-to-be," he murmured, his gaze alight with what looked like unholy fire to Aberdeen. "Will you walk outside with me, my dear?"

"I'm sorry that I can't," Aberdeen said. "My nieces wouldn't like me leaving them. We've just gotten in from a long day of traveling. I'm sure you'll understand."

Creed shot her a look of approval.

"That's too bad," Bode said. "There's someone I want you to meet."

"Is Sabrina outside?" Fiona frowned. "Why don't you bring her in?"

"Sabrina says she thinks she's coming down with a cold. She didn't want to give it to anyone." Bode shrugged. "I've just learned Sabrina is a fortune-teller. I wanted her to tell your fortune as a gift, Miss—"

"Donovan," Aberdeen said. "I don't believe in fortune-telling, Mr. Jenkins. Please tell your friend I'll be happy to meet her at another time when she isn't under the weather."

But then she realized that Fiona was staring at Bode, her brows pinched and low. Aberdeen sank back into her chair, glancing at Creed, who watched Bode like a hawk.

"Sabrina is a home-care provider," Fiona said, "who happens to have a gift. Why do you sound so irregular about it, Bode?"

He smiled at Fiona, but it wasn't a friendly smile. "I think you've tried to set me up, Fiona Callahan. And I don't take kindly to trickery."

"I don't know what you're talking about," Fiona snapped. "Don't be obtuse."

"Then let me be clear. You hired Sabrina McKinley to spy on me."

"Nonsense," Fiona shot back. "Why would I do that?"

"You'll do anything you can to save your ranch." Bode tapped his walking stick with impatience. "My daughter Julie figured it all out," he said. "She learned from one of your sons that Sabrina had been here one night."

"So?" Fiona said, her tone rich with contempt.

"So it was an easy feat for Julie to run a background check on Sabrina. Turns out she was traveling with some kind of circus."

"Is that a crime?" Jonas asked. "Last I knew, a circus was a place for hard-working people to have a job with some travel and do what they like to do."

"I'd be careful if I was you, Jonas," Bode said, his tone measured, "your little aunt can get in a lot of trouble for helping someone forge documents of employment and employment history."

Creed snorted. "How would Aunt Fiona do that?"

"Why don't you tell them, Fiona?" Bode stepped closer to Aberdeen, gazing down at the little girls she held. "I'd be cognizant, my dear, were I you, that this family loves games. And not games of the puzzle and Scrabble variety. Games where they use you as a pawn. You'll figure out soon enough what your role is, but only you can decide if you want to be a piece that's played."

"How dare you?" Aberdeen snapped. "Sir, I'll have you know that I'm a minister. I've met people from all walks of life, heard their stories, ached with their troubles, celebrated their joy. You know nothing about me at all, so don't assume I don't know how to take care of myself and those I love."

"I only wish to give you the gift of knowledge," Bode replied.

Aberdeen shook her head. "Gift unaccepted and unneeded. Creed, I'd like to take the girls to their room now." She stood, and Burke materialized at her side.

"I'll take Miss Donovan to her room," Burke said. "The golf cart should carry everyone nicely."

"I'm going out to see Sabrina," Jonas said, and Bode said, "She's not up to seeing—"

"She'll see me," Jonas snapped.

Judah trailed after Jonas. "I'm not being a bodyguard or anything," he told Bode as he walked by him, "I'm just damn nosy."

The two men left. Creed handed Lincoln Rose to Burke. Fiona stood, looking like a queen of a castle.

"You've caused enough of an uproar for one night, Bode. Out you go."

"We're at war, Fiona," Bode said, and she said, "Damn right we are."

"That's enough," Creed said. "If you don't go, Jenkins, we'll throw your worthless hide out."

Aberdeen followed Burke outside, with a last glance back at Creed. He'd stepped close to Bode, protectively standing between his aunt and the enemy, and Aberdeen realized that Creed was a man who guarded his own. He looked fierce, dangerous, nothing at all like the man who romanced her and seduced her until she wanted to do whatever it took to make him happy.

Yet, looking back at Creed, Aberdeen also realized she had no idea what was going on in this family. It was as if she'd landed in a strange new world, and the man she'd agreed to marry had suddenly turned into a surly lion.

Johnny took one of the girls in his arms, following her out, and as their eyes met, she knew her brother was re-thinking her cowboy fiancé, too.

"Busted," Sam said, and Creed nodded. Bode had left, his demeanor pleased. Whatever he'd come to do, he felt he'd succeeded.

"I think you are busted, Aunt," Creed said. "He knows all about your plan. I don't think Sabrina would have ratted you out unless he threatened her."

"Oh, pooh." Fiona waved a hand. "Bode is my puppet. He jumps when I pull his strings."

Creed crooked a brow at his aunt. "You told Sabrina to enlighten him with the fortune-teller gag?"

"Seemed simpler than having him fish around and find out she's actually an investigative reporter." Fiona shrugged, looking pleased with herself. "Now he thinks he knows something he probably won't go digging around in her background. At the moment, he thinks he stole her from me, so he's pleased. It's not that hard to do a search on the computer for people these days, you know."

Creed shook his head. "You deal with her," he told his brothers. "I have a fiancée and three little ladies to settle into the guest house."

His brothers looked as though they wished he would keep on with the line of questioning he'd been peppering the cagey aunt with, but he had promised romance to a pretty parson, and he was going to do just that.

Creed walked into the guest house right after Aberdeen had finished tidying the girls up and putting them in their jammies. The girls were tired, too exhausted for a bedtime story, so Aberdeen kissed them and put them in their little beds with rails—except for Lincoln Rose, who had her own lovely white crib. "Your aunt is amazing," she told Creed, who nodded.

"She amazes everyone."

"She's thought of everything." Aberdeen pointed around the room, showing the toys and extra diapers and even a tray of snacks and drinks on a wrought-iron tray on the dresser. "How did she do all this so quickly?"

"A lot of this is Burke's doing," Creed said, "but Fiona is the best. We were spoiled growing up."

"I could guess that." Aberdeen looked around the room. "It's clear that she spent a lot of time thinking about what children need to be comfortable."

Creed frowned. Aunt Fiona hadn't known about the girls. He hadn't told anyone, not even Rafe. He'd wanted them to get to know Aberdeen and the girls on their own, and not from anything he mentioned on a phone call.

Somehow Aunt Fiona had figured him out. He sighed. "No moss grows under her feet."

"Well, I'm very grateful. And now, if you don't mind, I'm going to bed." She turned her back on Creed, letting him know that he need not expect a good-night kiss. She wasn't ready to go into all the details of everything he was keeping from her, but at this moment she was bone-tired. And her nieces would be up early, no doubt. Tomorrow she'd make Creed tell her what was going on with the scary neighbor and Rancho Diablo.

At least those were her plans, until she felt Creed standing behind her, his body close and warm against her back. She closed her eyes, drinking in his nearness and his strength. He ran his hands down the length of her arms, winding her fingers into his, and Aberdeen's resistance slowly ebbed away.

He dropped a kiss on the back of her neck, sending a delightful shiver over her.

"I'm sorry about tonight," he murmured against her skin. "I had romantic plans for us."

"It may be hard to find time for romance with all the commotion you have going on here. I thought my family tree was thick with drama."

He turned her toward him, his dark gaze searching hers. "I know you're wondering about a lot of things. I'll tell you a few family yarns in between riding lessons with the girls."

"Not my girls," Aberdeen said, her heart jumping.

"No time like the present for them to get in the saddle." Creed winked at her. "And you, too. You'll make a wonderful cowgirl."

"Sorry, no." Aberdeen laughed. "Lincoln Rose is staying right in her comfy stroller. My other two nieces can look at the horses, but there'll be no saddle-training for them."

"We'll see," Creed said, his tone purposefully mysterious. "Learning to ride a horse is just like learning how to swim."

"Will not happen," she reiterated, and stepped away from his warmth. She already wanted to fall into his arms, and after everything she'd heard today, she'd be absolutely out of her head to do such a thing. If she'd ever thought Creed was wild, she had only to come here to find out that he probably was—at the very minimum, he lived by his own code. And the judge was looking for stability in her life before he awarded her permanent custody of her nieces. An adoption application needed to be smooth as well. She shot Creed a glance over her shoulder, checking him out, noting that his gaze never left her. He was protective, he was kind, he was strong. She was falling in love with him—had fallen in love with him—but there were little people to consider. Her own heart needed to be more cautious, not tripping into love just because the man could romance her beyond her wildest imaginings. "Good night, Creed," she said, and after a moment, he nodded.

"Sweet dreams," he said, and then before she could steel herself against him, he kissed her, pinning his fingers into her waist, pulling her against him.

And then he left, probably fully aware that he'd just set her blood to boil. Tired as she was, she was going to be thinking about him for a long time, well past her bedtime—the rogue. And she was absolutely wild for him.

She wished Creed was sleeping in her bed tonight.

Chapter 14

"You can't marry her," Aunt Fiona said when Creed went back to the main house. Fiona was sitting in the library in front of a window, staring out into the darkness. Burke had placed a coffee cup and a plate of cookies on the table. Creed recognized the signs of a family powwow, so he took the chair opposite Fiona and said, "I'm surprised you'd say that, Aunt. Doesn't Aberdeen fill the bill?"

Fiona gave him a sideways glance. "If there was a bill to be filled, I'm sure she'd do quite well. However, I don't believe in doing things in half measures, and I think that's what you're doing, Creed."

He nodded at the cup Burke placed beside him, and sipped gratefully. He didn't need caffeine to keep up with Fiona, but he did need fortification. It was going to be a stirring debate. "You're talking about the little girls."

Fiona shrugged. "They're darling. They deserve your best. We don't have a best to give them at the moment, as Bode's untimely visit indicates."

"We'll be fine. Give me the real reason you're protesting against me marrying her."

"Stability. We don't have that." Fiona sighed. "Have you told Aberdeen about this situation?"

"No. It didn't seem necessary. I'll take care of her and the children."

Fiona nodded. "I would expect that. However, we're at war here. Bode was sizing us up. I don't mind saying I'm afraid."

Creed shrugged. "I'm not afraid of that old man."

"You should be. He intends to make trouble."

"What's the worst he can do?"

Fiona looked at him. "You should know."

"I think the choice should be Aberdeen's."

Fiona nodded. "I agree. Be honest with her. Let her know that we're not the safe haven we may appear to be at first glance."

Creed didn't like that. He wanted to be able to give Aberdeen and the girls the comfort and safety he felt they needed. Protecting them was something his heart greatly desired. And yet, he knew Aunt Fiona's words of caution probably warranted consideration. "I'll think about it."

"Do you love her, Creed?" Fiona asked, her eyes searching his.

"Aberdeen is a good woman." He chose his words carefully, not really certain why he felt he had to hold back. "I think we complement each other."

After a moment, Fiona sat back in her chair. "Of course, you know that it's my fondest wish for you boys to be settled. I haven't hidden my desire to see you with families. But I wouldn't want to bring harm to anyone, Creed."

He stared at his aunt. Harm? He had no intention of causing Aberdeen any pain. Far from it. All he wanted to give her was joy. He wanted to take care of her. That's what they'd agreed upon between themselves: each of them needed something from the other. He intended to keep his side of the bargain.

But as he looked at his little aunt fretting with her napkin and then turning to stare out the window, searching Rancho Diablo in the darkness, he realized she really was worried.

For the thousandth time in his life, he wished Bode Jenkins would somehow just fade out of their lives. But he knew that wasn't going to happen. They just couldn't be that lucky.

"If I only believed in fairy tales," Fiona murmured. "But I have to be practical."

"You pitting us against each other for the ranch is very practical." Creed smiled. "Nobody is complaining, are they?"

Fiona gave him a sharp look. "Is the ranch why you're marrying her?"

Creed drew in a deep breath. Why was he marrying Aberdeen—really? Was he using the ranch as an excuse to bolster his courage to give up rodeo, give up his unsettled ways and get connected to a future? Aberdeen, a ball and chain; the little girls, tiny shackles.

Actually, Creed thought, he was pretty sure the little girls were buoys, if anything, and Aberdeen, a life preserver. Before he'd met them, he'd been drowning in a sea of purposelessness. "I can't speak to my exact motivation for marrying Aberdeen Donovan," Creed said.

"I haven't had time to pinpoint the reason. It could be gratitude, because I think she saved my life in the literal sense. It could be she appeals to the knight in me who feels a need to save a damsel in distress. It might even be that she's gotten under my skin and I just have to conquer that." Creed brightened. "Whatever it is, I like it, though."

Fiona smiled. "You do seem happy."

He grunted. "I haven't got it all figured out yet. But when I do, I'll let you know."

Two weeks later, the magic still hadn't worn off. Mornings bloomed so pretty and sunny that Aberdeen found herself awestruck by the beauty of the New Mexico landscape. Riding in the golf cart with Burke, who'd come to get her and the girls for breakfast, Aberdeen couldn't imagine anything more beautiful than Rancho Diablo on a summer morning.

And the girls seemed tranquil, curious about their surroundings, staring with wide eyes. Horses moved in a wooden corral, eager to watch the humans coming and going. Occasionally she saw a Callahan brother walking by, heading to work—they always turned to wave at the golf cart. She couldn't tell which brother was which yet, but the fact that Creed has such a large family was certainly comforting. She liked his family; she liked the affection they seemed to have for each other.

She was a little surprised that Creed was a twin, and that his brother, Pete, had triplets. What if she had a baby with Creed? What were the odds of having a multiple birth in a family that seemed to have them in the gene pool? The thought intimidated her, and even gave her a little insight into why Diane might have become over-

whelmed. *One at a time would be best for me. I'd have
four children to guide and grow and teach to walk the
right path. I wonder if I'll be a good mother?*

When Aberdeen realized she was actually daydream-
ing about having Creed's baby, she forced herself to stop.
She was jumping light years ahead of what she needed to
be thinking about, which was the girls and putting their
needs first. They were so happy and so sweet, and she
needed to do her best by them. She saw Johnny ride past
in one of the trucks with a Callahan brother, and they
waved at her and the girls, who got all excited when they
saw their uncle. Johnny, it seemed, was fitting right in.
He hadn't come into the guest house last night, and she
suspected he'd slept in the bunkhouse with the brothers.
"Your uncle thinks he's going cowboy," she murmured to
the girls, who ignored her in favor of staring at the horses
and the occasional steer. It was good for Johnny to have
this time to vacation a little. He'd had her back for so
long he hadn't had much time to hang out, she realized.
They'd both been tied to the bar, determined to make
a success of it, buy that ticket out of Spring, Montana.

She hugged the girls to her. "Isn't this fun?"

They looked at her, their big eyes eager and excited.
For the first time she felt herself relax, and when she saw
Fiona come to the door, waving a dish towel at them in
greeting, a smile lit her face. It was going to be all right,
Aberdeen told herself. This was just a vacation for all of
them, one that they needed. If it didn't work out between
her and Creed, it would be fine—she and Johnny and
the girls could go back home, create a life for themselves
as if nothing special, nothing amazing, had happened.

As if she'd never fallen in love with Creed Callahan.

She took a deep breath as Burke stopped the golf cart

in front of the mansion. Aberdeen got out, then she and Burke each helped the girls to the ground. Aberdeen turned to greet Fiona.

"Look who's here!" Fiona exclaimed, and Aberdeen halted in her tracks.

"Mommy!" Ashley cried, as she and Suzanne toddled off to greet Diane. Aberdeen's heart went still at the sight of her older sister, who did not look quite like the Diane she remembered. Cold water seemed to hit her in the face.

"Aberdeen!" Diane came to greet Aberdeen as if no time had passed, as if she hadn't abandoned her children. She threw her arms around Aberdeen, and Aberdeen found herself melting. She loved Diane with all her heart. Had she come to get her daughters? Aberdeen hoped so. A whole family would be the best thing for everyone.

"How are you doing?" Aberdeen asked her sister, leaning back to look at her, and Diane shook her head.

"We'll talk later. Right now, your wonderful mother-in-law-to-be has welcomed me into the fold," Diane said, and Aberdeen remembered that they had an audience.

"Yes. Aunt Fiona, this is my older sister, Diane." Aberdeen followed her nieces, who were trying to get up the steps to Fiona. Aberdeen carried Lincoln Rose, who didn't reach for her mother. The minute she saw Fiona, she reached for her, though. Fiona took her gladly, and Aberdeen and Diane shared a glance.

"I'm good with children," Fiona said, blushing a little that Diane's own daughter seemed to prefer her. "It's the granny syndrome."

"It's all right," Diane said quickly. "Come on, girls. Let's not leave Mrs. Callahan waiting."

"Oh." Fiona glanced back as they walked through the

entryway. "Please, just call me Fiona. I've never been Mrs. Callahan."

"This is gorgeous," Diane whispered to Aberdeen. "How did you hook such a hot, rich hunk?"

"I haven't hooked him," Aberdeen said, hoping Fiona hadn't heard Diane.

"Well, find a way to do it. Listen to big sister. These are sweet digs."

"Diane," Aberdeen said, "what are you doing here? And how did you get here?"

"Mom and Dad told me where you were, and it's not that difficult to buy a plane ticket, Aberdeen."

"What about the French guy?"

"We'll talk later," Diane said as Fiona showed them in to a huge, country-style kitchen. At the long table, the largest Aberdeen had ever seen, settings were laid, and each place had a placard with their names in gold scrolling letters. There were even two high chairs for the youngest girls, with their own cards in scrolled letters. Each of the children had a stuffed toy beside her plate, and so they were eager to sit down, their eyes fastened on the stuffed horses.

"I hope you don't mind," Fiona said. "We have a gift shop in town and the owner is a friend of mine. I couldn't resist calling her up to get a few little things for the girls."

"Thank you so much," Diane said, and Aberdeen swallowed hard.

"Yes, thank you, Fiona. Girls, can you say thank you?"

The older ones did, and Lincoln Rose saw that her sisters were holding their horses so she reached for hers, too. And then Burke brought them breakfast, and Aberdeen tried to eat, even though her appetite was shot.

They were being treated like princesses—but the thing was, she wasn't princess material. She eyed her sister surreptitiously; Diane seemed delighted by all the attention Fiona was showering on them, and Aberdeen felt like someone dropped into a storybook with a plot she hadn't yet caught up on.

"Quit looking so scared," Diane said under her breath. "Enjoy what the nice lady is trying to do for you. This is great." And she dug into the perfectly plated eggs and fruit as though she hadn't a care in the world.

"Diane," Aberdeen said quietly, so Fiona couldn't hear, even though she had her head in the fridge looking for something—a jam or jelly, she'd mentioned. "What are you doing here? Really?"

Diane smiled. "Little sister, I'm here to see my daughters. Who will soon be your daughters, by the looks of things."

"I think you should reconsider," Aberdeen said, desperation hatching inside her. "If you're not traveling with that guy, and you seem so happy now, I mean, don't you think…" She looked at her sister. "These are your children, Diane. You can't just abandon them."

"I'm not abandoning them." Diane took a bite of toast. "I simply recognize I'm not cut out to be a mother. I wish it were different, but it's not. I get depressed around them, Aberdeen. I know they're darling, and they seem so sweet and so cute, but when I'm alone with them, all I am is desperate. I'm not happy. I think I was trying to live a dream, but when my third husband left, I realized the dream had never been real." She looked at Aberdeen. "Please don't make me feel more guilty than I do already. It's not the best feeling in the world when a woman realizes she's a lousy mother. And, you know, we had a fairly dismal upbringing. I just don't want to do that to my own children."

Fiona came over to the table, setting down a bowl full of homemade strawberry jam. "I'm pretty proud of this," she said. "I had strawberries and blackberries shipped in special, and I redid my jam stock after I lost all of last year's." She beamed. "Tell me what you think of my blue-ribbon jam!"

Aberdeen tore her gaze away from her sister, numb, worried, and not in the mood for anything sweet. She glanced around at her nieces who seemed so amazed by all the treats and their stuffed horses that all they could do was sit very quietly, on their best behavior. They were obviously happy to see Diane, but not clingy, the way kids who hadn't seen their mother in a while would be. Aberdeen sighed and bit into a piece of jam-slathered toast. It was sweet and rich with berry taste. Perfect, as might be expected from Fiona, as she could tell from everything Creed had said about his aunt.

Her stomach jumped, nervous, and a slight storm of nausea rose inside her. Aberdeen put her toast down. "It's delicious, Fiona."

Fiona beamed. It *was* delicious. If Aberdeen had eaten it at any other time in her life, she'd want to hop in the kitchen and learn Fiona's secrets. There were probably secrets involved in making something this tasty, secrets that could only be passed from one cook to another. Her stomach slithered around, catching her by surprise. She felt strangely like an interloper, a case taken on by these wonderful people and Creed. That wasn't the way she wanted to feel.

And then he walked into the kitchen, big and tall and filling the doorway, her own John Wayne in the flesh, and sunshine flooded Aberdeen in a way she'd never felt before.

"It's wonderful jam," Diane said, and Aberdeen nodded, never taking her eyes off the cowboy she'd come to love. He grinned at her, oblivious to her worries, and if she didn't know better, she would have thought his eyes held a special twinkle for her. Ashley got down from her chair and tottered over to him to be swept up into his arms. Lincoln Rose and Suzanne sat in their high chairs, patiently waiting for their turns for attention from Creed. Creed walked over and blew a tiny raspberry against Lincoln Rose's cheek, making her giggle, and did the same to Suzanne. They waved their baby spoons, delighted with the attention.

Then Creed winked at Aberdeen, in lieu of a good-morning kiss, and Aberdeen forced a smile back, trying to sail along on the boat of Unexpected Good Fortune.

But life wasn't all blue-ribbon strawberry jam and gold-scrolling placards. At least not her life.

Diane poked her in the arm, and Aberdeen tried to be more perky. More happy. More perfect.

She felt like such a fraud.

Chapter 15

Pete and Jackie strolled in, carrying their three babies and a flotilla of baby gear, and the mood in the kitchen lifted instantly. Creed rose to help his brother and sister-in-law settle themselves at the breakfast table.

"We figured there'd be grub," Pete said, "hope you don't mind us joining you, Aunt Fiona."

She gave him a light smack on the arm with a wooden spoon. "The more, the merrier, I always say." She beamed and went back to stirring things up on the stove. Jackie seated herself next to Aberdeen.

"So, how do you feel about the royal treatment, Aberdeen?" Jackie asked.

"It's amazing. Truly." Aberdeen caught Creed's smile at her compliment. "Jackie, Pete, I'd like you to meet my sister, Diane."

Diane smiled, shaking her head at the babies Pete and

Jackie were trying to get settled in their baby carriers. "I had my babies one at a time and I still felt like it was a lot. I can't imagine it happening all at once."

Jackie smiled. "We couldn't, either. And then it did." She got a grin from her proud husband, and Aberdeen's gaze once again shifted to Creed. He seemed completely unafraid of all the babies crowding in around him—in fact, he seemed happy.

"It hasn't been bad," Pete said. "We're catching on faster than I thought we would. Jackie's a quick study."

Aberdeen didn't think she'd be a quick study. She pushed her toast around on her plate, trying to eat, wishing the nausea would pass. She caught Creed looking at her, and he winked at her again, seeming to know that she was plagued by doubts. Cold chills ran across her skin. She didn't think she'd be radiant sunshine like Jackie if she found herself with three newborn triplets. He'd probably be dismally disappointed if she didn't take to mothering like a duck to water. "Excuse me," she said, getting up from the table, feeling slightly wan, "I'm going to find a powder room."

"I'll show you," Jackie said, quickly getting up to lead her down a hall.

"Thanks," Aberdeen said, definitely not feeling like herself.

"You look a bit peaked. Are you feeling all right?" Jackie asked.

"I'm fine. Thank you." Aberdeen tried to smile. But then she wasn't, and she flew into the powder room, and when she came back out a few moments later, Jackie was waiting, seated on a chair in the wide hallway.

"Maybe not so fine?" Jackie said.

"I suppose not." Embarrassment flashed over her.

"I've always been a good traveler. I can't imagine what's come over me."

"Hmm. Let's sit down and rest for a minute before we go back to the kitchen."

Aberdeen sat, gratefully.

"It can be overwhelming here, at first."

"I think you're right." Aberdeen nodded. "Johnny and I live a much simpler life. And yet, everyone here is so nice."

"Did you know your sister was coming?"

Aberdeen shook her head.

"Well, you've got a lot going on." Jackie patted her hand. "Let me know if there's anything I can do to help."

"You have three newborns." Aberdeen realized the nausea had passed for the moment. "I should be helping you."

"We all help each other." Jackie looked at her. "Your color is returning. Are you feeling better? You were so pale when you left the kitchen."

"I feel much better. I've always been very fortunate with my health. I don't think I've had more than a few colds in my life, and I'm never sick. I can't imagine what's come over me." Aberdeen wondered if she was getting cold feet. But she wouldn't get cold about Creed. He made her feel hotter than a firecracker.

"Not that's it's any of my business," Jackie said, "but the nurse in me wonders if you might be pregnant?"

Aberdeen laughed. "Oh, no. Not at all. There's no way." Then the smile slipped slowly off her face as she remembered.

There *was* a way.

Jackie grinned at her. Aberdeen shook her head. "I'm pretty certain I'm not."

"Okay." Jackie nodded. "Can you face the breakfast table?"

Aberdeen wasn't certain. Her stomach pitched slightly. "I think so."

Jackie watched her as she stood. "You don't have to eat breakfast, you know. It's a lovely time of the day to take a walk in the fresh air. And I'd be happy to keep an eye on your little ones."

"I think… I think I might take your suggestion." Something about the smell of eggs and coffee was putting her off. She felt that she'd be better off heading outside until her stomach righted itself. "I'm sure it's nothing, but…would you mind letting Fiona know I'm going to head back to the guest house?"

"Absolutely." Jackie showed her to a side door. "Don't worry about a thing."

Aberdeen *was* worried, about a lot of things.

I can't be pregnant. I was in the safe zone of the month when we—

She walked outside, the early-morning sunshine kissing her skin, lifting the nausea. "No, I'm not," she told herself, reassuringly.

A baby would really complicate matters. As wonderful as Rancho Diablo was, Aberdeen felt as though she was on vacation—not at home. Being here was fairy-tale-ish—complete with a villain or two—and any moment she should wake up.

She didn't know how to tell Creed that as much as she wanted to keep to their bargain, she didn't know if she could.

Creed glanced up when Jackie came back into the kitchen, his brows rising. "Where's Aberdeen?"

Jackie seated herself, looking at him with a gentle smile. "She's taking a little walk. Fiona, she said to tell you she'd see you in a bit." Jackie smiled at her husband, and resumed eating, as though everything was just fine and dandy.

But Creed knew it wasn't. Jackie had high marks in this family for her ability to cover things up—look at how skillfully she'd gotten Pete to the altar. So Creed's instinctive radar snapped on. "Is she all right?"

"She's fine."

Jackie didn't meet his eyes as she nibbled on some toast. "Maybe I'll go join her on that walk," he said, and Diane said, "Good idea."

Jackie waved a hand. "I think she said she was looking forward to some solitude."

That was the signal. It just didn't sound like something Aberdeen would say. Creed got to his feet. "I think I'll go check on the horses."

Diane nodded. "My girls and I are going to sit here and enjoy some more of this delicious breakfast." She whisked her sister's abandoned plate to the sink. "Fiona, if I could cook half as well as you do, I might still have a husband."

Fiona grinned. "You think?"

"No." Diane laughed. "But I would have eaten better."

Diane seemed comfortable with Fiona and company, much more so than Aberdeen did. Creed got to his feet. "I'll be back, Aunt Fiona."

"All right." His aunt beamed at him, and Creed escaped, trying not to run after Aberdeen as he caught sight of her walking toward the guest house. "Hey," he said. "A girl as pretty as you shouldn't be walking alone."

Aberdeen gave him a slight, barely-there-and-mostly-fakey smile. Creed blinked. "Are you okay, Aberdeen?"

"I'm fine. Really."

"Hey." He caught her hand, slowing her down. "You trying to run away from me, lady?"

She shook her head. "I just need a little time to myself." She took her hands from his, gazing at him with apology in her eyes.

"Oh." Creed nodded. "All right." He didn't feel good about the sound of that. "Call me if you need anything. Burke keeps the guest house stocked pretty well, but—"

"I'm fine, Creed. Thank you."

And then she turned and hurried off, smiting his ego. *Damn.* Creed watched her go, unsure of what had just happened. He wanted to head after her, pry some answers out of her, but a man couldn't do a woman that way. They needed space sometimes.

He just wished the space she seemed to need didn't have to be so far away from him.

Aberdeen felt guilty about disappearing on Fiona, and Diane—and Creed. She didn't want to be rude, but she wanted to wash up, change her clothes, shower. Think. Just a few moments to catch her breath and think about what she was doing.

She felt like she was on the Tilt-A-Whirl at the State Fair, and she couldn't stop whirling.

At least I'm not pregnant, she told herself. *I'm a planner. Planning makes me feel organized, secure.*

I've got to focus.

"Hey," Johnny called, spying her. "Wait up."

He caught up to her, following her into the guest house. "It feels like I haven't seen you in days."

"That's because we're in this suspended twilight of Happyville." Aberdeen went into the bathroom to wash up. When she came out, Johnny was lounging in the common area.

"That didn't sound particularly happy, if we're hanging out in Happyville." Johnny shot her a worried look. "What's up?"

Aberdeen sat on one of the leather sofas opposite Johnny. "I don't know, exactly."

He nodded. "Feel like you're on vacation and shouldn't be?"

"Maybe." Aberdeen considered that. "I need to wake up."

"An engagement, three kids that aren't yours, a new place…" His voice drifted off as he gazed around the room. "Saying yes to a guy who lives in a mansion would freak me out, I guess, if I was a woman."

"Why?" Aberdeen asked, and Johnny grinned.

"Because your bar was set too low. Re-ride wasn't much of a comparison, you know?"

Aberdeen nodded. "I lost my breakfast, and Jackie wanted to know if I was pregnant."

"Oh, wow." Johnny laughed. "That would be crazy."

Aberdeen glared at him.

"Oh, wait," Johnny said, "is there a possibility I could be an uncle again?"

"I don't think so," Aberdeen snapped, and Johnny raised a brow.

"That's not a ringing endorsement of your birth-control method."

Aberdeen sighed. "I don't want to talk about it." The best thing to do was to concentrate, and right now, she just wanted to concentrate on what was going on with

Diane. "Johnny, have you noticed that Diane seems to like her children just fine?"

"Mmm. She's just not comfortable with them. She's like Mom."

Aberdeen felt a stab of worry. "I wonder if I'd be like that."

Johnny crooked a brow. "You're not pregnant, so don't worry about it. Unless you might be pregnant, and then don't worry about it. You're nothing like Mom and Diane."

"How do you know? How does any mother know?" Aberdeen was scared silly at the very thought that she might bring a child into the world she couldn't bond with.

"Because," Johnny said, "you're different. You were always different. You cared about people. I love Diane, but she pretty much cares about herself, and whatever's going on in her world. You had a congregation that loved you, Aberdeen."

Aberdeen blinked. "I miss it. Maybe that's what's wrong with me."

"Well, I don't think that's all that's going on with you, but—" Johnny shrugged. "The pattern of your life has been completely interrupted. The bright side is that you can build a congregation here, if you want. I'm sure there's always a need for a cowboy preacher."

Aberdeen wasn't certain she wanted a new church. "What if I want my old church? My old way of life?" she asked softly.

Johnny looked at her. "I think that bridge has been crossed and burned behind us, sis."

Creed burst in the door, halting when he saw Johnny and Aberdeen chatting. He was carrying a brown paper bag, which caught Aberdeen's suspicious gaze.

"Sorry," Creed said, "Didn't realize you two were visiting."

"It's all right," Johnny said. "I'm just taking a break from ranching. I think I'm getting the hang of this cowboy gig." He waved a hand at the paper bag. "Did you bring us breakfast or liquor?"

Creed set the bag on a chair. "Neither."

Aberdeen shot her fiancé a guarded look. "Is that what I think it is, Creed Callahan?"

"I don't think so," Creed said. "It's a…lunch for me. That's what it is. I packed myself a lunch."

"You're going to go hungry, then," Johnny observed. "You can't work on a ranch and eat a lunch the size of an apple."

"It's for me," Aberdeen guessed.

"It's for us," Creed said, and Johnny got to his feet.

"I'll leave you two lovebirds alone," he said, and Aberdeen didn't tell him to stay.

"Goodbye," Johnny said, and went out the door.

"Creed, that's a drugstore bag," Aberdeen said, "and since you just bought a huge box of condoms when we were in Wyoming, I'm betting you bought a pregnancy test."

He looked sheepish. "How'd you guess?"

"Because you looked scared when you ran in here, like your world was on fire. Jackie told you, didn't she?"

"Well, everyone was worried. We thought something was really wrong with you. And Fiona started fretting, worrying that you didn't like her food, and Jackie said it was a girl thing, and she'd tell Fiona later, and then Diane blurted out that maybe you were pregnant, and I—" He looked like a nervous father-to-be. "Could you be?"

"I don't think so." Aberdeen sighed. "I mean, I guess it's possible. But not likely."

"It wasn't likely for Pete to have triplets, either," Creed said. "Maybe we'd better find out."

"I don't have to pee," Aberdeen said, feeling belligerent. She didn't want everyone at Rancho Diablo discussing her life.

"I'll get you a glass of water," Creed said, jumping to his feet, and Aberdeen said, "No!"

"Well, I might get a glass of water for me. With ice. It's hot in here."

Aberdeen closed her eyes. Just the thought of being a dad clearly was making him nervous. He'd have four children, Aberdeen realized, all at once.

"It wouldn't be what we agreed on," Aberdeen said, and Creed said, "We'll make a new agreement. After I drink a tall glass of water." He went into the kitchen and turned the faucet on full-blast. "Do you hear water running, sweetheart?"

Aberdeen shook her head. "I'm not going to take the test."

He shut off the faucet and came back in with a glass of water. "We'll drink together."

"You pee in the cup." Aberdeen ignored the glass Creed set beside her.

"I didn't get a cup," Creed said cheerfully. "I bought the stick one. It looked more efficient. And it said it could detect a pregnancy five or six days before a skipped—"

Aberdeen swiped the bag from him. "I'm not going to do it while you're here."

"Why not?" Creed was puzzled.

"Because," Aberdeen said. "I need privacy. I have a shy bladder."

He grinned at her. "No, you don't. I happen to know there's nothing shy about you, my little wildcat."

Aberdeen looked at him, her blood pressure rising. "I just want to avoid the topic a little while longer, all right?"

"Well, I feel like a kid on my birthday trying to decide which present to open first," Creed told her. "Pregnancy will probably be a very healthy thing for me."

"Is this about the ranch?" Aberdeen asked, and Creed looked wounded.

"No," he said, "that's dumb."

"Why? You said yourself—"

"I know." Creed held up a hand. "I told you getting married was about getting the ranch. I'd have three built-in daughters, and it would get Fiona off my back. I told you all that, it's true. But it's not anymore."

She looked at him, wanting to kiss him. Maybe he was falling for her as hard as she was falling for him! "What is it, then?"

"Our agreement?" Creed considered her question. "I don't know. Grab out the pee stick and we'll renegotiate based on whether you come up yes or no." He rubbed his palms together. "It's almost as much fun as a magic eight ball."

Aberdeen closed her eyes for a second, counting to ten. "Did anyone ever tell you you're a goof?"

"No. They just call me handsome. And devil-may-care." He came to sit next to her with his icy glass of water. "Drink, sweetpea?"

Chapter 16

Twenty minutes later, Creed tapped on the bathroom door. It seemed like Aberdeen had been in there a long time. "Aberdeen? Are you taking a nap in there?"

"Give me a second," she said, and he wondered if her voice sounded teary. Was she crying?

His heart rate skyrocketed. "Let me in."

"No."

"Is something wrong?"

"I don't think so."

He blinked. That sounded foreboding, he decided. "Do you want your sister?"

"No, thank you."

He pondered his next attack. She couldn't be in there all day. He was about to relinquish his sentinel position outside her door when it opened.

Aberdeen walked out, and he saw at once that she *had* been crying. "Guess we're having a baby?"

She nodded.

He opened his arms, and she walked into them, her body shaking. Creed held her, and she sniffled a second against his chest, and then she pulled away.

He wanted her back. "I'm really amping up the pressure on my brothers," he said cheerfully, seeing a whole world of possibilities kaleidoscoping before him. He'd have a son to play ball with, to teach how to rope. Was there anything better than a boy to help him on the ranch?

Even if they didn't have a ranch anymore, he'd have a son.

"Aberdeen, sweetie, this is the best news I've had in my entire life. Thank you."

She looked at him. "Really?"

"Oh, hell, yeah." He sat down, checking his gut and knew every word he was speaking was true. "I feel like a superhero."

She wiped at her eyes, then looked at him with a giggle. "I feel strangely like a villainess."

"Uh-uh." He shook his head. "I mean, you're sexy and all, but there's nothing evil about you, babe, except maybe what you do to my sense of self-control. I don't suppose you'd like to have a celebratory quickie?"

She laughed but shook her head.

"It was worth a try." He liked seeing the smile on her face. "Hey, you know what this means, don't you?"

"It means a lot of things. Name the topic."

He felt about ten feet tall in his boots. "We need to plan a wedding."

She looked at him, surprised. "Isn't that rushing things a bit?"

"Not for me. I'm an eight-second guy. I'm all about speed and staying on my ride."

Aberdeen crossed her arms in a protective gesture, almost hugging herself. "When I met you, you hadn't stayed on your ride. In fact, you had a concussion. What if—"

"What if I decide to bail?" He grinned at her and pulled her into his lap. "Lady, you're just going to have to stick around to find out."

She looked down at him from her perch. "I'm way over my head here, cowboy. Just so you know."

"Nah. This is going to be a piece of cake. Fiona can help you plan a wedding. Or we can elope. Whichever you prefer." He nibbled on her neck. "Personally, I'd pick eloping. We'll get to sleep together faster. And you'll make a cute Mrs. Callahan. I'm going to chase my Mrs. Callahan around for the rest of my life."

"I can run fast."

"I know," he said, "but I think we just learned that I run faster."

She laughed, and he kissed her, glad to see the water-works had shut off. She'd scared him! No man wanted to think that the mother of his child didn't want him. But he was pretty certain Aberdeen did want him, just as much as he wanted her. It was just taking her a little longer to decide that she wanted him for the long haul.

He wasn't letting her get away from him. "When are you going to make an announcement?"

She sighed. "I think something was foreshadowed when you ran in here with a paper bag from the drug-store. I won't be surprised if Fiona has already ordered a nursery. And I don't even know anything about you." For a moment, she looked panicked. "You know more about me than I do about you."

He shrugged. "No mysteries here. Ask a question."

"Okay." Aberdeen pulled back slightly when he tried to nibble at her bottom lip. Maybe if he got her mind off the pregnancy, he could ease her into bed. He did his best romancing between the sheets, he was pretty certain. Right now, her brain was on overdrive, processing, and if she only but knew it, he could massage her and kiss her body into a puddle of relaxation. He felt himself getting very intrigued by the thought.

"Who's the scary guy who visited?" Aberdeen asked. "That Bode guy?"

Uh-oh. It was going to be hard to lure her into a compromising position if she was up for difficult topics. "He's just the local wacko. No one special."

"I felt like I'd been visited by the evil Rancho Diablo spirit."

He sighed, realizing he was getting nothing at the moment—even his powers of romance weren't up to combating a woman who was still trying to figure out if she wanted to be tied to his family, friends and enemies. "I'm a very eligible bachelor," he said. "You don't have to examine the skeletons in my closet. Why don't we hop down to Jackie's bridal shop and look at dresses?" he said. Surely if romance wouldn't do it, shopping might get her thinking about weddings—and a future with him.

"Bode Jenkins," she said. "Was he threatening me?"

"He was being a pest. We're used to him showing up uninvited, trying to throw a wrench into things. Don't take it personally."

"He wants your ranch."

"Yep." Creed shrugged. "I think he may be delusional. He doesn't really want the ranch. He just wants to stick it to us. That's my personal assessment." He nuzzled at her cheek. "I'll be a lot stronger in my fight against evil and doom if I'm married. Let's talk about our future, all right?"

She moved away from his mouth. "Quit trying to seduce me. You're trying to get me off topic, and it isn't going to work."

He sighed. "Most women in your shoes would be more than happy to talk about tying me down, sister."

She took a long time to answer, and when she did, it wasn't what he wanted to hear. "I can't get married at the snap of a finger, Creed. Mom and Dad would want me to get married at home—"

"We can fly them here."

"They would want me to have a church wedding—"

"But what do you want?" he asked, wondering why she was suddenly so worried about her parents. Her folks didn't seem to be all that interested in what she did. He moved his lips along her arm, pondering this new turn of events.

"I don't know. I just found out I'm having a baby. I can't really think about a wedding right now." She slid out of his lap and walked over to the window. "I'd better get back to the girls. I've left them alone too long."

"They're not alone," Creed said, surprised. "They're with their mothe—"

The glare she shot him would have knocked him back two feet if he'd been standing. She went out the door like a storm, and Creed realized he had a whole lot of convincing to do to get his bride to the altar.

In fact, it was probably going to take a miracle.

"I never thought it would be so difficult to get a woman to jump into a wedding gown," Creed told his twin a few minutes later, when Rafe sat down next to him in the barn. Creed still felt stunned by the whirling turn of events in his life. "I'm going to be a father. I want to be a husband. I don't want my son coming to me one day and saying, 'Mom says you were half-baked with the marriage proposal.'" He looked at Rafe. "You know what I mean?"

Rafe shook his head. "Nope."

Creed sighed, looking at the bridle he was repairing. Trying to repair. This should have been mental cotton candy for him, and he was muffing the repair job. His concentration was shot. "Imagine finding out the best news in your life, but the person who's giving you the news acts like you're radioactive. You would feel pretty low."

"Yeah. But I'm not you. I'd just make her say yes."

Creed looked at Rafe. "Thanks for the body-blow."

Rafe grinned and took the bridle from him. "Give her some time, bro. She's just beginning to figure out that you've turned her life inside out. She needs some time to adjust."

"Yeah," Creed said, "but I want her to be Mrs. Callahan before I have to roll her down the aisle in a wheelbarrow."

Rafe looked at him. "And you wonder why Aberdeen isn't running a four-minute mile to get to the altar with you. Is that the way you romance a woman? 'Honey, let's get hitched before my brawny son expands your waistline?'"

"I never said a word about that. I just want sooner rather than later. I don't really care if she's the size of an elephant, I just want her wearing white lace pronto." Creed scratched his head, and shoved his hat back. "Truthfully, I think I wanted to marry that gal the moment I laid eyes on her. Even in my debilitated state, I knew I'd stumbled on something awesome." He looked at Rafe. "Aberdeen *is* awesome."

Rafe considered him. "You really are crazy about her, aren't you? This isn't about the ranch for you."

"Nope. I've tried every song-and-dance routine I know to get her to take me on. I've offered short-term marriage, marriage-of-convenience and the real deal. She just doesn't set a date." He sighed, feeling worn down. "It's killing me. I really think I'm aging. And I'm pretty sure it's supposed to be the woman who plots to get the guy to wedded bliss. She sure can drag her feet."

"I don't know, man. All I know is you better shape up before the big dance tomorrow night."

Creed straightened. "That's not tomorrow night, is it?"

Rafe nodded.

"Oh, hell. I've got a bad feeling about this."

Aberdeen already seemed overwhelmed by the ranch, by Rancho Diablo, by him. How would she feel about a bachelor rodeo? He already knew. She would see his brothers hooting and hollering, trying to catch women and vice versa, and figure that he was no different from those lunkheads. That's how a woman thought. "I bet pregnant women probably jump to conclusions faster than normal, because of their hormones and stuff."

Rafe smacked him on the head. "Of the two of us, you are definitely the dumbest. Why do you talk like Aberdeen has no common sense? When beautiful, husband-hunting women are throwing themselves at you tomorrow night, she'll totally understand. It'll probably make her want you. Jealousy is catnip to a woman."

Creed groaned. If he knew Aberdeen the way he

thought he did, she was going to run for the mountains of Wyoming. She was like a piece of dry tinder just waiting for a spark to set her off. He could feel her looking for reasons not to trust him. Damn Re-ride, he thought. He'd convinced her that all men were rats.

"Most men are rats," he said, pondering out loud, and Rafe nodded.

"Very likely. And women still love us."

Creed didn't think Aberdeen was going to love him if she could convince herself that he was a big stinky rodent. "I've got to get her out of here," he said, but his twin just shrugged.

"Good luck," Rafe said, and Creed figured he'd need a turnaround in his luck pattern if he wanted his bride.

He knew just who could advise him.

Diane sat on a porch swing, watching her daughters play in a huge sandbox the brothers had constructed for all the new babies at Rancho Diablo. Maybe it was dumb, Creed thought, to make a sandbox when the babies were all still, well, babies. Ashley and Suzu were big enough to play in the soft sand dotted with toys, but Lincoln Rose would catch up in time, and so would Pete's daughters.

Creed couldn't wait to see all the kids playing together one day. The vista of Rancho Diablo land made a beautiful backdrop for children to view, panoramic and Hollywood-like. Burke had helped, drawing off precise measurements and finding the best type of sand to make wonderful castles.

And now Diane sat on the porch swing alone, watching her two oldest, and holding her baby. He watched her for a second, and then went to join the woman he hoped would be his sister-in-law one day.

"Hi," he said, and Diane turned her head.

"Hello."

"Mind if I join you?"

"Not at all. Please do." She smiled when he sat down. "My girls really like it here. There's something about this ranch that seems to agree with them."

He nodded. "It was a pretty great place to grow up."

Diane looked back at her girls. Creed realized her gaze was following her daughters with interest, not the almost cursory, maybe even scared expression she'd worn before.

"Are you comfortable here?" Creed asked.

"I am." She nodded. "Your aunt and uncle have been very kind."

Creed started to say that Burke wasn't his uncle, then decided the tag was close enough. Burke was fatherly, more than uncle-like, and a dear friend. "How long are you staying?"

She smiled, keeping her gaze on her daughters. Creed mentally winced, his question sounding abrupt to him. He sure didn't want Diane to think he was trying to run her off.

"Your aunt has offered me a job," Diane said, surprising Creed.

"She has?"

"Mmm." She turned to look at him, and he saw that her eyes were just like Aberdeen's and Johnny's, deep and blue and beautiful. But hers were lined with years of worry. She'd had it hard, he realized—no wonder Aberdeen and Johnny were so bent on helping her. "She says she needs a housekeeper/assistant. She says all her duties are getting to be too much for her. Yet your aunt Fiona seems quite energetic to me."

Creed shrugged. "I wouldn't blame Fiona a bit if she felt like she needed some help. She's got an awful lot she does on the ranch."

"So it wasn't just a polite invitation?" Diane looked at him curiously.

"I doubt it. While my aunt is unfailingly polite, she's never offered such a position to anyone else that I'm aware of, and she wouldn't fancy giving up any of the reins of the place if she really didn't feel the need." He smiled. "She's pretty fierce about doing everything herself."

"So why me? Because I'm Aberdeen's sister?"

He shrugged again. "Probably because she likes you. Fiona prefers to run her own business, so if she offered, she must have felt that you'd be an asset to the ranch."

"She doesn't discuss hiring with you?"

He laughed. "She may have talked to some of my brothers. I can't say. But Fiona's business is her own. So if you're interested in a job with her, that's a discussion between the two of you. The only tip I could positively give you is that if you accept her offer, you will work harder than you ever have in your life. Ask Burke if you don't believe me."

She finally smiled. "I'll think about it, then."

"Yeah. Well, glad I could help. Not that I have any useful information to impart." He grinned at the pile of sand the two little girls were pushing around in the box with the aid of a tiny tractor and some shovels. "So now I have a question for you."

"All right," Diane said. "You want to know how I can help you to get Aberdeen to marry you."

He blinked. "Well, if you could, it would help."

She smiled. "Look, Creed. I'm going to be just as honest with you as you were with me. Aberdeen doesn't always talk about what she's thinking. If she does, she'd go to Johnny first, and then maybe she'd come to me. I'm a lot older than Aberdeen, in many ways. But I can tell you a couple of things. First, she's afraid she's turning out like me. The fact that she's pregnant makes it feel real unplanned to her, for lack of a better word, and Aberdeen is all about planning everything very seriously. People who plan are *responsible.* Do you understand what I'm saying?" She gave him a long, sideways look.

Creed nodded. "Thank you for your honesty."

She went back to watching her daughters. "It's good to self-examine, even when it's painful. I know who I am, and I know what I'm not. I'm not a good mother, but I know I'm a good person. That probably doesn't make sense to you, but I know that in the end, the good person in me will triumph."

Creed thought she was probably right. There was a kind streak in Diane, a part of her that acknowledged strength in family, that he'd already noticed. "No one's perfect," he said. "Neither my brothers nor I would claim we've come within a spitting distance of perfect. So you're probably amongst like-minded people."

Diane placed a soft kiss atop Lincoln Rose's head. Creed wondered if she even realized she'd done it. "Back to Aberdeen. The B-part to my sister that I know and understand—though I'm not claiming to be an expert— is that there will never be another Re-ride in her life."

"I'm no Re-ride," he growled.

"I mean that, even if she married Re-ride again, it would be no retread situation. Aberdeen is not the same shy girl who got married so young. She would kick his butt from here to China if she married him and he tried to do the stupid stuff he did before."

"She's not marrying Re-ride," Creed said decisively, "and I'm no green boy for her to be worrying about marrying."

Diane sighed. "I'm sure Aberdeen is well aware that it was a real man who put a ring on her finger this time, cowboy. All I'm saying is that she's going to make her own decisions in her life now. She'll do things when she's comfortable and not before—and right now, I'd say she's not totally comfortable. Some of that is probably due to me, but—" She gave Creed a long look and stood. "I feel pretty comfortable in saying that most of her indecision is due to you," she said, kissing him on the cheek, "future brother-in-law."

He looked at her. "I don't wait well."

She smiled. "I guessed that. You may have to this time, if you really want your bride." Diane went to the sandbox and said, "Girls, we need to get washed up now," and they dutifully minded their mother. Creed watched with astonishment as they followed Diane like little ducklings. It was one of the most beautiful things he'd ever seen. He wondered if Diane had yet realized that she had no reason to be afraid of being a mother— she seemed to have all the proper components except confidence. He watched the girls go with a little bit of sentimental angst, already considering himself their father in his heart, knowing that they needed their mother, too. He'd have thought Lincoln Rose would have at least reached for him.

But no. They'd been content to spend time with their mother, an invisible natural bond growing into place.

Creed wished he could grow some kind of bond with Aberdeen. She seemed determined to dissolve what they had. "I'm not doing this right," he muttered, and jumped when Burke said, "Did you say something, Creed?"

Creed glanced behind him as Fiona's butler materialized with a tray of lemonade and cookies. "Are those for me?"

"They're for the little girls and their mother." Burke glanced around. "Are they done with playtime?"

"I'm afraid so. Bring that tray over here to me. I need fortification."

Burke set the tray down on the porch swing.

"There's only one glass," Creed said.

"Yes. The lemonade is for you. It has a little kick in it, which I noticed you looked like you needed about twenty minutes ago when you ran through the house."

Creed looked at Burke. "Okay. Tell me everything you're dying to say."

"I'm not really an advice column," Burke said. "I see my role more as fortifier."

Creed waved a hand, knocking back half the lemonade. "You're right. That does have a kick. And it's just what I needed."

Burke nodded. "The cookies are for the girls. They get milk with theirs, usually."

Creed blinked. "Well, my ladies have departed me. All of them, I fear."

Burke cleared his throat. "If you don't need anything else—"

"Actually, I think I do." Creed looked at the butler, considering him. "Burke, your secret is out. We all know you and Fiona are married."

Burke remained silent, staring at him with no change in expression.

Creed let out a sigh. "I guess my question is, how did you do it?"

"How did I do what?"

"How did you convince my aunt to get to the altar?"

Burke picked up the tray. "I sense the topic you're exploring is Miss Aberdeen."

"I could use some advice. Yes." Creed nodded. "Wise men seek counsel when needed, Burke, and I know you have some experience with handling an independent-minded female. My problem is that I've got a woman who seems a little more cold-footed than the average female, when it comes to getting to the altar."

"I may have mentioned my role isn't giving advice," Burke said, "but if I had any, I would say that the lady in question seems to know her own mind. Therefore, she undoubtedly will not take well to being pushed." Burke handed him a cookie. "I must go find the young ladies. It's past time for their afternoon snack and nap."

Creed nodded. "Thanks, Burke."

The butler disappeared.

"I'm not hearing anything I want to hear," Creed muttered. "I know a woman needs her space. But I'm no Re-ride." He munched on the cookie, thinking it would taste better if Aberdeen was there to share it with him.

Between Burke's special lemonade, the cookie and the advice, he thought he was starting to feel better. Not much, just a little, but better all the same.

He was going to be a father.

He wanted to be a husband, too.

He wanted Aberdeen like nothing he'd ever wanted in his life. If his aunt had sprung the perfect woman on him, she couldn't have chosen better. He would easily trade Rancho Diablo if Aberdeen would be his wife. He wanted to spend the rest of his days lying in bed with her, holding her, touching her.

He was just going to have to hang on.

Chapter 17

"I'm worried about Sabrina McKinley," Fiona said to Creed when he rolled into the kitchen. She was making a pie, blueberry, he was pretty sure.

For once, he had no appetite for Fiona's baking. "You mean because of Bode?"

"Well, I certainly didn't like his tone the other night. He made it sound like she was a prisoner or something. The man gives me the creeps." She shook her head and placed the pie on a cooling rack. "I begin to rethink my plan of planting her, I really do, Creed."

"Jonas checked on her. He'd know if something was wrong." Creed sometimes wondered if his oldest brother had developed a secret penchant for Fiona's spy. Then he dismissed that. Jonas was nothing if not boring. He'd never go for the Mata Hari type.

"I suppose." She fluffed her hands off over the sink,

brightening. "On the other hand, we have news to celebrate!"

"Yeah." Creed didn't know how his aunt always managed to hear everything lightning-fast. "I'm going to be a father." He beamed, just saying the words a pleasure.

Fiona's mouth dropped open. "You're having a baby?"

He nodded. "Isn't that the news you were talking about?"

She slowly shook her head. "I was going to say that we have one hundred and fifty beautiful, eligible bachelorettes attending the ball tomorrow night." Her gaze was glued to him. "Is the mother Aberdeen?" she asked, almost whispering.

"Yes!" He stared at his aunt, startled. "Who else would it be?"

"How would I know?" Fiona demanded. "You were gone for months. I thought you had only just met Aberdeen when you got thrown at your last rodeo."

He nodded. "Absolutely all correct."

"That means you two got friendly awfully *quickly*." She peered at him, her gaze steadfast. "Goodness, you've barely given the poor girl a chance to breathe! No wonder she left."

He blinked. "Left?"

Fiona hesitated, her eyes searching his. "Didn't she tell you?"

His heart began an uncomfortable pounding in his chest. "Tell me what?"

"That she was going back home? She left an hour ago."

Creed sat down heavily in a kitchen chair. Then he sprang up, unable to sit, his muscles bunched with tension. "She didn't say a word."

"I think she said something about a letter. Burke!" Her butler/secret husband popped into the kitchen. "Yes?"

"When Aberdeen thanked us for our hospitality and said she was leaving, did she leave a letter of some kind?"

Burke's gaze moved to Creed. "She did. I am not to give it to Creed until six o'clock this evening."

"The hell with that," Creed said, "give it to me now."

Burke shook his head. "I cannot. It was entrusted to me with certain specifications."

Creed felt his jaw tightening, his teeth grinding as he stared at the elderly man prepared to stick to his principles at all costs. "Burke, remember the chat we had a little while ago out back?"

Burke nodded.

"And you know I'm crazy about that woman?"

Burke nodded.

"Then give me the letter so that I can stop her," Creed said, "please."

Burke said. "Creed, you're like a son to me. But I can't go against a promise."

"Damn it!" Creed exclaimed.

Fiona and Burke stared at him, their eyes round with compassion and sympathy.

"I apologize," Creed said. He ran rough hands through his hair. His muscles seemed to lose form suddenly, so he collapsed in a chair. "I don't suppose she said why?" he asked Fiona.

Fiona shook her head. "She said she needed to be back home. I asked her to stay for the ball, and she said she felt she'd only be underfoot. However," she said brightly, "Diane, Johnny and the girls stayed."

"Good," Creed said, shooting to his feet, "I've got a future brother-in-law to go pound."

"He's a guest!" Fiona called after him. "He saved your life!"

Creed strode out to find Johnny—and some answers. Five hours later, at exactly six o'clock—and after learning that Johnny and Diane knew nothing at all about Aberdeen's departure—Burke finally presented Aberdeen's letter to Creed, formally, on a silver platter.

The envelope was white, the cursive writing black and ladylike. Creed tore it open, aware that his family was watching his every move. News of Aberdeen's departure—and pregnancy—had spread like wildfire through Rancho Diablo. No one had had a clue that Aberdeen had wanted to leave.

Of course he'd known. In his heart, he'd known she was questioning their relationship from the minute she'd seen the ranch and the jet to the moment she'd learned she was pregnant.

Creed,
I want you to know how sorry I am that I will be unable to keep our bargain. As you know, at the time we made it, I was under the belief that Diane wanted me to adopt her children. I had no idea when, or if, Diane might return. But now I am hopeful that, given a little more time with her daughters and the gentle comfort of Rancho Diablo, my sister is gaining a true desire and appreciation of what it means to be a mother. This is more than I could have ever hoped for. For that reason, I'm leaving her here, in good hands, as Fiona has offered her employment. I know Diane is happy

here, happier than I might ever be. It seems a fair trade-off.

My part of the bargain to you was that marriage might cure your aunt's desire to see you married to help keep Rancho Diablo. I don't think you'll need my help. All of you seem quite determined to keep fighting, and I pray for the best for you. Mr. Jenkins seems most disagreeable, so I hope the good guys win. After the ball tomorrow night, perhaps all of your brothers will find wonderful wives. That is something else I will be praying for.

As you know, I have a congregation and a life back in Lance that means a lot to me. When I met you, I believed you were basically an itinerant cowboy. Marrying you for your name on an adoption application didn't seem all that wrong, considering that you, too, had a need of marriage. Now that I've met your family, I know that it would be wrong for me to marry you under false pretenses. That's just not the kind of person I am. Yours is a different kind of lifestyle than I could ever live up to. In the end, though you are a wonderful, solid man, I realize that my life and your life are just too different. With Diane finding her footing with her girls, I think this is a happy ending. I have you and your family to thank for that. So I'd say that any debt that may have existed before is certainly wiped out.

I know too well that you will want visitation rights once the baby is born. You no doubt have lawyers available to you who can draw up any documents you wish to that effect.

I know we will be talking in the future about our child's welfare, so I hope we can remain friends.
All my best,
Aberdeen
P.S. I have entrusted Burke with the engagement ring. Thank you so much for the gesture. For a while, I did feel like a real fiancée.

He looked up from the letter, his heart shattered. "She left me," he said, and his brothers seemed to sink down in their various chairs.

The silence in the room was long and hard. No one knew what to say to him. His hands shook as he stared at the letter again. She didn't feel like a real fiancée.

How could she not? Had he not loved her every chance he got? "She says she didn't feel like a real bride-to-be," he murmured. "But she's having my baby. How can she not feel like she's going to be a real wife?"

Jonas cleared his throat. "Women get strange sometimes when they're pregnant," he said, and Fiona gasped.

"That's not kind, Jonas Callahan!" She glared at him.

"It's true," Pete said. "Jackie gave me a bit of a rough road when she found out she was pregnant. There we were, this perfectly fine relationship—"

"That went on and on," Sam said. "Every woman has heard that a man who sleeps with her for a hundred years isn't serious about her, so you were only a Saturday-night fling, as far as she knew."

Pete stiffened. "But that wasn't how I felt about her. She just saw our relationship on a completely different level."

"I am never going through this," Judah said, "and if I do find a bride—and I hope I don't—but if I do, I'm going to do it right. None of this bride-on-the-run crap." He leaned back in the sofa, shaking his head.

"Maybe it's not that simple," Rafe said. "Maybe she didn't like it here."

"She didn't seem quite herself," Creed said, "but I put it down to the fact that she was worried about her nieces." Yet he'd known deep inside that hadn't been all of it. "I guess she didn't love me," he said, not realizing that he'd spoken out loud.

"Did you tell her you did?" Rafe asked.

Creed glanced up from the letter. "Not specifically those very words. I mean, she knew I cared."

"Because she was clairvoyant," Sam said, nodding.

"Hey," Jonas said, "your time is coming, young grass-hopper. Go easy on Creed."

"I'm just saying," Sam said, "that it's not like she's some kind of fortune-teller like Sabrina."

Everyone sent him a glare.

"Well, I did think she was the more quiet of the two sisters," Aunt Fiona said. "I wondered about it, I must say. I put it off to her being shy, perhaps, and—"

"That's why you offered Diane a job," Creed said, re-alization dawning like a thunderclap. He sent his aunt a piercing look. "You knew Aberdeen wasn't happy here, and you were trying to keep her little nieces here at the ranch!"

Fiona stared at him. "Oh, poppycock. That's a lot of busybodying, even for me, Creed. For heaven's sake."

He was suspicious. "Did Aberdeen tell you she wasn't happy here? With me?"

Fiona sighed. "She merely thanked me for my hospi-tality and said she had parents and a congregation to get back to. It wasn't my place to ask questions."

"So she never told you we'd had an agreement based on her feeling that a husband might put her in a more favorable light to an adoption committee?" Creed asked.

"So when Fiona offered Diane a job, and Aberdeen could see that things might be working out for her sister, the marriage contract between you two could be nullified," Judah said, nodding wisely.

"Oops," Aunt Fiona said. "I had no idea, Creed. I was just thinking to help Diane get on her feet again."

It wasn't Fiona's fault. He and Aberdeen had an agreement which, to her mind, was no longer necessary, so she'd chosen to leave him. She couldn't be blamed for that, either, since he'd never told her that he was wolf-crazy about her. Creed grunted. "What happens if Diane doesn't accept your offer of employment?"

Fiona straightened. "She will." She looked uncertain for a moment. "She'd better!"

"Because you fell for the little girls?" Creed asked, knowing he had, too. It was going to drive him mad if they left—and yet, if Diane chose to leave with her daughters, he would wish them well and hide his aching heart.

"No," Fiona said. "I would never dream of interfering in someone's life to that extent. She just happens to have recipes from around the world, thank you very much, due to all her travels. And she has experience taking care of elderly parents. And I could use a personal secretary." Fiona sniffed.

Groans went up from around the room. Fiona glared at her nephews. "Oh, all right. Is there anything wrong with giving a mother time to bond with her daughters? Perhaps all she had was a little bit of the blues. Does it matter? I like Diane. I like Johnny. And I like Aberdeen."

She shook her head at Creed. "Of course I didn't mean to do anything that would give Aberdeen the license to leave you, but I didn't know the nature of your relationship. It was up to you to discuss your feelings with her, which I'm sure you did amply."

Creed grunted. "I was getting around to it."

A giant whoosh of air seemed to leave the room. His brothers stared at the ceiling, the floor, anywhere but at him. Creed's shoulders sagged for a moment. He hadn't, and now it was too late.

"Give her time," Fiona said. "If I was in her shoes, I'd want time."

He held on to this jewel of advice like a gold-miner. "You really think—"

"I don't *know*," Fiona said, "although all of you seem to think I know everything. I don't. I just think Aberdeen has a lot on her mind. I would let her figure it out on her own for a while, perhaps."

"It might be sound counsel, considering the lady in question is mature and independent-natured," Burke murmured in his soft Irish brogue. Burke didn't hand out advice willy-nilly, so he was sharing knowledge of how he'd won Fiona.

"And the baby?" Creed asked, his heart breaking.

Fiona shook her head, silent for once.

The minutes ticked by in still quiet. Creed read the letter again, feeling worse with every word. Judah got up, crossing to the window of the upstairs library. "The Diablos are running," Judah said, and though the joy of knowing the wild horses were still running wild and free on Callahan land sang in Creed's veins, he stared out at them, not really believing their presence portended mystical blessings anymore.

Chapter 18

Aunt Fiona's First Annual Rancho Diablo Charity Matchmaking Ball was a knock-out success, Creed acknowledged. Ladies of all makes and models came to the ranch by the carload. If he'd still been a single man, he might have been as holistically lighthearted as Sam, who was chasing ladies like a kid at a calf-catch. He thought Johnny Donovan garnered his fair share of attention, though the big man never seemed to do more than dance politely with any lady who lacked a partner. Jonas was his usual stuck-in-the-mud self. If anybody was ever betting on Jonas to finally have a wild night in his life, the bettor was going to lose his money to the house. Jonas was a geek, and that was all he was going to be.

The one shocker of the evening was that Judah and Darla Cameron—who'd had her eyes on Judah forever, not that his clown of a brother had the sense to realize it—

actually seemed to engage in a longer-than-five-minute conversation. The chat lasted about twenty minutes, Creed estimated, even more surprised to see his brother initiate said conversation. To his great interest, he saw Darla head off, leaving Judah standing in the shadows of the house. Creed spied with enthusiasm, watching his boneheaded brother watching Darla walk away.

And then, just when he thought Judah was the dumbest man on the planet, beyond dumb and moving toward stupid-as-hell, Judah seemed to gather his wits and hurried after Darla. Creed snickered to himself and drank his beer. "Dumb, but not terminal," he muttered to himself, and thanked heaven he'd never been that slow where a good woman was concerned.

Or maybe he was. Creed thought about Aberdeen being up north, and him being here, and fought the temptation to give in and call her. Johnny said Aberdeen was stubborn. And on this Creed thought Johnny probably had a point.

He was willing to give her time, but it seemed like the cell phone in his pocket cruelly never rang with a call from her.

Creed went back to pondering Aunt Fiona's wonderful party. As bachelor busts went, it was one for the ages. Any of them should get caught. *Not me, I'm already caught, even if my woman doesn't know it. But it'll be fun for us all to get settled down, and then we'll raise a bunch of kids together, and instead of marriage feeling like a curse, we'll all look back and laugh about how determined we were to stay footloose and fancy-free.*

Except for my dumb twin. Rafe is a worm that will never turn. He watched Rafe go by, stuck in wolf mode, a bevy of absolutely gorgeous women tacked on to him like tails pinned on a donkey. Disgusting, Creed thought, that anyone considered his brother deep-thinking and existential when he was really a dope in wolf's clothing. Rafe looked like a man on his way to an orgy, dining at the table of sin with great gusto.

Disgusting.

Johnny sat down next to him on the porch swing. "You're not doing your part, dude. Aren't you supposed to be dancing?"

Creed shrugged. "I danced with a couple of wallflowers, so Aunt Fiona wouldn't be embarrassed. But I'm wallflowered out now."

"Nice of some of the local guys to show up and help out with the chores of chivalry," Johnny said.

"Everyone loves a lady in a party dress," Creed said morosely. "Heard from your sister? She's not coming back tonight to make sure I have my dance card filled? Induce me to give up my swinging-single lifestyle?"

Johnny laughed, raised a beer to Creed. "You know Aberdeen. She's the kind of woman who'll let a man hang himself with his own rope."

Creed leaned back. "It's dangerous dating a woman who's fiercely independent."

Johnny nodded. "Tell me about it."

Creed gave him a jaundiced eye. "Oh, hell, no. You're not dating anyone. Don't give me that commiseration bit."

"I'm hanging on," Johnny said. "For the right one to come along and catch me."

"Yeah, well, good luck," Creed said. "I found the right one. She threw me back."

"Patience is a virtue," Johnny said, and Creed rolled his eyes. Patience was *killing* him. He'd never been a patient man. Fiona said that he'd always wanted everything he couldn't have. He was a worker, a planner, a man of action—the crusader who rode into a forest and plucked out a maiden in the midst of battle, if need be, even before he discovered treasure and liberated it from the evil dragon.

Princess first. Ladies first. Absolutely, always.

At least that's the way he'd always seen himself. Aberdeen had him sitting on the sidelines in his own fish story. He was chomping at the bit.

"Wanna dance, handsome?" Creed heard, and glanced up, fully prepared to wave off a charming and buxom beauty, only to realize she was staring at Johnny, her eyes fast to the man whom Creed had thought might be his brother-in-law one day.

"Mind if go do my duty?" Johnny asked Creed. "I hate to leave you here alone, nursing that dry bottle, but as you can see, duty calls, and it's a beautiful thing."

Creed waved the empty bottle at Johnny. "Never let grass grow under your feet."

"Nor your ass, my friend," Johnny said with a grin, and went off with a lovely lady dragging him under the strung lights and a full moon to join the other dancers.

Creed shifted, feeling as if grass might have grown under him, he'd sat here so long. Johnny was right: he was moping after Aberdeen. If he didn't quit, he was going to end up Rip Van Winkle-ish, waking up one day to find time had passed and nothing had happened in his life. The phone wasn't going to ring; Aberdeen wasn't going to call.

He was waiting on a dream.

He had a baby on the way, a child who would bear his name. But he couldn't force Aberdeen to love him.

He would just have to be happy with knowing that at least his future had a blessing promised to him. And he was going to be a hell of a father. Because he remembered how much it had hurt when he'd lost his own father, how much it had stung not to have a dad around on the big occasions. So maybe he couldn't be a husband, and maybe his Cinderella had thrown her slipper at his heart, but this one thing he knew: he was going to wear a World's Best Father T-shirt as if it was a king-size, golden, rodeo buckle.

And his kid would know he was there for him. Always.

Eight months later

Aberdeen had grown like a pumpkin: blue-ribbon, State-Fair size. At least that's the way she felt. Johnny worried about her incessantly. "You should have stayed, accepted the Callahans' offer of employment, because you're driving me nuts," she told her brother.

"I could have," Johnny said, turning on the Open sign at the bar door, "but my livelihood is here. I'll admit I toyed briefly with the idea of staying in New Mexico and working with the Callahans. They seemed to need the help. And they sure know how to throw a heck of a dance. There were ladies from everywhere just dying to find a husband. I had a feeling if I'd hung around, Fiona might have fixed me up with a wife, too. From what I've gleaned over the past several months, no weddings went off and no one got caught, though."

Aberdeen wondered if Johnny was trying to reassure her that no one had caught Creed. She decided to stay away from that painful subject. She nodded at his pleased grin. "You could use someone looking after you."

"Women are not that simple, as I know too well." Johnny smiled and wiped off the bar. "No, it was fun at the time, and I enjoyed the break, but I had to be near my new nephew."

She shook her head. "I don't know the sex of the baby. Quit angling for a hint."

Johnny laughed. "Okay. So what happens when the baby is born?"

"I'm going to keep doing what I'm doing. Occasionally preaching, working here, looking for a house."

Her answer was slightly evasive because she knew Johnny was asking about Creed. The truth was, she never stopped thinking about him. Yet she knew their bargain had been a fairy tale. He'd been grateful to her and Johnny; he'd wanted to help her out. She wouldn't have felt right keeping him tied to an agreement for which there was no longer a need.

"As soon as that baby is born, you know he's going to be here."

Aberdeen nodded. "That's fine." She was over her broken heart—mostly. "You know what the bonus is in all this? Diane is happy at the Callahan ranch. Her daughters are flourishing."

At that Johnny had to smile. He flew down there once a month to visit the girls and Diane, always bringing back reports of astonishing growth and learning skills. Teeth coming in. New steps taken. First pony rides. He'd even taken their parents down to visit once. They'd been impressed with the girls' new environment, and the change in Diane.

Johnny never mentioned Creed when he took his

monthly sojourn to New Mexico, and Aberdeen never asked. She knew he would come to visit his baby. It would be the right thing, for the baby's sake. And he would want his baby to spend time at Rancho Diablo. *It will all work out*, Aberdeen told herself. *We're two adults, and can make this work. We are not Diane and her ex-husbands, who turned out to be sloths and degenerates of the first order. Creed will be an excellent father.*

She turned her mind away from Creed and back to the new sermon she was writing. After the baby was born, she intended to go back to school for some additional theology classes. The bar would bring in some income as she did the books for Johnny, and then she could afford a separate house.

It might not be the kind of situation she'd dreamed of with her concussed cowboy—but those had been just dreams, and she knew the difference between dreams and real life.

She went upstairs to the temporary nursery, smiling at the few things she'd put in the small room. A white crib, with white sheets and a white comforter. A lacy white valance over the small window. Diapers, a rocker, some tiny baby clothes in neutral colors: yellow, white, aqua.

It had seemed better not to know if she was having a boy or a girl. She would love either.

In fact, she couldn't wait.

Voices carried up the stairs. Johnny was welcoming some customers. She'd be glad to find her own little house, she realized. Something about having a baby made her feel protective, made her need her own space.

Her tummy jumped with a spasm, bringing another smile to Aberdeen's face. This was an active child, always on the go. The ob/gyn had said that Aberdeen needed to take it easy; the baby could come any day now.

It was too hard to sit and wait, though. The feeling of nesting and wanting everything just right had grown too great for her to ignore. She touched the baby's tiny pillow, soft satin, and told herself that in a few days, she'd be holding her own precious child.

"Aberdeen," a deep voice said, and she whirled around.

"Creed," she said, so astonished she couldn't say anything else. Her heart took off with a million tiny tremors. The baby jumped again, almost as if recognizing that its father had walked into the room.

"I bribed Johnny to let me up here without telling you I was here. Blame me for that, but I wanted to surprise you."

"I'll yell at him later," Aberdeen said.

His gaze fell to her stomach. Aberdeen put a hand over her stomach, almost embarrassed at her size.

"You look beautiful."

"Thank you." She didn't, and she knew it. Her dress was a loan from a mother in her congregation. She hadn't wanted to spend money on clothes when she was too big to fit into much other than a burlap potato sack, the kind that could hold a hundred pounds of potatoes easily. "Why are you here?" she asked, not meaning to sound rude, but so shocked by his sudden appearance that she couldn't make decent conversation.

She'd never been so happy to see anybody in her entire life. She wanted to throw herself into his arms and squeal for joy that he'd come.

But she couldn't.

"I came to see you. And my baby," he said. "I didn't want to miss you having the baby."

She swallowed. "Any day now. I guess Johnny told you."

Creed smiled. "He gives me the occasional update."

Drat her brother. "I guess I should have known he would."

"So this is the nursery?"

She ran a hand proudly along the crib rail. "For now. At least until I find a small house."

He nodded. He gazed at her for a long time. Then he said, "I've missed you."

She blinked, not expecting him to say anything like that. "I—"

He held up a hand. "It was just an observation. Not said to pen you into a corner."

She shook her head. "I know."

Another cramp hit her stomach. Her hands went reflexively to her tummy.

"Are you all right?" Creed asked, and she nodded.

"I think I'll go lie down. It's good to see you, Creed," she said. "Thanks for coming."

He nodded. "Guess I'll go bug Johnny. He's promised to teach me how to make an Expectant Father cocktail."

"Oh, boy," Aberdeen said, backing toward the door. "You two just party on."

She disappeared into the hallway, but as she left, she glanced over her shoulder at Creed. He was staring at her, his gaze never leaving her—and if she hadn't known better, she would have thought he looked worried.

If he was worried, it was because of the baby. He'd never said he loved her, never told her anything except that he'd take care of her and Diane's daughters, so she knew she'd done the right thing by letting him go.

Another cramp hit her, this one tightening her abdomen strangely, and Aberdeen went to check her overnight bag, just in case.

"So, did the heart grow fonder in absentia?" Johnny asked.

Creed shook his head and slid onto a bar stool across from Johnny. "Can never tell with Aberdeen. She keeps so much hidden."

"Have confidence," Johnny said, putting a glass in front of him, "and a New Papa cocktail."

"I thought you were going to teach me about Expectant Father cocktails."

Johnny grinned and poured some things into the glass. Creed had no idea what the man was putting in there, but he hoped it took the edge off his nerves. He'd waited eight long months to lay eyes on Aberdeen again, and the shock, well, the shock had darn near killed him.

He'd never stopped loving her. Not one tiny inch, not one fraction of an iota. If he'd thought he had any chance with her, any at all, he'd ask her to marry him tonight.

And this time he'd spend hours telling her how much he loved her, just the same way he'd spent hours making love to her. Only now, he'd do it with a megaphone over his heart.

"Give her a moment to think," Johnny said, "and drink this. It's for patience. You're going to need it."

"I've never had to chase a woman this hard," Creed grumbled. "I'm pretty sure even a shot from Cupid's quiver wouldn't have helped. The shame of it is, I know she likes me."

Johnny laughed. "No, this is a drink for patience as you wait to become a father. The doctor said today was her due date. Did I mention that?"

"No," Creed said, feeling his heart rate rise considerably. "All you said was today was a great day to get my ass up here. Thanks, you old dog. Now I think I'm going to have heart failure."

"You are a weak old thing, aren't you?" Johnny laughed again. "Relax, dude. I predict within the next week, you'll be holding your own bouncing bundle of joy."

Creed felt faint. He took a slug of the drink and winced. "That's horrible. What is it?"

"A little egg, a little Tabasco, a little bit of this and that. Protein, to keep your strength up."

Creed frowned. "Ugh. It's not going to keep my strength up, it's going to bring my lunch up."

"Trust me on this. It grows on you."

Creed shuddered. And then he froze as Aberdeen's voice carried down the stairs.

"Johnny?"

"Yeah?" her brother hollered up the stairs.

"I think perhaps you might bring the truck around."

Creed felt his jaw give. His gaze locked on Johnny. "What does that mean? Is that code for kick me out?"

"No." Johnny flipped the open sign to Closed and locked the door. "I think it means she wants to make a little run to the county hospital."

Creed blinked. He felt fainter. "What am I supposed to do?" He jumped up from the bar stool. "Should I carry something? Help her pack?"

Johnny said, "Hold on," and went upstairs.

A moment later, he came back down. "You might jog

up there and keep an eye on her while I bring the truck around. I'll meet you out back in a minute."

Creed's anxiety hit high gear when he realized Johnny was totally rattled. The man knocked over a liquor bottle and broke a glass—Creed had never seen him anything but sure-handed around his bar—in his haste to put things away.

But he didn't hang around to analyze his friend. He shot up the stairs to check on Aberdeen. She sat on the bed, looking puzzled.

"Do you need something?" he asked. "A glass of water? A…hell, I don't know. What can I do?"

"Nothing," Aberdeen said, panting a little. "Except I have some concerns."

"Shoot," he said, "I'm your listening ear."

She gave him a wry gaze. "Are you going to want to be in the delivery room?"

"Nothing could keep me out of there," he said, "unless you don't want me, in which case I'm not above bribing you."

Aberdeen started to laugh, then quit abruptly. "Ugh. Don't make any jokes."

"I'm not joking in the least. I have to be there every step of the way."

"Okay." She took a deep breath. "You can't look under the sheet, and if things get tricky, you have to leave. Deal?"

"I don't know," he said, "you didn't keep to our last deal. I don't guess I can trust you with another one unless it's in writing."

"Creed!" Aberdeen said, looking like she was torn between laughing and crying.

"Oh, all right," he said, "although I reserve the right to judge what is tricky."

"If I say go, then you go," Aberdeen explained, with another gasp and a pant.

He sighed. "You'll want me there. Pete's already told me that my main role is to bring you ice chips and let you squeeze the skin off my fingers. Oh, and if you cuss me out, I'm to ignore all that and tell you how beautiful you are, and how you're the most wonderful woman in the world."

Aberdeen groaned. "If you can do all that, you'll be a true prince."

A truck horn honked outside, and Creed helped Aberdeen to her feet. "Guess I got here in the nick of time," he said, to make conversation. "Isn't that what princes do? Show up to help the fair damsel?"

Aberdeen didn't say anything for a moment.

But then she looked up at him, about halfway down the stairs. "Thank you for being here," she told him, and Creed's heart soared.

Maybe, just maybe…

Chapter 19

"I can't believe my mother had six of us," Creed said, after Aberdeen let out a loud groan. "Can't she have some medication to dull the pain?"

"She's too far along," the nurse said.

"Can I have some pain medication?" Creed asked.

The nurse smiled at him, at the edge of tolerance. "Perhaps you'd like to go sit outside in the waiting area. We'll take good care of Mrs. Callahan."

Aberdeen let out another gasp. Creed's gaze flew to her, his teasing spirit gone. He was panicked. There seemed to be a lot of pain involved, and he hadn't meant to do this to her. She was never going to become Mrs. Callahan.

She was going to hate him forever.

He went through his litany of jobs Pete had suggested: ice chips, tell her she's beautiful, stay out of the way except when she wants to squeeze your fingers to the bone. Try to be helpful. Try.

Creed stayed at the bedside, scared out of his wits. Good-and-stomped cowboys suffered, but even they hadn't seemed to be in this much agony.

Creed closed his eyes and prayed.

Thirty minutes later, Aberdeen gave one final shriek that went through Creed—he seemed to feel her every pain—and suddenly the doctor smiled with satisfaction.

"It's a girl," the doctor said, and Creed went light-headed. He sank onto a chair as nurses scurried to clean up baby and Aberdeen. He was out of breath; there was no more strength in his body.

Then it hit him. The baby that was squalling up a storm and being fussed over by the nurses was *his*. He jumped to his feet and hurried over to get a glimpse.

She was beautiful.

He went to tell Aberdeen. His heart constricted as he saw how exhausted she was.

"How are you doing?" he asked, and Aberdeen gave him a wan smile.

"How are you?" she asked. "I thought you were going to fade on me."

"No," he said. "I'm tough. Not as tough as you, though. You win." He bent down and kissed her on the lips, so she'd know she was beautiful. A kiss seemed to express his feelings better at this moment than words.

Then he remembered he was in this predicament because he'd never said the words (Sam's shot about clairvoyance came to mind), so he just threw himself out on the ledge. "You're beautiful," he told her. "I may never get you pregnant again, but I want you to know that I love you fiercely, Aberdeen Donovan. And this may not be the time to tell you, but if you don't put my ring back on your finger and marry me, I'm going to… I'm going to cry like my daughter."

Aberdeen smiled. But she didn't say anything for a long moment. She closed her eyes and he thought she looked happy. Content. He brushed her hair back from her face, thinking she really was the most beautiful woman he'd ever seen in his life. Of course he was in love with her, had been always, but now she'd given him an amazing gift, so he loved her even more.

"I saw him one day," Aberdeen murmured, and Creed said, "Who?"

"The Native American. He was on your ranch, probably a thousand feet from the house. He waved to me, so I went to talk to him. He was tall, and had long, braided hair and such kind eyes. He said he was watching over the horses."

"The Diablos?"

"He called them that, but I didn't know what he meant at the time. And he said not to be scared, that all things worked out for the Callahans. That you would know your parents through this baby."

He blinked. "He told you that?"

"I didn't understand what it meant. But now I do. He said he'd known your parents a long time ago, and this baby was a gift to them. And then he left."

Creed was shocked. He'd never spoken to Aunt Fiona's friend; neither had any of his brothers, as far as he knew. "Our parents died long ago," he said. "I'm not sure how a baby can be a gift to them. But I'm okay with the theory."

"Have you ever talked to him?"

Creed shook his head. "He comes around to talk to Fiona about once a year. I don't know why. It's one of those things Aunt Fiona is mysterious about—one of many things, I suppose."

"He was nice. I liked him. I've never seen so much peace in someone's eyes." She looked at him. "I'll marry you, Creed Callahan."

His heart soared. "You will?"

She smiled. "Yes."

A nurse came between them for a moment, handing Aberdeen her pink-blanket-wrapped baby, and a delighted smile lit Aberdeen's face. "She looks just like you."

"Don't say that," Creed said, "I want her to look just like her wonderful mother. There are no beauties in my family tree, just unfortunately unhandsome brothers."

"There's a beauty now." Aberdeen kissed the top of her baby's head. "She's so sweet."

"That she gets from your side of the family." Creed was so proud he was about to burst. "Are you really going to marry me?"

Aberdeen handed him the baby, which he took carefully, lovingly. "I am, cowboy. I've decided you're the prince I've been waiting for."

He was so happy he wanted to cry. "What took you so long?"

"I was afraid you might be the wolf in my fairy tale, not a prince. You had me fooled for a while." Aberdeen smiled. "I was determined not to make any more mistakes. But I never stopped thinking about you, and after a while, I knew you were the only man I could ever love."

"When were you going to tell me?" Creed asked. "Because I'm pretty sure the last several months have just about killed me."

"After you told me," she said simply, and he groaned.

"I'm going to tell you every day of your life how much I love you," Creed said. "I'm going to keep you convinced that you made the right decision."

"I am," Aberdeen said with conviction. "I know exactly what I'm doing. I'm marrying the most wonderful man in the world. Now name your baby."

He hesitated, glancing down at the sleeping child in his arms. "I don't know anything about naming babies. What if I pick something she hates later on?"

She smiled. "Don't you have a favorite female name?"

"Aberdeen," he said with a decisive nod.

That made her laugh as she lay back against the pillow. "I'm going to sleep now, but when I wake up, I want you to have named your little girl. Surprise me with your creativity."

"No pressure or anything," he said, and he looked down at the tiny lips, adorable closed eyes, sweet cheeks of his daughter, knowing the old Navajo was right: this baby connected him to the past he could barely remember. But he knew his parents had loved him, just as he loved this child. Joy filled him, and then it came to him. "Joy," he said, and Aberdeen opened her eyes.

"That's lovely," she said.

"It's what I feel when I look at you," he said, and she knew his heart was in his words. "And when I hold this little baby…" He leaned down to give Aberdeen a kiss. "Thank you is all I can say. And I will love you until the end of time."

"You're going to make me cry," Aberdeen said, but he sat down next to her, and touched her face, and suddenly Aberdeen didn't feel like crying, only smiling, with joy.

Creed Callahan wasn't loco, she knew. He was her

prince, her man, and the hottest cowboy she'd ever laid eyes on. All hers.

All her dreams come true.

Creed leaned against her and Aberdeen drifted, loving feeling him by her side, holding their baby. It was the sweetest moment, starting their family. She murmured, "I love you," and Creed said, "Joy says you'd better," and then he kissed her again.

It was perfect.

Joy.

Epilogue

In February, the month after Joy Patrice was born, Aberdeen finally walked down the aisle into Creed's waiting arms.

Only it wasn't that simple.

First, he had to convince her that baby weight was no excuse not to marry him. Then he had to tell her that getting married at Rancho Diablo on Valentine's Day during the coldest month of the year was a swell idea—red was a great color for bridesmaid's gowns. She only had one attendant and that was Diane, but still, it took some doing. Aberdeen kept talking about waiting until springtime, when she'd lost some weight, when Joy would be a little older, when the weather would be warmer—but he wasn't about to let her weasel out of marrying him for any reason.

He'd nearly lost her before. If he'd learned anything,

it was that he had to do a lot of talking with this woman. So talk he did.

And today, a day that dawned clear and sunny, he didn't relax until Aberdeen finally said, "I do." And even then, he asked her to say it again, which made her and the guests laugh.

Judah said later he'd never seen such a desperate case. Jonas told Judah he'd better hush, because one day it might be him begging some poor woman to marry him. Sam said he thought it was romantic, if a bit weinie, of his brother to go down on bended knee and promise to love and adore Aberdeen for the rest of their lives, and Rafe said his twin had finally showed some depth of character and soul. Pete said he didn't care as long as they hurried up and cut the cake because he was starving. Keeping up with the demands of three little girls kept his appetite fired up.

Valentine's Day was a perfect day to catch his bride, in Creed's opinion. When they were finally declared husband and wife, he swept Aberdeen off her feet and carried her back down the aisle, intent on putting her right into the waiting limousine.

He intended to spend their week-long honeymoon in Bermuda making love to her constantly, and as far as he was concerned, the honeymoon began *now*.

"Wait," Aberdeen said, laughing, "Creed, put me down. We have guests. There's cake to cut."

"Oh." He put her down, reluctantly. "I'm not letting you out of my sight, though."

She took him over to the three-tiered cake. "I know. But there are some duties required—"

"Cut fast," he told her, and she made a face at him.

"We have to dance, and tell everybody thank you

for coming," she said. "Creed, we just can't desert our guests. And there's Joy. I feel so guilty about leaving her. Don't you think we should wait for our honeymoon until—"

"That's it," he said, "here's the knife. Cut the cake, take a bite and let's shazaam before you get cold feet. I know you too well, parson, and I worked too hard to get you." He put cake into her mouth, waved at the applauding guests, let the photographer snap a few more photos of them and then went over to Aunt Fiona, who was holding Joy in her arms.

"This is a great party, Aunt," he said.

"But you're leaving."

He kissed her cheek. "Yes, we are. My bride wants me all to herself. Mrs. Callahan is demanding like that."

"Creed," Aberdeen said, laughing, as she bent to kiss Fiona's cheek, and then reached up to kiss Burke's.

"It's all right," Fiona said. "I've succeeded beyond my wildest dreams, so I just want to say welcome to the family, Aberdeen. And congratulations on catching Creed. I never thought I'd live to see the day, did you, Burke?"

Burke shook Creed's hand. "The limo has all your items in it, and is waiting for your call."

"Thanks for everything," Creed said, and kissed his aunt goodbye. Then he bent to kiss his baby's head. "Joy, you be sweet to your family. Aunt Diane is going to take very good care of you."

"Yes, I am." Diane closed her sister in her arms. "Congratulations, sis," she said, "I'm going to be as good an aunt to your daughter as you were to mine. I can never thank you enough for giving me time to figure out my life."

Aberdeen smiled. "I knew you would."

Johnny nodded. "I'm going to practice my uncle skills. I can't wait. Seems like I've been waiting months for this, and now I've got four babies to uncle. It's pretty cool."

"Yes," Creed said, prouder about new fatherhood than about winning all his rodeo buckles. "All these new women in my life. Who would have ever thought it?"

"I would," Fiona murmured to Burke, who hugged her as she gazed at her growing family. "I always knew he had it in him."

"I always knew I had it in me," Creed said to Aberdeen, and she kissed him.

"Let's go, cowboy," she said, for his ears only. "I've got a special gift to give you in the limo. Because I'm pretty sure you said I wasn't having you until I made an honest man of you, and now I have."

"Hot dang," Creed said. "I'm already there, my love."

They waved goodbye to their guests under a shower of pink paper hearts, and, as Creed helped his bride run to the white limo in her long, lacy gown, he caught sight of the black mustangs running, tossing their manes and pounding their hooves, free and wild, as they chased the spirits in the wind.

Enchanted.

* * * * *

Marin Thomas grew up in the Midwest, then attended college at the U of A in Tucson, Arizona, where she earned a BA in radio-TV and played basketball for the Lady Wildcats. Following graduation, she married her college sweetheart in the historic Little Chapel of the West in Las Vegas, Nevada. Recent empty-nesters, Marin and her husband now live in Texas, where cattle is king, cowboys are plentiful and pickups rule the road. Visit her on the web at marinthomas.com.

Books by Marin Thomas

Harlequin Western Romance

The Cowboys of Stampede, Texas

The Cowboy's Accidental Baby

Harlequin American Romance

Cowboys of the Rio Grande

A Cowboy's Redemption
The Surgeon's Christmas Baby
A Cowboy's Claim

The Cash Brothers

The Cowboy Next Door
Twins Under the Christmas Tree
Her Secret Cowboy
The Cowboy's Destiny
True Blue Cowboy
A Cowboy of Her Own

Visit the Author Profile page at Harlequin.com for more titles.

A COWBOY'S DUTY

MARIN THOMAS

To Lauren

When we first met, you were quiet and shy.
It wasn't until I got to know you better that
I began to see a strong, determined and
resourceful young woman. A woman who is
not afraid to rely on herself or face the unknown
without flinching. Hold fast to your dreams—
no matter how long they take to realize or
what roads you must travel to achieve them.
Believe in yourself, and there will be
no limit to what you can achieve.

Things turn out best for the people who make the
best out of the way things turn out.

—Art Linkletter

Prologue

"Ready?"

"I'll never be as ready as you are." Dixie Cash grimaced at her friend Shannon Douglas—one of the top female bull riders in the country.

Shannon was forever on the lookout for a rough stock competition and when Five Star Rodeos had agreed to sponsor women's bull riding in three summer events, Shannon had promised to find five women crazy enough to ride with her—Dixie being one of them.

"Here." Shannon held out a bank draft.

"I feel bad taking your money." Dixie shoved the check into the front pocket of her jeans.

"You're worth every penny."

When Shannon had mentioned the rodeos, Dixie had just been hired as a part-time receptionist for a construction company in Yuma. She'd wanted to help her friend but needed money to launch an internet business for her homemade organic bath soaps. Then Shannon had made Dixie an offer she couldn't refuse—a thousand dollars per rodeo.

"Looks like Veronica Patriot has set her sights on Gavin Tucker."

Dixie's gaze followed Shannon's pointer finger. Figures the blonde buckle bunny would target the handsome bareback rider. "If the cowboy knows what's good for him he'll avoid that tramp like the plague." Dixie had run into Gavin—literally—at the Canyon City Rodeo in June when she'd tripped over his gear bag and knocked him to the ground.

"The bull's more of a spinner than a bucker," Shannon said. "Stay centered." The tan Charbray stood docile in the chute, but once freed all hell would break loose.

"Ladies and gentlemen, turn your attention to gate two. Dixie Cash is about to tangle with Bad Mamajamma." The crowd stomped their boots against the bleachers and whistles filled the air.

"If the Cash name sounds familiar it's because Dixie's got six older brothers who rodeo. Earlier today, Merle Cash took third in the saddle bronc competition."

While Shannon and a rodeo helper fished the bull rope from beneath Bad Mamajamma, Dixie pulled on her riding gloves and adjusted her headgear with its protective mask.

Let's get this over with. Dixie straddled the fifteen-hundred pound nuisance, found her grip then nodded to the gate man. The bull pounced for freedom, the first buck almost unseating Dixie. Anticipating a wild ride, she held her breath through the first of two tight spins, squeezing her thighs against the animal's girth.

Bad Mamajamma decided he'd had enough of Dixie and kicked out with extra force. As if she'd been shot from a cannon, Dixie catapulted through the air. She hit the dirt hard, but instinctively curled her body into a ball and rolled away from the bull's hooves. The bullfighter stepped in front of Bad Mamajamma, affording Dixie an extra second to gain her footing. She ran for the rails and scrambled to safety.

"Well, folks, Dixie Cash gave it her best effort." The announcer discussed Shannon's upcoming ride, but Dixie stopped listening when her boots landed in front of Gavin Tucker.

"Good try," he said.

Try being the operative word. "Thanks." *Brilliant, Dixie. A cowboy with killer looks and nice manners goes out of his way to talk to you and you mumble "thanks"?*

"How long have you been riding bulls?" Gavin asked.

"Started this summer."

A dark eyebrow lifted. "Gutsy gal."

More like crazy. For the life of her, Dixie couldn't find her tongue. Turned out she didn't have to. Veronica Patriot materialized out of nowhere and sashayed her way between Dixie and Gavin. She placed her French-manicured talons on Gavin's chest and thrust her heaving bosom in his face. "Time to celebrate, cowboy."

Dixie despised Veronica. The woman had done a number on her brother Porter—used him to make another cowboy jealous then left him high and dry with a broken heart.

"Sorry, I've got plans." Gavin's soulful brown eyes beseeched Dixie.

"What plans?" Veronica propped her hands on her hips.

Dixie had read her share of silent *help me* messages from her brothers. The look Gavin sent her begged her to rescue him from the clutches of the evil buckle bunny. *What the heck.*

"Gavin and I have a date," Dixie said.

"Pardon?" Veronica frowned.

"That's right." Gavin inched closer to Dixie and the scent of dust and faded cologne went straight to her head. When he rested his arm across her shoulders a little shiver raced down her spine. Gavin couldn't have been more than six feet tall, but her five foot six inches fit perfectly tucked against him.

Veronica's gaze bounced between Gavin and Dixie. "What kind of date?"

"A boy-girl date." Dixie smiled sweetly.

"Honey, a girl like you can't handle a military man."

Dixie had heard that Gavin Tucker had been stationed in Afghanistan before he'd left the army. "What do you think, Gavin? Can I handle you?"

He grinned.

Disgusted, Veronica snorted like a pig and stomped off.

"Thanks." Gavin released Dixie and stepped back.

Wishing he still had his arm around her, she said, "No worries. Veronica can be a pest."

"Are you celebrating later with your lady bull rider friends?"

"Probably."

"I'm heading over to the Spittoon. Maybe I'll see you there."

"Maybe."

Gavin walked off and Dixie couldn't help but think he was exactly the kind of man she'd like to marry someday.

Gavin stepped inside the Spittoon, a bar on the outskirts of Boot Hill, and surveyed the crowd. The place was packed, noisy, and smelled like stale beer, dusty cowboys and easy women. And he hoped Dixie Cash was among the clientele—not that he thought she was a party girl. There was something about the petite, tomboyish cowgirl that drew him. She showed the same courage and spunk as the women he'd worked alongside in the army.

He made his way to the bar, ordered a beer, then found a dark corner away from the crush of bodies. Keeping his back to the wall he searched for the blue-eyed brown-haired girl-next-door. He spotted her at a table next to the dance floor engaged in conversation with her friends. As if she sensed his scrutiny, their eyes connected and Gavin felt the subtle stirrings of arousal.

A former soldier had no business being with a girl like Dixie—that fact in and of itself fed Gavin's desire, and adrenaline pumped through his veins. If there was one thing he was addicted to, it was adrenaline. After six years of living on the edge…living with danger…he was drawn to taking risks. And Dixie Cash was definitely a risk.

"Well, well, well."

Gavin jumped an inch off the floor. *Damn.* How the hell had Veronica Patriot snuck up on him? His temper flared but he counted to ten, as a therapist had once instructed him to do when he felt threatened.

"What happened to your boy-girl date?" The buckle bunny narrowed her eyes.

"Dixie's—"

"Here." Dixie sidled up to Gavin and slipped her arm through his. She stood close enough that her soft breast pressed against his biceps.

"You're not his type." Veronica sneered. "Besides, don't girls like you have curfews?"

"She's right, Gavin. We should leave. It's past my bedtime." Dixie batted her dark lashes and suddenly Gavin's jeans felt a size too small.

Reminding himself that Dixie's flirting was an act to help him out of a tight spot, he said, "Ready when you are."

"Don't you want a real woman, soldier?" Veronica thrust her bosom out, flaunting her attributes.

After a lengthy glare-down, Veronica stepped aside and Gavin led Dixie across the dance floor and out the door. It wasn't until they were almost to his truck that he realized he still held her hand. He stopped and glanced over his shoulder. Veronica had followed them outside.

"She doesn't give up easily, I'll give her that," Dixie said.

"How would you feel about leaving with me in my truck?"

"I don't know. Can I trust you?"

"Sugar, if I harm one hair on your head, your brothers will hunt me down."

"You're right. I'll go for a ride with you."

Ten minutes later… "She's still following us." Gavin glanced between the road and the rearview mirror. Dixie's stomach growled and he threw caution to the wind. "You up for Chinese takeout? We could eat at the motel.

If Veronica sees us go into my room together maybe she'll give up."

"I don't believe that woman knows the meaning of surrender, but I won't turn down a free meal."

Veronica trailed them to the restaurant and then the motel where she parked across the lot, facing Gavin's room. Ignoring their stalker, he and Dixie sat on the king-size bed, ate chop suey and watched the old spaghetti Western, *A Fistful of Dynamite*.

Near the end of the movie, Gavin peeked out the window. Veronica's Mustang was gone. The woman had finally left him alone. He checked his watch—half past one in the morning. Time to drive Dixie back to the Spittoon so she could be on her way home. "Coast is clear." He turned from the window.

Dixie lay curled in a ball on the bed, her hands folded neatly beneath her cheek, her chest rising and falling in deep, even breaths. In sleep, she appeared innocent and cuddly and he wanted to lose himself in all her sweet goodness. But Gavin didn't dare crawl onto the bed with Dixie and risk falling asleep. He couldn't take the chance he'd experience the recurring nightmare that had followed him home from Afghanistan. He lowered the volume on the TV and made himself comfortable in the chair. He'd gone many nights without a wink of sleep, but the longer he watched Dixie's slumbering body the more exhausted he became.

The sun streaming through a gap in the curtains woke Gavin at the crack of dawn. He wasn't sitting in the chair—he was lying on the bed. Sometime in the middle of the night he'd crawled under the covers. He rolled away from the light and came face-to-face with a wide-awake Dixie.

He held his breath, waiting for her to make the first move—she did. Her lips brushed his, then came back for more. One kiss turned into two…three…then clothes started flying off.

Chapter 1

"Hello, Gavin."

The saccharine voice raised a warning flag inside Gavin Tucker's head. Bracing himself, he stepped away from the bucking chute at the Piney Gorge Rodeo and faced Veronica Patriot with a groan. "Veronica."

The woman took buckle bunnying to a whole new level. She'd been pursuing Gavin since he'd joined the circuit back in May after he'd left the army. The middle of August had arrived and the blonde piranha showed no signs of tiring.

Gavin adjusted the spurs on his boots, hoping she'd take his silence as a hint and mosey along. At first, he'd found Veronica's infatuation amusing. He'd become accustomed to pretty women fawning over him whenever he'd worn his military uniform and the same held true for his cowboy getup—Wranglers, boots and a Stetson.

Gavin's ability to attract the opposite sex had come in handy during his furloughs from the army. One look at his combat boots and women had fallen into his bed willingly. He'd honed his survival skills on the battlefield and used them to pick ladies who wanted nothing from him but a good time and a goodbye. A sixth sense told him that Veronica had more on her mind than a quickie.

"You don't appear all that happy to see your biggest fan." She puckered her glossy lips.

A weaker man might tuck tail and run, but Gavin wasn't easily intimidated. "I'm not interested in hooking up." *Ever.*

"Did you and Dixie have a spat?"

Dixie Cash. The petite brunette hadn't crossed Gavin's mind since the morning he'd dropped her off in the parking lot of the Spittoon bar last month. He fought a smile as he recalled the first time he'd caught a glimpse of her—climbing onto a bull named Listless at the Canyon City Rodeo back in June. For an instant he'd seen in her a kindred spirit when Listless had thrown her. Dixie had limped from the arena with a smile on her pixie face as if she'd had the time of her life wrestling fifteen hundred pounds of orneriness, then she'd stumbled over his gear bag and right into his arms. Her face had burned red and he'd thought her embarrassment oddly sweet.

"Dixie's a friend." *Friend* sounded better than *one-night stand.*

"I can be that kind of friend, too." Veronica's gaze dropped to Gavin's crotch.

His face heated—not because of Veronica's lewd stare. He'd made a mistake when he'd crossed the line with Dixie, yet he'd had no choice but to move on and put that night behind him.

Short of being mean, Gavin said, "Pick another cowboy. I'm not interested in what you're offering."

"When you tire of your little bull rider and decide you want a real woman, I'll be waiting."

One of Gavin's competitors let out a wolf whistle as Veronica strutted off. "I wouldn't complain if she followed me through the copper state."

"Careful what you wish for," Gavin mumbled. Now that he was rid of the annoying buckle bunny he checked the arena for Dixie. He recognized Shannon Douglas mingling behind the chutes with a few of the lady bull riders from the Boot Hill Rodeo, but Dixie was nowhere in sight. She'd probably viewed their one-night stand as a mistake, too, and wanted to avoid running into him.

Turning his thoughts inward, Gavin focused on his ride as he secured his protective vest. After wearing bulletproof gear as part of his military uniform, he felt comfortable in the constricting rodeo garment.

"Welcome to the Piney Gorge Rodeo and Livestock Show!" A thunderous din reverberated through the small outdoor arena. Gavin loved rodeo fans. The men and women were die-hard loyalists to the sport much the way soldiers were dedicated to their units.

"Up next this fine Saturday afternoon is bareback riding! Bareback horses are leaner and quicker than those used for saddle bronc riding and the cowboys sure do take a beating in this event." The announcer paused.

A commotion in the cowboy ready area caught Gavin's attention. The Cash brothers had arrived. Dixie had mentioned that her mother had named her siblings after country-western singers. Right then Johnny, the eldest Cash brother, spotted Gavin. The speculative gleam in the man's eyes unnerved him. Had Dixie told Johnny she'd spent the night with Gavin in his motel room?

He and Dixie hadn't made a big deal over sleeping together. He'd enjoyed—make that had *really* enjoyed—making love to Dixie, but the country girl wasn't his usual type. The things he'd seen and experienced during his years in the military would only contaminate a young woman as pure as Dixie.

Johnny broke eye contact first, and Gavin shook his head to clear his thoughts. Today he intended to make it to eight. Luck hadn't been with him this summer—the highest he'd placed was fourth. If he didn't get his rodeo act together and pull off a few wins, he'd eat through his savings in no time flat and be forced to find a civilian job. Having to quit the circuit before he was ready was all the motivation Gavin needed to climb onto another wild bronc.

"Ladies and gentlemen, turn your attention to chute number three. Gavin Tucker from Phoenix, Arizona, is about to tangle with Cisco Kid, a bronc known for throwin' cowboys on their heads. Let's see if Tucker can best Cisco Kid."

Gavin blocked out the arena noise as he fussed with his rigging—a heavy piece of leather with a suitcaselike handle attached to it. He flexed his gloved fingers until his grip felt comfortable. A deep breath later, he nodded and Cisco Kid bolted from the chute. Gavin marked out, ignoring the jolting pain shooting through his shoulder caused by the gelding's powerful bucks and lightning speed.

The racket inside Gavin's head quieted as the thrill of the physical torture the horse inflicted rushed through his body. Cisco Kid made a final attempt to spin but

Gavin spurred harder and the bronc gave up. Feeling a victory at hand, he relaxed his guard too soon and Cisco Kid tossed him on his arse. Gavin missed the buzzer by one second. Back in the cowboy ready area he gathered his gear. This time he spotted Veronica before she startled him.

"Change your mind about me?" She'd brought a friend along—a redhead with glittery eye shadow. "Candi's up for a little fun," Veronica said.

A threesome? No thanks. Even in his wildest days, Gavin had never gotten into the kinky stuff. Call him old-fashioned, but one woman at a time was plenty. "Sorry, Veronica—" he swung his gaze to glitter girl "—and Candi. Gotta hit the road." A ride in Wickenburg awaited him.

Candi popped a pink bubble with her chewing gum. "Maybe next time?"

Not a chance. He touched a finger to the brim of his hat then grabbed his bag and left the arena. The sooner he put a few miles between him and those two the better.

An hour down the road, Gavin noticed a billboard advertising Millie's World Famous Hotcakes. He took the exit ramp and pulled into a parking lot crowded with eighteen-wheelers. Gavin found an empty stool at the end of the lunch counter. He rested his hat on his knee and flipped over the white mug in front of him.

A gray-haired waitress named Peggy strolled by with a coffeepot and filled the cup. "Didn't make it to eight?" She offered a sympathetic smile.

"Not today." *Not in a long while.*

"You ain't alone, handsome." Peggy nodded to a table where three cowboys sat, one with an ice pack strapped to his shoulder. "Special's barbecue ribs and corn bread."

"That'll do." While he waited for his meal he mulled over his schedule. The Wickenburg rodeo had a decent purse. If he made the final go-round he'd be guaranteed a share of the prize money. If he lost…he'd head down the road.

A self-admitted rodeo junkie, Gavin got high on the buzz and danger of riding bucking stock. Feeding his adrenaline addiction was his number one priority because it fueled his strength—strength he needed to run from the demons that had followed him home from war.

"How was the rodeo?" Dixie asked her brother Johnny when he walked into the kitchen of their grandparents' farmhouse early Saturday evening. She was dying for news about a particular bareback rider, but as soon as her brothers had returned from the Piney Gorge Rodeo they'd gone to their bedrooms to nap.

"Merle made it to the final round before getting thrown." Johnny grabbed a beer from the fridge, then sat at the kitchen table. "Shannon said she hopes your ankle feels better soon."

Dixie's cheeks warmed. She'd discovered she was pregnant two weeks after the Boot Hill Rodeo in July. She'd hated to disappoint Shannon and give up the third thousand-dollar payoff, but she hadn't dared risk the baby's health. She'd told Shannon and the other women about her pregnancy but had asked that they keep it a secret and to tell anyone who inquired after her whereabouts that she'd sprained her ankle—the excuse she'd given her brothers when she'd told them she wasn't competing today.

"Anything else exciting happen at the rodeo?" she asked.

"Depends on what you consider exciting."

"I suppose Veronica Patriot was there." Dixie fussed with the dishes in the sink while contemplating her dilemma—how to glean information about a certain cowboy without drawing her brother's suspicion.

"Veronica's hot on Gavin Tucker's tail." Johnny chuckled. "He got thrown in the first round then split."

"Did Veronica leave the rodeo with Gavin?" Drat, the question slipped from her mouth.

"Why do you care if Tucker went off with Veronica?"

"I don't." After Dixie had spent the night in Gavin's motel room she'd returned to the farm the following morning and confessed she'd stayed at a friend's house because she'd had too much to drink at the Spittoon.

Johnny tossed his empty beer bottle into the garbage and made a beeline for the back door.

"Hey, you promised to fix the shelf in the barn cellar."

"Conway said he'd take a look at it."

Conway Twitty was the fifth born Cash son. All six of her brothers had different fathers. Only Dixie and Johnny shared the same daddy. Her mother had come full circle in her quest for the perfect man and had reunited with her first love, Charlie Smith, only to become pregnant with Dixie. Aimee Cash had never married any of the men she'd slept with, so Dixie and her brothers had taken her surname—Cash.

Dixie and Johnny had the same dark brown hair and blue eyes, which they'd inherited from Charlie. Their brothers had brown eyes and various shades of blondish-brown hair like their mother. "Conway's preoccupied," Dixie said.

"Is he still pouting because Sara broke up with him?"

"I think so." Conway was the handsomest of her brothers and women fawned all over him, which derailed his love life on a regular basis. Each time he found *the one*, another woman would happen along and tempt him to cheat. Then when *the one* caught him two-timing, she'd send Conway packing and her brother would mope like a coon dog left home on hunt day.

"I'll look at the shelf before I leave tonight," Johnny said.

"You and Charlene have big plans?" Charlene was Johnny's longtime girlfriend. They'd been together six years and Johnny had yet to propose.

"We're going to the movies then back to her place afterward."

None of her brothers brought their significant others to the farm. Paper-thin walls and shared bedrooms prevented any privacy, not to mention having only one bathroom in the house.

"What about you?" Johnny winked. "Got a hot date?"

Right then Dixie's stomach seized and she bolted from the kitchen. She took the stairs two at a time then skidded to a stop in front of the bathroom door. One hand clamped over her mouth and the other pounding the door, she fought the urge to vomit.

"Go away! I'm reading," Porter Wagoner shouted.

Ignoring the bedroom doors creaking open behind her and Johnny's shadow darkening the top of the stairs, Dixie banged her fist harder. *Blast you, Porter.* She spun, intent on dashing outside, but Johnny blocked her escape.

Oh, well. Dixie threw up on his boots.

"Eew!" Willie Nelson chuckled.

"I'll fetch the mop." Merle Haggard leaped over the contents of Dixie's stomach and hurried to the kitchen.

"Sorry." Dixie wiped the back of her hand across her mouth.

"What's all the commotion?" Porter emerged from the bathroom, his eyes widening at the mess covering Johnny's boots.

"Have you been drinking Grandpa's pecan whiskey, sis?" Conway asked.

She ignored her brother's sarcastic joke.

"I see your ankle sprain has miraculously healed." Johnny's gaze drilled Dixie.

"You think it's food poisoning?" Buck Owens asked in his usual quiet voice.

"No. I drank too much coffee today and skipped supper." Growing up the youngest in the pack she'd learned from her brothers how to talk her way out of trouble.

Johnny pointed to the floor. "If all you've had to drink is coffee, what are those white chunks on my boots?"

Merle saved her from having to answer. "Here's the mop," he said, shoving the handle at Dixie.

Her stomach lurched and she tossed the mop back at her brother and fled to the bathroom, slamming the door behind her. Dixie offered up the remainder of her lunch to the porcelain god, then once her stomach settled, she sank to the floor between the toilet and the pedestal sink, too exhausted to face her brothers.

At only five weeks pregnant the morning sickness was hitting her hard. Amazing that her mother had gone through this so many times—by choice. Dixie holed up in the bathroom until the uproar in the hallway faded. Until Buck quit asking if she was okay. Until the shadows of her brothers' boots disappeared from beneath the door. Then she brushed her teeth and gargled with mouthwash. When she emerged from the bathroom, the hallway was empty save for Johnny sitting at the top of the stairs.

Through thick and thin her eldest brother had always been there for her. Dixie sank down next to him on the step. "I'm twenty-three, Johnny. A grown woman. I can take care of myself."

The hurt look in his eyes cut through her. She hated disappointing him and knew the last thing he wanted was for her to follow in their mother's footsteps.

"Are you pregnant?" he asked.

"Yes." She'd hoped to keep the secret a while longer—until she decided when and how to tell Gavin.

"Who's the father?" he asked.

"I'm not ready to say."

Johnny gaped. "The guy's got a right to know he's fathered a child."

"I'll tell him." *Eventually.* When she was certain she could hold her ground with Gavin. Dixie had plans for the future and wouldn't allow anyone—including the baby's father—to interfere with them.

"Why didn't you tell me the truth this morning when I asked why you weren't going with us to the rodeo?"

"'Cause I knew you'd be mad."

Johnny shoved a hand through his hair, leaving the ends sticking up. "I taught you about birth control."

"We used a condom," she said.

"Not the one I made you put in your purse when you were sixteen, I hope."

She dropped her gaze.

"What the heck, Dixie! That condom was seven years old."

"I know. I know. What does it matter now?"

"Do you plan to keep the baby or do I need to drive you into Yuma to one of those women's clinics?"

"I'm going to keep the baby."

"You sure?"

"Positive."

"Okay then." Johnny stood. "You've got one week to tell me who the father is or I'll make a big stink."

"You better not tell anyone I'm pregnant."

"One week, sis. I'm not letting this guy shirk his responsibility to you and the baby." As soon as the front door shut behind Johnny, various bedroom doors opened.

"Quit spying!" she shouted, then fled to the barn—her private sanctuary.

Chapter 2

"I'm heading into Yuma. Anyone want to come along?" Dixie asked as she waltzed into the kitchen Wednesday afternoon. Three of her brothers—the unemployed ones—played poker.

"I'll see your five Lemonheads and raise you two." Conway pushed the candy to the center of the table.

"Stupid move, bro," Porter said.

"I'll see your two, little brother, and raise you five." Buck grinned.

"Hey, did anyone hear my question?"

Three heads swiveled in Dixie's direction and her brothers spoke in unison. "What?"

"I've got an appointment with the owner of Susie's Souvenirs in Yuma. Who wants to go with me?"

Conway gaped as if she'd left her brain upstairs in the bedroom. "We're in the middle of a poker game."

"Well, excuse me for interrupting." She grabbed her purse from the counter and stepped onto the wash porch.

"Man, she's touchy," Conway said.

"I heard that!" The smack of the screen door punctuated Dixie's shout.

Halfway to the truck Porter's voice rang out.

"Hey, Dix, wait for me!"

"If you're coming along to pry the name of the baby's father out of me, you might as well stay here," she said when he skidded to stop in front of her.

Porter's smile flipped upside down. "How'd you know?"

Dixie hopped into her 1982 red Ford truck, then cranked the engine and turned on the air conditioner. As soon as her brother shut the passenger-side door, she shifted into Reverse and backed away from the barn. Porter wasn't the brightest member of the Cash clan but Dixie had a soft spot for the brother closest to her age. "They sent you to do their dirty work because you're the youngest—"

"No, you're the baby of the family." He shook his head. "A baby having a baby. That doesn't sound good when you say it out loud."

She glanced in the rearview mirror. Buck and Conway stood on the porch arms crossed over their chests, faces sober.

"I'm not saying who the father is, so you might as well finish your poker game." She stopped the truck.

Porter checked the side mirror. "Nah. I'll go with you."

Chicken.

At the end of the dirt drive, Dixie turned onto the county road and drove west. The trip into Yuma took less than a half hour once they reached the interstate. "You could look for a job while we're in town."

"No one's hiring."

Porter was lazy. She supposed he didn't know any better. His engaging smile and puppy-dog eyes made people want to take care of him and Porter never snubbed a helping hand. "Wouldn't hurt to fill out an application," she said.

"Drop me off at the bowling alley. I'll ask if they're hiring."

And if they weren't, Porter would bowl a few games. When her brother wouldn't stop fidgeting, she asked, "What's the matter with you?"

"How come you didn't tell us you had a boyfriend?"

"I don't have a boyfriend."

His mouth sagged. "You mean, you just…you know…"

"Yes, Porter. I had sex."

"But you've never dated anyone, except for that guy in the high-school band."

"Rick McKee? He wasn't my boyfriend." But Rick had taken her virginity in the backseat of his car the night of the junior prom—an unremarkable experience.

"You're not supposed to have sex with a guy if he's not your boyfriend."

"I bet you've had sex with a girl and you never saw the girl afterward."

"It's different for guys."

"You're such a chauvinist."

"Jeez, are all pregnant women as crabby as you?"

"Sorry." Dixie had kept her emotions bottled up inside her since she'd discovered she was pregnant. If only her grandmother were alive to help her navigate this uncertain time. "I'm scared, Porter."

He turned down the radio. "Scared of what?"

"Of losing my dream."

"What dream?"

"Never mind." She rarely shared her plans for the future with her brothers—mostly because they wouldn't understand. Dixie's dream was really her grandmother's dream. When Ada Cash passed away, Dixie had stood before her open casket and vowed to find a way to make her grandmother's family soap recipes famous.

"I used to have a dream," Porter said.

"What was it?"

"I wanted to be a monster truck driver."

Dixie's dream had a better chance of becoming a reality than her brother's.

"Doesn't matter anymore," he said.

But dreams did matter. Grandma Ada had wanted to sell her soaps to Colgate but Grandpa Ely had insisted she was "plum off her rocker" if she believed a big corporation would buy a few fancy bars of soap from a nobody. Dixie was determined that even in death her grandmother would not remain a *nobody*.

"Why monster truck driving?" she asked.

"Can you keep a secret?"

"Of course." None of her brothers had been able to get her to confess the name of her baby's father and all of them had given it their best shot.

"Remember back in March when I drove up to Phoenix?"

"You said you were helping a friend move into an apartment."

"I lied." Porter lowered his voice. "I went to the Phoenix Monster Truck Rally."

"Why do we have to keep it a secret?"

"Because I did something stupid."

Dixie couldn't believe how *stupid* she'd been to accompany Gavin Tucker to his motel room. If Veronica hadn't hounded the handsome cowboy, Gavin would have never given Dixie the time of day.

She'd had no intention of sleeping with Gavin, but when she'd awoken the following morning to find herself staring him in the eye she hadn't had the power to resist kissing him. When she'd pressed her mouth to his, he'd returned the kiss and the rest had been the stuff of her fantasies.

Porter remained silent, so Dixie prodded him. "Don't leave me hanging. What stupid thing did you do?"

"I wanted to impress a girl I'd met so I told her I was a mechanic for Bob Patton's monster trucks. She asked me why I was in the stands and not with the crew."

"So you snuck your way into the pit area," Dixie said.

"Yeah. Everything was cool until one of the mechanics handed me a wrench and told me to tighten a screw or bolt—I can't remember which—on one of the trucks. I stood there like a dope."

Dixie winced. "What did they do when they figured out you were an imposter?"

"They flung mud balls at me. The TV cameras were playing the video on the JumboTron. The announcer told the fans that this is what happens to boys when they pretend to be monster truck drivers."

Ouch. Wanting to lighten the mood, Dixie changed the subject. "What's everyone doing this weekend?"

"Conway said he's driving to Tucson to visit an ex-girlfriend and Buck and Willie might go with him. Me, Merle and Johnny are heading up to the Growler Stampede."

Dixie wondered if Gavin would be at the stampede. Didn't matter. She'd track him down once she decided how she'd support herself and the baby, while at the same time launch her internet business. She wasn't afraid to tell Gavin he was going to be a father, but she worried what role he'd insist on playing in their baby's life and the possibility that he'd interfere with her entrepreneurial plans.

If Gavin had been a normal cowboy, she'd take for granted he'd *try* to do right by her. He'd *try* to send her money for the baby. He'd *try* to visit between rodeos. Cowboys *tried* at everything but usually came up short— at least the ones she'd lived with all her life. Gavin was a different breed—a soldier cowboy. She had no experience with soldiers, but she didn't need a high IQ to understand that to be successful in the military a soldier had to be dependable, courageous, loyal and unselfish. The unselfish trait worried Dixie—she didn't want or expect Gavin to change his future plans for her or the baby.

"Why are you shaking your head?" Porter asked.

"I was thinking about how to convince Susie to increase her inventory of my soaps." *Another fib.* They sure slid off her tongue easily these days.

"Don't know why you're gung ho on selling soap." Porter pointed to her stomach. "When you marry the father, you won't have time to make soap."

Not if Dixie could help it. She tried to summon a smidgeon of anger toward Gavin. For what—being handsome? Charming? Behaving like a gentleman? Shoot, he hadn't forced her to get into his truck and drive off with him. No one had put a gun to her head and insisted she shuck her clothes at the Shady Rest Motel. She was the sole proprietor of the mess she was in.

Regardless, she wanted nothing to do with marrying a martyr. The fact that Gavin had apologized profusely after they'd made love was proof he'd regretted the act. Why suffer through the pomp and circumstance of a wedding ceremony when a few months down the road they'd end up divorced—a divorce she'd have to file for because Gavin was too principled to initiate the split.

"Look out!"

Dixie slammed on the brakes. If not for Porter's warning she'd have blown through the four-way stop on the outskirts of Yuma.

"Didn't realize being pregnant impaired a woman's driving."

"Ha. Ha." Dixie drove six more miles, then swung into the Desert Lanes Bowling Alley. "I'll text you when I leave Susie's," she said.

"Take your time." Porter nodded to a bright yellow Mustang parked near the entrance. "Hailey's working. She lets me bowl for free."

If only Dixie had her brother's charisma she might have talked the online marketing company into setting up her business website for free. When she reached Yuma's historic Main Street, she parked in the lot behind Susie's Souvenirs.

"Susie? It's Dixie," she hollered, stepping into the shop.

"Be right down!" Sandals clacked against the stairs that led to an apartment above the store. Susie greeted Dixie with a smile. "You look good."

"I do?"

The older woman moved closer and studied Dixie's face. "Your skin is glowing." Susie dropped her gaze to the wicker basket in Dixie's hand. "Which one made your complexion so radiant?"

She'd used the same olive soap this morning that she'd washed with the past three years and until today no one had ever used the word *radiant* to describe her.

It's because you're pregnant.

Dixie set the basket on the counter and selected the organic peppermint soap. "This is what I'm using." She held the bar beneath Susie's nose.

"That smells amazing. What's in it?"

"Sunflower, palm, coconut and peppermint oils." Along with wheat and barley grass, alfalfa, parsley and grapefruit-seed extract. "I also brought along a Christmas soap I'm experimenting with." Dixie handed Susie a star-shaped bar.

"How pretty. I love the threads of red and green that run through the soap." She sniffed. "Pine boughs, fresh fruit and spices. Very nice."

"I was hoping you'd consider using a display instead of leaving the soaps next to the register."

"I won't know if I have room for a stand until I finish stocking the Christmas merchandise," Susie hedged.

Dixie's soaps were available in other stores along Main Street, but Susie's Souvenirs was the most popular tourist shop in Yuma and Dixie made more money here than the other places combined. "Can you find room if I pay you a fifteen-percent commission instead of the usual ten?"

"What else did you bring?" Susie peered inside the basket.

"Eucalyptus and spearmint." Dixie lined up the soaps on the counter. "Lemongrass. Desert Sage. Oats and Spices." Each bar was a unique shape wrapped in colored tissue

paper and a frilly ribbon with a hand-stamped label—
Dixie's Desert Delights, Inc. $6.99.

"I'll find room for a display."

"Thanks, Susie. I put extra business cards at the bottom of the basket."

"I'll give you a jingle when inventory gets low."

Dixie could only hope she'd sell all forty bars before Christmas.

Where the hell was he?

Gavin stood in the dark shivering. He knew he was in the desert, because coarse grains of sand pricked his feet. But where in the desert? And what had happened to his weapons? He wore nothing but his sweat-soaked fatigues. The booming sound of a rocket-propelled grenade sent him running, his lungs burning with each gasp of air.

The target exploded in the distance and streaks of bright light lit up the night sky.

Nate! Nate, where are you?

Gavin glanced over his shoulder and a second explosion illuminated the darkness. In that instant of clarity Gavin spotted Nate a hundred yards behind him.

Run, Nate! Catch up!

Something wasn't right—Nate wasn't moving. Gavin turned back, determined to reach his friend, but with each step, his feet sank deeper into the ground as if the desert had turned into an ocean of quicksand.

Nate reached out his hand for help and time passed at a crawl as Gavin pressed forward, muscles burning, sweat stinging his eyes. Fifty yards from Nate another explosion rent the air and suddenly half of Nate disappeared. Gavin stared in horror. Where were Nate's legs?

A thud hit the ground by Gavin's combat boot. He looked down. Half buried in the sand was Nate's leg.

Gavin woke with a start and bolted from the motel bed. He stumbled into the bathroom, ran the cold tap and splashed his face, choking on the water that hit the back of his throat.

Damn it.

He lowered the toilet cover and sat with his head in his hands. He hadn't had a nightmare like this in weeks. Why now?

Maybe he was pushing himself too hard.

Or maybe you're not pushing yourself hard enough.

Whatever the reasons behind his recurring nightmares, as long as Gavin ignored them they'd eventually go away.

"Another tough night for Gavin Tucker," the announcer said at the Growler Stampede Rodeo in Growler, Arizona.

Gavin picked himself up and dusted off his jeans, then waved his hat at the crowd as he jogged out of the arena. *Dumb bronc.* Thunder Rolls had tossed him on his head as soon as he'd cleared the gate. Ignoring the twinge in his wrist, Gavin stuffed his gloves into his gear bag.

"Better luck next time, soldier." Mitch Farley, a Colorado rancher approached.

Gavin shook hands with the retired marine. Mitch's son had been stationed with Gavin in Afghanistan. "How's Scott? Still overseas?"

"Yep. He's coming home for Christmas." Left unsaid…*if he doesn't get killed first.*

"What are you doing in Arizona?" Gavin asked.

"Drove down with a neighbor to watch his nephew

compete in bull riding." Mitch cleared his throat. "What made you decide not to reenlist?" The older man had spent twenty-five years in the military before taking over the reins of his family's cattle ranch.

Gavin didn't mind discussing his military career with fellow servicemen and women, but he didn't care to share the information with his rodeo competitors. He grabbed his gear and motioned for Mitch to walk with him. "After Nate got killed nothing was the same over there." Nate had been Gavin's best friend. They'd gone to high school together and had joined the army on a whim.

"Is it true one of the villagers you were helping planted the roadside bomb?"

"Yeah." After that day, the goodwill Gavin possessed toward the Afghan people had died a quick death. Gavin thought of the sacrifices he and Nate had made while living in the hostile region. And for what? Nate had given his life and Gavin couldn't shake the dreams that had followed him home.

"You did good work in Afghanistan, son." Mitch clasped Gavin's shoulder. "Don't let one idiot take that away from you."

"After Nate died—" Gavin shrugged off Mitch's touch. The last thing he wanted was pity "—I knew I wasn't going to be any use to the army, so I checked out."

"What about a military position stateside?"

Staying in one place wasn't an option. Keeping on the move was the only way Gavin felt as if he could breathe. "I wanted a change."

Mitch chuckled. "Getting your ass kicked by a wild bronc sure is a change."

"It'll come back to me." Gavin and Nate had competed in rodeos throughout high school and during their military leaves, but admittedly Gavin was rusty and needed a heck of a lot more practice before he'd become competitive.

"You can't rodeo forever. You got a plan B if you end up injured?"

"Not really."

"When you get ready to call one place home, come see me. I could always use a good ranch hand."

The word *home* generated an uncomfortable feeling in Gavin. Settling down was the last thing on his mind. "Nice to know there's a place to hang my hat if I need one."

"Take care." Mitch walked off.

Now what? The next rodeo on Gavin's schedule was in Chula Vista, California—a week from today. He should hit the road but a sixth sense warned him not to be in a rush to leave the Grand Canyon State. His years in the military had taught Gavin to never ignore his instincts.

He chalked up the doom-and-gloom thought to his recent nightmare. He sure in hell didn't want a repeat of that terrifying hallucination. Maybe a drink would settle his nerves and numb his brain while he listened to eight-second stories. The one thing he missed about the army was the camaraderie of fellow soldiers.

"Hey, Waters." Gavin called across the parking lot. "Where's everyone hanging out after the rodeo?"

The calf roper tossed his gear into the back of his pickup. "Mickey's. A few miles east of here."

"Thanks." Gavin got in his truck and checked his cell phone for messages. None. A short time later he parked at Mickey's. Standard cowboy bar—a dump, save for the fancy red door. Neon beer signs brightened the windows, reminding Gavin that he was hungry and thirsty.

The smell of sweat, spilled beer and cigarette smoke greeted his nostrils inside. A thirty-foot bar sans stools stretched along one wall behind which a pair of bald, tattooed bartenders filled drink orders. The rest of the place was crowded with mismatched tables and chairs.

A country-western song wailed from the jukebox as Gavin zigzagged through the maze of rowdy cowboys. "Bud Light." He tossed a five-dollar bill on the bar.

"You win or lose today?" asked the barkeep with a snake tattoo slithering up his neck.

"Lost."

"Tough draw?"

"Not really." He took his beer and strolled through the crowd listening to a country ballad of love gone wrong. Why the lyrics made him think of Dixie he had no idea. He'd regretted making love to her, even though it had been a long time since he'd been intimate with a woman. If only the taste of her bold kiss hadn't drowned out the warning voice in his head.

He'd had a hunch he was the first cowboy she'd ever had a one-night stand with. Thank God she'd had a condom in her purse, because Gavin's protection had been out in the glove compartment of his truck.

He moseyed over to a table near the dartboard where a pair of inebriated cowboys tried to hit the target.

"Hey, Kramer!"

Gavin's senses went on high alert when he recognized the gravelly voice—Johnny Cash. He tuned his ears to the conversation behind him.

"You see my ride?" Cash asked Kramer.

"Yep. Too bad you didn't win."

"Sanders drew a better bronc," Cash said. "You got a minute?"

"Sure. What's up?"

"You were at the Boot Hill Rodeo this past July, weren't you?"

"I bit the dirt on Short Fuse." Kramer chuckled. "Your sister rode a bull in that rodeo, didn't she?"

Gavin tensed.

"Speaking of my sister," Cash said. "Were you at the Spittoon that night after the rodeo?"

"Sure was."

"You happen to see who my sister left the bar with?"

"If I did, I can't remember." Then Kramer asked, "Wasn't Dixie supposed to ride in Piney Gorge this month?"

"Yeah. She withdrew."

"Your sister plan to do any more bull ridin' in the future?"

"Not for nine months."

The blood drained from Gavin's head and pooled in his stomach, making him nauseous.

Kramer lowered his voice. "You sayin' some guy knocked her up after the rodeo?"

"Yep, that's what I'm saying. I'd like to find the jerk and wring his neck."

"If I hear any rumors, I'll be in touch," Kramer said.

"Thanks. And, Kramer?"

"Yeah?"

"Keep this to yourself."

"Sure. No problem." Kramer headed to the bar and Cash followed.

Gavin didn't give himself time to think; he bolted for the door. Once outside, he cut across the parking lot, hopped into his truck and headed south. After he'd driven an hour he could no longer suppress his anxiety.

He pulled off the road, turned on the flashers then left the truck and started walking.

The longer he walked the lower the sky fell and the higher the ground raised, compressing him until each breath felt like he was sucking air through a straw.

Damn his frickin' intuition. If he'd ignored his sixth sense, he'd have been on the road to Chula Vista by now and been none the wiser about Dixie's condition.

Chapter 3

Gavin pulled up to a pump at the Chevron station in Stagecoach. The sudden downpour he'd driven through ten miles back had left behind a rainbow in the sky, and the smell of steamy pavement and wet clay permeated the air. He filled the gas tank, then entered the convenience store.

"Howdy." A slim man with gray whiskers and a toothy smile greeted Gavin. "Passin' through or visitin'?"

"Passing through." Gavin hoped. "I'm looking for the Cash place."

"Was good people... Ely and Ada Cash. Solid, Christian folk." The old man shook his head, dislodging a hank of oiled hair from the top of his noggin. The strand fell across one eye. "A shame, you know."

"What's that?"

"Ely and Ada's only child, Aimee, couldn't keep her legs crossed long enough to find a decent man."

Gavin had heard the gossip on the circuit—that all six Cash brothers had different fathers. He sensed the old man didn't get many customers each day and if he didn't cut to the chase he'd be stuck listening to back-in-the-old-days stories. "There an address for the Cash property?"

The clerk shook his head. "Go back through town and turn right on Route 10. 'Bout eight miles down the road you'll run into the pecan farm."

"Any landmark I should look for?"

"There's a billboard advertisin' Vera's Lounge fer Gentlemen." The geezer chuckled. "Vera ain't runnin' her bawdy house no more, but Peaches, the girl on the billboard, still gives private dances if yer interested."

Gavin wasn't. "Thanks for the directions." He made it to the door before the clerk's voice stopped him. "Don't know what business ya got with the brothers, but don't cross 'em. They'll bring ya down like a pack o' wolves."

Although Gavin's *business* was with Dixie not her brothers, the warning reminded him to watch his back. With each passing mile along Route 10, his confidence slipped. He'd had ample time to mull over the news that Dixie was pregnant. Like a scratched record, his mind replayed the morning-after minutes in the motel room. Dixie wouldn't make eye contact when he'd apologized for letting things get out of hand. He'd guessed that she'd been embarrassed about their lovemaking—now he wasn't sure.

What if Dixie had been in a relationship with another man and they'd had a fight? Then she'd gone to Gavin's motel room and when she woke the next morning, she realized she'd cheated on her partner. Guilty feelings would explain Dixie's withdrawal and the fact that she'd never contacted him about her pregnancy—because her boyfriend was the father of her baby, not Gavin. He sure in hell hoped that was the case. In any event, he wouldn't rest easy until he knew the truth.

And if the baby's yours...

Gavin shoved the thought from his mind when he spotted the dilapidated billboard in the distance. The sun had faded the sign, but the outline of Peaches's voluptuous curves remained visible. He turned onto a dirt road. Rows of pecan trees for as far as the eye could see escorted him through the property. After a quarter mile, a whitewashed farmhouse came into view. Dixie's truck sat parked out front.

The two-story home was in need of a little TLC. The black shutters could use a coat of paint. The front porch sagged at one end and a handful of spindles were missing from the railing. A swing hung at an odd angle from the overhang and a collection of empty flowerpots sat near the screen door.

Gavin parked next to Dixie's truck and turned off the ignition. He waited for a barking dog to announce his presence but the farm remained eerily quiet. A gray weathered barn with a tin roof sat across the drive. There was no sign of harvesting equipment and Gavin questioned whether the pecan farm was in production anymore. He climbed the porch steps but before he raised his fist to knock, a loud bang echoed through the air. Switching directions he walked to the barn where he found Dixie.

The first sight of her sent an unwelcome spark of excitement through Gavin. There was nothing sexy about Dixie's attire—jeans, a faded oversize Arizona Cardinals T-shirt and rubber gloves that went up to her elbows. She sifted through a large metal tray filled with river rock, then walked to the rear of the barn and dropped a handful of stones into a wooden cask mounted on a brick base. Next, she retrieved several bunches of straw, which she added to the barrel, and she scooped a small bucketful of ash from an old-fashioned potbelly stove with a chimney pipe that vented out the side of the barn.

"What are you making?"

A squawk erupted from her mouth. "Gavin."

His name floated toward him in a breathless whisper. He couldn't recall ever feeling this off balance around a woman. Dixie wasn't a flashy girl with showy attributes, but the aura of warmth that surrounded her attracted Gavin. Her average looks, compassionate blue eyes and long brown hair made him feel safe, encouraging him to let his guard down. The night he'd spent in the motel with her he'd almost forgotten he'd been a soldier. Forgotten where he'd been and what he'd seen.

Forgotten he was broken inside.

He motioned to the workbench crowded with scales, liquid-filled jugs, colored glass bottles that resembled jars from an ancient apothecary shop, potted herbs and tin molds. "Are you and your brothers running a meth lab out of your barn?"

She didn't laugh. "Nothing as exciting as drug-trafficking. I'm making soap."

Soap?

Dixie dumped the remaining ash into the cask. "What are you doing here?" He gave her credit for not beating around the bush.

"Verifying information I heard in a bar."

"Oh?"

"Johnny told a friend you were pregnant." He studied Dixie, searching for the slightest sign he'd hit upon the truth.

Nonchalantly she returned to the workbench and sifted through tin molds. "I am."

Gavin held his breath, waiting for her to confirm he was the father. When she didn't offer any details relief left him light-headed. He'd guessed right—she'd been involved with another man before she'd slept with Gavin. On the heels of relief came an unsettling feeling— disappointment. He was far from old-fashioned but he'd never pegged Dixie as the kind of woman who'd cheat on her man.

For his own peace of mind, he wanted confirmation. "I'm not the father, am I?"

A stare down ensued. Dixie balked first—rubbing her fingers over her eyes.

Tears? "I didn't know lady bull riders cried." His attempt at humor failed miserably. Unaccustomed to dealing with female emotions Gavin gently tugged a lock of her hair, but Dixie kept her watery gaze averted.

"I'm sorry."

Gavin tensed. "'Sorry' meaning… I *am* the father?"

She nodded.

The truth hit him like a fist in the gut. "We used a condom."

"I know," she said, a disgusted note in her voice. "My brother gave me that condom when I was sixteen years old before I went on my first date."

"How old are you now?"

"Twenty-three."

Gavin stifled a groan.

"How was I supposed to know it wouldn't be any good?" She peeled off her gloves and jabbed a finger at Gavin's chest. "You're the guy. You should have had protection in your wallet."

Accepting his share of the blame, he asked, "When did you plan to tell me?"

"Eventually."

"Eventually when?"

"When I was good and ready."

He doubted she'd have been *good and ready* anytime soon. Conflicting emotions raged inside him but beneath the chaos, he was pleased to learn Dixie wasn't another Veronica.

Dixie turned her back to Gavin and scooped more ash into the bucket. This was not how she'd imagined breaking the news to Gavin that he was about to become a father. She peeked at him beneath her lashes. He appeared to be taking the news well. Maybe a little too well—then again when an army man received bad news, he soldiered on.

"What are you doing with the ash?" he asked when she dumped the contents of the bucket into the casket. He didn't want to discuss the baby—fine by her.

"I'm making lye for the soap."

"Isn't lye a dangerous chemical?"

"It is for those who don't know what they're doing." Years ago a burn on her thigh from the caustic liquid had taught Dixie the importance of taking safety precautions when working with the liquid.

"Will breathing that stuff hurt the baby?"

Maybe the baby did matter to him. "I'm careful not to breathe any fumes." The doors at both ends of the barn were open and two industrial-size fans circulated the air.

"You shouldn't make soap until after the baby's born."

This is why she'd wanted to hold off telling Gavin

about her pregnancy. She didn't want him questioning her every move or believing he had a say in what she did or didn't do. Besides, putting off marketing her soaps for nine months wasn't an option. The company she'd contracted with to create her business website charged five thousand dollars for their service—a thousand dollars less than the normal fee if she paid them in full by the end of November.

After a lengthy silence, Gavin asked, "We need to discuss what happens next."

Dixie's throat swelled with panic and she swallowed hard. She'd known from the get-go that Gavin was an honorable man and once he learned he'd fathered her baby he'd insist on doing his duty and marry her. She'd never admit as much, but making love with Gavin had been an incredible experience and she found the notion of waking up each morning in the same bed with him mighty appealing. She shook her head, clearing the X-rated vision from her mind.

Although she respected Gavin for wanting to do right by his child, he was a soldier used to controlling situations and making split-second decisions in the heat of battle. He called the shots and expected his orders to be followed. There was only one problem—Dixie answered to no one.

"Gavin—"

"Dixie—"

"You go first," she said, bracing herself for a marriage proposal.

"I'm not sure what the answer to our predicament is, but I do know that I'm not ready to marry and settle down."

Stunned by his confession, Dixie leaned against the

workbench and stared unseeingly at the scattered supplies.

"I want to do right by the baby, so I intend to help you financially."

Her face warmed with embarrassment. What an idiot she'd been to believe Gavin wanted to marry her. Shoving her bruised pride aside, she focused on the positive—he didn't want to be involved in her or the baby's life.

"I don't want to marry, either," she said, wincing at the crack in her voice. Gavin's expression softened and Dixie lifted her chin. If there was one thing she hated—it was people feeling sorry for her. She'd grown up subjected to sympathetic murmurs from teachers and neighbors who'd known about her mother's loose morals.

And look at you now...following in your mother's footsteps by having a baby out of wedlock.

No. Dixie refused to believe she was anything like her mother. When she'd slept with Gavin she'd had no intention of trapping him into marriage. If anything, her pregnancy made her more determined to become financially independent—the one goal her mother had never achieved.

"Rest assured I'm not walking away from my responsibility to the baby," he said.

Of course not. Gavin was America's hero—just not hers.

"You can count on me to help with medical expenses."

"That won't be necessary. I have health insurance." She and her brothers were covered under the same policy. The income brought in by leasing the pecan groves paid the property taxes, monthly insurance premiums, and expenses like utilities, food and the cell phone bill.

"I'll help buy whatever you need for the baby." He

nodded as if trying to convince himself of his sincerity. "Crib, high chair…diapers."

If Gavin took care of the baby supplies, Dixie could save the cash she earned from her soap sales in Yuma to pay the rest of what she owed for her website. Accepting help from Gavin would relieve some of the financial pressure, but she feared his contributions might lead him to believe he had a vote in how she raised their baby.

Feeling the strain of pretending their discussion about the baby was everyday run-of-the-mill conversation, Dixie said, "If there's nothing else you wanted…"

He reached past her, his arm brushing her shoulder. The contact sent a zap of electricity through her body. Would a simple touch from Gavin always ignite a powerful reaction in her? He grabbed a Sharpie marker and scribbled a phone number on the bench.

"Call me if you need anything." He pulled out his cell phone, then asked, "What's your number?"

Dixie hesitated. She didn't want Gavin checking up on her, but if she didn't give him the number he'd ask one of her brothers. She recited the digits, warning, "I don't always carry my phone with me."

His dark eyes drilled into her and Dixie got the uncomfortable feeling he could read her mind. "I'll leave a message on your voice mail."

A sudden urge to weep overcame her—*pregnancy hormones.* She walked to the stove and stirred the ashes. *Leave, Gavin.* When a minute passed and he hadn't spoken, she glanced over her shoulder. He was gone. On shaky legs she hurried to the barn door and caught the taillights of his truck.

Dear God, how would she keep her attraction to

Gavin from showing if he came and went as he pleased in her life?

She glanced at his phone number, startled by the stack of twenty-dollar bills resting on the worktable.

Gavin's first child-support payment.

Gavin made it as far as the end of the drive on Dixie's property before hitting the brakes. Three pickups pulled onto the one-lane dirt road. The Cash brothers had returned from the rodeo in Growler.

Johnny drove the first truck and kept on coming, stopping inches from Gavin's bumper. He made no move to back up, which meant Gavin had to back down. Keeping his gaze on the rearview mirror, he shifted into Reverse and pressed the gas pedal. Once he reached the farmhouse he shut off his truck. The Cash brothers circled their vehicles like a wagon train.

Gavin's senses were on high alert as he stepped from the truck. He and the brothers faced off. A sweat broke out across his brow. The cotton material beneath his armpits dampened and his blood pumped through his veins like a white-water rapid.

"What's going on?"

Dixie's voice penetrated Gavin's military fog and the buzzing in his ears weakened as she marched across the yard, arms swinging.

"What's Tucker doing here?" Johnny asked.

Gavin held his tongue, deferring to Dixie to inform her siblings that he'd fathered her baby.

"He's interested in my soaps," she said.

Did she really think her brothers would buy the lie?

Johnny moved closer, crowding Gavin's personal space.

One...two...three...

"Since you drove all this way to check out my sister's soaps, the least we can do is invite you to supper."

Four...five...

Johnny stepped back and Gavin sucked in a deep breath, the lungful of oxygen easing his anxiety. He glanced at Dixie. Her eyes pleaded for him to leave. "I'll stay."

"Willie, grab some beers." Johnny nodded to the porch. "Take a load off, Tucker."

An hour later, Merle took the half-empty beer bottle from Gavin and handed him a fresh one. "For a soldier, you drink like a sissy," he said.

Gavin wasn't going to be bullied into getting drunk so he'd spill his guts about his relationship—whatever it was—with their baby sister. He checked his watch—5:00 p.m. and no one had fired up the grill. He set aside his beer and stood. "I need to hit the road." A beefy hand on his shoulder pushed him down on the porch step.

"Dixie, when are the burgers gonna be ready for the grill?" Johnny called.

The screen door smacked against the house and Dixie shoved a platter of raw meat at Johnny. "Quit yelling." She whapped his chest with a spatula then retreated inside the house.

Porter appeared with a sack of charcoal and dumped the entire bag into the belly of the large Weber grill. He then stuck his hand through a hole in the latticework covering the lower half of the porch and pulled out a large can of lighter fluid. After soaking the briquettes, he tossed a lighted match into the cooker. A fireball shot into the air.

"Hey, Tucker," Merle said. "Why'd you leave the army?"

"After my buddy Nate Parker died I didn't want anything to do with the military." Following Nate's death Gavin had been forced to attend several sessions with a shrink. He'd decided if there was any hope of putting his time in Afghanistan behind him he had to walk away from everything associated with the military.

Johnny spoke. "Never knew you and Parker were friends."

"Parker's story hit all the TV stations throughout the state," Merle said. "It'd been a while since Arizona had lost one of its own."

"We were up in Flagstaff at a rodeo the weekend the news broke," Johnny said. "There was a moment of silence for Parker."

"Nate would have appreciated that."

"You should have stuck to soldiering, Tucker." Willie snickered. "You suck at bareback riding."

"Rodeo suits me fine."

"I'm sorry about Parker," Buck chimed in.

Gavin missed the good old days when he and Nate had traveled the circuit together. As the only child of a single mother, Gavin thought of his army buddy as a brother. "Nate was a damned good soldier. He didn't deserve to die." Didn't deserve to have his body blown into pieces.

Merle went inside, then returned a minute later with a guitar. He played "Song for the Dead" by Randy Newman—a tribute to a fallen solider. Merle's baritone voice was easy on the ears and Gavin's thoughts drifted to the good times he'd shared with his childhood friend. When the song ended, he said, "That was nice. Thanks."

Johnny motioned for Gavin to follow him to the cooker. "What's going on between you and my sister?"

Gavin suspected the eldest Cash brother believed he'd fathered his sister's baby. "We're just…friends."

The look in Johnny's eyes called Gavin a liar. "Where's your home these days?"

"Nowhere in particular. I'm not itching to put down roots."

"We all—" Johnny nodded to his brothers on the porch "—grew up hearing people call our mother a tramp, a slut and a gold digger."

Gavin knew where Johnny was heading with this speech.

"Dixie's not like our mother. She doesn't deserve being called names."

"I've never believed Dixie was anything but a nice girl."

"Good. 'Cause I better not hear one bad word about her on the circuit."

"Mind if I ask you a question?" Johnny had piqued Gavin's interest about the Cash family.

"Fire away."

"Is it true you and your siblings all have different fathers?"

"Only Dixie and I share the same father."

"Do your brothers keep in touch with their fathers?"

"Nope. What about your family?"

"I'm an only child. My mother lives in Phoenix and works for the parks and recreation department."

"I can't imagine growing up an only child."

"No fights for the bathroom."

The joke fell flat. Shoot, the soldiers in Gavin's army unit had thought he was a funny guy.

"You plan to make rodeo a career?" Johnny asked.

"For the time being."

"Willie's right—you stink at rodeo."

"You're not so great, either." Gavin changed the subject. "How long has Dixie been making homemade soap?"

"Since she was ten or eleven. Dixie sells the bars in tourist shops in Yuma." Johnny lowered his voice. "Between you and me…she's got this harebrained idea she can sell our grandmother's soap online."

Gavin was impressed with Dixie's ingenuity but worried with the baby coming that now wasn't the best time to start up a new business.

A movement near the porch caught Gavin's attention. Dixie spread a plastic cloth over a picnic table in the yard. She made several trips in and out of the house for plates, glasses, condiments, buns, and pitchers of lemonade and iced tea. Gavin was astonished that none of her brothers offered to help. Instead, the men sat on their backsides, jawing. A newborn would bring added stress to Dixie's life—a life already busy with soap-making, starting a new business and catering to six grown men.

You're no better than the Cash brothers—you're walking away from Dixie.

"Burgers are done!" Johnny shouted.

The brothers raced to the picnic table and Dixie motioned for Gavin to sit at the opposite end from her. He pulled out his chair and there resting on the seat was the cash he'd left Dixie in the barn. He glanced down the table and her steely-eyed glare told him exactly what he could do with his money.

Shove it up his you-know-what.

Chapter 4

Not again.

Gavin halted in his tracks when he caught sight of Conway and Willie Cash jawing with the cowboys near the bull chutes. The San Carlos Roundup Rodeo took place the first weekend in September—two weeks after he'd learned about Dixie's pregnancy—and darned if he hadn't run into one or more Cash brothers at the events he'd competed in. He presumed the men concluded that he'd knocked up their baby sister and weren't letting him out of their sight.

Too bad Gavin couldn't blame his dismal performances on the constant scrutiny. Instead, impending fatherhood disrupted his focus. Dixie was close to eight weeks pregnant and thoughts of her and the baby wandered through his mind 24/7. How was Dixie feeling—did she have any food cravings? Had she gained weight?

What about morning sickness—did she suffer from that? The questions hammered his brain nonstop making him irritable and edgy.

Ignoring Dixie's siblings, Gavin focused on the bronc he'd drawn for today's competition. Jigsaw had a proven track record of bucking off experienced riders. The rodeo announcer introduced the cowboys competing in the bareback event, offering stats on the better athletes. Gavin was described as the former soldier turned cowboy, which drew the loudest applause. He was humbled by the fans' heartfelt appreciation for his service to their country. Once each weekend he felt like a hero even though he was the furthest thing from a Caped Crusader.

"Let's see if Tucker can end his losing streak," the announcer said.

Gavin climbed the chute rails and eased onto Jigsaw's back. *Keep your balance.* An image of Dixie collecting ash from the potbelly stove in the barn flashed before his eyes.

Stay focused.

Fearing Dixie would disrupt his thoughts again, Gavin ignored his chute routine and nodded to the gate man. The door swung open, and Jigsaw demonstrated his superiority in the sport. The bronc's rump twisted in the middle of a buck. Gavin lost his rhythm and his spurring became choppy. Then Jigsaw spun in a tight circle and Gavin was history. He sailed through the air and landed on his belly, the hard ground knocking the wind from him. The pickup men attempted to corner the bucking horse, but Jigsaw evaded capture.

The earth beneath Gavin shook and instinctively he rolled left. Too late—Jigsaw's hoof grazed his shoulder and a searing pain shot through the muscle. As if he'd made his point, the bronc trotted from the arena without an escort. Gavin struggled to his feet, his fingers tingling as numbness spread through his arm.

"Close call." Willie Cash met Gavin when he returned to the cowboy ready area.

Arm hurting like hell, Gavin wasn't in the mood to spar with the Cash brothers.

"Where's your next rodeo?" Conway asked.

"Check with your spies...they'll know where I'm riding."

The brothers spoke in unison. "What spies?"

"Your brothers. One of you always turns up wherever I ride."

Conway grinned. "Johnny said we're not to let you out of our sight."

Gavin wouldn't have a moment's peace until he did right by Dixie. He grabbed his gear, wincing at the throb in his shoulder. "See you at the next go-round." He stopped short of leaving the chute area when he heard Shannon Douglas's name over the loudspeakers.

"Folks, we got a special treat tonight before we kick off the men's bull riding competition. For those of you who haven't heard, Shannon Douglas from Stagecoach, Arizona, has been riding bulls since high school. She competed in three Five Star Rodeo events this past summer and earned a sponsorship from Wrangler."

The JumboTron flashed images of Shannon at the rodeos in Canyon City, Boot Hill and Piney Gorge. Gavin moved closer to the cowgirl's chute and watched her wrap the bull rope around her hand.

"Shannon's about to tangle with Persnickety, a bull from the famed Red River Ranch in Oklahoma."

The chute door opened and Persnickety launched himself into the arena. Shannon's compact body undulated with the bull's explosive bucks and sharp spins. Gavin glanced at the JumboTron…5…4…3…

Persnickety reared and Shannon lost her seat, sliding off the back of the bull. As soon as she landed on the ground she scrambled to her feet and ran for the rails.

"Too bad, folks. I thought Shannon might best Persnickety but not today!"

Gavin turned to leave when he heard his name called. Shannon jogged toward him.

"You almost had that bull," Gavin said.

"I'll get him next time." She sucked in a deep breath. "I haven't been back to Stagecoach in over a month. How's Dixie feeling?"

Gavin supposed Dixie had told Shannon about her pregnancy when she'd scratched at the Piney Gorge Rodeo. "Fine, I guess."

"You guess? Aren't you keeping in touch with her?"

Gavin didn't care to go into detail about his and Dixie's relationship—whatever it was. *You're about to have a baby together and you can't define your relationship?* "I saw Dixie a couple of weeks ago and she looked good." More than good.

Shannon lowered her voice. "She's going to have the baby, right? Or did she…?"

Stunned, Gavin couldn't respond. Dixie having an abortion had never crossed his mind, but that didn't mean it hadn't crossed Dixie's.

"Gavin?"

"I gotta go." He left the arena and cut across the parking lot to his truck. He stowed his gear in the backseat, then started the engine and cranked the air-conditioning.

While the cab cooled, he grabbed his cell phone from the glove compartment and checked messages. Nothing.

Call her.

When Dixie had returned his money, the message had been loud and clear—don't interfere.

At first Gavin had been relieved Dixie had expected nothing from him, but the long hours of driving between rodeos had left him with too much time to think. He'd reflected on his father—a deadbeat dad who'd never been there for his son. Once Gavin had joined the military he'd lost all contact with his father and to this day didn't know his whereabouts.

Dixie had grown up without a father, too. Gavin had the power to make sure their child had a father—that is if Dixie hadn't taken matters into her own hands.

Gavin hit three on his speed dial. "Hey, Mom. Gotta minute?"

"What's wrong, honey? You never call on Saturday nights."

"I need some advice."

"Sure." She laughed. "I love telling you what to do."

There was no easy way to say it. "I got a girl pregnant."

A sigh filled his ear. "How old is she?"

"Twenty-three."

"Poor girl."

Poor girl? Dixie, the bull rider turned soap maker was not a *poor* girl.

"What are you going to do?" his mother asked.

Gavin wasn't marriage material, but how could he walk away from Dixie when he'd seen firsthand how tough it had been for his mother to raise a child on her own.

Dixie isn't alone. She has six brothers.

Admittedly his career in the military had left Gavin with rough edges, but he wasn't so sure the Cash brothers would be better role models for his son or daughter. The *uncles* would turn the kid into a hooligan.

"I offered money to buy things for the baby but she threw the cash back in my face."

"You're not marrying this girl?"

"She isn't interested in marriage."

"You mean you proposed and she said no?" When he didn't answer his mother asked, "What's scaring you, honey?"

"I'm not ready to settle down." Gavin was an emotional and mental mess. He was in no shape to be in a committed relationship. In order to function normally when he'd returned from Afghanistan he'd made sure to keep emotionally distant from the world around him. He doubted Dixie wanted to marry a man who acted as though he didn't care about anything.

After leaving the military, Gavin had promised himself no long-term commitments and raising a child was sure in heck a lasting stint. Dixie was stubborn, bossy and independent. He worried that a marriage between them would be doomed to fail.

"What's this girl's name?" Gavin's mother asked.

"Dixie."

"That's cute. Where does she live?"

"Stagecoach."

"Never heard of the place."

"It's a small town outside of Yuma. Her mother's dead and her father's out of the picture but she has six brothers."

"What do her brothers say about the situation?"

"The eldest expects me to marry Dixie and the rest have me trained in their crosshairs."

"The more I learn about Dixie and her family the more I like."

"Then you'll appreciate hearing that she rode bulls in a couple of rodeos this past summer and she makes homemade organic soap."

"Intriguing. Is she pretty?"

"Sure."

"She must be nice if you've spent time with her."

Dixie was nice. She was kind and compassionate and had been willing to help him out of a tight spot when Veronica Patriot had put a bull's-eye on his chest.

"No one can force you to marry, but whatever you decide I'm here if you need to talk."

"Thanks, Mom. Everything okay on your end?"

"Barney and I have a new neighbor."

Barney was the five-year-old bulldog Gavin had given to his mother the Christmas before he'd shipped out on his first military assignment.

"Ricardo owns a Chihuahua named Chica and we've been taking the dogs on walks together."

"Does Ricardo know your son is a former army soldier?" Sylvia Tucker was forty-four years old and very pretty, which made Gavin all the more protective of her.

"Don't go all military on me, young man. Ricardo is a gentleman and we're just friends."

Gavin heard the doorbell chime in the background.

"Keep me posted on what you and Dixie decide to do."

"Mom?"

"What?"

"I don't want to disappoint you."

"You're a good man, honey. You'll figure out what's best for everyone."

Gavin tossed the phone onto the seat. Was marriage the answer for him and Dixie? The old-fashioned way to deal with an unplanned pregnancy was a hasty wedding, but a legal document wasn't necessary for Gavin's child to use his last name or for Gavin to be involved in his or her life.

Think, man. Think.

Gavin had survived his tour in Afghanistan. Figuring his way out of this mess with Dixie should be a piece of cake.

Or not.

"Hey, Dixie, it's Susie. Could you drop off more of your soaps?"

"You sold out my supply?" Dixie set aside the utensils she'd been cleaning in the barn.

"A guy came in today and purchased every last one. Said he was putting them in goody bags for a corporate shindig."

Dixie grabbed a marker and wrote *corporate goody bags* next to Gavin's cell number. What a great promotional idea for her online business. "Did the man say where he was from?"

"Nope." Susie laughed. "I thought he was pulling my leg."

"Why's that?"

"He was dressed like a cowboy."

Cowboy? Dixie's excitement fizzled. "What did he look like?"

"Like all the others—Stetson, Wranglers, boots. He smelled nice. Hmm…maybe he wasn't a real cowboy."

"Describe his hair." Dixie's brothers wore their hair on the long side because they preferred spending money on rodeo entry fees rather than barber visits.

"Short and he was clean-shaven. He had nice teeth, too."

Gavin.

He hadn't phoned her—not that she expected him to, although part of her had hoped he'd check in with her. After her first doctor's appointment a week ago she'd considered informing him that the baby was fine, but she'd chickened out.

What did Gavin intend to prove by buying her soap inventory?

You threw his money back in his face.

"There'll be lots of tourists in town for the start of the Scarecrow Festival tomorrow," Susie said.

"I'll pack up a basket of soaps right now. See you soon." Dixie ended the call and went into the storage room at the rear of the barn. She opened a door in the floor then flipped on the light switch and descended the stairs. Instead of dank, damp earth the cellar smelled like utopia—a mixture of nature's best scents.

She remembered the adoring expression on her grandmother's face when Grandpa Ely had installed electricity in the barn. No longer had her grandmother been forced to use kerosene lamps when she'd worked late at night.

Dixie gathered the remaining twenty-seven bars and left the cellar. She didn't care for the way Gavin had wanted to make his point—that he intended to support the baby whether she wanted his help or not.

Maybe she'd acted childishly when she'd returned the cash he'd left in the barn, but he'd bruised her pride when he'd insisted he wasn't ready to marry. *Next time take his money and save yourself the aggravation.*

Dixie didn't leave a note before she drove to Yuma—all six of her brothers had left before sunup for who-knew-where and who-knew-how-long. As she drove down the dirt road, she contemplated being a single mom. Not only would she face financial struggles raising her baby but becoming pregnant had taken away her childhood dream of marrying. Eligible men did not chase after hardworking single moms, and in no way was Dixie taking a page from her mother's book—how to land a man and lose him in less than nine months.

Aimee had been a pleaser—a woman who'd gone to great lengths to make a man feel appreciated and valued. Men had preened in her presence because she'd made them feel worthy—even when they'd been unemployed or drunk. In the end, what had drawn men to Aimee had also sent them fleeing. She'd inflated a man's self-esteem to the point where he'd believed he'd risen above her and deserved a better woman. Off he'd run, leaving her high, dry and pregnant.

Dixie knew some guys wouldn't object to raising another man's child, but she refused to make a fool out of herself to attract one. Her brothers were prime examples of males expecting women to flatter them at every turn. Dixie blamed her siblings' cocky attitudes on their mother, who'd insisted at every turn that her sons were the handsomest young men in all of Arizona. However, when it came to Dixie, her mother had said, "Don't worry, child, you'll grow out of your tomboy looks."

For the most part her mother had been right—the sharp angles of Dixie's face had softened over time but she wasn't and never would be the beauty her mother had been. Combine her average looks with having a child out of wedlock and her prospects of marrying Prince Charming were slim to none.

At the end of the drive, Dixie turned left onto the rural road. She traveled less than a mile when the steering wheel locked up on her. "Damn." She wrestled the wheel, managing to guide the car onto the shoulder where she shut off the engine and set the emergency brake. She didn't know a lot about engines but guessed the truck was leaking power-steering fluid.

The weather channel had forecasted 101 for the day's high. She didn't dare risk the last of her inventory melting into a puddle of goo. She placed the basket of soaps in the shade on the floor then got out and wiggled beneath the truck to check for leaks.

Amber-colored fluid formed a puddle on the ground beneath the engine. *Wonderful. Frickin' wonderful.*

Instead of using the three hundred dollars waiting for her at Susie's shop to help pay for her website, she'd have to use the money for truck repairs.

The truck parked on the shoulder of the road near the turnoff to the Cash pecan farm looked suspiciously like the red Ford Dixie drove. Worried it might be hers, Gavin made a U-turn and parked behind the vehicle. He walked up to the passenger side and poked his head through the open window. A basket of Dixie's soaps rested on the floor.

Where was she? He shielded his eyes from the sun and looked down the road. Had she found shade beneath a scraggly bush or had she hiked back to the farm? She wasn't crazy enough to walk in hundred-degree heat while pregnant, was she?

Don't answer that.

"Dixie!"

Maybe a passing motorist had offered her a lift. Apprehension exploded into a full-blown anxiety attack as his mind invented all kinds of scenarios—none comforting. What if she passed out from heat exhaustion and lay in a ditch? Or worse, what if the person who'd given her a lift had abducted her and taken her across the border?

The fear gathered steam inside Gavin and triggered a flashback of Nate's death. Gavin's heart pounded so hard he thought the organ would burst through his chest wall. Breaking out in a sweat, he struggled to take deep breaths but only managed to wheeze. In an attempt to block out the flying body parts, Gavin closed his eyes, but the action only intensified the vision and he stopped breathing all together when an image of Dixie bound and gagged in the trunk of a strange car flashed through his mind. He opened his mouth but terror smothered his vocal chords and her name came out in a gasp. Cursing, he summoned his inner strength and shouted, "Dixie!"

"I'm right here."

Gavin spun, then stumbled in shock. He slammed his palm against his chest, jump-starting his stalled heart.

Breathe. She's okay.

"What's the matter?" Dixie took a step toward Gavin but froze when he backed up.

The relief Gavin felt that nothing evil had befallen Dixie was so acute his chest physically ached. He opened his mouth to suck in air but his lungs drew in a gasp.

"You're scaring me, Gavin."

Shit. He was scaring himself. "I'm fine." He rubbed his brow, swallowing a curse when he noticed his trembling hand.

The only explanation he could come up with for his over-the-top reaction was that he cared about Dixie more than he'd believed.

She's pregnant with your baby—it's natural to be concerned about her. Worry was fine but anything more was out of the question—for her sake and his.

Feeling as if his insides had been sliced open with a hunting knife, Gavin pulled himself together and studied Dixie's flushed face and perspiring brow. Sweat stains marked her T-shirt and the strands of hair that escaped her ponytail stuck to her damp face and neck. "What happened to the truck?"

"It's leaking power-steering fluid. I was under the truck checking the engine when you drove up."

"You have no business crawling on the ground in your condition. What if another vehicle had rear-ended the truck? You could have been killed." He spread his arms wide. "And why are you out in this heat? You should be at home resting in front of a fan."

Dixie wiped her brow, the gesture propelling Gavin in action. Taking her arm he escorted her to his truck. After starting the engine, he directed the air-conditioning vents toward her face then handed her a water bottle from the cooler in the backseat. "Drink."

"Yes, sir." Dixie guzzled the water. "Would you please fetch the basket from the truck? I don't want the soaps to melt."

Gavin did Dixie's bidding, setting the basket on the backseat.

"I've got a bone to pick with you," she said after Gavin got into the truck.

"Pick away." Gavin didn't think—he just did it—and brushed a strand of sweaty hair off her cheek. He swore he heard her sigh but it must have been his imagination, because her eyes flashed with anger.

"What point did you hope to make by buying every last one of my soaps from Susie's Souvenirs?"

"She told you?"

"Susie said a cowboy purchased them for corporate goody bags." Dixie quirked an eyebrow. "Unless I'm plum dumb, rodeos don't qualify as corporate events and cowboys don't care to shower with lavender-oatmeal soap."

"You wouldn't take my money, so you left me no choice."

She crossed her arms and tapped the toe of her shoe on the ground.

"We'd better figure this out right now, Dixie, because I'm not going to play the money game with you. You're carrying my child and I have an obligation to support—"

"I'm not an obligation!"

Bad choice of words. Gavin reined in his temper. In a neutral voice he asked, "Where were you headed before your truck broke down?"

"Yuma. The Scarecrow Festival kicks off tomorrow and I was taking Susie the rest of my supply." She leaned over the seat and grabbed the shopping bag filled with the soaps Gavin had purchased from Susie's store. "Instead, I'll return these."

After checking the mirrors he pulled onto the road. When they reached Stagecoach, he asked, "Would you like to stop for a bite to eat before driving the rest of the way into Yuma?"

"No, thanks."

Gavin turned on a country music station and focused on the lyrics of the song in an effort to cleanse his memory of the terror he'd experienced a short while ago. When he felt close to normal he glanced across the seat, expecting to find Dixie snoozing. Instead, she gazed out the window in a trancelike state.

"I went to my first doctor's appointment a few days ago." She kept her eyes averted. "They did blood tests and everything checked out fine."

His fear that Dixie might have changed her mind about having the baby died a quick death. "You're eight weeks now?"

"About."

"Did the doctors give you a due date?"

"March 24, but she said first babies are usually late."

March twenty-fourth. Gavin could barely think ahead to his next rodeo never mind the birth of his child. In the military he'd kept his thoughts in the present and had never jinxed himself by contemplating the future. Too many guys made plans then ended up wounded or dead.

"Gavin?"

"Yeah?"

"If you really want to help support the baby, then you can loan me a thousand dollars."

The amount didn't faze Gavin—he had a decent-size savings account. "Your insurance didn't cover the cost of the doctor's visit?"

"I don't need the money for bills. I need cash to pay the marketing company that's designing my website."

"They're charging you a thousand dollars?"

"Five thousand. I saved two grand on my own, then Shannon Douglas offered to pay me a thousand dollars per rodeo to compete in bull riding events this past summer. I would have had five grand by now but when

I discovered I was pregnant I withdrew from the Piney Gorge Rodeo in August."

Dixie had taken a heck of a chance for a measly two thousand dollars. Her recklessness worried Gavin. What kind of a mother would she be if she had no qualms about risking life and limb for a few bucks?

"I'd pay you back a little at a time," she said.

"If I become an investor in your company does that mean I have a vote in your business's practices?"

She stiffened. "Absolutely not. I make all the decisions. Your money would be a loan not an investment."

"Is now the right time to be starting a new business?"

"Why not? There's no stopping the baby from coming."

"Exactly. The baby should be your main focus, not selling soap."

"You expect me to park my butt in a chair and do nothing but read magazines and drink lemonade all day?"

Yes. "No, but slaving over hot soap molds and working with dangerous chemicals isn't good for the baby." *Or you.*

She snorted. "Now I understand why you get along with my brothers—you're a chauvinist."

"Am not. I think it's great that you have aspirations to start your own company."

"But?"

"It would be best if you waited until a few years after the baby's born."

"A few years?"

"Three or four. Once the kid's in school—"

"How interesting that I have to sacrifice my plans to care for the child, while you do as you please."

Gavin opened his mouth to object but couldn't think of a damn thing to say in his defense.

"Whether you approve or not, I intend to work while I'm pregnant and continue working after the baby's here."

Dixie wasn't backing down and Gavin reluctantly admired her spunk. "Okay. I'll give you the thousand dollars."

"You'll *loan* me the money. I'm paying you back—with interest."

Investing in a soap company wasn't the way Gavin pictured supporting his child, but if it got the job done, who was he to complain?

Chapter 5

"Your truck's gone," Gavin said, waking Dixie from her nap in the front seat. After they'd eaten at a diner outside of Yuma, she'd slept the rest of the way to Stagecoach.

"One of my brothers probably towed the truck to the farm—" Dixie yawned "—when they got home from the rodeo."

Hair mussed and eyes swollen from sleep, she looked like a pixie. An image of a little girl with brown pigtails popped into Gavin's mind and he wondered if Dixie was carrying his daughter—not that he had a preference regarding the child's sex.

"Is the farm in production anymore?"

"Yes, but after my grandparents died and my brothers began rodeoing, we leased the acreage to a company, which operates other farms in the area."

"How long is your contract with the company?" Gavin asked.

"Four years."

"What will you do with the property if you can't lease the land anymore?"

"This is home and I speak for my brothers when I say that we'd never sell the land or the house."

"Small house for seven people."

"That's for sure. Sharing a bathroom with six smelly men is not fun."

Gavin pulled up to the farmhouse and surveyed the trucks parked helter-skelter in the yard. "I don't see your pickup."

"Maybe they took it to Troy Winter's place. He fixes cars for real cheap." Before Dixie had a chance to unsnap her seat belt, the porch door opened and all six Cash brothers walked outside—none of them smiling.

Gavin got out of the truck, rounded the hood and held open the passenger-side door for Dixie.

"We thought you'd been abducted when we found your Ford stranded on the side of the road," Johnny's said.

"Yeah, sis," Willie spoke up. "How come you didn't call? We left messages on your cell phone."

"Sorry." Dixie didn't sound a bit apologetic. "Gavin happened to drive by and rescued me."

"You're a regular knight in shining armor, aren't you, Tucker?" Merle said.

"Where have you been?" Johnny asked when Dixie stopped in front of the porch.

"Delivering inventory to Susie's."

Johnny opened his mouth but Dixie cut him off. "Susie sold out of my soaps and with the festival tomorrow I didn't want to miss an opportunity to make more money." She climbed the steps, pausing when the group blocked her path. "Move. I have to use the bathroom." Her brothers parted like the Red Sea.

As soon as Dixie disappeared inside the brothers switched their focus to Gavin. "We need to talk, Tucker." Johnny trotted down the steps and headed toward the barn. Feeling as if he was being led behind the woodshed for a whipping, Gavin trailed the eldest Cash sibling.

"What are your intentions toward my sister?" Johnny stopped inside the barn. He crossed his arms over his chest and leaned against the workbench.

"My intention is to do the right thing, but your sister isn't cooperating."

"You proposed to Dixie?"

"No!"

Johnny's eyes rounded.

Gavin shoved a hand through his short-cropped hair. "We're not at a point in our relationship where we're ready to discuss marriage."

"You two passed that point back in July."

"Has Dixie said anything about wanting us to marry?"

"Are you kidding? She still won't say who the baby's father is." Johnny narrowed his eyes. "But we both know who put a bun in my sister's oven."

Jeez. He didn't need to make what Gavin and Dixie shared sound dirty.

"My brothers and I are the only family Dixie has and our job is to look out for her." Johnny paced between the bench and the potbelly stove. The man was wound up tighter than a yo-yo.

"I expect you to marry my sister and make a decent woman out of her."

Gavin was used to giving orders not taking them. "This isn't the eighteen-hundreds, where women are ostracized for becoming pregnant out of wedlock."

"Our family has been talked about and ridiculed all of our lives because of our mother's wild ways. I won't allow Dixie to suffer any more than she already has."

Gavin hated that people might mistreat Dixie because she had a baby out of wedlock, but he feared the one thing guaranteed to protect her against public condemnation—marrying him—would cause her as much if not more pain and misery.

"Dixie and I need time to feel our way through the situation."

"Time is running out, Tucker. In another month she'll sport a baby bump."

The words *baby bump* echoed through Gavin's mind and his skin broke out in a cold sweat. "Dixie wants to focus on selling her soaps."

"That's another reason she needs to marry." Johnny shook his head. "She's got all these crazy business ideas running through her head. She needs a man to keep her in line."

Gavin smothered a smile behind a cough. Johnny didn't know his baby sister well if he believed Dixie would toe the line for Gavin, or any man for that matter.

"She thinks marketing her soaps on the internet will make her rich."

Gavin doubted the online business would earn enough money to improve Dixie's standard of living. That she'd protested vehemently when he'd suggested she set aside her soap-making while she raised the baby hinted that there was more behind her desire to sell suds than money. Gavin's gaze zeroed in on the phone number he'd scribbled on the workbench. Dixie had drawn a red heart around the digits. A surge of protectiveness filled him.

"It takes money to run a business," Johnny said. "Where's Dixie going to find the extra cash when she's raising a kid by herself?"

"I intend to help support the baby."

"But you won't be available to babysit so Dixie can make the soaps or fill online orders, will you?" Gavin didn't have a chance to defend himself before Johnny added, "You're not good enough to make a living at rodeo."

"So you've said."

"How do you intend to support yourself as well as a kid if you don't have a nine-to-five job?"

"I could ask you the same question," Gavin said.

"First of all, I don't have a kid on the way, and second, I don't need a job—even though I work as a seasonal cowboy for the Triple D Ranch. The income from leasing the pecan farm supports me and my siblings."

"What happens when all of you marry? Will pecans still pay the bills and take care of your wives and children?"

Johnny glared.

"I'm not ready to quit rodeoing." Rodeo was the only thing helping Gavin ease back into civilian life. The thought of giving up the sport cold turkey was enough to make him physically ill.

"What happens if you get injured and can't rodeo?"

"Then I'll find a civilian job." He hoped that didn't happen anytime soon but if it did, his experience with water conservation and reclamation projects should help him find employment with a city water district.

"You need to look for work now rather than later."

Refusing to be bullied, Gavin said, "You need to let your sister and me figure things out."

Johnny backed off. "If you hurt Dixie, you'll have me and my brothers to answer to."

Gavin wasn't afraid of a fight—he'd been through several hand-to-hand scuffles in boot camp and his tour in Afghanistan, but he didn't want the situation between him and Dixie's brothers to escalate to that level. "Consider me warned."

"Warned about what?" Dixie waltzed into the barn.

Without missing a beat, Johnny said, "Your cooking. What's for supper?"

"I don't know." Dixie crinkled her nose. "What are *you* making?"

"I can cook," Gavin interrupted the squabbling pair. "I make a mean chili."

"Yeah, right," Johnny said.

"Be happy to show you." Maybe he could win Johnny over with food.

"Okay. The meat freezer is in the dining room."

Gavin trailed Johnny from the barn, leaving Dixie with her mouth hanging open.

"This is the best chili I've ever tasted," Porter said. Grunts of agreement followed the pronouncement.

Dixie silently fumed. She sat at the picnic table in the shade and scowled at her brothers who wolfed down the famous chili recipe Gavin had once cooked for the soldiers in his unit. His attempt to win favor with her brothers appeared to be working. She sampled another spoonful of the spicy concoction and covered her mouth to prevent a moan of appreciation from escaping.

"What's in this stuff?" Conway asked.

"Ground beef, Italian sausage, peppers, tomatoes and secret spices."

"Did you write down the recipe, Dix?" Johnny slurped a heaping spoonful.

"If you like it so much, you can make Gavin's chili next time," Dixie said.

Merle slouched in his chair and rubbed his belly. "How'd you learn to cook like this, Tucker?"

"I was raised by a single mom and she taught me to cook and sew."

"You sew?" Dixie blurted.

Gavin grinned. "I can sew a button on a shirt and I iron my own clothes."

The cowboy was Martha Stewart in disguise.

"What happened to your dad?" Buck, always the last to join a conversation, spoke up.

"He didn't stick around after I was born."

"What made you choose the army?" Willie asked, bombarding Gavin with more questions.

"Couldn't make enough money at rodeo and didn't want to go to college, so the military seemed like a good option."

"What'd you do in the army?" Buck asked.

"Provided Afghan villagers with clean drinking water in an effort to win their trust."

"Did it work?" Merle asked.

"Not really." Gavin's emotionless expression caused a pang in Dixie's heart. War left soldiers with scars—some visible, most invisible. What kind of baggage did the conflict in Afghanistan leave Gavin with?

Porter pushed his bowl aside. "What's for dessert?"

"Nothing." Dixie stood. "Gavin and I need to run an

errand in town. We'll be back later." She cut across the yard and hopped into Gavin's truck.

"I guess we have an errand to run." Gavin set his spoon aside.

"Mind if I...?" Porter nodded to the chili remaining in Gavin's bowl.

"Help yourself."

"What do you think you're doing?" Dixie asked as soon as Gavin slid behind the steering wheel and started the truck.

"What are you talking about?"

"Cozying up to my brothers with delicious food and—"

"You think my chili's delicious?" He drove out of the yard.

"Never mind the chili. If you believe befriending my brothers will make me change my mind about allowing you to—"

Gavin slammed his boot on the brake and they rocked to a stop. Without warning he leaned across the front seat and kissed Dixie.

She'd dreamed of the kisses they'd shared in the motel room, but none of her fantasies had done justice to the real thing. When he pulled away, she pressed her fingers to her tingling lips. "What did you do that for?"

"You were getting too riled and that's not good for the baby."

The baby. Gavin had kissed her because he worried about the baby—not because he was attracted to her and couldn't help himself.

"I am not riled. I'm simply telling you that no one bosses me around, including my brothers."

"Where are we going?" Gavin turned onto the county road leading into Stagecoach.

"The drive-through."

"You could have had more chili."

"I'm not hungry. I want a root beer."

Gavin's gaze dropped to her stomach. "Are you experiencing cravings already?"

"No." She sighed. "I needed to get away from my brothers."

"I guess having six of them can be overwhelming."

After they'd passed the second mile marker, she asked, "Were you lonely growing up an only child?"

"Sometimes."

"Did you have a best friend?" Dixie considered Shannon Douglas her best friend. They'd hung out together in high school but after graduation Shannon had spent most of her time traveling the circuit, seeking out women's rough stock events to compete in and Dixie didn't see her friend as often as she'd like to.

"Nathan Parker was my best friend. We rodeoed in high school." Gavin chuckled. "During our first competition Nate got his front tooth knocked out and I broke my wrist."

"But the injuries didn't stop you from climbing onto another bronc."

"Nope. We rode the circuit after we graduated and when we ran out of entry-fee money we went down to the recruiter's office. Ended up going through boot camp together and got assigned to the same unit in Afghanistan."

"Is Nate still in the army?" If she hadn't been staring at Gavin's hands she would have missed the way his knuckles whitened against the wheel. A sense of forbidding spread through her. "You don't have to answer that. I have a bad habit of being nosy."

"It's all right. I told your brothers about him. Nate was killed three months before I left the military."

"I'm sorry, Gavin." She wanted to learn more about his best friend but hated for Gavin to relive painful memories, so she kept her questions to herself.

They arrived at the drive-through and a teenager stopped at Gavin's window. "What can I get you?"

"A number five meal and two large root beers." Gavin glanced at Dixie. "You made me leave before I finished my supper."

"Be ready in a jiffy." The teenager dropped off their order with the cook, then meandered over to a car crowded with teenagers and chatted.

"Do you want to sit in the truck or outside?" He nodded to a table in the shade.

"Outside."

Once they were situated at the table, Gavin spoke. "Nate was killed by a roadside bomb."

Gavin's baggage from the war. Dixie's heart ached for him.

"I've gone over and over that day in my head, but I can't figure out what I missed."

"What you *missed*? I don't understand."

"We were installing an in-ground water filtration system. The people in the village had never given us any trouble and acted as if they appreciated our efforts to provide them with clean drinking water."

Dixie closed her eyes and pictured a dusty, barren village in the middle of mountainous terrain.

"I must have overlooked a clue—a warning the villagers were plotting against us. Late one afternoon we packed up to return to base camp and Nate wanted to drive the first Humvee in line. It was his birthday so I let him. When Nate walked up to the front of the vehicle, he stepped on a trip wire and set off the explosion."

Grasping Gavin's hand, Dixie squeezed hard. Nate had been blown up and Gavin had witnessed the tragic event—there were no words of comfort for that kind of horror.

Fearing his emotions would spiral out of control if he allowed himself to recall the details of that fateful day, Gavin gazed into Dixie's teary eyes, soaking in the sympathy and comfort shining in the blue depths. Their color reminded him of the Arizona sky on a cloudless day and slowly the tightness in his chest eased.

Their order arrived and he dug into his burger, disgusted by how easily he'd opened up to Dixie. At least he'd stopped babbling before he'd shared the gory details of Nate's death.

"You haven't told anyone about the baby, have you?" Dixie asked.

"I spoke to my mother," he said. "She knows."

Dixie stiffened. "And…?"

"She supports whatever decision we make about our situation."

"There's no decision to make." Dixie slurped the last of her root beer through the straw. "I'm not forcing you to be involved in the baby's life. You can come and go as you please."

A part of Gavin wished Dixie expected more from him. He was used to soldiers relying on him to solve problems and lead the way, but he also knew the best thing for Dixie and the baby was for him to keep his distance.

"How come you haven't told your brothers I'm the father?" he asked.

"Because they'd force you to marry me."

If Dixie discovered Johnny had already guessed on his own and had begun a marriage campaign on her behalf, she'd throw a fit.

"Marriage isn't an option." She made "I do" sound akin to torture.

He thought of his mother raising him alone and working two jobs to keep a roof over their heads. Sure, his situation with Dixie was different because he intended to pay child support, but what if Dixie carried a boy? There were times during his childhood when he'd yearned for a father to throw the baseball with or to coach his little league team. A father to help him buy his first car. To give him advice on girls. He'd missed not having a male role model in his life.

The sad truth was that no matter how Gavin might want to be involved in his child's life he didn't dare become a permanent fixture. But he'd show his son or daughter that he cared by making sure their mother didn't have to struggle financially, and he'd do his best to visit his child a few times a year.

Again Gavin's thoughts turned to his mother. Dixie hadn't been the only one who'd been teased because her father hadn't married her mother. Sylvia Tucker had also been a victim of gossip—neighbors, teachers and others in the community talking behind the single mother's back.

Marriage appeared to be the only way Gavin could protect Dixie and their child from vicious, hurtful ridicule.

"I've changed my mind," he said. "We're getting married."

"That sounds like a military order not a proposal." Dixie grimaced. "Why the sudden change of heart?"

Gavin couldn't ignore his deep sense of honor, but he also feared in doing the right thing he'd be the one making all the sacrifices. "You shouldn't have to raise our child alone." In reality, though, she would raise the baby without his help because he intended to remain a safe distance from them most of the time.

"Thanks, but no thanks." Dixie stood so fast she toppled her empty root beer mug. "I have my own plans and I won't allow you or anyone else to derail them."

"How would marrying me upset your plans?" To Gavin's way of thinking, he and Dixie would go their separate ways and come together on occasion for the baby's sake—birthdays and holidays.

She opened her mouth then snapped it shut. Rubbed her brow. Shook her head. Waved a hand in the air. She looked darn cute all fired up.

"Do you find the idea of marrying me repulsive?"

"Ha-ha." Her gaze zeroed in on Gavin's mouth, raising his body temperature several degrees. "You know you ooze sex appeal."

The disgusted tone in her voice equated *oozing sex appeal* to a draining-pustule disease.

"How long do you guess a marriage between us would last? A month? Just until the baby was born? Maybe a year afterward?" Dixie asked.

"Don't sound so optimistic."

"I'm serious. You and I know that you'd never have given me the time of day if Veronica hadn't been stalking you at the Boot Hill Rodeo."

That wasn't necessarily true but he doubted arguing the point would change Dixie's view. He studied the stubborn tilt of her chin. This was one fight Gavin would not win. He changed tactics. "What if we get engaged but hold off on a wedding until we know each other better." If Dixie still didn't want to marry then Gavin could walk away believing he'd done his duty.

"I have better things to do than spend time getting to know a man."

If Gavin wasn't able to support her and their child emotionally, he'd do it financially. "I'll invest in your soap company."

"Oh, no. I don't mind you offering me a loan like you already agreed to but I don't want you having a stake in my business."

"Why not?"

"Because, then you'd have a say in how I manage things."

"I don't want to tell you what to do with your soaps, Dixie." Investing in her company would be investing in his child's future.

"You'd give me money and not tell me what to do with it?"

"Consider me a silent partner." Dixie would find out soon enough how good he was at keeping things bottled up inside him.

"If I don't accept your engagement proposal will you rescind your previous offer to loan me a thousand dollars?"

He hadn't been thinking along those lines but since Dixie jumped to that conclusion he went with it. "We get engaged and you get the thousand dollars and access to more money if you need it." He crossed his arms over his chest and waited, confident she'd cave in.

Finally, her shoulders sagged. "I'll agree to the engagement as long as you understand it doesn't mean I'm agreeing to marriage."

"Deal." Her sassy demeanor amused Gavin. Beneath all that stubbornness was a sweet soul he found more and more difficult to resist. "Shall we seal our pact with a kiss?"

She slapped her open hand against his chest. "Whoa, soldier. Just because I agreed to a trial engagement doesn't mean you can have your way with me."

"It's a simple kiss, Dixie." He didn't give her time to reject him. He swooped in, pressing his mouth to hers, deepening the embrace—because she let him. Because she tasted of hope and goodness. Eventually the need for oxygen forced him to end the kiss.

"Gavin?"

"What?"

"Let me break the news to my brothers about our engagement."

That was one duty Gavin was willing to pass off to Dixie.

Chapter 6

"Where's Gavin?" Johnny's question greeted Dixie when she entered the farmhouse kitchen. Her eldest brother sat alone at the table, nursing a beer.

"He left." As soon as they'd returned from town. Dixie assumed Gavin hadn't wanted to stay for fear she'd change her mind about their engagement.

"Did you ask him where he was headed?"

It was bad enough that her pregnancy caused occasional bouts of morning sickness, excessive sleepiness and numerous trips to the bathroom in the middle of the night—she had little energy left to contend with bossy brothers. "What Gavin does is none of my business." And he had no say in what she did.

Johnny leaned across the kitchen table. "Tucker's whereabouts sure in heck oughtta be your business, little sister."

Dixie had had enough of well-meaning men for one day. She planted her fists on her hips and ignored the squeaking sounds of the bedroom doors in the upstairs hallway. "Gavin has his life and I have mine."

"The hell you say!" Johnny's fist slammed against the table. "He's the father of your baby."

Although Dixie hadn't come right out and said Gavin was the father, she believed Johnny had guessed the first time Gavin visited the farm. "So what if he is the father?" The heat and the fact that she had a craving for chocolate when there were no sweets in the house made her irritable.

"You and Tucker are getting married pronto."

"Oh, really? Do you plan to drag me to the church by my hair?"

Voices whispered in the upstairs hallway—no doubt her brothers were holding a family conference, debating how best to defend her honor.

"After what Mom put us through, how can you consider raising your baby out of wedlock?"

Johnny had gone for the jugular. He, more than the others, understood how difficult it had been for her to be the only daughter of a promiscuous mother. "Don't get your tighty-whities twisted in a knot. Gavin proposed this afternoon."

She neglected to tell Johnny that the engagement was a sham and she had no intention of marrying Gavin. Once word spread that she and Gavin were engaged and she was expecting his baby, they'd become old news and people would move on to greener gossip pastures. She'd wait a month or two after the baby was born then end their engagement and raise the child alone—as she'd planned to do all along.

"About time you came to your senses."

Dixie opened her mouth to argue but yawned instead.

"You're tired."

"I hate it when you do that," she said.

"Do what?"

"Tell me what I'm feeling."

Johnny raised an eyebrow. "You need a nap."

Swallowing a sarcastic retort, Dixie left the kitchen, her brother stalking her through the hallway.

"When's the wedding?" he asked.

"We haven't settled on a date."

"Why not?"

Her brothers had gathered on the landing, their gazes shifting between Dixie and their big brother.

"I'm going to take a nap." She climbed the stairs and shoved her way through the human barricade. "Leave me alone." She punctuated the command with the slamming of her bedroom door at the end of the hall.

After Dixie's birth, her grandfather had expanded the linen closet into the attic, turning the space into a nursery. The room's slanted ceiling made it impossible for her brothers to stand up straight without hitting their heads, so they rarely ventured inside the room. A window air conditioner kept the cramped quarters cool. She stretched out on the twin bed and stared at the ceiling. Her throat grew thick. Her eyes burned and chest ached.

I will not cry. The silent declaration opened the floodgates and tears leaked from her eyes.

Dixie's heart had stopped beating when Gavin had insisted they marry, and for an instant, she'd believed he'd wanted to make him, her and the baby a real family.

Stupid. Stupid. Stupid.

She lifted the corner of the sheet and dabbed her tears.

Her reaction had been childish. It had only been a matter of time before Gavin insisted on marriage—for the baby's sake, not hers. She cursed herself for agreeing to a trial engagement, realizing now that she'd set herself up for more heartache and—

"Mind if I come in?"

"I'm napping, Porter."

As if the statement had been an invitation, Porter ducked inside. Shoulders hunched, he crossed the room and sat at the foot of her bed.

"Johnny said you and Gavin are engaged."

She flipped onto her side, facing the wall.

"Aren't you happy the father of your baby's going to do right by you?"

"Gavin doesn't need to marry me to send child-support checks."

"You don't want to marry him?" Porter stood and knocked his head on the ceiling. "Ouch."

"I don't love Gavin." As soon as she said the words, a voice inside her head mocked her with laughter. Dixie rolled away from the wall. "Would you marry a girl you got pregnant if you didn't love her?"

Porter's cheeks turned red. "I guess, if I had to."

Dixie rolled her eyes.

"Gavin seems like a nice guy. He fits in with the rest of us and he can cook a mean pot of chili. You could do worse than him for a husband."

"Gavin's a saint, that's for sure."

"Johnny thinks you're going to sabotage your engagement."

Darn her older brother for seeing through her. "Exactly how would I do that?"

Porter shrugged. "Johnny says you should quit selling your soap and focus on Gavin and the baby."

She refused to put aside her goals and desires for the baby. Other women had careers while raising children—she could do it, too. "Get out."

Her brother hunch-walked to the door. "Did Gavin give you an engagement ring?"

Since she had no intention of dragging out their engagement charade longer than necessary, she didn't expect Gavin to waste his money on a diamond. Still…a ring would quiet the gossipmongers. "Leave me alone."

Shaking his head Porter left her in peace. Murmurs from the hallway drifted beneath the door but Dixie ignored them and placed a hand over her tummy. She concentrated on the baby growing inside her; her final thought before drifting off to sleep was whether or not the baby would have Gavin's brown eyes.

Gavin tightened his leather riding glove then flexed his fingers. Almost two weeks had passed since he'd proposed to Dixie and they'd spoken only a few times on the phone. Aside from polite, meaningless conversation, she never brought up the baby and neither did Gavin.

He'd had plenty of time to contemplate the future during the long, solitary drives between rodeos, but he'd yet to come to terms with his impending fatherhood. That didn't bother him as much as the realization that when he was apart from Dixie he missed her.

The few times they'd spoken, he'd asked when the marketing firm would have her website up and running, but Dixie hadn't given a clear answer and had changed the subject. Maybe she believed his interest in her business was self-serving since he'd loaned her money. He should be grateful she kept him at arm's length, but he found her coolness irritating.

If anything good had come from proposing to Dixie it was that the Cash brothers had quit following him on the circuit. If only he could find his seat again and make it to eight on a bronc, he'd feel better about the future. His confidence faltering, Gavin worried that the rodeo career he'd mapped out for himself was nothing more than a pipe dream. The only consolation after each loss was that when he closed his eyes at night and saw Nate's mutilated body, he focused on Dixie and eventually the blood and gore gave way to sleep.

Dixie was an enigma—stubborn, bossy and opinionated. Yet, when he'd held her in his arms and had made love to her she'd been soft, sweet and achingly vulnerable. He clung to the memory of her sexy sighs and gentle caresses, which carried him to a peaceful place each night.

"Fans, Gavin Tucker's up next in the bareback riding competition!" the rodeo announcer said.

Pushing Dixie to the far reaches of his mind, Gavin climbed the chute rails and straddled Twinkle. He'd picked the Blythe Rodeo on a whim, hoping the added practice would prepare him for the next go-round in Bullhead City the following weekend where the pot was ten grand.

"Tucker's drawn Twinkle." The announcer chuckled. "Twinkle's got the personality of a rattler. Cowboys never know when this bronc's gonna toss 'em on their head."

Gavin had heard his competitors gossiping about the horse earlier in the day. The bronc was an arm jerker—a stout horse that bucked with a lot of power. If a cowboy managed to keep his seat on Twinkle, he'd earn big points. Gavin tested his grip, then took a deep breath and nodded to the gateman.

Twinkle leaped for freedom and it took all of Gavin's strength to hold on. He leaned back and spurred the gelding. So far so good. Twinkle switched direction every other buck, forcing Gavin's thigh muscles to work overtime as he fought to keep his balance. Sweat ran into his eyes but he ignored the sting, as he gauged the bronc's next move. Right before the buzzer sounded, Gavin's arm gave out and Twinkle sent him sailing through the air. He landed face-first on the ground and swallowed a mouthful of dirt.

As Twinkle trotted from the arena, Gavin slowly got to his feet. The first few steps were the toughest—testing his muscles, evaluating injuries. Today he'd gotten off easy—a few aches, pains and twinges.

"Looks as if Twinkle outsmarted Tucker. Better luck next time, cowboy!"

Gavin waved his hat to the crowd, then hobbled into the cowboy ready area where he collected his gear. He'd grab a hotdog from the concession stand and hit the road.

"Long time no see, soldier."

Gavin's stomach clenched at the sound of the silky voice. He turned and came face-to-face with Veronica. He'd thought he'd seen the last of her a month ago.

"Are the rumors true?"

He played dumb. "What rumors?"

"The ones sayin' you're engaged."

"Who'd you hear that from?"

"Porter Cash. He's been telling everyone he runs into that you're marrying his sister."

Gavin didn't blame the Cash brothers for wanting

folks to know Dixie was engaged before news of her pregnancy spread. "It's true. We're engaged."

The corner of Veronica's mouth curled. "You knocked her up, didn't you?"

He'd never believed in his wildest imagination that he'd get a girl pregnant by accident but thank God the girl had been Dixie and not Veronica. Gavin hoisted his gear bag onto his shoulder. "Enjoy the rest of the rodeo."

Long, red talons sank into his forearm when he attempted to pass Veronica. "If things don't work out with Dixie…"

He yanked his arm free and moseyed off.

"Dixie can't handle a man like you," she called after him.

Gavin kept walking and ignored the looks of his competitors. Forgetting about his hotdog he left the arena and zigzagged through the parking lot to his truck. While he waited for the air conditioner to cool off the interior, he checked his phone for messages. None. He shifted the truck into Drive and sped away.

Another rodeo. Another loss. Another solitary night on the road.

Except for the losing part—exactly what he'd wanted when he'd quit the army. He should feel fortunate that the woman carrying his baby had no plans to interfere with his nomadic life, instead, he resented Dixie's stand-offish attitude.

Maybe she senses a darkness inside you.

Was it possible that Dixie might be leery of getting closer to Gavin? The only way to find out was to ask Dixie if she was afraid of him and Gavin sure in heck wasn't opening that can of worms.

The next time he paid attention to the highway signs

he discovered he'd missed his turnoff and was driving south. Like a homing pigeon his instinct was to return to Dixie. He had five days until his next ride. He might as well blow them on the Cash pecan farm.

Gavin flipped on the turn signal and took the exit for Stagecoach. With each passing mile, his heart beat faster. His and Dixie's one-night stand had been a fluke, yet there was no denying they'd hit it off in bed. He wanted to make love to her again but feared the closeness would weaken his resolve to keep his distance from her and the baby.

Squirming against the snugness of his jeans, Gavin slowed the truck at the edge of town. He stopped at the only traffic light and tapped his fingers against the steering wheel. He should bring Dixie a present. Glancing along the block of storefronts he studied his options.

Food. Liquor. A gift certificate from the Bee Luv Lee Hair Salon. Did the grocery mart at the gas station sell flowers? The light turned green and he drove another block before hitting the brakes in front of the Pawn Palace. He studied the gadgets in the store window, his gaze zeroing in on a sparkly object in the corner.

A diamond ring.

Crap. He'd been so focused on doing the right thing that he'd gone about it backward. He must have hurt Dixie's feelings when he'd proposed to her without an engagement ring. He put the truck in Park and went into the store. Fifteen minutes later and a hundred-fifty bucks poorer, Gavin drove out to the pecan farm.

He didn't expect a pawn-shop ring to win him any points, but when he pulled up to the house, Gavin was contemplating ways to steal a kiss from Dixie before the evening ended. Her pickup was the only vehicle in the yard. He'd forgotten about the truck breaking down and was relieved it had been repaired. In her condition Dixie shouldn't be without reliable transportation.

He parked by the barn, figuring Dixie would be in her workshop but all the lights were off. He did an about-face and returned to the house, knocking twice on the front door. No answer. He peered through the window, but the foyer was empty. He tried the doorknob—unlocked. "Dixie!" he shouted when he stepped inside.

He checked the kitchen. Empty. Where was she? He left through the back door and hiked into the pecan grove. Maybe she was gathering herbs or flowers or whatever she used to make organic soap. He'd walked a quarter mile when his ears perked. He stopped and listened to a hollow thudlike sound, then switched directions, cutting through a row of trees before pulling up short.

Dixie stood ten yards away, throwing stones at the trunk of an ancient pecan tree. A pile of rocks rested at her feet. Throw after throw the rocks whittled a divot in the bark. If Dixie's soap business tanked she could try out for a major league baseball team—the girl's aim was dead-on.

"Strike three, he's out!" Gavin shouted.

Dixie spun, stumbling off balance. Gavin rushed forward, offering a steady hand.

"Sorry. I didn't mean to frighten you."

"What are you doing here?" She swiped angrily at the tears staining her cheeks.

"You're crying."

"I'm sweating." *Darn.* The cowboy popped in and out of Dixie's life at the most inconvenient times.

"I was passing through the area and thought I'd see how you're doing."

"Just because we're engaged doesn't give you the right to check up on me."

He raised his hands in the air. "Are you upset because I've been on the road?"

"Don't get a big head." She scrunched her nose. "You're not the reason I'm crying."

"You said you were sweating."

She sniffed, then kicked the pile of rocks she'd spent an hour gathering.

Gavin inched closer and tucked a strand of hair behind her ear. His fingers lingered against her skin and she shivered at the intimate touch. "Tell me why you're upset. I want to help," he said.

It took more effort than expected to rein in her emotions. She'd had herself a good cry, now she had to decide on the next course of action. "You can't fix this."

"Try me."

Dixie was no match for Gavin's sympathetic gaze. "Today I learned that the marketing firm I paid five thousand dollars to design my business website turned out to be a bogus company." Lord, she couldn't believe how gullible she'd been. She braced herself, expecting Gavin to implode. He didn't.

"What do you mean 'bogus company'?"

"My design agent disappeared off the face of the earth. His 800 number's been disconnected and the internet address for the company's website no longer exists."

"Have you reported this to anyone?"

"I contacted the Internet Crime Complaint Center and filed a report."

"Did you call your bank to put a hold on the check?"

"Yes, but the creep had already cashed it." Through veiled eyes she studied Gavin.

Her brothers, who were technically challenged except when it came to playing video games on their Xbox had warned her not to do business with an internet company. But Dixie had done her homework—or so she'd believed. The scam artist had posted bogus reviews for his company and must have had friends involved in the con, because the woman she'd emailed asking questions about her experience with the marketing firm had given Dixie all the right answers and a link to her newly designed website, which Dixie discovered had also disappeared from the internet. "Go ahead and say it."

"Say what?"

"I told you so." Gavin remained silent. "I'll pay back the money you loaned me." Who knew how long it would take to save up a thousand dollars? The tears that were never far from the surface these days dribbled down her cheeks and she batted away the wetness. "All I ever wanted was to make my grandmother's dream come true."

Gavin took her hand and led her to the tree she'd used for target practice. They sat on the ground and leaned their backs against the trunk. He didn't pressure her to talk and after a few minutes she relaxed. She wasn't used to sharing her fears or dreams—blame it on pregnancy hormones, but Dixie needed to vent.

"My grandmother was more of a mother to me than my own mom," she said. While Aimee Cash had chased after men, Grandma Ada had spent time teaching Dixie to keep house, cook and make the family soap recipes, which dated back six generations in France.

"Grandma Ada dreamed of selling her soaps to a big

company like Colgate, but my grandfather told her that she was foolish if she believed they'd take notice of her homemade soaps."

Gavin wiped the tears marring Dixie's cheeks. Her long, brown lashes swept down, concealing her blue eyes. The need to hug her was powerful, but he hesitated. Along with wanting to comfort Dixie came a strong urge to help fulfill her dream.

He blamed his years in the army for his need to step in and take over. He was a problem solver. A fix-it man. But it was more than instinct that prompted him to lead—he genuinely cared about Dixie. "I'll loan you the money to work with another marketing firm."

"Thanks, but no, thanks. I'm finished doing business online."

Time passed and neither spoke, and then Dixie's head bumped Gavin's shoulder and he realized she'd dozed off. The weight of her resting against him felt right. Comfortable.

Now that he understood Dixie's passion for soap-making was tied to her love for her grandmother he was determined to do everything possible to help her succeed. The sun drifted lower in the sky, casting shadows across the trees and darkening the grove. He wasn't sure how long they sat when the rumble of pickups reached his ears.

Gavin gently nudged Dixie's shoulder but she burrowed deeper against his side. Taking advantage of her sleepiness he lifted her chin and pressed his mouth to hers. Her lashes flew up and he waited for her to object—instead she curled her arms around his neck and opened her mouth wider. The tip of her tongue touched his lips and his arousal shot off the charts. He drowned in Dixie—her soft breasts rubbing against his chest, the taste of her sweet mouth, the scent of her honeysuckle shampoo. He pressed his erection against her thigh and groaned.

Dixie popped open the snaps on his shirt. When her cool fingers stroked his naked chest, Gavin lost what little control he had. He pulled the hem of her shirt from her jeans and slipped his hand beneath the cotton. Sliding his fingers across her warm skin, he cupped her breast and thumbed her pert nipple through the silky fabric of her bra.

The sound of a throat clearing brought Gavin back to his senses and he pulled away from Dixie. The Cash brothers had crashed his party. Johnny, Merle and Buck scowled. Porter grinned. Willie and Conway appeared indifferent to catching their sister lip-locked with Gavin.

Dixie continued kissing him. "We've got company," Gavin mumbled against her mouth.

She sucked in a quiet breath, then scrambled to her feet and attempted to straighten her shirt and smooth her mussed hair.

When Johnny's gaze zeroed in on the front of Gavin's unsnapped shirt, Gavin quickly fixed the problem. Shoot, it wasn't as if he and Dixie had been caught frolicking beneath the pecan tree buck naked.

"Dixie—"

"Don't say a word." Brushing the dust off her fanny, she marched past her brothers, leaving Gavin alone to face the firing squad.

"Until my sister's wearing an engagement ring, you keep your hands to yourself, Tucker," Johnny warned. The remaining Cash brothers nodded in agreement and followed their sister back to the farmhouse.

Gavin stuffed his hand in his jean pocket and touched the pawnshop ring box. Now was probably a good time to officially propose. When he got back to the house Dixie's brothers were lounging on the porch. He stopped at the bottom step. "Dixie!"

The screen door squeaked open and she stepped outside.

Gavin had hoped for a more private place to present Dixie with the ring. He climbed the steps and took her left hand in his, then slipped the silver band with diamond chips onto her finger.

Dixie frowned. "What's this?"

"An engagement ring."

The Cash brothers gathered close and examined the piece of jewelry. They twisted Dixie's hand one way then the other, lifting it toward the light. "I can't tell," Merle said. "Are those diamonds or cut glass?"

"I'll buy you a bigger diamond, if you want," Gavin said.

"Don't bother." Dixie retreated inside.

"Way to go, Romeo." Conway spat tobacco juice into the bushes, then the brothers filed into the house, leaving Gavin alone outside.

Well, hell. He'd done what Johnny had asked, hadn't he? Gavin descended the steps and walked to his truck. After the heated kiss he and Dixie had shared, they needed time to cool off—who knows how far things would have gone between them if her brothers hadn't interrupted. At least nothing had happened—this time.

If Gavin knew what was good for himself he'd make sure there was no next time.

Chapter 7

"Oh, for goodness' sake, spit it out," Dixie said. Her brothers sat at the dining-room table playing with their fries and chicken wings, while casting puzzled glances her way. She supposed they questioned why she hadn't invited Gavin for supper after he'd given her the engagement ring.

Johnny pushed his plate aside, then nodded to the band on Dixie's finger. "You haven't set a wedding date."

"So?"

"You'll be showing soon and people will wonder when you and Gavin are tying the knot," Johnny said.

"Let them wonder."

"It's not a big deal, Dixie. Pick a damn date and we'll speak to Reverend Thomas about—"

"I'll get married when—" *and if* "—I want to." Dixie ignored her brothers' gapes and continued eating. If she told the truth—that she'd hoodwinked Gavin into agreeing to an engagement on a trial-run basis, allowing him to believe she'd succumb in the end and marry him when in reality she had no intention of doing so—her brothers would carry her bound and gagged to the altar.

Buck's quiet yet firm voice broke the silence in the room. "You're wearing Gavin's ring."

Dixie's eyes stung at the reminder. That Gavin had bought her an engagement ring as an afterthought shouldn't hurt, but it did.

"A ring means you intend to marry." Johnny scowled.

"I'm twenty-three years old. Stop telling me what to do." She tossed her napkin on the table. "I'll be in the barn."

Dixie had more to worry about than booking a Saturday wedding at the local chapel. She still hadn't told her brothers she'd been scammed out of five thousand dollars by a bogus online marketing firm. Inside the barn she switched on the lights and surveyed the messy worktable covered in spools of decorative ribbon and sheets of colored tissue paper. The tears she'd struggled to hold back during supper dribbled down her cheeks. Darn her seesawing hormones.

What to do... Although Dixie appreciated Gavin offering her additional money to hire a new marketing company, she'd lost her entrepreneurial courage and self-doubt had gained a foothold inside her. She'd been a naive fool to believe she could bring her grandmother's dream to life.

Forcing the morose thoughts aside, she organized her supplies and stowed the herbs in airtight containers. She lost track of the time and not until headlights swept across the barn doors did she realize the sun had set. Thinking Gavin had returned, Dixie smoothed her hair and straightened her shirt before stepping from the barn and spotting Shannon Douglas's white extended-cab pickup. Hiding her disappointment she pasted a smile on her face.

"Hey, Shannon." Dixie's smile faltered when her friend's expression remained sober. "Congrats on being sponsored by Wrangler." Johnny had told Dixie the news.

"Thanks." Shannon's green eyes dropped to Dixie's stomach. "How are you feeling?"

"Fine. Why?"

Shannon stepped past Dixie and examined the soap molds. "I haven't heard from you in forever."

Shannon and Dixie used to talk once a week, a simple how's-it-going call. They'd chat about Shannon's latest ride, or a cute cowboy one of them had run into.

"I was afraid you were still mad at me for bailing on you at the Piney Gorge Rodeo."

"I'm not mad, Dix." Shannon frowned. "Why are you here at the farm while Gavin's riding the circuit?"

"Where else would I be?"

"With him."

"It's not like that between us." Dixie rubbed her thumb over Gavin's phone number inside the heart she'd drawn. "We're not jumping into marriage but he is going to support the baby."

"You're wearing an engagement ring." Shannon's gaze shifted to Dixie's hand.

"Gavin doesn't want people to think bad of me."

"Are you dragging your feet, because Gavin doesn't seem like the kind of guy to dodge responsibility?"

There was that damned word again—*responsibility.* "I've got six brothers who are fit to be tied over me getting pregnant. I don't need my best friend upset with me, too."

"I'm not upset," Shannon insisted. "But I know what you went through when people ridiculed your mother."

"Times have changed."

"People haven't, Dixie. Maybe you don't care what folks say about you but think of the baby."

"Gavin and I plan to remain engaged until the baby's born."

"Then what—Gavin's off the hook?"

No, I'm off the hook. Dixie felt guilty that Gavin appeared the bad guy when in truth she was the villain. "Gavin's not walking away from his responsibilities. He's committed to his child."

Shannon opened her mouth, then shook her head and changed the subject. "I dropped by to invite you to the Bullhead City Rodeo next Saturday. If I win, Wrangler will fly me to Florida to compete in a special women's rough stock event which will be broadcast live on TV."

"I'd love to watch you ride," Dixie said.

"Bullhead City is four hours away. You shouldn't make the drive alone in case—"

"I'm pregnant, not dying from an incurable disease."

Shannon laughed. "I can't picture you a mother."

"Thanks."

"I hope it's a boy."

"Why?"

"Because you're a tomboy and you wouldn't know the first thing about playing with dolls or having tea parties."

"You can leave now if you're through badgering me."

"Yeah, yeah, I'm going." Shannon hugged Dixie. "Take care of yourself."

"I will. And, Shannon…thanks for stopping by."

"No problem. I want to make sure that kid knows I'm his favorite aunt."

Dixie watched the taillights of Shannon's truck disappear. Resting a hand over her tummy, she asked, "Are you a boy or a girl?" At only ten weeks pregnant Dixie hadn't felt the baby kick. The doctor told her to expect a fluttering sensation between the sixteenth and eighteenth week—the time Dixie had hoped to launch her website business. She'd so wanted a game plan in place for supporting her child before she felt the first kick and the baby suddenly became *real*.

She closed her eyes and thought back to earlier in the afternoon when Gavin had kissed her in the pecan grove. He was an accomplished kisser—just the right amount of pressure, tongue, nibbles and nuzzles to make her crave more.

After discovering she'd been ripped off by the phony marketing firm she'd channeled her fear into anger. When Gavin had caught her throwing rocks at the tree, the anger had given way to fear again. The impulse to rush into his arms and trust him to right the wrongs done to her had scared Dixie to death. Her grandmother had taught her to be self-sufficient and relying on Gavin would only hurt her in the long run. When the wanderlust bug bit him, he'd return to rodeo and leave Dixie with a broken heart.

Dixie was certain she'd pegged Gavin correctly— so why had he bothered with an engagement ring? She twirled the band on her finger. As far as rings went this one was old-fashioned—certainly nothing that spoke of a man's undying love and passion for his bride-to-be.

Was there a chance Gavin might one day possess real feelings for her—not thoughts of responsibility toward her and the baby, but genuine, heartfelt caring? Did she dare believe she and Gavin could make it as a couple?

No. The only reason Gavin remained a part of her life was because of the baby. To believe anything more would bring heartbreak—hers.

Her gaze returned to Gavin's cell number. She was capable of driving four hours to a rodeo and back home the same day. Besides, one or more of her brothers was probably headed to the same rodeo. A four-hour inquisition from her brothers was enough to convince her to call Gavin. She pushed two on her speed dial.

"What's wrong, Dixie?"

Gavin's abrupt question startled her, leaving her speechless.

"Dixie? You there?"

"I'm here and nothing's the matter."

"You never call. I thought…"

"Got a minute?"

"Sure."

Instead of discussing the upcoming Bullhead City Rodeo, she said, "You didn't stay for supper."

"I wasn't invited."

"In case you weren't aware," she said, "my brothers and I haven't had the privilege of attending Miss Manners Charm School."

"Are you being funny, Ms. Cash?"

Dixie smiled at the note of humor in Gavin's voice. "Hardly."

"What's on your mind?"

"Do you plan to ride in the Bullhead City Rodeo next Saturday?"

"I had planned to. Why?"

"Shannon Douglas wants me to watch her compete and I thought maybe I could hitch a ride with you."

"I'll pick you up early in the morning."

Silence filled the connection, then they spoke simultaneously.

"Gavin."

"Dixie."

"You go first," he said.

"No, you."

"Never mind, it was nothing. See you Saturday," he said.

"Okay, sure."

"And, Dixie?"

"What?"

"I'm sorry about the jerk who stole your money."

Dixie's throat swelled with emotion. "Good night." Gavin was far from perfect but he was a decent, caring— *sexy*—man.

You keep forgetting you're not his type.

Baby aside, if Gavin had his pick of women, no way would he choose a pecan farmer's granddaughter. Dixie would just have to settle for Gavin coming in and out of her life to visit the baby. Now, if only he'd cooperate and stop making her want him.

Wow.

Gavin's eyes were glued to Dixie who stood on the porch waiting for him as he barreled up the drive. She looked *h-o-t* in the denim miniskirt and bandanna-print tank top. Red boots drew his attention to her sexy legs. No man on earth would look at this woman and suspect she was pregnant.

Gavin shifted into Park and frowned. Why was Dixie

dressed to kill? They were going to a rodeo, not a night on the town and besides, she *was* pregnant *and* engaged.

Maybe she dressed that way for you.

Yeah, right. Dixie's lack of excitement when he'd slid the engagement ring on her finger was proof enough she had reservations about him. *What did you expect?*

Okay, so his official proposal wasn't exactly a romantic bended-knee declaration of undying love, but she could cut him some slack—her brothers had been watching.

You gave her someone's cast-off ring.

Gavin hopped out of the truck and rounded the hood, opening the passenger-side door and offering Dixie a hand up. *She painted her nails.* The bright red color was at odds with the down-to-earth woman he knew.

"Thanks for letting me tag along to the rodeo." She tugged her hand free and shut the door in his face.

They hadn't seen each other in six days—didn't that at least merit a smile?

The past week had been a whirlwind of activity as he'd come to accept that if he pushed Dixie too hard about marriage she'd flee across the border to Mexico to escape exchanging vows with him. In any event, he decided that if he got to pursue his own itinerary Dixie should be allowed to do the same.

When he got in the truck, the scent of honeysuckle surrounded him—better than the usual fast-food and coffee smells. "You look nice," he said, starting the engine.

"Thanks."

"Are your brothers competing today?"

"I think Merle and Buck are. They left at the crack of dawn."

They drove in silence to the main road. "When's your next doctor's appointment?"

"I had one yesterday."

He waited for Dixie to tell him how she and the baby were doing but she didn't. "Everything okay with—"

"The baby's fine."

"What about you?"

"What about me?"

She had to know he was concerned about her health, too. "Did the doctor say you're fine, as well?"

"Yes."

Communicating with an Afghan villager was easier than conversing with Dixie. Maybe she wasn't comfortable discussing the changes in her body. He pushed her. "Do you have morning sickness?"

"I did, but this past week it tapered off."

"What about cravings?"

"Pickles."

He chuckled. "No sweet cravings like ice cream or pie?" Gavin's mother had told him that she'd loved banana splits while she'd been pregnant with him.

"Not yet, thank goodness. I'm hoping I don't gain too much weight with this pregnancy."

"You won't have a problem losing whatever you gain." He cast an appreciative glance across the seat. "You're in great shape." His compliment turned her cheeks pink.

"What have you been up to lately?" she asked.

Aside from seeing Dixie's dream come to fruition… "I competed in a small rodeo up in Blythe this past Sunday. A one-day event."

"How'd you—"

"Lost." *Again.*

"Did you run into Veronica Patriot there?"

"Yep." That Dixie worried about the buckle bunny convinced Gavin she wasn't as immune to him as she'd have him believe. "Veronica wanted to know if the rumors were true." He looked at Dixie. "If we were engaged."

"What did you tell her?"

"The truth."

"She must have freaked out."

"She wasn't happy."

Dixie drummed her fingers on the armrest. "Mind if I ask a personal question?"

"Go right ahead."

"When you're not rodeoing...where's home?"

If he said his truck would she think him pathetic? "My mother's place in Phoenix." A partial truth. On occasion he visited his mother but never stayed the night. Mostly he lived in motel rooms or slept in the backseat of his truck.

He turned on the radio, exhaling a shaky breath when Dixie reclined in her seat and closed her eyes. He'd keep quiet so she could catch a nap before they arrived in Bullhead City. He wanted her in a good mood later tonight when he stopped in Yuma to show her the surprise he'd put together this week for her.

Delayed by construction on Highway 95, Gavin didn't pull up to the fairgrounds until almost noon. When he didn't grab his gear from the backseat Dixie frowned. "I thought you were riding today?"

"Changed my mind," he said. No way would he have been able to concentrate, knowing Dixie was in the stands watching him. They weaved their way through the crowd inside the arena.

"What made you change your mind?" she asked.

"I tweaked my shoulder during the last rodeo and it's still sore," he fibbed.

"Maybe you should see a doctor."

The concern in Dixie's voice surprised Gavin. He couldn't remember anyone, save for his mother, worrying about him. "I'll get to a doctor if it's not better in a week."

"Probably a pinched nerve. Conway suffered one in his neck last year and was a bear to live with until the pain went away."

Thanks to the army the words *suck it up* had been drilled into Gavin's brain and he rarely complained. What would it be like to come home at the end of the day to a woman who listened to his grumbles and offered a sympathetic hug? Gavin guided Dixie past a group of chattering teens.

"Here we are." He led Dixie through the row until they located their seat numbers. "Are you hungry?" he asked.

"Not really."

"How about a drink?"

"A water would be nice," she said.

"Comin' right up." Gavin headed for the concession stand, but halfway there Veronica Patriot stepped into his path.

"Hello, Gavin." Her gaze traveled over his body, her eyes widening when she saw his dress boots. "You're not competing today?"

"Nope." He attempted to move past her but Veronica slid sideways and he bumped into her triple D's.

"Why in such a hurry?" Her mouth curved in invitation.

Frustrated, Gavin swallowed a cuss word. "I'm here with Dixie."

Veronica's mouth curled in a snarl. "Your fiancée?"

He considered telling the pesky tramp to go screw a fence post and leave him alone but instead walked off without a word.

As Gavin stood in the concession line, he reflected on the past few nights in which he'd drifted off to sleep with his thoughts on Dixie. He'd learned that as long as he focused on her, the nightmares that had haunted him since leaving Afghanistan lost their razor-sharp edges.

He'd gotten so caught up in his plans for Dixie this past week that he had to remind himself that what he'd done had been for the baby, too—not just for Dixie, although pleasing her made him feel good. And worthy.

Dixie affected Gavin in a way no one had since he'd left the army. He didn't understand the spell she'd cast over him, but he was beginning to believe that tying himself to one person for the rest of his life might not be as scary as he'd once thought.

Chapter 8

"Ladies and gentlemen, welcome to Bullhead City's sixty-first annual Cowboy Festival and Rodeo." The JumboTron flashed still photos of the cowboys competing in the day's events. Dixie ignored the pomp and pageantry and wiggled in her bleacher seat. Gavin took up his space and part of hers, making it impossible to prevent their legs from touching. The heat radiating from his thigh was distracting and downright arousing.

"They wrote about Shannon." Gavin pointed to the article in the brochure he'd purchased from a program hawker.

"What does it say?" Using the write-up as an excuse to lean against Gavin's arm, Dixie closed her eyes and breathed in the clean masculine scent of his woodsy cologne.

"A spokesperson from Wrangler says… 'Shannon

Douglas is the first female rodeo athlete to come along who has the skill, determination and stamina to compete with the men.'" Gavin straightened in his seat. "I hope she can back that statement with a winning ride."

"She will." Like Dixie, Shannon had grown up with brothers—no sisters. In order to survive the physical roughhousing and teasing among their siblings, they had both developed a mental and physical toughness.

"Folks, we have a special event this afternoon sponsored by Wrangler." The fans applauded. When the noise died down the announcer continued. "For those of you who aren't familiar with the name Shannon Douglas—" a chuckle followed "—you will be in a few minutes. Shannon and Wrangler have teamed up to promote women's rough stock events. We all know cowgirls are tough inside and out but only the toughest gals ride bulls."

Music and action photos of Shannon's summer rodeos flashed across the JumboTron. "Shannon Douglas is a native of Stagecoach, Arizona, and one of the few women in the United States who'll take on fifteen hundred pounds of buckin' rage." The fans stomped their boots on the bleachers and Dixie winced at the ear-splitting din.

"Shannon's gonna kick off the men's bull ridin' event by showin' us she can compete with the best cowboys on the circuit. Turn your attention to gate number five. Looks like C. J. Rodriguez is placin' a bet with Shannon right now."

Dixie spotted Shannon seated on the bull in the chute and C.J. perched on the rails next to her. Money exchanged hands and the audience cheered.

"Hey, C.J.!" The announcer's shout echoed through the arena and C.J.'s head popped up. "You bettin' Shannon makes it to eight?"

C.J. shook his head *no* and the crowd roared, half booing C.J. the other half cheering him.

"C.J. that ain't very supportive," the announcer teased.

Shannon smacked C.J. in the chest with her hat and he held it while Shannon placed a protective helmet and mask over her head and face. Before she signaled the gateman, she and C.J. fist-bumped, and then the cowboy dropped out of sight and the chute door opened.

"Here comes Shannon Douglas on Boilermaker!"

Dixie clutched Gavin's rock-hard thigh and held her breath as she counted off the seconds. Boilermaker fell into a pattern of bucking twice then spinning. The bull flung, whipped and jerked Shannon's body every which way but the cowgirl hung on.

Six...seven...eight! Dixie popped out of her seat, stuck her fingers in her mouth and whistled for all she was worth. Amid the thunderous applause the bullfighters helped Shannon free her hand from the rope. As soon as she landed in the dirt she rolled to her feet then scampered toward the rails, Boilermaker hot on her heels.

The bull gained ground on Shannon and a collective gasp echoed through the arena. Boilermaker rammed his horns into the rails inches from Shannon's boots, but C. J. Rodriguez was there to lift her to safety.

"Congratulations, Shannon Douglas!" the announcer said. "Shannon is the first woman ever to make it to eight on Boilermaker." The JumboTron cut to the cowboy ready area where C.J. twirled Shannon in his arms. If Dixie didn't know better she'd guess the pair was a couple, but Shannon was too smart to attach herself to a womanizing cowboy like C.J.

"Let's see what the judges think of Shannon's ride." The fans kept their gazes glued to the JumboTron. "An eighty-two! Not bad for an eight-second day at the office."

"Shannon was amazing. She deserves better than an eighty-two," Dixie said.

"I agree."

"You do?"

"I'm not stupid enough to disagree with a pregnant lady."

His smile was so innocent and sweet Dixie couldn't help but laugh. "Don't poke fun at me, Gavin Tucker."

He slapped a hand over his chest. "I would never tease a preg—"

She elbowed him in the ribs. "Cut it out with the pregnant-lady jokes."

Gavin nuzzled her ear. "Shannon might be the best female bull rider in Arizona, but no one looks as sexy as you do on the back of a bull."

Thrilled but embarrassed by the compliment, Dixie buried her face against Gavin's shirt. "Maybe one day I'll prove I can make it to eight."

"You're not riding any more bulls in this lifetime."

A red flag waved inside Dixie's head and she pushed away from Gavin. "You're not the boss of me."

"Maybe not but I'm half the boss of him." He placed a hand against her stomach.

The intimate touch rattled Dixie and her words came out in a breathless wheeze. "What if *him* is a *her*?"

"All that matters is the baby is healthy." He sat down and Dixie took her seat. "Just so I understand…you're not really considering competing after the baby's born?" he asked.

"No. My bull riding days are over." Although exciting, the sport was too risky. If anything happened to her who would take care of the baby? God forbid she died unexpectedly and her brothers had to raise their niece or nephew.

Gavin will raise the baby. Would he? They both knew he'd proposed to her out of duty not love. A man like Gavin didn't care to be tied down by a family—or a child.

What if you're wrong?

Dixie ignored the clowns entertaining the crowd and lost herself in thought. What if she did die suddenly and Gavin stepped in to raise their son or daughter? If she and Gavin never married, then he'd be a stranger to his own child. A vision of a sobbing toddler fearful of being left alone with Gavin flashed before her eyes.

Agitated, Dixie twirled the ring on her finger. It had been her bright idea to insist on a trial engagement—mostly because her pride wouldn't accept that the only reason Gavin had spent the night with her had been to escape the clutches of Veronica Patriot.

Don't blame Gavin. You were the one who suggested leaving the bar together.

Dixie refused to argue with herself about who was or wasn't at fault for her and Gavin's predicament. Until now she'd only considered doing what was best for her—not what was in the best interest of the baby. Did she dare change her mind and give marriage to Gavin a real shot—for the baby's sake?

What if she opened her heart to Gavin and after a time fell in love with him—then a few years down the road, he became restless and wanted out of their marriage?

Dixie glanced at Gavin whose attention remained on the cowboys behind the chutes. Waking up every morning and seeing his handsome face resting on the pillow next to her would hardly be torture—not to mention she had none…zero…nada complaints about his lovemaking.

Can you make him happy?

That was the million-dollar question—one she wouldn't know the answer to until she and Gavin hung around more. The baby wasn't due for months—plenty of time to decide if marriage was a real option for them. If, after the baby was born, Dixie believed parting ways was best…so be it. Gavin would be none the wiser. Shoving her worries aside, Dixie allowed herself to enjoy the rest of the day in the company of a handsome cowboy.

"Folks, we're takin' a thirty-minute break before the women's barrel racin' event. Check out the live band near the food court and for those of you who haven't tasted the best churro in Arizona, stop by Rosie's, she's givin' away free samples."

Gavin chuckled as the stands cleared. Food sampling was a hit at small-town rodeos. "Are you hungry?" he asked Dixie.

"We ate hotdogs less than an hour ago." Her blue eyes twinkled. "Unless you think because I'm pregnant I'm starving all the time."

"I have no clue how the pregnant female body works." He grinned. "Give me a heads-up when you're getting hungry so I can feed you before you become cranky."

"Ha-ha. Be happy you won't be making midnight runs to the grocery store to pacify my cravings."

Gavin marveled at the change in Dixie's usual stubborn demeanor. He liked the teasing, lighthearted girl. When she shifted in her seat, Gavin asked, "Want to stretch your legs?"

"Let's see if we can find Shannon."

They left the stands and headed to the livestock barns. "This is my favorite time of the year," Dixie said.

A cowboy walking a palomino blocked their path and Gavin pulled Dixie out of the way. After the coast was clear they continued walking. He waited for Dixie to release his hand—she didn't. He tightened his hold on her fingers as they strolled past the horse stalls and admired the bucking stock. "Why do you like autumn so much?"

"The middle of October kicks off the start of the pecan harvest," Dixie said.

"How long does the harvest last?"

"Some years up until Christmas. If my grandfather had difficulty hiring seasonal workers, then me and my brothers stayed home from school and picked pecans."

"Did that happen often…not having enough help during harvest?"

"Johnny said way back in the day when our mother was a baby that my grandfather hired fifty or more pickers each harvest. I guess there were times when he had to turn families away."

"Your grandfather must have been a good man to work for."

"When Mexicans searching for agricultural work crossed the border they hiked straight to Stagecoach and Grandpa's farm."

"Did your grandfather use illegal immigrants as laborers?"

"I'm sure some of them were. Border security wasn't the hot topic then that it is today."

Growing up in Phoenix, Gavin was used to the TV news reporting sting operations to weed out undocumented workers. "I'm still surprised the authorities didn't stop at the farm to check the workers' green cards."

"Grandpa and Grandma treated the migrant workers very well and the families always returned to Mexico after the harvest. I think the sheriff and his deputies focused their attention on real criminals."

"I didn't notice any migrant-worker cabins on the farm." Then again Gavin had only walked through part of the orchard the afternoon he'd come upon Dixie using a tree trunk for target practice.

"The families slept outside in tents. Grandpa rigged up an outdoor latrine and shower and Grandma Ada gave the women her homemade bath soap, which I'm sure they loved."

The mention of Grandma Ada's soaps reminded Gavin of the surprise waiting for Dixie in Yuma. "Did you want to stay and watch your brothers compete this afternoon?"

"I guess so, why?"

"I was hoping to leave early. There's something I want to show you."

"That's fine. My brothers won't care if I'm cheering them on or not."

"Okay, then. Let's say goodbye to Shannon and be on our way."

Gavin and Dixie left the barn and returned to the cowboy ready area behind the chutes. They weaved through the throng of rodeo personnel until they found Shannon talking to a reporter. They hung back, waiting for the cowgirl to finish the interview. When the reporter left, Dixie caught Shannon's attention.

"Congratulations, Shannon," Dixie said.

The women hugged and then Shannon glanced at Gavin. "Thanks for bringing Dixie today."

"Sure thing. That was a hell of a ride."

"Yeah, it was, wasn't it?" Shannon's smile widened.

"What's up with the little show you and C. J. Rodriguez put on for the audience?" Dixie asked.

"Wrangler wants us to travel together for the next year and compete in the same rodeos."

"Why?"

"The production managers want the fans to believe there's a romance between me and C.J. because they think it will increase ticket sales." Shannon lowered her voice. "I'm not complaining. What girl wouldn't want to travel the circuit with C.J.?"

Dixie ignored Gavin's grin and said, "C.J.'s a player."

"I know what they say about cowboys—"

"What's that?" Gavin interrupted Shannon.

"You can't trust 'em to stick around longer than the time it takes their horse to drink from a water trough," Dixie answered for her friend.

"No worries. Things between me and C.J. are friendly but not too friendly. He just broke up with a barrel racer from California. He won't admit it, but he's nursing a broken heart."

"Be careful, Shannon."

"I will." The women hugged and Shannon strolled off.

Gavin took Dixie's hand and they left the building. Once they reached his truck, he said, "What I want to show you is in Yuma. Mind if we grab supper there instead of stopping on the way?"

"Sounds good." Dixie hopped into the front seat and fastened her belt then yawned. Five minutes later, she was fast asleep.

Gavin parked in front of a cinder-block single story home at the end of Main Street in Yuma. A banner reading Sold had been slapped across the For Sale sign in the window. Heart pumping with excitement he gently shook Dixie awake. "We're here."

Dixie's eyelashes fluttered up and she straightened in the seat. "Where's here?" She glanced out her window.

"Dixie's Desert Delights."

Her brow scrunched. "What are you talking about?"

He nodded to the vacant house.

"I don't get it. We're parked in front of an ugly, run-down home that's…" Dixie looked at Gavin with wide eyes—like a child who'd caught a glimpse of Santa Claus sneaking up the chimney. "You bought this property?"

Gavin grinned. "Yep." He hopped out of the truck, skirted the hood, then opened her door and helped her out. They stood on the sidewalk and studied the cracked window at the front of the house.

"It's not in great shape, but with your brothers' help, we'll give it a face-lift. You'll have to decide on a paint color for the outside." He walked to the front door and inserted the key then flipped on the lights and stood back.

In a trancelike state Dixie stepped inside and spun in a slow circle.

Gavin crossed the room and stood before a crumbling adobe fireplace. "The Realtor said you might have to do some extra advertising to draw people down here to the end of the block." Dixie's mouth hung open as she wandered about the room.

"There's a bathroom and a small kitchen that will come in handy for making your soaps." When Dixie remained silent, Gavin became nervous. "The original owners sold the house in the late fifties when the property was zoned for business. Through the years it's functioned as a coffee shop, an antiques store and a lawyer's office, but the past four years it sat empty."

Dixie's face remained a blank slate and the excitement Gavin had felt all day fizzled. "What's the matter? You don't like the place?"

"I don't understand, Gavin." Her voice broke, his name escaping her mouth in three syllables.

What did she not understand? He crossed the room and stood before her. "This is where you're going to sell your soaps."

"Why...how...when—"

He pressed a finger against her lips. "Why...because you're the mother of my child. How... I had money saved up, which I used for a down payment. When... I contacted a Realtor last week and she showed me the house. I thought it could easily be turned into a gift shop."

"What was the down payment?"

"Don't worry, I'm not destitute." He chuckled. "You won't have to support me."

"This isn't funny, Gavin."

"I didn't buy this property to make you cry."

"No, you did this because you felt sorry for me, didn't you?" Dixie backed up a step. "Stupid Dixie gets taken to the cleaners by an online scammer and—"

"I never said you were stupid."

"But you thought it." She wiped a tear from her cheek. "I don't know where I'm going to get the money to pay you back."

"I don't want to be paid back." Gavin wouldn't allow Dixie's pride to stand in the way of him helping her.

"I can't accept this as a gift."

Thinking quick on his feet, Gavin said, "I didn't buy this for you, Dixie. I bought this for the baby, so our child would have the security he or she deserves." Sort of the truth…in a roundabout way.

"What do you mean?"

"I agreed to pay child support but I wanted you to have a means of supporting yourself."

"I've taken care of myself since my grandmother passed away. I don't need you or—"

"Before you say anything more, check out the place. If you don't believe this will work for a gift shop then I'll have the Realtor put the property back on the market."

She gasped. "You already signed the papers?"

He nodded.

Dixie looked away first. Gavin wished he knew what was going on in her pretty head, but he stood there like a dope, waiting for her to make the next move. She did— in the direction of the kitchen. Gavin remained in the front room.

Way to go, idiot. He'd expected his gift to make Dixie happy. Instead, he'd upset her. Gavin shuffled to the front window and glanced down the block. The streetlights had come on and local businesses were locking their doors.

Had he misread the situation? He'd sworn he'd heard passion and excitement in Dixie's voice when she'd told him about her plans to market her grandmother's soaps. He'd thought for sure she'd be thrilled to manage her own business.

"Gavin?" Dixie's silhouette darkened the kitchen doorway.

"What?"

"It's perfect."

Chest aching with relief, he said, "Good. Because

your brothers are meeting me here tomorrow and we're working on the place."

Dixie moved toward him and he met her in the middle of the room. "I'll help, too," she said.

"You'll be busy making soap." He cupped her cheek. "You need inventory before you open a business."

"You're right. I'll need to stock up on supplies and, oh, there's a new soap mold in a catalog I've been eyeing. Then Christmas is right around the corner and—"

Gavin leaned in and kissed Dixie. He'd wanted to kiss her all day. He intended to keep it light and innocent but Dixie hugged him, pressing her breasts to his chest and he lost all self-control. He backed her up against the wall and nudged his thigh between her legs. She moaned, her arms squeezing his neck harder when he threaded his fingers through her hair. He could have kissed her forever if he hadn't needed air to breathe. Gasping, he pulled away. "Everything will work out, Dixie. You'll see."

Chapter 9

"I don't know what to say." Dixie clung to Gavin. She never expected to sell her grandmother's soaps in a boutique—that's why she'd attempted to start an internet business. After being scammed out of five thousand dollars she'd believed her promise to her grandmother would never be realized. Now Gavin was bringing her dream back to life in an amazing way.

In light of his kindness, how could she not give Gavin the benefit of the doubt and try to make their relationship work? Of course there were risks involved—mainly to her heart. Dixie slammed the door on her negative thoughts. She'd spent an entire day with Gavin and not once had she wished to be anywhere else. Not once had she worried about her and the baby's future or how she intended to support herself. With Gavin by her side she felt secure and safe. She tightened her hold and kissed his cheek, his five o'clock shadow tickling her nose.

Gavin threaded his fingers through her hair, and holding her head in place he plunged his tongue into her mouth. Lord, the cowboy could kiss. *Careful...* She'd best move slowly with Gavin or physical desire would shove aside common sense and she'd fall head over heels in love. Then where would she be if he changed his mind about her and the baby and decided he wanted nothing to do with them?

The reservations still existed—a part of her feared Gavin wouldn't always be there for her and their child— but buying this property proved he wanted to make her happy. Clinging to that scrap of hope Dixie decided the only surefire way to know if Gavin was with her for the long haul was to stop throwing roadblocks in his way and open her heart to him.

He broke off the kiss. "We'd better slow down, honey."

"I don't want to." She locked gazes with him, hoping he'd read the sincerity in her eyes.

"I didn't buy this property to coax you into my bed," he said.

"This has nothing to do with the shop." *And everything to do with giving our baby...us...a chance to be a real family.*

Gavin dipped his head and kissed her neck. "If and when we make love, it won't be against a wall or on the hard floor."

"Let's go back to the farm."

"And have your brothers stand outside your bedroom door eavesdropping?" He nuzzled her neck.

Gavin was right—her brothers would be a problem. "What about the barn?"

He grinned. "How many gentlemen friends have you entertained in the hayloft?"

"You'd be the first." Gavin was the first man she'd slept with who was skilled in bed, and unlike her mother's boyfriends he hadn't run from his responsibility.

"I'm tempted to roll in the hay with you, but we can't forget the baby. You've had a long day and need a good night's sleep."

Dixie dropped her gaze before Gavin read the disappointment in her eyes. How were they supposed to grow closer if he always thought of the baby before her? Determined to give it one more try, she stood on tiptoes and poured her heart and soul into her kiss.

Gavin responded with gusto, snuggling her body against his arousal. But a few seconds later he stepped back and winked. "Once this place is fixed up, we'll christen it properly."

Heart breaking, Dixie said, "I'm going to hold you to your promise."

"Honey, that's one promise I intend to keep."

"Well if it isn't the newest entrepreneur in town."

The unenthusiastic statement greeted Dixie Monday morning when she stopped in at Ed's Graphic and Design, a printing shop on Main Street in Yuma. "Hello, Mrs. Hinkle."

Mildred Hinkle owned the Penny Saver Market across the street from Susie's Souvenirs. Last year she'd asked Mrs. Hinkle if she'd sell Dixie's organic soaps in her store but the old woman had snubbed her nose at Dixie's request.

"I hear you plan to sell those little soaps you make in that run-down hovel at the end of the street." Mildred frowned, her wrinkled mouth drawing into a pucker.

Only two days had passed since Gavin had revealed

his surprise—darned if Dixie would allow Mrs. Hinkle to put a damper on her excitement. "Yes, I'm turning the house into a gift shop." And since she had more space than she needed for just the soaps, Dixie planned to experiment with other products and develop a line of bath salts and lotions as well as doing custom-made gift baskets. She was even considering offering do-it-yourself classes on organic soap-making.

"Have you decided on a name for your business?" Ed, the owner of the printing shop stepped from the back room.

"I have." She smiled at the tall, middle-age man. "Dixie's Desert Delights."

"That sounds right nice."

Dixie ignored Mildred's scoff.

"I'm guessing you're here to order a sign to hang out front of your business," Ed said.

"I was hoping—"

"Make sure she follows the rules the chamber of commerce created," Mrs. Hinkle interrupted. "Your sign has to be the same size as the rest of the businesses along Main Street." She gathered her sales flyers and marched out the door.

"Don't pay attention to Mildred. She doesn't want anyone's business outshining hers."

Dixie hadn't considered that other merchants might view her as a threat. She guessed with the struggling economy that most people were pinching pennies and local businesses had to compete for customers.

"I hear your brothers are busy sprucing up the place."

"The inspection report on the property wasn't bad," Dixie said. "The wiring has to be updated, but the structure itself is sound."

Ed pulled out a three-ring binder from beneath the counter. "What kind of sign are you interested in and what's your budget?"

"I was thinking of a design that resembled one of my gift-wrapped soaps." She removed a bar from her coat pocket.

Ed studied the soap. "It's doable. What colors did you have in mind?"

"The cinder block is being painted an olive-green so I thought rose for the tissue paper color and buttercream for the bow."

"Black lettering?" Ed asked.

"No, chocolate-brown."

"That'll work. After I create the design you can make any last-minute changes."

"Do I have a choice of font styles?"

Ed flipped through the binder, then spun the book toward Dixie.

After perusing the pages, she pointed to a script she believed her grandmother would have approved of. "I like this one." There was a touch of feminine flourish to each letter yet the font was bold, clean and readable.

"I'll have this finished by the end of the business day tomorrow."

"And the cost?"

"Depends on the size," Ed said.

"Mrs. Hinkle said the sign had to be the same dimensions as others along the block."

"That's just Mildred bellyaching. You can have any size sign you want."

"What about the chamber of commerce? I can't afford a fine."

"The only rule the chamber enforces is that a business sign can't block a traffic light. Other than that buy whatever size you can afford."

"Since I'm the farthest away from the middle of town I'd like the biggest sign."

"That'll run you twelve hundred. Included in the price are the poles and hardware to attach it to the shop and a special UV coating to prevent the colors from fading in the sun."

Twelve hundred was a lot of money. "I'll think about it and let you know when I stop in tomorrow to view the design."

"Sure thing."

"Thanks, Ed." Dixie left the print shop and strolled down the block, studying the signs hanging outside each business. When she reached Dixie's Desert Delights she decided she needed to purchase the largest sign. The twelve hundred dollars would have to go on her credit card.

"Watch out." Johnny rounded the corner of the house, carrying a load of two-by-fours. She followed him inside.

Her brothers and Gavin had made remarkable progress in less than forty-eight hours and the once neglected house was becoming a quaint little gift shop. Fresh paint, repairs to the fireplace and new shelving mounted on the walls gave the inside a cozy feel. "Where's Gavin?" she asked after Johnny laid the boards on the floor.

"Outside talking to the plumber."

The last she'd heard, the toilet flushed fine. "What's wrong with the plumbing?"

"Not sure." Johnny nodded to the pile of wood. "Where do you want the counter for the cash register?"

"By the back wall facing the front door."

"Makes sense." Johnny began taking measurements.

"When Merle gets here send him over to the hardware store. Gavin's got an order of supplies waiting to be picked up." Johnny finished measuring, then left to fetch another load of wood.

Our dream is coming true, Grandma.

"Hey, you're here." Gavin stepped through the kitchen doorway wearing no shirt and a tool belt slung low on his jean-clad hips. If rodeo didn't work out for him he'd make a sexy handyman. He grinned when he caught her staring and her pulse skipped a beat.

"I ordered a sign for the front of the shop." As if Gavin sported a huge magnet glued to his chest, Dixie's feet glided across the floor. She stopped before him and brushed at an imaginary speck of dirt sticking to his sweaty shoulder. Her fingers lingered longer than necessary—ever since she'd decided to give her relationship with Gavin a real chance, she couldn't resist touching him.

"Porter and Buck took off." Gavin's gaze fastened onto Dixie's mouth and she swayed closer.

Mesmerized by his dark eyes, she said, "That wasn't nice of them to leave you shorthanded."

"I asked Buck to keep Porter busy. Your brother means well but he can't hammer nails worth a damn."

"I'll help you."

"Thanks, but I don't want to take any chance of you hurting yourself."

There he went...worrying about the baby.

"Once the shop is finished, you'll be busy setting up your inventory." He stroked a finger across her cheek and her skin tingled at the simple caress. "Have lunch with me."

Hypnotized by his brown eyes Dixie nodded. The

batch of cinnamon-citrus soap waiting in the barn back at the farm could wait a while longer. "I'll grab sandwiches from the deli across the street."

"Give me a half hour." He kissed the tip of her nose and walked off, leaving her yearning for more. When she turned away she caught Johnny spying at the front door.

"Why the change of heart?" her brother asked.

"What are you talking about?"

"You and Gavin. You're acting lovey-dovey all of a sudden. A week ago you bristled when he got too close."

Dixie wasn't about to share her feelings with her brother.

"You two decide on a wedding date?" Johnny asked.

A few days ago Dixie would have balked at going through with a wedding. Now the ceremony was a real possibility. "Not yet." She crinkled her nose. "You'll be the first to know when we do." She stopped at the door. "I'm off to the deli."

"I'll take a—"

"Sorry, you're on your own for lunch." She closed the front door behind her, ignoring her brother's scowl.

Thirty minutes later, deli food in hand, Dixie entered the backyard behind the shop. She placed the food on a stone wall beneath the shade of a piñon tree and waited for Gavin to join her.

"Thanks for getting lunch." He sat next to her and she handed him a sandwich.

"Are you antsy yet?" Dixie opened a bag of chips.

"Antsy about what?"

"Returning to rodeo."

Gavin considered Dixie's question, then answered honestly. "I haven't given rodeo much thought the past few days." He'd been so involved in whipping the property into shape that he hadn't had time to miss busting broncs. Was it possible that the incessant urgency he felt to push himself to the limits dissipated when he focused on making Dixie happy? Rodeo had been the vehicle of choice to feed his addiction to danger after he'd left the army. The fact that lately he hadn't felt the need to take risks gave Gavin pause.

He reflected on the previous night when he and Dixie had worked side by side in the shop. The mellow sounds of country music had played on the radio while Dixie painted a stencil on the wall and Gavin tiled the bathroom floor. There'd been no need for conversation—both of them comfortable with the silence. Gavin had never felt more at peace with himself than when he was with Dixie. Since the rodeo in Bullhead City the intensity of his nightmares had tapered off. There was no doubt in his mind that Dixie was good for his soul.

"You must be tired after having to sleep on the blow-up mattress."

Dixie had loaned him the mattress so he could stay at the shop and work late into the night, then wake at the crack of dawn and begin all over again. "You won't hear any complaints from me. It beats sleeping on the hard ground."

There were times in Afghanistan when he and his men had been forced to sleep in their bedrolls on the rocky soil. Dixie had offered to give up her bedroom at the farm but Gavin insisted she needed a good night's rest more than he did. To tell the truth he thought she was pushing herself too hard.

"Maybe you should head home after lunch and take a nap."

"I can't afford to rest. I need to make more soap."

"You have to think about the baby, Dixie."

She stiffened and for the life of Gavin he couldn't figure out why she bristled each time he mentioned the baby. Wasn't a father supposed to show interest in his child?

Although she didn't look pregnant, the more time he spent with Dixie the more real the baby became. Last night Gavin had lain in the dark and envisioned buying a home in Yuma. Dixie and the baby would head to the gift shop each morning and Gavin would drive to a civilian job. At the end of the day their little family would eat a cozy meal followed by a long walk through the neighborhood—Gavin pushing the stroller.

The midnight musing should have caused a panic attack because settling down threatened his plan to stay on the move and keep one step ahead of the memories of Nate's death.

You've hardly thought of Nate the past few weeks.

The realization shook Gavin. Nate had been more than a friend—he'd been a brother. *Nate wouldn't want you to feel guilty over his death.* Yeah, well, Nate hadn't seen the look in his mother's eyes when Gavin had stopped at her home to deliver the few possessions Nate had accumulated while in the army.

"Have you given any thought to baby names?" Dixie asked.

"No, have you?"

"If it's a girl I'd like to name her after my grandmother." Dixie peeked at Gavin. "But Ada's old-fashioned."

"Is Ada short for anything?"

"Adelle. My grandmother's people were French."

"Adelle is a nice name. Maybe we could call her Addy instead of Ada."

"I like that."

"I have a suggestion for a boy's name," Gavin said.

"As long as it isn't a country-western singer."

Gavin chuckled. "I was hoping…if you agreed… maybe naming him after my buddy Nate." Gavin couldn't go back in time and save his friend but he could honor Nate's memory by naming his son after him.

"Nathan. That's a nice strong name," she said.

"You're sure?"

"Positive."

Changing the subject, Gavin asked, "Are you planning a grand opening for the shop?"

"I guess I should," Dixie mumbled.

"What's the matter?" Gavin snagged her hand and rubbed the callused pad of his thumb across her knuckles. "Having doubts about managing your own business?"

"No." She sighed. "I'm worried I won't sell enough inventory to pay the mortgage."

"My child-support checks will make up the difference if sales fall short."

"It's going to be difficult to watch the store and keep up with making new products."

"You'll figure out a way." With Johnny's help Gavin had poured a cement slab in the backyard for the potbelly stove, which they'd brought from the barn and hooked up yesterday. "What else is troubling you?"

"Susie gave me the cold shoulder when I picked up the rest of my soaps from her shop."

"You're her competition now."

"I guess, but I worry that you wasted your money,

Gavin. Dixie's Desert Delights is just one of several gift shops along Main Street. What if I don't make enough money to reimburse you for the down payment?"

"I don't want to be reimbursed." He threaded his fingers through hers. "We should set a wedding date and tie the knot before the baby's born." Gavin hated the thought of his child being labeled a bastard, but the desire to marry Dixie had more to do with making Gavin feel safe. With Dixie by his side there was hope that he'd conquer the demons chasing him and live a normal, fulfilling life—as normal as possible for a soldier returning from the war front.

Fearing if he revealed the truth behind his proposal, Dixie would run for the hills, he focused on what was best for the baby, not him. "Most people today don't give a hoot if a couple marries before, after or if ever once the baby's born, but I care, Dixie. I want to be married to the mother of my child before my son or daughter makes an entrance into the world."

"I thought—"

"I realize we're still feeling our way as a couple, but I hope I've proved my intentions are sincere."

"You have."

"Then pick a date."

"What about your rodeo schedule? Would you continue to ride after the baby's born?"

"That depends," he said.

"On what?"

"On whether or not you want to make this a real marriage."

Chapter 10

"Dixie, I swear I've never smelled anything better than this." Skylar Riggins held up a bar of soap from Dixie's Christmas collection.

"That's one of my favorites." The Christmas-tree-shaped bar spawned fond memories of Dixie and her grandmother experimenting with herbs and oils in the barn. The Christmas before her grandmother had passed away they'd worked on a new holiday scent, and when Dixie had suggested adding nutmeg to the recipe her grandmother had hugged her and said with pride, "I'll rest easy knowing my recipes will be in good hands."

"Have you seen my new romance line?" Dixie nodded to the decorative hatbox brimming with delicate heart-shaped pink and peach soaps. While Skylar walked off to do more sniffing, Dixie milled about the customers—all women—attending Dixie's Desert Delights Grand Opening Saturday afternoon.

Gavin and her brothers had worked tirelessly all week to ready the shop for business and Dixie had spent endless hours making soap and putting up flyers in town advertising the event. Next to the front door she'd placed a basket of soap samples and a gift certificate to a local restaurant to be given away in a drawing to one lucky customer who stopped by the store today. Dixie couldn't have asked for a better turnout and was surprised and pleased when the gals she'd rodeoed with this past summer had showed up to support her.

"Dixie," Hannah Buck spoke from across the room. "Do you have any soap for men?"

The question caught the attention of several women. "I do." Dixie opened the glass door of her grandmother's dining-room hutch and pointed to the bars on the top shelf. "The scents are called Bad Boy, Charmer, Swashbuckler and Cowboy." Several women rushed over to examine the products.

"My favorite is Cowboy," Dixie said. After smelling Gavin's cologne all week she'd been inspired to create a line of soap for men. Cowboy contained a hint of sandalwood and musk.

"Mmm. Sexy. I'll take a Cowboy and a Bad Boy." The woman winked at Dixie. "Either of these will be an improvement over what's waiting for me at home."

"Dare I ask who's waiting at home?" Dixie smiled.

"The mailman." The women laughed.

"You think that's bad, I've got a mechanic at my house."

Dixie took Hannah by the elbow and led her to the checkout counter. She nodded at the soap in her friend's hand. "Who's the lucky guy?"

"I don't want to jinx anything but I met this really nice

guy at work and I think he likes me except…" Hannah waved a hand in the air. "Never mind."

"What she's not saying—" Kim Beaderman joined the women at the counter "—is that this really nice guy is my brother."

Dixie waggled an eyebrow. "Sounds like a soap opera… *As the Yuma Medical Center Turns.*"

"Mike and I are just friends," Hannah insisted, her cheeks turning pink.

Dixie gave Hannah the sale's slip to sign. "Thanks for coming by today. I was worried about a poor turnout."

Kim waved a hand. "The place is packed. Your store's a hit."

"I hope things stay this way through Christmas." She pointed to the raffle gift by the door. "Don't forget to fill out your email address for the drawing."

The women walked off, and Dixie turned her attention to the front window. Each time she caught a glimpse of Gavin using his cowboy charm to hawk her soaps and entice women into her shop, Dixie's heart melted.

Instead of heading off to a rodeo, Gavin had remained in Yuma for her grand opening. Last night her brothers had informed her that they were competing in Payson today, so when Gavin waltzed into the store this morning with breakfast burritos and orange juice she'd been caught off guard. He'd done so much for her already and she'd felt guilty he'd passed up a rodeo to stay behind and help her. Although she insisted she could handle the opening by herself, Dixie was secretly grateful for Gavin's support.

"So…" Wendy Chin slipped behind the counter and hugged Dixie. "I hear congratulations are in order."

Wendy's gaze dropped to Dixie's stomach. "When's the baby due?"

"March."

"How are things between you and the baby's father?" Wendy nodded to the front window.

"We're fine. Why?"

"Judging by the way Gavin ogled you a few minutes ago I'd say you two are more than fine."

Gavin had been watching her?

"He was staring at you like a serial killer eyes his next victim."

Dixie gaped.

Wendy flashed a cheeky grin. "I don't read romance books. I read thrillers. It was meant as a compliment."

"Gavin's a great guy." No matter how things turned out between them, Dixie would always hold him in high regard. "He's been a huge help—"

"Oh, yeah, I bet he has." Wendy laughed.

"What's so funny?" Julie Kenner asked.

Dixie moved from behind the counter and hugged Julie. "Thanks for stopping in."

"Sorry, I'm late. I had to work a half day." Julie motioned to the crowd of women. "The store looks great, Dixie. I can't believe you opened your own business."

"I couldn't have done this without Gavin's help." Dixie spied him chatting with Mildred Hinkle. He handed her a soap sample and darned if he didn't make the old biddy blush.

"Excuse me a minute." Dixie cut through the crowd. "Hello, Mrs. Hinkle," she said when Mildred stepped through the door. "Nice of you to drop by. While you're browsing help yourself to cookies and punch in the kitchen."

"Never mind refreshments. That nice young man out front told me if I use this—" she held up a sample from Dixie's romance collection "—my Walden's headaches will completely disappear."

Dixie swallowed a laugh, then guided Mildred to the pink hatbox. "Use any of these soaps from my romance collection and Walden won't be able to keep his hands off you."

"The sign in the window says you'll refund my money or offer an exchange if I don't like the soap."

"That's right. Return it and—"

"You want customers to bring back used soap?"

"I certainly do. Have you heard of Clean the World?" Mildred shook her head. "Clean the World is a soap recycling program that collects bars of used soap and distributes them to needy communities all over the world."

"How awful to give someone dirty soap."

Dixie laughed. "All the used bars are run through a sanitization process first."

"Hmm. Never heard of the group but I guess it's nice to help people when you can."

"Why don't you try one bar and if Walden doesn't care for it, exchange the soap for a different scent until you find his favorite."

"All right. I'll do that." Mildred handed Dixie a bar wrapped in rose-colored ribbon and followed her to the cash register. "Is that young man outside related to you?"

Dixie didn't want Mildred to know that she and Gavin were engaged. If things didn't work out between them she'd have to answer the woman's nosy questions. "He's a friend."

"Well, you should work harder at making him more

than a friend, young lady. Men like him don't come along often."

Dixie couldn't agree more. She handed Mildred her change and gift bag. "Thank you for stopping in, Mrs. Hinkle."

"You're welcome, dear."

Dear? There went another reason Dixie needed Gavin—he converted her enemies to friends.

"Hey, Dixie, we're heading over to the Dude Ranch if you and Gavin want to stop by later," Hannah said. The Dude Ranch was a saloon, which featured local country music bands and a huge dance floor.

"Maybe next time." Dixie hadn't gone out with the girls in forever—since the Boot Hill Rodeo in July, but her dogs were barking and the day wasn't over.

"Don't be a party-pooper, Dix," Shannon said. "Next week I'm heading to Florida with C.J. I won't be back for at least a month."

"Thanks for the invite, but it's been a long week." Not to mention she couldn't drink alcohol and she wasn't in the mood for loud music and greasy buffalo wings. Her gaze drifted to the window. With her brothers away at a rodeo she had the house to herself tonight. What really appealed to her was soft music and sharing the porch swing with Gavin.

"Take care, Dixie," Skylar said. The rest of the gang waved goodbye and left.

Three hours until closing.

Three hours until she was alone with Gavin.

Gavin stood by the door watching Dixie straighten the gift shop for tomorrow's crowd. She looked frazzled, tired but happy. Her stomach growled and he chuckled. "I heard that all the way over here. C'mon. You need to eat."

"I want to get things ready for tomorrow."

While Dixie locked up the cash and credit card receipts in the small safe Gavin had installed in a kitchen cupboard, he mulled over the day. He knew diddly-squat about women's buying habits and fancy-smelling soaps but he'd kept track of the number of people who'd visited the shop with his handy dandy counter gadget. If half the hundred-thirty-two customers purchased a bar of soap then the grand opening of Dixie's Desert Delights had been a success.

"Okay, I'm ready." Dixie flashed a tired smile as she put on her coat.

Gavin held the door for her, then took the key from her fingers and secured the lock.

"I'm not so tired that I'm unable to lock the door," she grumbled.

He handed her the key. "I locked the outside shed earlier."

"I forgot about the shed. I'm used to leaving the barn doors wide-open and not worrying about thieves."

Gavin grasped Dixie's elbow and escorted her to the side of the house where he'd parked his truck. "This area of downtown seems safe but I wouldn't test your luck and leave the doors or shed unlocked."

"I promise I'll be more vigilant."

He helped Dixie into his truck and slid onto the driver's seat. "What are you hungry for?"

"Anything."

Gavin had ordered a sandwich for Dixie at noon and had had it delivered to the shop but he doubted she'd eaten it. He refrained from lecturing her about taking better care of herself for the baby's sake because he didn't want to ruin what had been a great day for her. He opened his mouth to suggest a nice meal at a sit-down restaurant but Dixie yawned. "We'll stop at the drive-through in Stagecoach and grab a couple of burgers to go. How does that sound?"

"Great." Dixie slouched into a comfortable position. "Go ahead and turn on the radio—" she yawned again "—while I rest my eyes for a minute."

She was fast asleep before Gavin left Yuma city limits. He switched on the radio, lowering the volume, then sang along in his head with Kenny Chesney. The city lights faded to black in the rearview mirror and snoring sounds escaped from Dixie's mouth. She looked soft and kissable.

Gavin gripped the wheel tighter and willed his libido to cool. This past week he'd woken each morning with a hard-on. Shoot, he hadn't been this horny since the age of thirteen when he'd wanted to kiss Stephanie Quaker in study hall.

Get a grip, man.

He managed to steer his thoughts and the truck onto the county road that led into Stagecoach. He decided not to stop at the drive-through because he hadn't the heart to wake Dixie. They'd scrounge up something to eat at the farm. Fifteen minutes later he turned onto the road to the Cash property. The house was dark when he pulled into the yard. He shut off the truck and set the brake.

Dixie remained sound asleep…tempting him. He unsnapped his belt, leaned across the seat and kissed her neck. She swatted at him but missed. Grinning, he blew in her ear. This time she jumped, the movement sending her shoulder cracking against his jaw.

He rubbed his chin and chuckled. "Ouch."

Dixie blinked. "We're home."

Home. An unfamiliar yearning pulled at Gavin's heartstrings. He hadn't considered anyplace *home* in years. He tried to envision him and Dixie raising a handful of kids with a pecan grove for a backyard. Three months ago his mind would have been a blank slate but now… He could see himself walking out the door and down the porch steps to get in his truck and leave for work.

"You were sleeping so soundly I didn't want to wake you. I thought we could eat here."

"Sure, that's fine." Dixie led the way into the house and into the kitchen. "I haven't had time to grocery shop this week." She opened the fridge door—the shelves were bare.

Gavin peeked over her shoulder. "Any soup in the pantry?"

Dixie confiscated two cans of chicken noodle and a box of saltines. "This won't fill you up."

"Don't worry about me. I'll stop for a snack when I head back to Yuma." Gavin had been making the round-trip every day while they'd worked on the store. He hadn't minded the drive until tonight. Lack of sleep was catching up with him.

"Do you care if I take a quick shower while you heat the soup?" Dixie paused in the doorway. "If I don't grab one now my brothers will use up all the hot water when they return from the rodeo."

"Go ahead." Gavin listened to Dixie's light footfalls on the stairs and closed his eyes, envisioning her naked body standing beneath a spray of water.

The pipes rattled and clanked behind the kitchen wall

and Gavin's willpower diminished. He'd kept his hands to himself all week—no easy task when Dixie *accidentally* bumped into him. Or he'd caught her staring at his backside when she thought he wasn't looking.

Dixie wants you as bad as you want her.

They were engaged. What the heck were they waiting for?

Gavin decided to take matters into his own hands. He didn't know why Dixie hadn't answered him when he'd asked if she'd intended to make their marriage a real one after they tied the knot, but as far as he was concerned, the more *real* their relationship became the better the chances of their marriage succeeding. He climbed the stairs, stopping in the hallway to strip. He left his clothes on the floor outside the door.

Dixie's humming greeted him when he stepped into the bathroom. A light-colored shower curtain enclosed the claw-foot tub and Gavin could see her silhouette through the sheer fabric.

Hoping not to startle her too badly, he slid the curtain aside at the end of the tub and stepped in. Dixie's back faced him, offering a view of her firm little fanny and curvy hips. Arms raised above her head, she shampooed her hair.

Gavin moved closer and braced his hands against the wall on either side of her body, and then he pressed his chest to her back. Dixie gasped, the action causing her to suck in a mouthful of water. She coughed, sputtered and spun. Eyes wide she opened her mouth to speak but Gavin caressed her breasts and instead she moaned. He didn't wait for permission. He nibbled a path across her shoulder, up her neck and ended with a kiss beneath her ear.

"We were supposed to christen the gift shop not the shower." She leaned heavily against him.

"I've been thinking about making love to you all week and when I heard the shower go on…"

Dixie clasped his face between her hands and stood on tiptoe. "Don't stop." She pressed her mouth to Gavin's and ignored the voice in her head insisting she proceed with caution. She wanted no reminders of what happened when she'd allowed her emotions and desires to take the lead. Dixie was tired of pretending she didn't need Gavin.

Right now. Right here. She needed him more than anything. She understood the risks involved in making love, but Gavin had squeaked through her defenses when he'd surprised her with the gift shop. The reasons they shouldn't be a couple no longer mattered. Dixie was willing to risk her heart because she had the baby in her corner. Gavin cared about the baby and the baby was inside her. They were a package deal.

She wiggled closer, loving the feel of his powerful body. She tried to express what he meant to her through kisses and caresses…safer than saying the words out loud. With each touch she intended to show him that she was committed to their relationship. "Please, Gavin."

"I couldn't stop if I wanted to, honey."

"Hey, Dixie! Where's Gavin?" Johnny's voice echoed through the upstairs hallway.

Dixie gasped and Gavin clamped a hand over her mouth. She giggled at the stern look he gave her. They'd played in the shower until the cold water had forced them out. Good grief they were both adults having a baby together. So what if her brother caught them naked?

"Dixie?" Johnny pounded on the bathroom door.

Gavin wrapped Dixie in a towel, then tied one around his waist before opening the door. She peeked over Gavin's shoulder. Johnny stood in the hallway holding Gavin's clothes. Before anyone had a chance to speak the rest of her brothers skidded to a stop in the doorway.

"Well, now. That's a cozy sight." Willie expelled a grunt after Buck jabbed an elbow into his stomach.

Poor Buck. Finding his baby sister almost naked with a man was more than his prudish brain could process. "I didn't expect you until later tonight," she said.

"Obviously." Porter snickered.

Gavin raised his hand. "Before you interrogate your sister, give us some privacy to—"

"The last thing you two need is more privacy." Johnny shoved Gavin's clothes at him. "You're supposed to save that stuff for the honeymoon."

Conway came to Dixie's defense. "She's twenty-three, Johnny. Old enough to have sex. Hell, you were poking Ilene back in ninth grade. She was only—"

"Shut up, Conway."

"No you shut up, Johnny. Just because you're the oldest doesn't mean you can—"

"Hey," Willie interrupted. "Is that why Ilene wouldn't go to the school dance with me when I asked her? Because you were banging her in Grandpa's truck?"

Buck interrupted before Johnny had a chance to defend himself. "Didn't Grandpa find a condom on the floor of the backseat of his truck?"

"Shoot. Grandpa accused *me* of having sex with a girl. All along it was you." Willie shoved his finger in Johnny's chest.

"That was years ago. Besides, you never liked Ilene because she had small…you know." Johnny's face turned red.

"I wouldn't have cared if her boobs were no bigger than pecan nuts if she'd have let me under her skirt," Willie said.

"I thought you were in love with Marsha, Will?" Merle joined the conversation. "You said Marsha was your first love?"

"When did I say that?" Willie argued.

"When you got drunk two years ago and Merle had to haul your ass out of the bar," Johnny said. "You were foaming at the mouth about some girl named Marsha in your high-school class."

Dixie chanced a peek at Gavin and found him staring at her brothers in fascination. She supposed he'd never seen anything the likes of a Cash brothers' argument. Growing up an only child Gavin had missed out on all the action Dixie had seen in her younger years.

"Are we talking about Marsha Bugler?" Buck asked.

It amazed Dixie that no matter how loud or raucous her brothers became Buck's quiet voice always caught their attention.

"Yeah, that's the Marsha we're talking about. Why?" Johnny asked.

"Marsha and I were friends," Buck said.

"Friends?" Willie scoffed. "She never mentioned you when we were together." Willie's eyes narrowed. "Just how good of friends were you?"

"Good enough that she told me you'd gotten her pregnant."

Dixie gasped and her brothers' jaws dropped. "Is that true?" Johnny asked Willie.

No one spoke a word. Moved a muscle. Or breathed as they waited for Willie's answer.

"It's true."

"How come you didn't tell Grandpa or Grandma?" Dixie asked.

"Marsha told me not to tell anyone because she wasn't going to keep the baby," Willie said.

Dixie rested her hand over her tummy as if to protect her unborn child from her brother's confession.

Like a dark cloud hovering overhead, silence filled the hallway as everyone digested Willie's confession. Then Buck asked, "Do you ever hear from Marsha?"

"No. Why would I? She moved to California."

Without another word, Buck retreated to his room, the sound of his clunking boot heels echoing in the air.

"What's up with Buck?" Willie asked Johnny.

"How should I know?" Johnny pointed at Gavin. "Get dressed and meet me outside." The Cash brothers dispersed… Porter and Merle heading to their rooms, the rest following Johnny downstairs.

Dixie shut the bathroom door and leaned against it. "Sorry about the interruption."

Gavin wasn't. Standing naked, save for a skimpy towel and her long hair dripping wet, Dixie had never looked more appealing. If she didn't leave the bathroom soon, he wouldn't let her. He picked up her clothes from the floor and held them out.

As if sensing Gavin's arousal, Dixie mumbled, "I'll get dressed in my room."

Gavin pulled on his jeans. He caught a glimpse of himself in the mirror above the sink and stared long and hard, seeking answers about his and Dixie's future.

He'd spent a lot of time with Dixie lately and had

learned a few things about himself in the process. One—
her smile produced tiny twinges in his chest. Two—he
knew what she was thinking before she spoke out loud.
Three—not an hour in the day went by when he didn't
want to kiss her. Four—he hadn't missed riding the circuit as he'd anticipated. Five—he'd learned that if he
focused his thoughts on Dixie before he fell asleep, the
chances of dreaming of Nate's death greatly decreased.

Tonight with Dixie clinging to him in the shower he
admitted that he yearned for her to need him not because he provided her and the baby a sense of security,
but because she desired him the way a woman desires
a man she loves.

Until now, Gavin hadn't admitted to himself that he'd
purchased the shop in Yuma because he'd wanted to be
tied to Dixie by more than the baby. He turned away
from the mirror and slipped into his shirt. He couldn't
regret getting Dixie pregnant, because she and his unborn child had become his anchor. Dixie and the baby
made sense when nothing else did.

He shoved his feet into his boots and went outside
where he found Johnny waiting on the porch swing with
a shotgun resting across his lap.

"Are you going hunting?" Gavin asked.

"As soon as Dixie gets out here we're all taking a
drive to visit Reverend Thomas."

Johnny would get no argument from Gavin.

Dixie's brother narrowed his eyes. "You're not leaving Stagecoach until you marry my sister."

"Says who?" Dixie stepped onto the porch and planted
her fists on her hips.

"Says me." Johnny stood.

"Over my dead body."

Johnny cocked the rifle. "Fine by me."

"Settle down, you two," Gavin said. Johnny was all bluster but Gavin didn't appreciate Dixie's adamant refusal to marry him. Hadn't their lovemaking in the shower meant anything to her?

"I won't be rushed," Dixie insisted.

Gavin came to her rescue. "I believe your sister would like a real wedding…the kind with a guest list and a reception afterward."

"That takes time to plan," Dixie added.

"You two had better get planning then because there will be no more hanky-panky in this house until you're married."

"Don't talk stupid, Johnny." Dixie looked at Gavin. "I'm starving." She waltzed off the porch and hopped into Gavin's truck.

"If you string my sister along, Tucker, you'll answer to me and my brothers."

If anyone was doing the stringing, it was Dixie, not Gavin.

Chapter 11

"You're awfully quiet," Dixie said.

Gavin bit into his Chicago-style hotdog and shrugged. He'd been lost in thought since they'd pulled into Vern's Drive-In fifteen minutes ago.

"You shouldn't let my brothers get to you."

Easier said than done. After Johnny had accused him of leading Dixie on, Gavin had questioned his intentions toward their sister. On the surface he'd convinced himself marrying Dixie was the right thing to do—the one sure way to step up and accept responsibility for his actions. And he admitted that Dixie had a calming effect on him and made him feel more in control of his emotions and his ability to close himself off from the demons that haunted him at night. But after they'd made love in the shower…he'd felt a strong urge to be a good father and provide his child with a stable, normal upbringing—

the opposite of what he and Dixie had experienced. This *urge* was gaining steam inside Gavin and scaring him.

What if he didn't turn out to be a good father? "My dad was never in the picture when I was a kid." Hell, Gavin didn't know the first thing about a father's role in the family.

"Did you have any contact with him?" she asked.

"Once. I was fourteen and he scared the crap out of me."

"What happened?"

"I was waiting at a bus stop after dark and he approached me." Gavin remembered that Friday night as if it had happened yesterday. His father had been filthy, his clothes torn, his hair hanging in greasy strands over his shoulders. His breath had smelled putrid—like rotting teeth and beer. His father had said, "What's the matter, son? Don't you recognize me?"

"What did your dad want?"

"Money. He was living on the street." Gavin had given him what was in his pocket—four dollars.

"What did your mother say when you got home and told her?"

Gavin hadn't told his mother right away. He'd slipped into his room and sat on the bed, shaking with disgust and fear. When he'd finally confessed to seeing his father, his mom had been furious and concerned for Gavin's safety. "She was upset and she felt bad that I had to see how destitute my father had become."

"How did he get so bad off?"

"He was a drug addict." Gavin got the creeps when he thought about all the times he'd ridden the city buses alone through the years and how his father could have approached him at any time.

"I'm sorry." Dixie gripped his thigh and his muscle warmed. "I know the feeling of not having a father give a damn about you."

Gavin wanted to show his child he cared by being there in person. But a real marriage to Dixie meant he had to stop running for good…forever. No matter what his fears were, Gavin felt compelled to try—for his child's sake.

"Dixie, you do know that when I asked you to marry me it was with the assumption that we were going to live together."

She removed her hand from his leg, leaving behind a chill where her fingers had touched him.

"I don't want to see my kid every other weekend or just when I'm passing through town on my way to a rodeo. I want to be there every day." In order to do that Gavin would have to land a civilian job and put down roots—the very things he swore he'd steer clear of when he'd left the army.

He credited Dixie with the reprieve he'd experienced from the nightmares that had plagued him after returning from Afghanistan, but could he trust the horrible memories to remain at bay forever? He pictured himself lying next to Dixie in bed, holding her close then awakening to her screams because he dreamt she was the enemy and he'd pinned her to the mattress.

"Will you be truthful with me if I ask you a question?" she said.

Gavin nodded.

"Is the real reason you're pushing marriage because of the shop in Yuma?"

"What do you mean?"

Dixie squirmed, her eyes shifting between Gavin and

the neon sign above the drive-in. "Are you worried I won't be a good manager and the shop will go bankrupt?"

The thought hadn't entered his mind. "No. If things don't work out between us and we split, the shop remains yours." Gavin believed as long as Dixie had a means of supporting herself and he refrained from interfering she wouldn't worry about him threatening her independence. "I'm not marrying you to take care of you," he said. "I'm marrying you so that our child has a shot at a normal life." If there was such a thing these days.

Dixie's silence worried Gavin. If he pushed her into marriage before she was ready, would she panic and run as soon as they said "I do"? Evil laughter echoed through his head. If anyone ran it would be *him* not Dixie.

"Okay." The quietly spoken word sounded like a firecracker exploding inside the truck.

His blood pumped hard through his veins. "Okay what?"

"Okay, I'll set a wedding date. But nothing fancy. I can't afford a big shindig and you've already spent too much money on the gift shop."

"Small suits me fine, but I'd like there to be enough time for my mother to make arrangements to come."

"I forgot about your mother."

"She's eager to meet you."

Dixie worried her lower lip. "I've been without my mother and grandparents for so long I forgot my pregnancy doesn't just affect us."

"My mother won't interfere in our decisions about the baby if that concerns you."

"Not at all. My grandmother meant the world to me

and I want our baby to have a close relationship with your mother."

"How soon can you put a wedding together?"

"What's your rodeo schedule like the next couple of weeks?"

"I can pick and choose." Gavin wasn't rodeoing for the money, that was for sure.

"Today's date is…"

"October 16."

"Would the first Saturday in November work for you and your mother? I'll check with the church to see if it's available."

"I'll phone my mom on the way back to the store tonight."

Dixie smiled. "Why drive back to Yuma just to sleep?"

"I've been doing it all week."

"My brothers caught us taking a shower together. If we tell them we've picked a wedding date they won't care if you share my bed."

The temperature inside the truck shot up ten degrees as Gavin imagined cuddling Dixie in bed. Now that they were committed to going through with a marriage ceremony, there was no reason they couldn't make love whenever and wherever the mood struck. And after their tryst in the bathroom today, Gavin knew without a doubt that Dixie enjoyed making love with him.

"All right. I'll spend the night at the farm." Her brothers would just have to get used to their sister and Gavin sneaking off to be alone—at least until they decided where they'd live after the wedding. *Don't forget about finding a job.*

Gavin would begin looking for civilian work once he

and Dixie were legally married. They'd need time to become used to marriage and living together. He wouldn't push her to find an apartment in Yuma until the baby came and he quit rodeo. He ate the last bite of hotdog, then started the engine and backed out of the parking spot. "I think we should tell your family together," he said.

"That's fine. You can do all the talking."

This was one time Gavin looked forward to confronting the Cash brothers.

"I made a to-do list for the wedding." Conway's abrupt statement as he waltzed into the kitchen Monday morning startled a drowsy Dixie as she ate her oatmeal.

The instant Gavin had announced that they'd selected Saturday, November 4 for their wedding her slick-talking, bucking-bronc rodeo-junky brothers had morphed into wedding planners.

"I want a quiet, family-only ceremony." Dixie shoved her empty bowl across the table and suppressed the growing anxiety that she'd made a mistake in agreeing to a wedding date. Then she remembered the shower she and Gavin had shared two days ago and her heart sighed.

"What's up with the dreamy look on your face?" Conway poured himself a mug of coffee and joined Dixie at the table.

"Sleepy, not dreamy. I wish I could catch a nap before heading into Yuma to open the shop."

"How come Gavin left early this morning?"

Gavin had slept on the sofa and risen at the crack of dawn. She smiled at the memory of him sneaking into her bedroom and waking her with a kiss and a whispered, "I'll call you later."

"Gavin's off rodeoing."

"Where? The next event's in Casa Grande."

"He mentioned California." Dixie assumed Gavin needed some space before they got married in a couple of weeks and she also appreciated the breathing room.

"When will he be back?" Conway asked.

"He didn't say."

"Guess it doesn't matter. You can call him for his opinion on wedding themes."

Themes? "Conway, what are you up to?"

"Your wedding has to have a theme and since you own a soap shop I thought we'd use bubbles."

Dixie sputtered. "Bubbles?" Good Lord, if Conway gave each guest a bottle of bubbles the inside of the church would look like a wash machine gone wild.

"No bubbles," she said. "Besides, we don't have the money for anything extravagant, so the guest list is limited to a handful."

Conway frowned. "I suppose that means the reception has to be at the farm?"

"We'll clean the barn and set up tables in there. Cook barbecue and—"

Conway snapped his fingers. "A pig roast—what a great idea, sis."

"No pigs on a spit!" She winced and lowered her voice. "Pulled-pork barbecue."

"What's going on?" Porter strolled over to the fridge. "Who drank all the juice?" He swished the half inch of orange liquid in the plastic container.

"Sorry," Dixie said. "I gave up soda until after the baby's born."

Merle joined his siblings in the kitchen. "Are you going to breast-feed?"

The kitchen was becoming much too crowded. "I don't know. I hadn't thought that far ahead." Besides, this wasn't a conversation sisters had with brothers.

"If you breast-feed, you can't eat junk food." Merle grabbed several slices of white bread to go with his morning coffee. "You have to eat healthy stuff."

"Since when have you become an expert on lactating women's diets?" she asked as Merle dunked a piece of bread in his coffee, then shoved the sopping mess into his mouth and grinned.

"When do you have time to shop for a wedding dress?" Conway asked.

"I plan to wear Grandma's." The plain, unadorned silk had aged to a beautiful ivory color and was lovingly packed in a box beneath her bed.

"What about bridesmaids?" Conway said. "Gavin'll have groomsmen plus a best man."

"Who's Gavin gonna pick for a best man?" Merle asked.

Conway scribbled a note on the pad of paper in front of him. "I bet he picks Johnny."

"Who's picking Johnny for what?" Willie joined his siblings.

"Best man," Porter answered.

"Hold on everyone." Dixie scooted her chair back and stood. "Gavin and I aren't having a big wedding. Johnny will give me away but no bridesmaids or groomsmen."

"Why's everyone in the kitchen?" Buck came in from the wash porch.

Porter, Conway, Willie and Merle pointed at Dixie. "We're trying to plan a wedding but she's putting up a stink," Conway said.

"It's *my* wedding. I can put up a stink if I want to."

"Cold feet?" Buck's quiet voice silenced her brothers.

"No." *Maybe.* "Conway thinks I need a fancy-schmancy wedding and I want to keep things simple." She didn't dare tell her brothers that one of the reasons she didn't care for an extravagant affair was because she didn't want Gavin believing she was head-over-heels about him—just in case things didn't work out and they parted ways after the baby was born.

Her brothers' gazes swung to Buck, waiting for his response. "Dixie's the bride. She has the final say."

"Thank you, Buck. You're my favorite brother." She placed her juice glass in the sink. "Now, if you'll excuse me, I have a business to run." She stepped outside and took a deep breath, filling her lungs with cool morning air. She loved the month of October—daytime highs in the eighties and nighttime lows in the sixties—perfect sleeping weather. October made suffering through the unbearable heat of Arizona summers worthwhile. As soon as she got in her truck and cranked the engine she flipped on the radio, hoping the noise would block out her concerns over marrying Gavin.

No such luck.

Gavin's arguments in favor of marrying were sound—she was all in favor of him being involved in their child's life, but recognized from her mother's experience that a man and woman living together for the sake of a child always led to a breakup. Dixie didn't want to suffer the same heartache and bouts of depression her mother had endured as a result of failed relationships.

Then don't let Gavin steal your heart.

Too late. After all he'd done for her, there was no way Dixie could not love the man—at least a little.

Feel appreciation and gratitude, but stop there.

No can do. Their lovemaking had touched her deeply and convinced her that Gavin cared about her—how much, time would tell. The one thing that saved her from a panic attack was the knowledge that if Gavin tired of her or decided he wanted out of the marriage, she retained the gift shop in Yuma. As long as she had a means of supporting herself and the baby she'd survive without Gavin.

Dixie's cell rang. Keeping one eye on the road she stuck her hand into her purse and rummaged through the contents until her fingers bumped the phone.

"Hello."

"It's me."

Her heart stuttered at the sound of Gavin's sexy voice. "Everything okay?"

"Yep. Just calling to see how things are going with you."

"Fine." Dixie smiled. "Where are you?"

"Chula Vista."

"You're rodeoing there?"

"No. Passing through. I'll be in San Dimas this weekend."

Because she was content working in her store each day, it didn't bother Dixie a bit that Gavin would spend the week traveling through California.

"I might look up a few army buddies while I'm out here." He cleared his throat. "How are the wedding plans going?"

"Fine."

Silence followed by, "Let me know if you need any money."

Gavin had already done more than enough and Dixie would not ask him to help pay for a wedding. "My brothers want to know if you'll be picking a best man." Dixie winced as soon as she asked the question. She hadn't meant to remind Gavin of the loss of his best friend.

"I don't have anyone in mind for a best man."

"That's fine because I'm not having a maid of honor." Shannon was the only friend she'd consider asking and Shannon was in Florida for who knew how long.

"Dixie, you don't have to—"

"No, it's all right, Gavin."

"I've got to go. Traffic is a nightmare."

"Okay. And, Gavin…thank you—" she swallowed the lump in her throat that formed when she thought of his generosity "—for buying the shop."

"Talk to you later."

The call cut off and Dixie felt a keen sense of loss. She slowed down as she drove through Stagecoach and shifted her thoughts to the gift shop and brainstorming ideas to increase sales and publicity.

"Where the hell have you been, Tucker?"

Gavin grinned in the cowboy ready area at the San Dimas Western Days Rodeo in San Dimas, California. "What's the matter, Murray, afraid I'll win?"

Fellow bareback rider Ryan Murray snorted. "Army man, I can beat you with both hands tied behind my back."

Gavin shook hands with Murray—the wiry cowboy reminded him of Nate—always teasing people. "I had business to take care of in Arizona." Gavin dropped his gear bag.

"Thought maybe you had an epiphany and realized you weren't a bona fide bareback rider."

A group of competitors nearby chuckled and tipped

their hats to Gavin. He'd missed sparring with the guys when he'd taken a break from the circuit to help Dixie with the store. "Why've you been hanging out in Arizona?" A cowboy named Pete Santali invited himself into the conversation. Santali was a bull rider who'd joined the circuit right out of high school and had yet to finish higher than tenth in a rodeo.

"You recall the Canyon City Rodeo in Arizona this past July?" Gavin spoke to the men.

"Sure. I rode Caramel Delight and he kicked my butt into the stands," Santali said.

"Remember the female bull riding event?"

"Hell, yes! Prettiest dang girls I ever seen ride bulls." Murray spit tobacco juice at the ground. "You hook up with one of them beauties?"

"As a matter of fact, I did. I'm engaged to Dixie Cash."

Murray whistled between his teeth. "Man, are you crazy? I sure as hell wouldn't want the Cash cowboys as brothers-in-law."

"They're not so bad." Gavin took comfort in knowing that while he was on the road, the brothers would be there to help Dixie if she needed anything.

"You gonna keep rodeoing after you marry?" Santali asked.

"Not sure." The past week he'd enjoyed being by Dixie's side and as far as small towns went, Stagecoach wasn't bad. Commuting into Yuma for a job wouldn't bother him—not if Dixie worked in her gift shop. He liked the idea of meeting her for lunch or dropping into the store to check on her and the baby during the day.

"When's the wedding?" Santali asked. "We invited?"

"Nope. We're having a family-only ceremony next month."

"You gonna look for a real job?" Murray asked.

"Eventually."

Santali chuckled. "Hell, I wouldn't know where to apply if I had to get a real job."

"I've got experience with water reclamation projects," Gavin said. "I'm hoping to find work with the city of Yuma."

"Good luck to you, man." Murray shook Gavin's hand and Santali did the same, and then the cowboys walked off.

Gavin approached chute eight and studied his draw— a horse named Tiny Dancer—when the gelding bucked, he gave the illusion of walking on air. The horse had a fifty-fifty win streak going so Gavin had a shot of making it to eight. He rummaged through his gear bag and removed his rope and glove. The announcer droned on about the winners of the bareback event from the previous year's rodeo. Gavin appreciated that the announcer attempted to make the event sound important or relevant to the current rodeo standings, but the truth was the cowboys riding today weren't good enough to compete for the bigger purses. The Western Days rodeo was comprised of young hotheads trying to gain experience, old has-beens who refused to hang up their ropes and Gavin—guys whose lives were in limbo.

"Next up is Gavin Tucker! He's riding Tiny Dancer!"

Gavin stuffed his hand into his riding glove, then climbed the chute rails and settled on the gelding's back. He played with his grip on the rope handle, trying not to overthink his ride. He'd gotten caught up in attempting to predict a horse's moves before the chute door opened and the horse never performed as expected—most of the time Gavin sailed through the air after a few bucks.

One more twist of the rope and he nodded to the gate-man. Tiny Dancer vaulted into the arena. Gavin rode out the first three bucks in succession and then the gelding got serious and added a spin to his repertoire of moves. Gavin—cocky from three seconds of success—sailed over the horse's head. He landed on the ground, skidding across the dirt on his stomach then came to a stop in a tangle of arms and legs. The fans' lukewarm applause embarrassed him as he crawled to his knees and retrieved his hat.

"Tucker," Santali hollered when Gavin stepped behind the chutes. "Hope you make a better husband than you do a rodeo cowboy."

So did Gavin.

Chapter 12

"Dixie, I've got to have another bar of that romance soap you sold me last week." Mildred Hinkle marched through the gift shop and stopped in front of the counter where Dixie rang up a customer. "You'll want another bar of that one." Mildred pointed to the pink-wrapped soap among the woman's purchases. "Use it to wash your delicates and I guarantee your husband will notice."

The customer nodded and Dixie added another bar from the romance collection. "That will be twenty-eight dollars and thirty-six cents." She ran the woman's credit card through the machine, then handed her a receipt to sign. "The bottom one is yours."

"Thank you for the recommendation." The woman smiled at Mrs. Hinkle.

"Happy to help."

If Dixie didn't know better, she'd swear sourpuss Mildred had become Ms. Congeniality. Left alone with the old woman she said, "I'm glad your husband approves of the soap."

"He more than approves." Mildred winked. "He came to bed before the ten o'clock news before every night this week. Hasn't done that in seventeen years."

Dixie swallowed a chuckle. "I'm working on a new Thanksgiving soap—citrus spice." She motioned for Mildred to follow her into the kitchen at the back of the store. Each night Dixie stayed late to make soap after the shop closed—better to keep busy than sit at home and think of Gavin. She expected to miss him, but hadn't anticipated her every other thought to focus on him... What was he doing? Who was he with? Was he thinking of her?

Gavin had made a habit of phoning Dixie in the evenings to wish her good-night. He had no idea that when she answered his calls she was on the road driving back to Stagecoach. She didn't tell him she'd worked late, knowing he'd disapprove of her driving home alone at night. Or he'd insist she wasn't getting enough rest. Dixie had agreed to a wedding—not to having Gavin dictate her every move.

Mildred studied the bowls of spices and herbs on the kitchen table while Dixie fetched the sample soap and waved it beneath Mildred's nose.

"Lovely...almost good enough to eat. Is that nutmeg?"

"Yes." Dixie held up a leaf and a pumpkin-shaped mold. "Which one do you prefer?"

"Both. Have you thought of adding additional shapes like gourds and Indian corn? A bowl of harvest-scented soaps would make a terrific holiday display."

"That's a great idea. Thank you, Mrs. Hinkle."

Mildred glanced at the wall clock. "I'd better return to my store."

Dixie followed her to the front door, happy to see another customer come into the shop. She hoped the steady stream of clientele this week foreshadowed the upcoming holiday spending habits of the locals and tourists.

"Where's that handsome young man who helped you during your grand opening?"

"Gavin's rodeoing."

Mildred's gaze narrowed. "Oh, he's one of those cowboys?" She waggled a finger in front of Dixie's face. "You best keep an eye on him, dear." She leaned closer. "I know from experience that traveling men stray."

Dixie watched Mildred cross the street and walk up the block to her store. She considered the older woman's words, then discarded them. Gavin wasn't the kind of man to stray. She honestly believed when he'd proposed to her—yes, for the sake of the baby—that he planned to honor their marriage vows. Honorable intentions aside, there was the chance that after the baby was born and they set up house and established a routine that their relationship might hit a bump in the road.

There was no guarantee she and Gavin and the baby would remain a family forever, but she had to try—for the baby's sake *and* her sake. She'd rather live with the stigma of a divorce than hear gossip about her being an unwed mother. A tramp. Or worse—that she'd followed in her mother's footsteps.

"Let me know if I can answer any questions." Dixie smiled at her customer.

"I'm just browsing, thank you."

A dull twinge spread through Dixie's stomach—the third one in as many hours. She pressed her fingers against her side and returned to the kitchen. She shouldn't have eaten the pickle that came with the tuna sandwich she'd ordered from the deli.

"Gavin! What are you doing here?" Gavin's mother hugged the life out of him while he stood on the welcome mat outside her apartment.

"Miss me?" Gavin teased.

"Of course." She tugged him inside and shut the door. A baritone woof greeted him.

"Hey, Barney."

"Barney's disappointed you're not Ricardo asking us to join him and Chica on a walk."

"So it's like that between you and Ricardo?" Gavin tossed his Stetson on top of his mother's coffee table, removed his phone from his pocket and turned off the ringer before sitting on the couch next to the old bulldog. He scratched Barney behind the ears.

"Ricardo and I are friends. Nothing more." His mother retrieved a can of Gavin's favorite cola from the fridge.

"What's the expiration date on this?"

"Ha-ha. Maybe you should visit your mother more often." She patted his cheek. "I'll make you a sandwich—"

"No thanks, Mom. I ate on the way into town."

His mother returned to her recliner. "Why didn't you tell me you were coming to Phoenix? I would have asked for time off from work."

"I can't stay. I'm on my way to Winslow."

"Another rodeo?"

"Yep."

"Looks like you've been staying healthy unless you're hiding a cast under that shirt."

"No broken bones. Sore muscles and achy joints but that's nothing new."

"How's Dixie?"

"Good."

"Just good?"

"We set a wedding date."

"Then things between you two are better than good." His mother smiled. "Have you decided where you'll live after you marry?"

Gavin read between the lines of his mother's question. She wanted him to settle near her in Phoenix. "A lot has happened since we last talked."

"And whose fault is that? You only phone every two weeks."

"I'll try to do better." Gavin smiled sheepishly. After years in the military where he'd been in the habit of phoning home once a month he had trouble keeping track of the time between calls to his mother.

Yet you remembered to check in with Dixie every night this past week.

"Dixie and I bought a gift shop in Yuma and she's selling her homemade soaps there." His mother would only worry if she discovered Gavin had taken out the loan but the store belonged to Dixie.

"Does this mean you're going to retire from rodeo?"

"Not yet. Perfumed soaps aren't my thing. Dixie's in charge of the store."

"How long do you plan to rodeo, then?"

Gavin sympathized with his mother worrying over his health and safety. She'd spent six years fretting about him in the army. He'd come back alive from a war zone and she still had to worry he'd get his head stomped in by a bronc. "I'll rodeo until the baby's born."

"And Dixie's due date is…?"

"Sometime in March. I'm planning to look for a civilian job after Christmas. Hopefully I'll find work in Yuma."

"So you and Dixie intend to stay in Yuma?"

"No. Dixie's lived her entire life in Stagecoach, Mom. The family farm means a lot to her and they lease the pecan groves to a business corporation so she'll want to be close by to keep an eye on things." Her six brothers could do the eye-keeping, but in truth, Stagecoach had grown on Gavin.

When he'd left the army he'd planned to live in a big city where he could go about his daily routine with a good amount of anonymity. With a baby on the way and he and Dixie marrying, Gavin believed the best environment for their child was among friends and family.

"Would you consider moving to Yuma? It's not that far from Stagecoach." It had always been the two of them—Gavin's grandparents had disowned his mother when she'd turned up pregnant.

"Is that your roundabout way of asking if I'll take care of the baby while you and Dixie work?"

"Not at all. Dixie's going to bring the baby to the shop with her."

If push came to shove, Gavin would admit fatherhood was scarier than fighting the Taliban and he'd appreciate having his mother's support and guidance.

"I'd like nothing better than to live closer to you and the baby, but I love my job with the parks department and Ricardo…" Her cheeks turned pink.

His mother had never dated while she'd raised him— at least not to Gavin's knowledge. "You love this man?"

"Not love. I like Ricardo very much. He's a widower and we enjoy each other's company."

"No pressure, Mom. I want you to be happy. Just know you can visit Dixie and me as often as you want."

"I will do that. Are you planning to live at her farm, then?"

Gavin cringed at the prospect of sharing a house with the Cash brothers. "For a while, I guess."

"What's the matter, honey? You seem—" his mother waved a hand in the air by her face "—unsettled."

Needing to voice his fear out loud, he said, "I'm not sure Dixie's as committed to making our marriage work as I am."

"Go on."

"Dixie and I have gone about this whole thing in an unconventional way." He ran his fingers through his hair. "She didn't tell me she was pregnant. I had to confront her. In the beginning I wasn't ready for marriage and only wanted to offer financial support." Gavin popped off the couch and paced by the front door. "Then I had a change of heart."

Because being with Dixie makes you feel good inside.

"I insisted that Dixie and I marry for the baby's sake."

His mother's eyes widened.

"I know it sounds bad, but Dixie grew up without a father, too, and I thought she'd appreciate my gesture."

"I'm guessing she didn't."

"No. She rejected my proposal and…"

"And what?"

"I was relieved."

"Why?"

"I wasn't ready to settle down, Mom. I've been on the move with the army for so long I didn't think I could stay in one place and be happy." Gavin's explanation was weak at best.

"Then Dixie and I spent more time together and got to know each other better. So I thought, why not do what was best for the baby and maybe along the way we'd all become a real family."

"Dixie didn't see things your way?"

"No. She agreed to an engagement but wanted to wait to marry until after the baby was born."

"What changed her mind about setting a wedding date?"

That was the million-dollar question. "I don't know." He didn't want to believe Dixie felt indebted to him for buying the shop in Yuma. Or that after making love in the shower she'd allowed her hormones to speak for her. Gavin hoped her feelings for him were deepening.

"Have either of you said the words *I love you*?"

Gavin dropped his gaze to the tips of his boots. "No."

"Then maybe the wedding should wait."

Dixie was skittish enough about marrying. If Gavin suddenly got cold feet and suggested they postpone their nuptials he'd never convince her to pick another date. "I think it's best we marry now not after the baby's born."

"All right. You can count on me to be at the wedding."

"Thanks."

"And, honey, I'm always here for you if you need to talk."

Gavin hugged his mother. "I know."

"I hope Dixie appreciates your integrity and all you're willing to do for her."

"She does." Appreciation wasn't the problem, but convincing Dixie to commit a hundred percent to their marriage was an obstacle he'd yet to overcome. Being away from Dixie this week had taught Gavin how much he needed her. With Dixie by his side, he could defeat the enemies who stalked him at night. Without Dixie... Gavin feared the worst—a life on the run and no relationship with his own child.

"Johnny," Dixie gasped.

"Hey, sis, what's up?"

Another sharp pain stabbed Dixie in the side and she broke out in a cold sweat. "Are you busy?"

"I'm on my way into Yuma to pick up a new pair of jeans. The back pocket ripped the other day and—"

"Meet me at the Yuma Regional Medical Center."

"What happened?"

She gripped the clipboard in her hand until another pain passed. "It's the baby." Finished filling out the medical forms, Dixie stood. As soon as she took a step, a rush of warmth spread between her legs. Horrified, she glanced down. A dark stain spread across the crotch of her jeans. Feeling faint, she collapsed on the chair and the phone dropped into her lap.

The redheaded nurse behind the station desk summed up the situation and called for a wheelchair. An orderly appeared and they helped Dixie into the chair, then wheeled her into a curtained-off cubicle where the nurse assisted her in putting on a hospital gown. When Dixie caught sight of her bloody underwear tears filled her eyes.

"Hang on, dear." The nurse helped her onto the hospital bed and stuffed a pad between her legs before picking up the phone and calling for a doctor. The nurse returned to Dixie's side and took her vital signs. "How far along are you?"

"Fourteen weeks."

The nurse patted Dixie's hand. "The doctor will be here soon."

"Am I losing the baby?"

"I don't know, but we'll do everything we can to help you."

Left alone in the sterile room Dixie closed her eyes and prayed for her baby.

A few minutes later a middle-age man flung the curtain aside and stepped into the cubicle. "I'm Dr. Davidson." He scanned Dixie's medical chart. "Did you fall or hurt yourself today?"

"No." She hadn't fallen. Hadn't bumped into anything. "I began feeling sharp twinges this morning and they became worse after lunch."

"What have you eaten today?"

"Toast, orange juice. A pickle and a tuna sandwich."

"Let's take a look at you." The nurse rolled an ultrasound machine next to the bed and the doctor squirted cold jelly across Dixie's stomach. She gave him credit for maintaining a poker face. The nurse watching the monitor wasn't a good actress—she wouldn't make eye contact with Dixie.

I'm losing the baby.

"I'm sorry. The placenta tore away from the uterine wall and the baby no longer has a heartbeat." He squeezed Dixie's arm gently. "Sometimes these things happen and there's no explanation why." He scribbled on the medical chart then asked, "This was your first pregnancy?"

Dixie nodded, still struggling to process the news that she'd lost the baby.

"You'll be able to try for another baby as soon as your body has had time to heal."

I won't be able to try again—not with Gavin. Her throat thickened and she struggled to catch her breath.

"I'll need to perform a D and C once you expel the fetus." He looked at the nurse. "Call me when she's ready."

As soon as the doctor left the room the nurse started an IV and a few minutes later, Dixie felt contractions. Offering words of encouragement and sympathy, the nurse held her hand and it was over in twenty minutes. After administering a sedative, the doctor performed a D and C. Dixie had no idea how much time had passed when he peeled off his gloves, patted her shoulder and told her to follow up with her gynecologist as soon as possible. Then he was gone.

"Would you like to see your daughter?" the nurse whispered as if the baby were sleeping and not dead.

My daughter?

The nurse held a towel between her hands, and there in the middle of the cloth lay a teeny-tiny baby approximately four inches long. The most beautiful little being Dixie had ever seen.

"You can hold her," the nurse said.

Tears blurred her vision as Dixie cradled the towel in her lap. Gently she brushed the tip of a finger over her daughter's head. *I love you, sweetheart. I'm so sorry. So sorry. Your daddy loves you, too.* Dixie pressed the pad of her index finger against her daughter's lifeless heart. *Find Grandma Ada, sweetie. She'll take care of you in Heaven and one day we'll be together again.* Dixie pressed a kiss to the baby's face, then handed her back to the nurse.

"Have you picked a name?" The nurse's eyes shone with unshed tears.

"Adelle. Addy for short. After her great-grandmother."

"It's a beautiful name." The nurse gently placed the towel on the instrument tray. "We have a chaplain on duty."

Dixie shook her head no.

"Would you prefer the hospital make arrangements for the baby or did you—"

"She's going home with me." Dixie would bury little Addy in the family plot next to her great-grandmother.

"Who should we call for you while you're recovering?"

"My brother's on his way."

"Try to rest. Once the bleeding slows down and you feel well enough to stand and walk, you'll be released. When your brother arrives I'll send him in to sit with you."

"Thank you."

"I'm sorry you lost your little girl." The nurse slid the curtain closed, allowing Dixie privacy to mourn.

Alone at last, tears leaked from her eyes, dribbled down her temples and pooled in her ears.

Gavin, where are you? I need you.

Dixie cried herself to sleep. When she woke all six of her brothers stood by her bedside. They might be the most bothersome, demanding, opinionated, bossy brothers a girl could have but they'd dropped whatever they'd been doing and had rushed to her side.

Johnny leaned down and hugged her. "I'm sorry, Dix."

Throat aching she glanced at each brother through watery eyes. "Did the nurse tell you?"

"Tell us what?" Merle asked.

"The baby was a girl."

Johnny cleared his throat. "She told us you wanted to take her home to bury her."

"If we had a girl, Gavin and I had decided to name her Adelle. I want to bury her next to Grandma Ada."

"That's a good idea," Porter said. "Grandma would be real honored you picked her name."

"Have you told Gavin?" Conway asked.

Dixie shook her head. "I called a couple of times but his phone went straight to voice mail. I didn't leave a message." It didn't seem right to tell Gavin she'd lost their baby in a voice message.

"We'll track him down," Johnny said.

She squeezed Johnny's fingers. "Tell Gavin that I don't want to see him." What was the point? There was no baby so there would be no marriage.

"What about the wedding?" Merle asked.

"There isn't going to be one."

Her brothers frowned.

"What do you mean there won't be a wedding?" Conway asked.

"Gavin's off the hook." Dixie grimaced at the sight of her soiled clothes resting on the chair. "I can't wear my jeans."

"The nurse left a pair of scrubs for you." Johnny pointed to the outfit at the foot of the bed.

"Give me some privacy to dress. I want to go—" her voice broke "—home." Dixie wished her grandmother waited for her at the farm—Grandma Ada always knew how to heal a hurting heart.

Chapter 13

"Why the hell haven't you been answering your cell, Tucker?"

Gavin held the phone away from his ear. The irate caller sounded like Dixie's brother. "Johnny?"

"I've been trying to get ahold of you since Monday."

"Sorry. My phone's been turning off on its own. I need a new—"

"Never mind your phone. It's Dixie."

Fear shot through Gavin, leaving him cold. He'd left a voice mail on Dixie's cell after the rodeo in Winslow on Sunday but she'd never returned his call. Figuring she'd been busy with the store or she'd gotten tired of him phoning, he'd backed off and hadn't attempted to contact her the past two days. He wanted to surprise her and show up in person at the gift shop tomorrow. "What's wrong, Johnny? Is she okay?"

"Dixie's…fine. Get here as soon as you can."

Gavin checked his mirrors, then pulled over to the side of the road and waited for three vehicles to pass. Coast clear, he made a U-turn and headed west on I-8. "I'm three hours away."

"Drive safe." *Click.*

Whatever was going on with Dixie must be serious if Johnny wouldn't say over the phone.

Don't jump to conclusions.

Maybe there'd been trouble at the gift shop. Had the place been robbed or vandalized? Or had Dixie changed her mind about the wedding—again. Was she back to wanting to marry after the baby's birth in March or worse…wanted to cancel the wedding altogether.

What if it's the baby?

As soon as the thought entered his mind, Gavin rejected it. Worrying wouldn't get him to the farm any faster. He put the pedal to the metal and pushed the truck to eighty. He could afford a ticket on his untarnished driving record. Hoping to keep his thoughts from straying to Dixie he turned on the radio and listened to a sports talk show.

Gavin cruised through Stagecoach at 10:15 p.m. His stomach growled, but he ignored the hunger pangs as he zipped through town, which was dead on a Wednesday night. Only the bars remained open, their neon beer signs glowing in the windows.

Tonight the Arizona sky was darker than usual—not even the silhouette of the Gila Mountains was visible to the southwest. He slowed the truck as he approached the turnoff to the farm. When he pulled up to the farmhouse, lights blazed from the windows on both floors and the Cash brothers' pickups were scattered about the yard.

Gavin parked behind Merle's truck and hurried to the house, taking the porch steps two at a time. He didn't bother knocking. When he stepped into the kitchen he found Dixie's siblings playing cards, Halloween candy substituting for poker chips.

Six somber faces stared at Gavin. He got the chills all over again.

Johnny stood. "Let's talk in the living room."

Gavin followed Dixie's eldest brother down the hall and Johnny shut the French doors behind them.

"Where's Dixie?" Gavin asked.

"Upstairs sleeping. I'd wake her but she's had a rough time of it and needs her sleep." The dull sheen in Johnny's blue eyes socked Gavin in the gut.

"Why hasn't Dixie been sleeping?"

"Look, Gavin. I shouldn't be the one telling you this, but if it were left up to Dixie who knows when you'd find out."

"Find out what?"

"She lost the baby on Monday."

The blood drained from Gavin's head and he sank onto the sofa. He hadn't wanted to believe something had happened to the baby but his instincts had been right all along. "Is Dixie okay?"

"Physically...yes. Emotionally she's a wreck."

Dixie taking the loss of their baby hard comforted Gavin in an odd way. They hadn't planned this pregnancy. Neither of them had been ready for parenthood, yet Dixie mourned for their child despite the fact that she was suddenly free of any long-term obligation. His chest felt numb...his hands cold. "How did she lose the baby?" He envisioned Dixie tumbling off a stepladder at the shop or tripping on the sidewalk.

"The doctor said sometimes these things happen and there's no real explanation why."

"She's been working too hard." He'd gone off to rodeo and left Dixie to handle the shop on her own. "I should have stayed and—"

"Don't blame yourself, Gavin. It wasn't your fault or Dixie's. It just happened." Johnny cleared his throat. "I'm sure you'll want to see her in the morning."

Did Dixie want to see him?

"I'll scrounge up an extra blanket and pillow. You can sleep on the couch." Johnny paused at the door. "And, Gavin?"

"What?"

"Keep things light between you and Dixie in the morning. She needs cheering up."

Dixie woke to the sun shining through her bedroom window. She squinted at the bright light. There was nothing *sunny* about the day ahead. She shifted on the mattress, the dull ache inside her still present. Her eyes misted. She'd cried so hard and so long Monday night after she'd returned from the hospital that there weren't any tears left inside her...just mist.

Her gaze fixated on the jewelry box her grandmother gave her. If she focused on an inanimate object long enough maybe she'd find the strength to dress for the day. She couldn't afford to spend another twenty-four hours in bed dwelling on the baby. She had to keep busy. Occupy her mind with other things. After breakfast she'd drive into Yuma and open the shop.

She swung her legs off the side of the mattress and sat up. She breathed deeply then grimaced. She needed a shower and her hair needed a shampoo. As if removed from her body, she shuffled across the room and rummaged through the dresser drawer. Clean clothes in hand she padded down the hall, noticing her brothers' bedroom doors stood open. Hopefully they'd left for the day—she wanted the house to herself.

The warm shower felt wonderful and Dixie stood beneath the pulsing water until it cooled. After drying off she smoothed lotion on her body and brushed her teeth. Once she blew her hair dry, she secured the long strands in a ponytail and went downstairs. She froze in the hallway.

Gavin. Asleep on the living room couch, his sock feet hanging over the edge.

Her eyes misted. Again.

Damn her brothers for interfering. She'd insisted she'd tell Gavin about the baby when she was ready. She was *not* ready right now. She fled to the kitchen where she found a note on the fridge, held in place by a saguaro magnet.

Porter and Buck opened the gift shop today. The rest of us are heading over to the Johnsons' to put a new roof on their barn. Call if you need anything. Johnny.

More mist in her eyes. Maybe by the end of the day she'd produce enough moisture to form a teardrop.

Dixie removed the carton of orange juice from the fridge, then promptly returned it to the shelf and shut the door. Her reason for eating healthy was…gone. She started a pot of coffee and gazed out the window above the sink. She had no idea how to handle things between her and Gavin.

Now that there was no baby she couldn't expect Gavin to keep paying the mortgage on the gift shop and she couldn't afford to buy him out. She supposed they'd have to put the place up for sale. Dixie didn't know how long she gazed out the window before Gavin's image materialized in the sparkling glass. Bracing herself, she faced him.

He looked tired and rumpled after a night on the couch. Their gazes locked. Neither moved. Neither spoke. The air thickened and silence echoed through the room in thunderous waves. Just when she feared she'd pass out from holding her breath, Gavin moved across the room and pulled her close, his hug firm.

Dixie's defenses were at an all-time low and she had no willpower to resist Gavin. In fact she desperately welcomed his sympathy. She could have stood in his arms forever—warm, safe and protected from reality. But touching Gavin…absorbing his comfort…breathing his scent…would only make the goodbye more difficult.

Slowly, as if her arms were lead pipes instead of flesh and bone, she released her hold and attempted to pull away.

Gavin held her prisoner, tightening his hold. Then he did the unthinkable—he kissed the top of her head, the gesture weakening her defenses.

Hadn't she bawled enough since Monday? She collapsed against Gavin, her tears soaking the front of his shirt.

He caressed her shoulders, uttered meaningless phrases in her ear and kissed her neck, his rough whiskers pricking her jaw. She cried forever—until the rumble of his deep voice filtered into her ear.

"What?" she choked out.

"Coffee's done."

She slipped from his embrace, wiped her eyes on a dish towel and poured two mugs of coffee. They sat across from each other at the table, Gavin's face sober. Sad. Concerned. Self-consciously she touched her cheeks. Three days of sobbing had left her with puffy eyes and blotchy skin. "What time did you get here last night?"

"After you'd already gone to bed." He frowned. "If you called me, I'm sorry. My phone's been turning off on its own. I need to upgrade to a new model."

She'd attempted to contact Gavin from the hospital before she'd lost the baby. Afterward, she hadn't had the courage to tell him. "Are you hungry?"

He shook his head.

Dixie hated beating around the bush. "Did Johnny tell you?"

"I'm sorry, Dixie."

She watched for a sign of how deeply the loss of their baby affected him, but his face remained expressionless. Playing the *tough guy* came naturally to a man who'd been in the army.

"How are things at the shop?" he asked.

Startled by the change in subject, it took Dixie a moment to formulate a response. "Fine."

"Christmas will be here soon," he said. "Are you going to run any specials?" He grinned. "Two-for-one deals?"

"I haven't thought that far ahead." That he didn't ask questions about the baby hurt. He must be relieved to be free of the responsibility of fatherhood.

"Do you ski?" he asked.

Why were they talking about skiing? "I went skiing

once with Shannon. I sprained my knee and never tried it again."

"I might head up to the White Mountains this winter and take a few lessons."

Gavin rose from his chair and took his mug to the sink. "It's a beautiful day. You feel like taking a drive and grabbing breakfast out?"

Sunshine didn't equate to a beautiful day. And no, she didn't feel up to a drive. "I'm not in the mood, thanks."

"There's a rodeo in Goodyear next weekend."

That Gavin kept bringing up the future pointed to the obvious—he didn't view himself as tied down anymore. He was off the hook for being a father and a husband. So why all the chitchat? Why didn't Gavin come right out and say he intended to hit the road for good?

He's too honorable. Gavin was principled to the core and would not end their engagement or call off the wedding, because he was a man of his word and when he made a promise or a pledge he saw it through. He'd wait for Dixie to sever their relationship.

"You could come to the rodeo in Goodyear if one of your brothers will watch the gift shop."

"Gavin, stop." Ignoring his startled stare she said, "You don't have to do this."

"Do what?"

"Pretend nothing has changed between us."

"I'm not following."

Dixie had lost Gavin—a man who'd turned out to be more than she'd ever dreamed of. "There's no baby so there's no need for a wedding."

He remained silent—more proof in Dixie's mind that calling off the wedding was exactly what he'd hoped she'd do.

"We don't need to make any decisions right away," he said.

Darn him for pretending to care. "I'll try my best to cover the mortgage payments on the shop."

"The shop was a gift. As far as the monthly mortgage I'm more than happy—"

"No."

He studied her for a long while, but Dixie wouldn't back down. Nor would she take charity. *Then why did you accept the gift shop in the first place?* She'd done it for the baby—not herself.

"I'll finish the repairs to the store that I didn't get to before the grand opening."

"Thanks, but my brothers can handle a few minor fix-it problems."

Gavin cleared his throat. "Then I guess there's no reason to stay."

Dixie wanted to scream, "Stay for me. For us." The words stuck to the sides of her throat. "You're free to go."

The stillness in the room suffocated her and she feared she'd pass out. Gavin inched toward the door. "See you…"

She hoped not. The nicest thing Gavin could do for her was remain as far away as possible. Running into him would remind her of what she'd almost had—a baby…a husband…a family of her own.

She felt compelled to speak as she followed him to the door. "Good luck with your rodeo career." Now that she was no longer his obligation, Gavin could concentrate on his bareback riding.

"If you need anything…call."

"Thanks, but I won't…" *Need you.*

Hand on the knob he glanced over his shoulder and

Dixie yearned to kiss him one more time. *Don't you dare.* If she kissed Gavin she'd never have the courage to kick him out of her life. She'd resort to every female trick in the book to keep him by her side.

The only way to end this torture was to part ways. "Safe travels, Gavin." After the door shut, she peeked out the window and watched him walk to his truck. He paused, fingers on the door handle, as he studied the ground for the longest time.

Go, Gavin. Get in the truck and leave. Please don't make this any harder than it already is.

Dixie spun away. Leaning her back against the wall, she lowered herself until her rump hit the floor. Drawing her knees to her chest she buried her face in her hands. The rumble of Gavin's truck engine echoed outside. Then blessed silence.

There. It was done. Over. Finished.

Dixie was back to being alone again.

Gavin left Stagecoach and drove with no particular destination in mind, afraid if he stopped, he'd think. He didn't want to reflect on Dixie losing the baby. Him losing Dixie. His survival instincts kicked in and a numbness settled deep in his bones, protecting him from the pain. He drove for hours, stopping for gas and food once.

Fatigue and hunger compelled him to pull into a Love's Travel Plaza at 10:00 p.m. *Where the hell am I?* He must have passed a dozen highway signs yet he hadn't read any of them. He parked next to a car with a New Mexico license plate and got out. He winced as a muscle spasm gripped his calf when he took his first step. He limped on, his wobbly gait drawing stares from an older couple leaving the building. Inside the truck stop he noticed a banner above the entrance to the convenience store—Welcome to Albuquerque.

After using the bathroom Gavin sat at a table in the adjoining restaurant and flipped over the white mug. A waitress named Heather filled the cup with coffee and left a menu. "Be back in a jiffy."

Gavin perused his options until the waitress returned. "What can I get you?" she asked.

"Are there any specials?"

"Sorry." Heather shook her head, her blond curls bouncing against her face. "Mac—" she nodded toward the kitchen "—cooks a mean breakfast."

Gavin skimmed the breakfast items. "I'll take the Number 1 with wheat toast and sausage instead of bacon."

"Sure thing." Heather placed silverware on the table then hurried off.

Gavin sat in a stupor, sipping his coffee. A baby's shrill cry interrupted his trance. A woman toting an infant carrier walked through the dining area and picked a table in the middle of the room—right in Gavin's line of vision. He was powerless to look away as the young mother placed the carrier on a chair and removed the baby. She pressed her lips to the top of the infant's fuzzy head and the baby's cries softened to a whimper.

The numbness that had protected Gavin from his thoughts slowly melted and a burning tingle spread through his chest as he acknowledged what he and Dixie had lost. Their baby had been real…yet not real. Shoot, Dixie hadn't begun showing before she'd lost the baby. And sadly he hadn't gone to a doctor's appointment and seen his child's image through an ultrasound nor had he felt the baby kick in Dixie's stomach.

The infant across the room was dressed from head to booties in blue—a boy. When a young man joined the woman and reached for the baby, Gavin curled his fingers into a fist. What would it have felt like to hold his child? He wished he'd asked Dixie if the baby had been a boy or girl.

A son or a daughter.

Losing their child was painful but Dixie cutting him loose was crippling. She'd been his reason…his strength to move forward with his life and put the ugliness of his past behind him. Without her by his side, Gavin feared all the progress he'd made toward burying his demons would be lost.

He guessed it didn't matter what *he* wanted because what he wanted—Dixie—didn't want him back. Gavin was left with no choice but to move on.

To what?

To the one thing he sucked at—rodeo.

Chapter 14

"Thank you for stopping in." Dixie flashed a saccharine smile. As soon as the woman left the store another walked in. Keeping her smile in place she said, "Let me know if I can help you with anything."

Dixie glanced at the wall calendar behind the counter. Today was Friday, November 3. A dull ache spread through her chest. Tomorrow would have been her and Gavin's wedding. The days since he'd left Stagecoach dragged by for Dixie—probably because her every other thought drifted to Gavin.

Where was he?

Did he mourn the baby they'd lost?

Did he miss her?

The bell on the door jingled again. Mildred Hinkle. The old biddy had dropped by every day since she'd heard about Dixie's miscarriage—thanks to Johnny's big mouth. Worried about her depression her brother had asked Mildred to keep an eye on her. She appreciated that Millie—Dixie had joined the Main Street Merchants League and was now allowed to call Mrs. Hinkle by her nickname—had offered a sympathetic ear if Dixie felt like discussing her miscarriage and broken engagement. Dixie preferred to keep her feelings to herself.

"Hello, Millie. How's business at your end of the block?"

"Oh, fine, dear." After years of being a curmudgeon, Mildred had little experience cheering people up, but Dixie appreciated her efforts. Mildred motioned to the half-empty Christmas display on the counter. "Your pre-holiday sales are doing well."

"Sales this week have been incredibly…"

Mildred blinked. "Incredibly what, dear?"

Was Mildred behind the increase in shoppers browsing Dixie's Desert Delights the past few days? "Millie, have you been sending your customers my way?"

"I might have suggested they check out your soap selection…"

Annoyed by Mildred's confession, Dixie swallowed a sharp retort. If people didn't stop pitying her she'd never gain the strength to forget Gavin—as if that was even possible. "Thank you for the referrals, Millie, but everyone's on tight budgets these days. You can't afford to turn down sales."

"I've been in business for over twenty years and I have more loyal customers than I know what to do with."

No use arguing with the Main Street matriarch. "I think I'll close up early today," Dixie said. Pretending to be happy exhausted her.

"Good idea. You need your rest."

Dixie walked Mildred to the door.

"You're feeling better now?" Mildred asked.

A loaded question if ever there was one. "I am."

"Good. See you tomorrow."

As soon as Dixie shut the door behind Mildred she flipped the sign in the window to Closed. When she turned away she came face-to-face with a customer. "Good grief, I'm sorry. I didn't mean to lock you inside."

"That's all right. If it's not too late, I'd like to buy these." She held out three bars of soap.

"Certainly." Dixie rang up the purchase then thanked the woman and let her out. Dixie spent an hour straightening the shop for the next day. When there was nothing more to do, she resigned herself to heading back to the farm—her *least* favorite place to be now.

The farm had once been her refuge but memories of Gavin followed her everywhere—from the barn to her bedroom to the kitchen to the pecan grove behind the house. If confronting Gavin's memory at the farm wasn't difficult enough then her brothers' attempts to cheer her up threatened to send her across the border.

Resigned to her fate, Dixie drove to Stagecoach. As she passed through town an unbearable urge for a cold beer hit her and she swung into the parking lot of Gilly's Tap House. A handful of trucks sat parked outside and none of them belonged to her brothers.

Loud music smacked Dixie upside the head when she entered the tavern. A raucous game of pool competed with the whiny sounds of a steel guitar blaring from the juke-box. An older couple, heads bent in conversation, occupied a table in the corner and two cowboys—probably local ranch hands—sat at the bar. Dixie chose a stool at the far end—she wasn't in the mood for company—especially the cowboy kind.

"Tough day at the office?" The barkeep slapped a drink napkin on the bar.

"You could say that. Coors Light, please." A frosty bottle appeared in front of her. "Keep a tab."

The bartender nodded, then meandered back to the cowboys and launched a discussion of the most recent NASCAR race.

Dixie's first swallow of beer was refreshing.

The second sip tasted like paradise.

The third made her belch. She wiped the back of her hand across her mouth. She'd better slow down since she was drinking on an empty stomach. She kept snacks at the store but had been too busy to eat. Come to think of it, she'd skipped lunch every day this week. She hadn't gotten on the scale since... She assumed she'd lost more than the baby weight she'd gained before the miscarriage.

There she went again thinking about the baby. She chugged the beer. Before she'd finished the bottle, the barkeep placed another one in front of her and nodded to the cowboys a few stools away. Dixie glanced sideways and the men saluted her with their beers.

She smiled her thanks. While Dixie nursed her beer, she surrendered the fight to ban Gavin from her thoughts. Like a drug addict giving up cocaine, Dixie acknowledged the road ahead would be painful and filled with failed attempts to forget Gavin—but it was a path she had to travel if she intended to heal.

Dixie's thoughts drifted back in time to when she and Gavin first met. There had been something intriguing and mysterious about the soldier cowboy. She knew from the get-go that she wasn't the kind of woman men like Gavin pursued but that hadn't stopped her from chasing him.

There. She admitted it. She was to blame for the mess she was in.

The barkeep delivered a third beer. The mellow voice of Patsy Cline singing "I Fall to Pieces" echoed from the jukebox. How long would Dixie continue to fall apart until there were no pieces of her left and she hit rock bottom?

"You're not drunk, are you?"

The voice startled Dixie and she jumped inside her skin. "What are you doing here?"

"I could ask you the same question." Johnny signaled the bartender for a beer.

"Leave me alone."

"Feeling sorry for yourself?"

Dixie gasped but her outrage was cut off by a hiccup. Go figure her eldest brother would use meanness to bully her out of a funk.

Sheesh. Where was a woman to go to find a little peace if not a bar? "How'd you know I was here?"

"I was on my way into Yuma and spotted your truck in the lot."

"You should have kept going. I'm not in the mood for socializing." She guzzled the remainder of her beer and signaled for a fourth.

"How many have you had?" Johnny asked.

Not nearly enough to banish Gavin from her memory. "Bug off."

"You haven't strung two nice words together since you lost the baby."

Johnny was the only brother who wasn't afraid to say the word *baby* in front of her. The others avoided the subject because they feared any reference to the miscarriage would send their sister over the edge.

A lump formed in Dixie's throat. "I never expected things to turn out like this," she said. She had volunteered to go with Gavin to his motel room that fateful night but she honestly hadn't planned on getting pregnant.

And you never expected to fall in love with him.

"Lots of women lose babies. Yeah, it hurts but life goes on and one day you'll wake up and be pregnant again," Johnny said.

Dixie snorted. "You suck at making people feel better." She chugged her beer. "It's not just the baby."

Johnny leaned closer. "Then what is it, Dix?"

"Gavin." She rested her head against Johnny's shoulder. "I tried not to fall in love with him." All that nonsense in the beginning when she refused to marry Gavin had been a feeble attempt to avoid admitting she was falling under his spell.

"Don't confuse appreciation for Gavin buying you the gift shop with love."

"I'm not." The moment her eyes had connected with Gavin's at the Canyon City Rodeo she'd sensed his decency and time had validated her intuition. Gavin was a great guy. She recalled the nice things he'd done for her. The sacrifices he'd made for her and the baby. He'd turned out to be more than she'd ever dreamed of…hoped for…desired.

And she'd lost him.

"There will be other babies and other men," Johnny said.

"I know you mean well, but you're making me feel worse."

"You really love Gavin?"

"With all my heart."

"Then why'd you let him walk away?"

"Because he acted like he didn't care that I'd lost the baby."

"What did he say?"

"He said he was sorry about the baby and then he said it was such a nice day we should take a ride. Then he talked about skiing this winter and rodeoing. He didn't even ask me—" Dixie shook her head "—if the baby was a girl or a boy."

"Damn." Johnny hugged her. "That's my fault. I warned Gavin not to mention the baby because you were depressed."

"You're such a dumb-ass." Dixie punched his arm.

"Hey, don't blame me. Any time one of us mentioned the baby you bawled your head off."

"Doesn't matter." She wiped her runny nose on Johnny's shirt. "Now that there's no baby, there's no reason for Gavin to be with me."

"What if he loves you?"

"He doesn't." That he'd left her and Stagecoach in the dust was proof of that.

"Did you tell Gavin you love him?"

"No."

"Did you ask him if he loved you?"

She drew in a quick breath. "Of course not."

"Then I guess you don't have much choice."

Dixie squirmed out of Johnny's hold and wiped her tears away. "What do you mean?"

"Find Gavin and tell him how you feel."

What if she spilled her guts like a lovesick fool only to have her worst fear confirmed—Gavin's feelings for her had been tied to the baby and without the baby, those feelings were gone? "And if he doesn't love me?"

"Then you come home and get on with life."

And cry. Oh, Lord, would she cry.

Johnny was right. She had to find Gavin and confess her feelings for him. Only then would she know how he truly felt about her. Dixie couldn't live with herself if there was the tiniest chance he might love her. She slid off the stool and stumbled sideways, her head buzzing from too many beers.

Johnny steadied her. "Where're you going?"

"To find Gavin."

"Tomorrow's soon enough. Right now you need a good night's sleep."

Johnny escorted her out of the bar, but Dixie put the brakes on in the middle of the parking lot. "I didn't pay for my drinks."

"I took care of the tab." He guided her to his truck. "I'll have Merle and Porter fetch your pickup later. They're going barhopping tonight in Yuma."

"Johnny." Dixie crawled into the front seat. "Will you come with me to find Gavin?"

"Sorry, baby girl." Her brother hadn't used her pet name in years. "You've got to do this on your own," he said.

"What about the store?" she asked.

"Porter will watch over it. He loves talking to women."

"He'll probably sell out my inventory," Dixie muttered.

As they pulled away from the bar, Johnny pointed out the windshield at a passing van with the words Pony Express written in bold letters across the doors. "That's the new taxi service for drunk cowboys."

"What?"

Johnny grinned. "You may need that number if Gavin doesn't want you back."

"You're such a snot."

"Hey, that's what big brothers are for…making little sisters miserable."

Dixie was miserable. She shifted her gaze to the starry heavens. *Grandma, help me win Gavin back.*

You think we can leave the village early today?

In the far reaches of Gavin's subconscious he knew how this conversation would end and fought to ignore the strong pull of Nate's voice.

My mom sent cookies for my birthday—chocolate peanut butter. I bet they're waiting for me back at base.

Gavin struggled to open his eyes but only darkness filled his vision as if someone had placed his IBA vest over his face. The Interceptor Body Armor smelled of dust, blood, urine and sweat. He hated that stinking desert ghetto.

We got a leave coming up next month. After we visit our moms do you want to head to Texas to rodeo?

Hands and feet throbbing, Gavin opened his mouth wider but the pressure building in his chest blocked the gasps of air from reaching his lungs. His heart raced faster and faster as if the organ were held hostage on a runaway train.

Can I drive the lead Humvee back to the base? C'mon, Gavin, it's my birthday. Let me drive it.

A loud explosion was followed by a light so bright it burned Gavin's eyes and they watered. Red. Lots of red. Blood everywhere. Muted screams ringing in his ears. Soldiers running helter-skelter, calling out commands while Gavin stood immobile, the rubber soles of his boots melting into the hot desert sand.

The echo of Nate's voice propelled Gavin up the line of armored vehicles to the lead Humvee where Nate's torso lay. Gavin dropped to his knees, cradled his friend's head in his lap and looked into his lifeless eyes.

Don't touch him! Gavin waved off his comrades who approached to help. Gently he set Nate on the ground. Rage filled him—unlike anything he'd experienced since entering combat duty. He wanted to kill something—no, someone. A life for a life.

He stumbled fifty yards into the desert to collect Nate's legs. He found the left leg first, then switched directions and retrieved the right leg. He returned to the Humvee and placed the legs beneath Nate's torso where they were supposed to be. Then he turned his rage on the villagers, wielding his firearm threateningly, demanding they turn over those guilty of planting the roadside bomb.

Wait… Something wasn't right.

The scent of honeysuckle—not blood and burned flesh—drifted up his nostrils. A fresh wind—free of dust—blew in his face. Where was Nate? Someone had moved his body and covered him with a blanket. Gavin stumbled to the body and dropped to his knees. He peeled back the edge of the covering.

"Noooo!"

Gavin woke, startled to find himself standing next to the motel bed. He touched his naked chest and the heat radiating off his body burned his palm. He grabbed his keys and bolted outside to his truck. Once he started the engine, he blasted the air conditioner at his face. In less than a minute Gavin went from sweltering to shivering. His teeth chattered and his fingernails turned blue.

He sat in his truck, mesmerized by the blinking sign above the office of the Coral Motel in El Paso, Texas. Never before had the nightmare ended with Dixie's lifeless eyes staring up at Gavin.

God help him if he ever had the same dream again.

"You should have stayed in the army, Tucker. The more you ride, the worse you get." Chuckles followed the barb.

So much for the cowboy camaraderie Gavin had hoped to find on the rodeo circuit when he'd left the army. Ignoring the jeers of his competitors, he limped through the cowboy ready area of the Eldorado Arena in Eldorado, Oklahoma. He couldn't very well deny Trevor Mandela's accusation, mainly because it was dead-on. Gavin collected his gear and left the building.

He stood in the parking lot, staring at the sea of vehicles and livestock rigs. Where had he parked the truck? He dug his keys from his pocket and started walking, the light dusting of snow crunching beneath his boots. He pushed the panic button on the fob every few feet as he meandered through the rows. When he reached the middle of the lot a horn went off and he spotted the pickup's flashing headlights. He hit the panic button again to disengage the alarm. Once he stowed his bag in the backseat he hopped inside the cab and revved the engine. What now?

Today was November 4—the day he and Dixie were supposed to get married. Instead, he'd gotten his butt kicked at another rodeo and now he had nowhere to go.

If a bruised backside and a breaking heart weren't bad enough, he no longer enjoyed busting broncs. The adrenaline rush he'd come to depend on for his survival had deserted him, leaving him a hollow shell of a man—and it was all Dixie's fault. He'd fallen in love with a woman who was better off without him.

He glanced at the rearview mirror and grimaced. His cheeks were sunken hollows in his face and the dark circles beneath his eyes made him resemble a villain not America's hero—all because of a recurring nightmare. Since the last time he'd seen Dixie he'd resorted to sleeping in snatches, fearing if he rested too long the nightmare would hold him prisoner.

You can't go on like this.

Lack of sleep was affecting his physical strength and his will to win. What was the point anymore?

He fished his phone from his pocket and checked for messages. None. When he'd purchased a new cell phone a while back he should have changed the number, but he hadn't the courage to make a clean break from Dixie. Maybe he should have because Dixie's silence convinced him that she'd moved on with her life.

If only he could find a way to do the same.

The holidays were breathing down Gavin's neck. He doubted he could come up with a plausible excuse for not spending them with his mother. When he'd phoned to inform her of Dixie's miscarriage and the wedding being called off, she'd insisted he drive up and spend some time with her. He'd politely declined the invitation. Sympathy from his mother would weaken his resolve to put Dixie and the baby behind him.

That's the coward's way out.

Running was easier than coming to terms with the past—a process he wasn't sure he'd survive.

Don't run. Face your demons—for Dixie.

Dixie had carved a place for herself in Gavin's heart

and he hadn't realized until she'd lost the baby how much she'd come to mean to him. In a short time she'd become his reason for living and had taught him to find joy in the little things life offered. Dixie had given him hope that one day he might be absolved for the role he'd played in Nate's death.

Dixie had become his everything.

Now she's your nothing.

Go see her. Tell her you want—no need—her in your life.

Gavin closed his eyes and envisioned himself barreling up the dirt drive to the farm, honking the horn. Dixie would step from the house wearing a welcoming smile. The only way that scenario would come to life was if he got help. He'd used Dixie, the baby, then the impending wedding as excuses to avoid confronting the demons that had followed him home from war.

The baby wasn't in the picture, the wedding had been called off and Dixie deserved better than sharing her life with a man and his tormented soul. The only way he could return to Stagecoach and ask Dixie to spend the rest of her life with him was if he sought professional help.

You have nothing to lose.

Nothing—save the woman who'd come to mean everything to him.

And Dixie was worth fighting for.

Chapter 15

The third week in November Dixie pulled into the apartment complex and parked in a visitor's spot. After chasing empty leads on the rodeo circuit, she was tired and grumpy and darn weary of hauling her heavy broken heart around with her. If Sylvia Tucker didn't know her son's whereabouts then Dixie was calling it quits and returning to Stagecoach.

An urgency she hadn't felt before now accompanied her as she strolled along the sidewalk of the first building. When she spotted apartment 112, she took a fortifying breath and rang the bell. The door opened and a loud woof sounded in the background.

"May I help you?"

"I hope so." Dixie flashed a weak smile. "Are you Sylvia Tucker?"

"Yes, I am. Who are you?"

"Dixie Cash, ma'am." She paused not knowing if she should add "the girl your son got pregnant. The girl who miscarried your son's baby. The girl who's in love with your son and doesn't know how she'll live without him."

The door opened wider and Gavin's mother waved her inside. Dixie followed her into the kitchen. "Sit down. I was just about to make tea."

Tea would be welcome. "Thank you, Ms.—"

"Call me Sylvia." She smiled as she filled the teapot at the sink. "I was hoping you'd show up here."

Dixie's eyes widened. "You were?"

Sylvia set the kettle on the stove and joined Dixie at the table. She squeezed Dixie's hand. "I'm sorry about the baby, honey."

The heartfelt words touched Dixie. "Thank you."

"My son needs you."

And I need him. "Do you know where Gavin is?"

"He's at his therapy appointment."

Therapy? "Did he injure himself in a rodeo?"

"Not that kind of therapy." The kettle whistled and Sylvia spent the next few minutes preparing the tea. When she sat down again, she said, "Gavin's seeing a psychologist."

"For what?" Had losing the baby affected him more than Dixie believed?

"It's not my place to tell, honey."

"I need to talk to him." *I need to tell him I love him.*

Sylvia's teeth worried her lower lip as if uncertain about confiding in Dixie. Finally she rose from the table and scribbled on a notepad by the phone. She tore off the paper and held it out. "His appointment ends in thirty minutes. If you hurry, you could wait for him outside the building."

Dixie grabbed the address and rushed to the door. "Thank you, Sylvia," she called over her shoulder. As soon as Dixie got in the truck, she input the address in the GPS system Johnny had insisted she use when she'd left to search for Gavin. The medical building was less than ten miles away.

The Phoenix freeways were busy and full of crazy drivers, forcing Dixie to concentrate on the road and not allow her thoughts to wander to Gavin. The GPS signaled her to exit the freeway and the medical building was only a mile up the street. She pulled into the parking lot and drove past the various entrances, reading the numbers etched into the glass on the doors. When she spotted 130B she pulled into a space nearby and waited.

She didn't have to wait long. Gavin emerged from the building, pausing to put on his sunglasses. Dixie honked the horn and he froze, his gaze scanning the lot. She got out of the truck. Like cement blocks, her feet dragged across the pavement as she walked toward him. She knew the instant he spotted her—his shoulders stiffened and he glanced along the sidewalk as if seeking an escape route. Dixie's heart sank. She stopped short of the sidewalk and swallowed hard. *Please be happy to see me, Gavin.*

"I've been looking all over for you," she said. No sense pretending she'd just happened to be in the neighborhood.

"How did you find out I was here?"

"Your mother. She gave me the address."

His mouth pressed into a thin line.

"I need to tell you something, Gavin."

Gaze fastened to the pavement, he removed his sunglasses and pinched the bridge of his nose. When he finally lifted his head, the wounded look in his eyes broke Dixie's heart. "Don't say anything." He shook his head. "Just…don't. Please."

She wasn't letting him off the hook that easy. "I love you, Gavin. I didn't want to admit it, but I began falling for you the night we went to your motel room after the Boot Hill Rodeo."

"You can't." He shook his head and fisted his hands.

"Can't what?"

"Love me."

If she could just touch him… Show him the depth of her feelings… "Why can't I love you?"

"I'm not…" He walked away then stopped and faced her. "I'm not well."

"What do you mean?"

"I'm sick, Dixie." He punctuated the remark by poking himself in the head.

"Are you trying to scare me away?"

He took her by the arm and escorted her to her pickup where he opened the door and all but shoved her into the driver's seat. Once he shut the door, his shoulders relaxed as if relieved to have a barrier between them.

"I've been diagnosed with PTSD," he said. "That should damn well scare you."

Dixie had heard stories of soldiers returning from war who struggled with the medical condition. Things didn't always end well for many of them. The thought of Gavin suffering alone made her heart physically ache. "But you're working on getting better." She motioned at the door to the medical office.

"Being with you made me feel better so I ignored my problems and convinced myself that you could heal me." He rubbed a hand over his exhausted face. "That wasn't fair to you."

"I'm glad you're getting professional help, but you don't have to push me away."

"There's no cure for PTSD, Dixie."

"So this is it? You're going to take the coward's way out and use your PTSD as an excuse to run from what we have?"

The muscle along his jaw bunched—the only signal that her words had angered him. "You can learn to manage your symptoms, Gavin. It doesn't have to keep you from living the life you deserve."

"Easier said than done."

"Let me help you."

"No." He raised his hands as if warding her off. "I can't trust myself not to hurt you."

"But you've never lost control before."

"I have nightmares, Dixie. Horrible nightmares and they're becoming more intense."

"Why?"

"My shrink thinks it's because of the baby and—" He looked away. "You."

Dixie understood losing the baby might cause a relapse, but...*her*? "What have I done to distress you? Tell me and I'll stop doing it."

"You've done nothing wrong." He slammed his fist against his chest. "Not a damn thing except make me love you."

"You love me?" Tears leaked from her eyes and her heart swelled with hope.

"I love you enough to know that I'm not the right guy for you."

"But—"

"Just go, Dixie."

"I'll wait for you."

"No. You have to move on with your life."

"Well, that presents a problem, Gavin. I can't and I won't get on with my life without you." Dixie paused, giving him a chance to speak. When he remained silent she grasped at straws. "The love I feel for you isn't something I can turn on and off like a faucet. My love won't fade away just because we're not together."

He stared into the distance and Dixie felt her hope slipping away.

"Can't you find enough strength inside you for one more battle, Gavin? For me? For us?"

Please, Gavin. Please fight for me because without you... She couldn't finish the thought. She started the truck and shifted into Reverse. "Take as long as you need to get better, because I'm not going anywhere." Dixie backed out of the spot. Before leaving the medical plaza she checked the rearview mirror. Gavin watched her, the desolate expression on his face tearing her apart.

Find your way back to me, Gavin.

Late that night Dixie pulled into the farm and Johnny met her at the door. "You look like hell. What happened?"

She waltzed past him into the kitchen, then sank onto a chair at the table. "I found Gavin."

Johnny poured her a cup of coffee. "Where was he?"

"In Phoenix at his mother's place."

"Well...?"

"He's seeing a psychologist for PTSD."

"That's rough."

"I told him it didn't matter. That I still loved him." The tears she'd held inside her during the drive back from Phoenix threatened to escape. "Gavin doesn't want us to be together unless he can trust himself not to lose control."

"Does he love you?"

"Yes." But he'd made loving her sound as if it tortured his soul. "He told me to move on with my life and not wait for him."

"Is that what you plan to do?"

"Shoot, no. I'm staying right here until he comes to his senses and realizes that I'm the key to finding the peace he's searching for."

Johnny grinned. "Now, that's the spirited girl Grandma Ada raised."

His words made Dixie smile. "I better get to bed if I'm going into the store early tomorrow."

"Speaking of the store, you were right," Johnny said.

"Right about what?"

"Porter damn near sold out your inventory."

"Looks like I'll be putting in longer hours." She shuffled from the room but stopped when Johnny called after her.

"Dixie?"

"What?"

"I'll talk to Gavin if you want me to."

"Thanks but this is something Gavin has to work through on his own." Dixie just hoped that knowing she waited for him—that she wasn't giving up on their love—was enough to help Gavin find his way back to her.

Christmas came and went as did New Year's and still no word from Gavin—just a holiday card from his mother informing Dixie that he'd continued to see his therapist and was working a part-time construction job.

Tomorrow was February 1—almost twelve weeks had passed since Dixie had confronted Gavin outside his therapist's office.

Several times a day she picked up her phone intent on calling him just to hear his voice. It was doubly hard, like now—during the long ride home after a day at the gift shop—to resist reminding Gavin that she was still waiting. Her resolve to remain strong and give him the space he needed weakened with each passing day. The excitement of running her own business had waned in the wake of Gavin's absence. Even the sunrise and sunset had lost its glow.

Dixie took the turn off to the farm, glad tomorrow was Monday and the gift shop was closed. She'd use the day to catch up on housework and laundry and think about Gavin and how much she missed him. She slowed the truck as she drove into the yard and parked by the barn. Halfway to the house she stopped, her heart pounding.

Gavin's truck sat among her brother's vehicles.

He came home.

Switching directions, she walked over to Gavin's pickup and placed her hand on the hood. Cool to the touch. How long had he been here? How long did he intend to stay?

"Gavin?" she hollered when she stepped through the front door.

"He's not here," Buck's voice floated down the hallway.

Dixie hurried into the kitchen. Her brothers were playing cards at the kitchen table—what else was new. "Gavin's truck is parked outside." She stated the obvious. "Where is he?"

"Out back," Willie answered.

Out back comprised two hundred acres. "Can you narrow it down?"

Johnny cleared his throat and her brothers tossed their cards down and shuffled from the room.

"Oh, God. It's bad, isn't it?"

"I don't know, Dixie. When Gavin got here, he asked to speak with you."

"What'd you tell him?"

"That you were still in Yuma at the store." Johnny nodded to the door. "Go talk to him. He went to Addy's grave."

The blood drained from Dixie's face. "How long has he been out there?"

"Over two hours."

She stared at the back door until Johnny's hand on her arm broke her trance. "He needs you, Dixie."

She yearned to believe her brother, but what if Gavin only returned for answers about the baby? Maybe his therapist had sent him to learn if they'd had a daughter or a son.

"I'm a mess." She smoothed a hand over her hair.

Johnny spun her around and unraveled her braid. After detangling the strands, he spread her hair across her shoulders. "There. Now you're pretty."

"You'll be here when I get back?"

"We'll all be here," Buck said. Her brothers hovered in the doorway. They were pains in the ass, but Dixie felt blessed to have their support. She left the house and cut through the backyard, walking east into the rows of pecan trees. The family plot was hidden behind a rocky knoll.

The sun shone brightly. No clouds—only blue sky.

Crystal-clear blue. The day looked like a million other Arizona days. Somehow it didn't seem right that the world went on undisturbed, unmarred and unchanged after Addy had passed on. At the very least her little girl deserved ominous clouds, booming thunder and gale-force winds—a storm to protest her passing. Dixie trudged on, too tired to shake her fist at the heavens.

The graveyard came into view and she slowed her steps. The small rectangle was enclosed by a three foot high iron gate, which Gavin had left open. The rusty hinges groaned in the breeze.

The closer Dixie drew to the plot the more strength each step required. Gavin knelt at the foot of Addy's grave—the mound so tiny he could easily reach out his hand and touch the heart-shaped marker Johnny had ordered for his niece. Fresh flowers lay beneath the headstone—Gavin must have brought those.

She stepped past the gate, her gaze landing on her grandmother's grave. A breath of wind hit Dixie in the face—Grandma Ada giving her encouragement. Dixie sank to her knees beside Gavin. They knelt in silence for the longest time and then Gavin reached for her hand. She gripped his fingers as if they were a lifeline.

Tears she'd already cried for her daughter filled her eyes again and she sniffed. Gavin folded her in a hug and they cried together—his shoulders shaking and her tears dampening his shirt.

Dixie had no idea how long they held each other, but she was grateful that they were finally mourning for their daughter together.

"I wanted to know if we'd had a girl or a boy."

"She was so tiny, Gavin. So precious."

"Addy's with your grandmother now," he said.

"Grandma Ada will take good care of our daughter until we see her again."

The sun sunk lower in the sky, smearing the horizon with a warm pinkish-purple hue. "I'm sad we lost Addy, but…" Gavin swallowed hard.

"But what?"

His gaze returned to her face and eyes damp with moisture beseeched her. "I don't want to lose you, too."

She flung her arms around his neck and held him tightly. "I've waited forever to hear those words, Gavin."

"I love you, Dixie." His rough, callused hands clasped her face. "I've made progress with my therapist but the scars will never go away."

"Scars don't scare me, Gavin, but living without you does."

He brushed his lips across her forehead. "I don't know what I did to deserve you. I tried like hell to walk away from you, but I couldn't."

"Gavin, I promise—"

He pressed a finger to her lips, silencing her. "I realized that I hurt more from not having you in my life than from all the pain and heartache I suffered in Afghanistan."

She hugged him tight. "I love all of you—the healed and the hurting."

"I'm going to need therapy for a long time."

"Doesn't matter. We're in this together for a lifetime."

"Be sure, Dixie. Once you're mine, I'll never let you go."

She caressed his cheek. "I've always been yours and there's nowhere I want to be except by your side."

"Will you marry me, Dixie?" His kiss was a gentle

caress…soft, fleeting, a whisper of devotion, need and desire.

"Yes, I'll marry you." Dixie deepened the kiss, wanting there to be no doubt in Gavin's mind that she'd stand by his side and love him no matter what his struggles were.

When the kiss ended, Gavin reached into his jeans pocket and removed a jeweler's box. "This time I'm doing it, right."

"You already gave me a ring." Dixie hadn't taken off the ring since Gavin had slipped it on her finger months ago.

"You deserve better than someone's castoff." He opened the ring box to reveal a one-carat marquise diamond.

She gasped. "Gavin…it's stunning." Good Lord, this must have cost a fortune. "It's too expensive." She shook her head. "I can't accept it."

Ignoring her protests, he removed the pawn-shop ring from her finger and slid the new diamond on. "I want everyone to know you're mine, Dixie." He kissed her once again and this time when they came up for air, Gavin stood and helped Dixie to her feet. "Where are we going to live?"

"Right here on the farm."

"There are six other men in that house."

"My grandmother left the farm to me, Gavin. It's mine. My brothers are allowed to live here until they reach the age of thirty-five or get married—whichever comes first."

Gavin's gaze settled on the heart-shaped headstone. "I like the idea of being close to Addy." He grasped Dixie's hand. "Let's go tell your brothers to start looking for wives or apartments."

"No need," Dixie said. "They're building a bunkhouse behind the barn."

"What for?"

"To sleep in after we're married."

"You were that sure I'd come back for you?"

"I never doubted for a minute."

Hand in hand they walked back to the house and for the first time since her miscarriage, Dixie was able to draw a deep breath without her chest hurting. "I'd planned to give you until the beginning of the summer to come to your senses," she said.

"Or what?"

"Or I'd have driven up to Phoenix and fetched you home."

"Like a stray dog, eh?" Gavin's booming laughter echoed through the pecan grove and drew Dixie's brothers onto the back porch.

They stopped in the yard and Gavin pulled her close, his mouth hovering over hers. "You're my one and only, Dixie. I love you."

"I guess this means we'd better finish the bunkhouse sooner rather than later," Willie said.

"No one's moving out of this house until they tie the knot." Johnny sent Gavin a stern look.

Dixie and Gavin approached the porch. "Porter," Dixie said. "You'd better contact Reverend Thomas right away." Her brother dashed into the house.

"This isn't a joke, is it, Dixie?" Willie asked.

She held up her ring finger and smiled.

Willie let out a low whistle. "Now, that's a proper engagement ring."

Johnny descended the steps and stopped in front of Gavin. "This better be for real, Tucker, or you'll have me and my brothers to answer to."

"It's for real, Johnny." Gavin smiled at Dixie. "I love your sister and I'll do everything in my power to make her happy." He swooped in for another kiss but stopped when the porch door banged against the side of the house.

"Wait!" Porter hollered. "No more kissing. Reverend Thomas said he'd marry Dixie and Gavin right now."

"How'd you get him to agree to officiate a wedding on such short notice?" Buck asked.

"I said if he didn't, Johnny was getting out the shotgun."

"You're such a drama queen, Porter," Merle said.

"What about your mother?" Dixie asked Gavin. He was Sylvia Tucker's only child and Dixie assumed she'd want to be present when her son married.

"My mother wants me to be happy, Dixie. And marrying you…right now…makes me happy."

Willie let out a whoop and leaped off the porch. "Let's get going!"

"Wait. Give me ten minutes." Dixie raced into the house and up to her bedroom where she pulled out the plastic bin from beneath the bed. She removed her grandmother's silk wedding dress and spread it across the mattress. With loving hands she smoothed the wrinkles and then searched through the closet for the cream-colored heels she'd purchased three years ago but had never worn because they pinched her toes. Next, she opened her jewelry box and took out her grandmother's pearl necklace and matching earrings. She raised the bedroom window and hollered, "Conway! Get up here now!"

While she waited for her brother, she put on her nicest bra and panty set and slipped into the wedding gown just as the bedroom door flung open.

"What's the matter?" Conway panted.

"Help me button this." She presented her back and the double row of pearl buttons.

"My fingers are too clumsy." Conway cursed under his breath.

"You're the one who wanted a big shindig, be happy I'm wearing a wedding gown."

Conway grumbled but finished the job. He spun her around. "Did grandma have a veil?"

"No."

"Fix your hair. It's a mess." He handed her the hairbrush from the top of her dresser. Dixie gathered the long strands and pinned them to her head in a messy bob.

"That'll do." Conway kissed her cheek.

Arm in arm they walked through the house. When they stepped outside Gavin's slow, sexy smile made promises she intended to hold him accountable for later that evening.

"You look beautiful," he said.

"Wait. The camera." Conway went back into the house and came out a second later. "Okay. We're ready."

Johnny grabbed Gavin's arm. "You're riding with me...in case you get cold feet."

"I'll take the bride." Conway snagged Dixie's hand and tugged her across the yard to Willie's pickup. Porter jumped in with them while Buck and Merle went in Johnny's truck.

Maybe it was a good thing Johnny was escorting Gavin to the chapel, because as soon as Gavin realized he wasn't just marrying Dixie but also her six crazy brothers, he really might make a run for it.

As the pickups sped down the dirt road, Dixie swiveled in her seat and stared out the rear window at Johnny's truck. Gavin was grinning from ear to ear.

Dixie lifted her smile to the heavens. *Thank you for bringing Gavin into my life, Grandma Ada. He not only made your dream come true, but he made mine, too.*

* * * * *

"Sorry," she said. "I just feel so helpless. Talk away. I'll keep my mouth shut."

"I don't want that." Then he caused her to catch her breath by sliding down the couch until he was right beside her. He slipped his arm around her shoulders, and despite her surprise, it seemed the most natural thing in the world to lean into him and finally let her head come to rest on his shoulder.

"Holding you is nice," he said quietly. "You quiet the rat race in my head. Does that sound awful?"

How could it? she wondered, when she'd been amazed at the way he had caused her to melt, as if everything else went away and she was in a warm, soft, safe space. If she could offer him any part of that, she would, gladly.

"If that sounds like I'm using you…"

"Man, don't you ever stop? Do you ever just go with the flow?" Turning and tilting her head a bit, she pressed a quick kiss on his lips.

"What the…" He sounded surprised.

"You're analyzing constantly," she told him. "This isn't a mission. Let it go. Let go. Just relax and hold me, and I hope you're enjoying it as much as I am."

Because she was. That wonderful melting filled her again, leaving her soft and very, very content. Maybe even happy.

"You are?" he murmured.

"I am. More than I've ever enjoyed a hug." God, had she ever been this blunt with a man before? But this guy was so bound up behind his walls and drawbridges, she wondered if she'd need a sledgehammer to get through.

But then she remembered Al and the distance she'd sensed in him during his visits. Not exactly alone, but alone among family. These guys had been deeply changed by their training and experience. Where did they find comfort now? Real comfort?

Her thoughts were slipping away in response to a growing anticipation and anxiety. She was close, so close to him, and his strength drew her like a bee to nectar. He even smelled good, still carrying the scents from the storm outside and his earlier shower, but beneath that the aroma of male.

Everything inside her became focused on one trembling hope, that he'd take this hug further, that he'd draw her closer and begin to explore her with his hands and mouth.

Don't miss
A SOLDIER IN CONARD COUNTY by Rachel Lee,
available February 2018 wherever
Harlequin® Special Edition books and ebooks are sold.

www.Harlequin.com

Looking for more satisfying love stories
with community and family at their core?

Check out **Harlequin® Special Edition**
and **Harlequin® Western Romance** books!

New books available every month!

CONNECT WITH US AT:

Harlequin.com/Community

 Facebook.com/HarlequinBooks

 Twitter.com/HarlequinBooks

 Instagram.com/HarlequinBooks

 Pinterest.com/HarlequinBooks

ReaderService.com

**ROMANCE WHEN
YOU NEED IT**

HFGENRE2017R

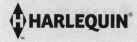

LOVE
Harlequin
romance?

Join our Harlequin community to share your
thoughts and connect with other
romance readers!

Be the first to find out about promotions,
news, and exclusive content!

Sign up for the Harlequin e-newsletter and
download a free book from any series at
www.TryHarlequin.com

CONNECT WITH US AT:

Harlequin.com/Community

 Facebook.com/HarlequinBooks

 Twitter.com/HarlequinBooks

 Instagram.com/HarlequinBooks

 Pinterest.com/HarlequinBooks

ReaderService.com

 **HARLEQUIN**®

**ROMANCE WHEN
YOU NEED IT**

HSOCIAL2017

Reward the book lover in you!

Earn points from all your Harlequin book purchases from wherever you shop.

Turn your points into *FREE BOOKS* of your choice
OR
EXCLUSIVE GIFTS from your favorite authors or series.

Join for FREE today at
www.HarlequinMyRewards.com.

Harlequin My Rewards is a free program (no fees) without any commitments or obligations.

MYR17